Sea
of Grey

Sea
of Grey

An Alan Lewrie
Naval
Adventure

Dewey Lambdin

THOMAS DUNNE BOOKS
ST. MARTIN'S GRIFFIN ✠ NEW YORK

THOMAS DUNNE BOOKS.
An imprint of St. Martin's Press.

SEA OF GREY. Copyright © 2002 by Dewey Lambdin. All rights reserved. Printed in the
United States of America. For information, address St. Martin's Press, 175
Fifth Avenue, New York, N.Y. 10010.

www.stmartins.com

Library of Congress Cataloging-in-Publication Data

Lambdin, Dewey.
    Sea of grey : an Alan Lewrie naval adventure / Dewey Lambdin.
        p. cm.
    ISBN 0-312-28685-6 (hc)
    ISBN 0-312-32016-7 (pbk)
    1. Lewrie, Alan (Fictitious character)—Fiction. 2. Great Britain—History,
Naval—18th century—Fiction. 3. Haiti—History—Revolution, 1791–1804—
Fiction. 4. British—Haiti—Fiction. I. Title.

PS3562.A435 S43 2002
813'.54—dc21   2002069293

In memory of "Genoa"

who passed over last Memorial Day weekend. Don't worry, hon . . . good cats go to heaven. If they didn't, what's the point of people getting there? Sleep safe, and say hello to Sister Foozle 'til we all meet again.

And to the two new "Bubbas"

who turned up like the shepherd in Terry Kay's *To Dance with the White Dog* on the counter of the vet's office like serendipity. Mostly white-furred, playful, mischievous, clever, impish, and talkative Mosby and Forrest! You boys get outta the dish cabinet right now, hear?

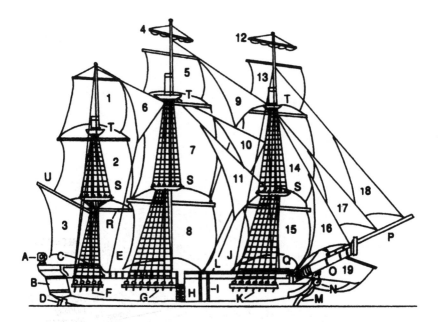

Full-Rigged Ship: Starboard (right) side view

1. Mizen Topgallant
2. Mizen Topsail
3. Spanker
4. Main Royal
5. Main Topgallant
6. Mizen T'gallant Staysail
7. Main Topsail
8. Main Course
9. Main T'gallant Staysail
10. Middle Staysail
11. Main Topmast Staysail
12. Fore Royal
13. Fore Topgallant
14. Fore Topsail
15. Fore Course
16. Fore Topmast Staysail
17. Inner Jib
18. Outer Flying Jib
19. Spritsail

A. Taffrail & Lanterns
B. Stern & Quarter-galleries
C. Poop Deck/Great Cabins Under
D. Rudder & Transom Post
E. Quarterdeck
F. Mizen Chains & Stays
G. Main Chains & Stays
H. Boarding Battens/Entry Port
I. Cargo Loading Skids
J. Shrouds & Ratlines
K. Fore Chains & Stays
L. Waist
M. Gripe & Cutwater
N. Figurehead & Beakhead Rails
O. Bow Sprit
P. Jib Boom
Q. Foc's'le & Anchor Cat-heads
R. Cro'jack Yard (no sail fitted)
S. Top Platforms
T. Cross-Trees
U. Spanker Gaff

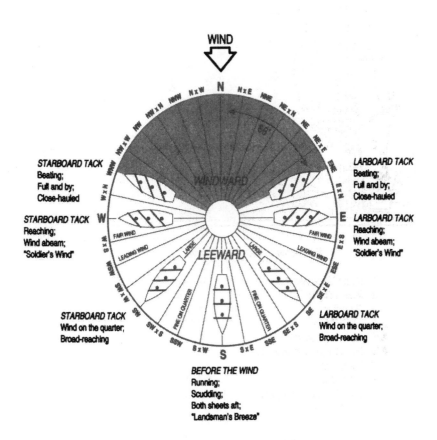

POINTS OF SAIL AND 32-POINT WIND-ROSE

PROLOGUE

Troubles hurt the most when they prove self-inflicted.

SOPHOCLES

CHAPTER ONE

Supping with his father was not exactly Alan Lewrie's idea for how he had intended to complete his personal celebrations, after a day of honour and fame, but after the disastrous shambles in Hyde Park he found himself at rather greater than "loose ends," with his only ally in the world that cynical Corinthian, that shameless old rake-hell and charter member of the infamous Hell-Fire Club; to wit, Major-General Sir Hugo St. George Willoughby, Knight of The Garter, with his sardonic, acidic jollity, with his perpetual leer for all things feminine. . . .

But he *was* paying, so . . .

Given Sir Hugo's "sportin' " nature, it was no wonder that they had ended the evening at The Cocoa Tree, one of the fastest gambling establishments in London. Ostensibly a proprietary coffee-house where men of the Tory persuasion were wont to gather, it set a magnificent table, and was all "the go" with those wealthy enough (or foolish enough!) to riffle the cards in the Long Rooms or lay side wagers, even to take an "insurance policy" on someone *else's* life; i.e., to wager just when a certain cove would croak!

Least it ain't a "cock and hen" club, Lewrie thought, most pleasantly stuffed and "whiffled" by then; *I'm in enough trouble.*

For a time, it had seemed as if one of those shadier establishments *might* feature in the afternoon and night's activities, as he and his father had made the rounds. First had come a gentlemanly tavern, near Sir Hugo's old haunts in St. James's Square for a few badly needed stiff ones, followed by a saunter east to the theatre district for a lively farce, which was followed by a patriotic display in honour of Admiral Duncan and the Battle of Camperdown—with offers of gallons of free drink from fellow theatre patrons near their box, and Sir Hugo gallantly stroking the mustachios he did not have (reducing the slaver, Lewrie thought it) as he boldly gazed down the bodices of the promising young ladies, or leered at the eager young orange-sellers.

Followed by a traipse through Covent Garden's vast and crowded arcade, where anything or anyone could be had at a decent price if one but haggled a bit, where smuggled French champagne had been prominently featured (Lewrie was *pretty* sure); thence here, to The Cocoa Tree, and a lashing or two more of wine accompanying supper, along with the odd "revivor" brandy, now the port.

Squinting only just a tad to maintain focus, Lewrie studied the many ladies present, strolling and flouncing past the communal table at which he and his father had shared supper with a pack of strangers. A lively pack of roisterers, in the main, but new to both of them.

The Cocoa Tree maintained a certain air of proper decorum, just as the resort at Bath did. Only true ladies welcome in Society, with a requisite purseful of "chink," and the itch to risk it, were allowed.

Quite unlike his dissolute youth, in the pre-Navy days, when he and his usual mob of bucks-of-the-first-head had frequented places like The Spread Eagle in the Strand, The Highflyer at the Old Turf Coffee-House, or The Free And Easy, where after the theatre (or long before!) the fast, the poor, and the criminal could commingle, drink, and chorus with the prettier doxies of whatever class or station, and arrange what sport they wished upstairs, at a nearby *bagnio* or by-the-hour rooming house. Oh, how he'd crowed back then, all cock-a-whoop in harmony with the "hens!" *Spending money like a drunken . . . sailor,* which he squiffily realised he was, both in the nautical and the "drunken" sense.

" . . . just a bloody nuisance," his father Sir Hugo was saying in aspersion as he wiped his mouth with a napkin as his plate of pudding was whisked away by a table-servant. "Women should not gamble anymore than they should attempt to smoke, or curse." To which their companions at-table grunted their amiable and dismissive agreements. "Had I the 'tin,' I'd found a man-only club, gentlemen. *Somewhat* like The

Cocoa Tree, White's, Almack's, or Boodle's . . . with the ladies allowed in to *dine* and be decorative, surely, but shoo them out by midnight. Make a male sanctuary, before they overrun all our masculine institutions by the battalions. Dash it all, a place where men may rest 'twixt entertainments, perhaps with lodgings, where a feller may let down his hair and put up his feet. . . ."

"Hear, hear!" one of their fellow diners cheered. "Gentlemen of standing and quality only allowed," he posed, drawing agreement from several others who had been seated by twos or singletons at their long table, hit-or-miss.

"An in-town retreat for serving officers, say," another opined. "Reasonably priced, of course, so we won't have to hunt high and low for lodgings each time we come up to London. Like a regimental mess, a ward-room, or . . ." the gentleman in Army uniform, a captain of foot, proposed. He was well turned out, but half his worth was surely on his back, Lewrie thought, not in his purse or with his banker. "What say you, Captain Lewrie?" the Army man asked him. "An intriguing idea?"

"Most," Lewrie answered, which was about all he could manage as a belch arose, redolent of baked sole, roast beef, pigeon pie, and wine. "A refuge from . . . domesticity," he glumly supposed.

To which sentiment, all eight men present voiced an earnest "Ever and amen" with a hearty, rumbling cheer, though his father peered over at him with a chary, cutty-eyed look of pending disapproval. Sir Hugo had warned him that, should he turn maudlin and weepy, he'd deny knowing him, and leave him to stew in his own misery!

"Quite intriguin'," Captain Browne," Sir Hugo mused, louder than necessary, perhaps to draw attention from his son to himself, after a stern, silent warning, which came off, as most of Sir Hugo's facial expressions, as a nettled falcon's leer, before prosing on.

"The best part of a coffee-house in the mornings, with rafts of daily papers. Good conversation, good wine cellar . . . with decent sets of rooms to let for members-only when down from the country, Members of Parliament, for serving officers, as you suggest, Captain Browne . . . an establishment that offers only the freshest victuals, so that no one dies for tryin' the fare at a two-penny ordinary, haw!"

"Exactly, General Willoughby," another of their fellow diners opined in a plumby voice, "with annual dues and daily charges just high enough to dissuade the lower orders, but within the reach of purses of most gentlemen. With requirements, mark you, sirs, for good character and decorous gentlemanly behaviour."

The very idea of a reference from one's vicar as part of one's *bona fides* set them back in a stunned silence for a moment. The fellow *was* sober-dressed, spare and gaunt-lookin'; was he a Dissenter, one of those Kill-Joys?

Well, that'd let me out, and Father, too, Lewrie told himself.

"Within the club, of course, sirs," the fellow amended quickly, seeing the response he'd drawn. "Mean t'say, run riot on your own . . . but damme if I'll tolerate hoo-rawin' drunks who drop their shoes and giggle, past my bedtime. Schoolboy antics, sons down from university with all their silly carryings-on!"

Well, that was alright, then! One of their fellow diners looked ready to call for quill, ink, and paper to begin setting down the bylaws, *instanter!*

Grandly liveried waiters set out fresh glasses, dishes of grapes and berries, plates of sliced cheeses with both sweet and salted biscuits before them, along with baskets of assorted nuts, with shell bowls and nutcrackers.

Sir Hugo sternly proposed a toast to the King; safe to do, with the water glasses removed, so toasting Hanoverian George III could not be rendered into one for the exiled Stuart claimant, the "king over the water," by a sly pass of one's port glass!

"Gentlemen, allow me to propose our second," Captain Browne said as he got to his feet. "In honour of our dining companion who fought at Camperdown, and won us the marvellous victory all England celebrates tonight . . . to the Royal Navy, and Camperdown!"

"Navy . . . and Camperdown!" they concisely echoed, on their feet. Lewrie, too, rose, though a naval officer never stood to toast the King if he valued his scalp. Low deck beams made their own tradition.

Which sentiment was quickly followed by a toast to Admiral Duncan, now made Baron Duncan of Lundie and Viscount Duncan of Camperdown; then followed by a toast to Lewrie himself, as a representative of the fleet that had won the victory, through which he modestly sat, forming turns of phrase in his head for the expected gallant response.

"Gentlemen, my thanks to you for the honour, though I must confess that my part in the battle was not *that* significant," he answered in kind, though the gold Camperdown Medal bestowed upon him by the King that afternoon tinkled against the matching Battle of Cape St. Vincent Medal.

"Pshaw!" Sir Hugo objected. "You took one of their frigates!"

Their boisterous toasting and cheering had drawn enough notice from the elegant crowd in the dining rooms, but his father said it loud enough to turn it into an attention-getting boast on the "spawn of his loins."

"Allow me to answer with a three-fold proposal," Alan said as he got to his feet a trifle unsteadily, making a supportive triangle from the fingers of his right hand for a moment, before taking up a refilled glass of port to hold before him and peer into its semi-opaque redness as if for inspiration.

"First, for my ship, the *Proteus* frigate, the finest, soundest Fifth Rate that ever swam. Secondly, to her crew, the bravest tars ever plied rammer, rope, or cutlass. From highest to lowest, *they* produced victory, ev'ry man jack! And lastly to our recent foes, the Dutch. They fought us English-fashion, hull-to-hull, yardarm-to-yardarm, and held stout to the last, past the time when their hopes were gone. Gentlemen, I give you HMS *Proteus*, her crew, and a worthy foe!"

"*Proteus* . . , tars/sailors/yer crew . . . the Dutch/foes!" others babbled, mangling his toast. Lewrie feared it would be too much for them, but to Blazes with that, he thought; they were lusty and loud, and that was what counted—loud enough to raise "Huzzahs!" from the onlookers, too, who'd been drawn by the noise at their table.

"Tryin' t'prove yer sobriety?" his father teasingly said as he seated himself again. "Showin' how you can still form compound sentences this late?"

"Wanted it out and done, before I went under the table," Lewrie told him. "Else we'd all be half-seas-over before we got round to the toasts to the ladies!"

Quite a few of the onlookers were fashionably dressed ladies in company of male companions, or two women out together despite the rigid rules of London Society; dashing, unconventional morts who ogled him as openly as he'd ogle them, given the chance, A mixture of hero worship, sympathy for his nobly-wounded "wing," that broken left arm still hung in a neat sling—one or two licking their lips and half-lidding eyes.

"Here, Captain Lewrie," the elegantly dressed man, Mr. Lumsden, whom they'd discovered was a City banker, demanded. "The papers don't tell us half of how 'twas done. Do give us your account of it. Tell us the whole tale!"

"Aye, and leave nought out!" another pressed.

"Well . . ." Lewrie said, unwillingly forced to his feet again by their enthusiasm and the chance to preen for an audience. "I will need the biscuits, nuts, and such, if you really insist."

A row of salted biscuits quickly formed the Dutch coast, while walnuts became ships of the line, and smaller hickories became frigates and sloops of war. Lewrie looked at his creation, trying to picture a bird's view from the confused, smoke and haze-riddled scene he'd had from his quarterdeck, wondering where or how to start to explain it at all. How does one re-organise chaos?

"When we sighted them, the wind was out of the Nor'Nor'west and fairly strong," he said, arrowing a hand, slant-wise, at the long line of Dutch ships. "I'm told they had been sailing Easterly, making for Calais and the Channel, but came about when our scouting frigates got hull-up on 'em."

"Running," the abstemious gentleman pronounced.

"Or luring us into shoal water, where their shallow-draught ships could fight, sir," Lewrie corrected him. "The coast was only five miles or so to loo'rd, and it shoals quickly, like tilting this table just a bit . . . at low tide, a man could wade out half a mile, and be only up to his chest by then. Last cast of the log showed ten fathom . . . only sixty feet of water."

"We'll need a translator, for all the nautical jargon!" one of the diners hooted.

"The Dutch had sixteen ships of the line . . . well, lighter than ours, really, and not all of 'em built as warships. Converted Dutch East Indiamen trapped in home ports," Lewrie went on. "Admiral Duncan had eight ships in his division, with his flagship, *Venerable,* in the very lead. Here," he said, pointing to the easternmost gaggle. "And Vice-Admiral

Onslow's division, with *Monarch* in the lead, were quite a bit West of Duncan's, strung out all higgledy-piggledly, d'ye see, in no proper order, since some of the older ships were poor sailers, even off the wind. 'Round eleven of the morning, Admiral Duncan even had to haul up to windward and beat back towards Onslow's group, so we could go in as a fleet, not a complete shambles."

Venerable, Ardent, and *Triumph* had led, two 3rd Rate 74s, with a two-decker 64; a following wedge was made up of a lone 74-gunner, *Bedford,* flanked by a pair of 64s, *Lancaster,* and Capt. William "Breadfruit" Bligh's HMS *Director.* A third trio in loose order was even further astern; *Belliqueiux,* a 64-gunner, supported by two old two-deck 50-gun 4th Rate ships, *Adamant* and *Isis.*

Vice-Admiral Onslow's group to the West had his flagship *Monarch* in the lead, with *Powerful* and *Monmouth* echeloned off to her right and stern, another pair of 74s with a 64; aft of them sailed a brace of 3rd Rate 74s, *Russel* and *Montagu*; trailing them was another pair, the 64-gunned *Veteran* and the 40-gun frigate *Beaulieu.*

Well, there should have been a third 64-gun 3rd Rate with them, HMS *Agincourt,* but she was far astern, and *damn* her Capt. Williamson for hanging back the entire three hours of the battle!

"Not the strongest fleet, gentlemen," Lewrie said, after naming them. "The rest, we frigates and gunboats, were in the centre. *Rose, Active,* and *Martin* were line-ahead together . . . a pair of twelve-gunned sloops, with a sixteen-gunner. Near their larboard side were *Diligent* and *King George,* hired cutters with six and twelve guns. *Speculator,* astern of them, was a hired lugger with only eight guns! The *Circe* frigate was here, East of the sloops and cutters, and my own ship was here . . . a bit East of *Circe,* and nigh level with Captain Bligh's ship, *Director* . . . well, perhaps a tad ahead of her, nearer the *Bedford,*" he said, shifting a hickory nut forward a half-inch.

"We were about four miles to windward of 'em when Duncan gave a signal to bear down and engage 'em. We repeated the signal, then bore off Easterly, with a touch of Southing, to pin the Dutch against their own coast, as it trends Northerly. . . ."

"Translator!" an idle stroller who had come to observe over the others' shoulders cried.

"This way." Lewrie grinned, employing a nutcracker for use as a wind-pointer. "With the wind large on our larboard quarters. Admiral Duncan hoisted orders as we neared them; first, to pass through their line and engage from leeward, meaning to break their line apart with a pair of hammer-blows 'gainst their centre and rear. It was cloudy and hazy, so how many ships got that signal, I can't say. After that, he flew 'Close Action.' I really do think, did he have to go aground and fight them on dry land, he'd have done so. Admiral Duncan is a terror, sirs . . . a right terror."

Duncan, that giant with the full, unruly mane of snow-white hair on his head, that tall, athletic form that towered over six-feet-four, of the massive calves that made the ladies swoon when he donned silk stockings . . . as hardy and strong as a Scots *ghillie* who had coursed the Highlands like an elkhound since childhood!

" 'Twas said of him that during the recent naval mutiny at the Nore, and his own harbour of Great Yarmouth, Duncan had seized one of the ringleaders by the scruff of the neck, held him out arm horizontal, dangling a full-grown man over the side of his flagship 'til the canting bastard squealed for mercy!" Lewrie related.

A man of great anger, too, who'd prefer the ancient punishment for blasphemy of searing the malefactor's tongue with a hot iron, was he able to get away with it; a man who wore an odd double ring on his left hand encircling little finger and ring finger so he still had use of that hand. He'd broken it and turned those fingers numb by smashing the skull of a rioter in a street melee in Edinborough in 1792—the churl had insulted the King, raising Duncan's Old Testament wrath!

"Sirs, Admiral Duncan would fight you for a rowboat!" Lewrie proudly boasted, happy to have been even for a short time a part of the man's fleet. Though how long that would last was open to question, he took time to fret. After his row with his wife in Hyde Park with both Lord Spencer and Mr. Nepean watching. . . .

"The proper place for frigates is not in the line, sirs," Lewrie continued, striking a lighthearted air, "but out in clear air, where one repeats signals for other ships to see, or stands by to assist any disabled ships of the line. Had I not made an error, we'd have been merely awed witnesses, but . . . we'd gotten too far ahead and *Circe* was crowding us, sailing on starboard tack cross our stern, and all of the cutters and such crowded us, as well. Did the Admiral wish us to break the Dutch line and fight on their landward side, we should have broken through with him. But for the wind, that had blown all the powder smoke alee of us, towards the shore. I *should* have borne away . . . and stayed up to windward but that became impossible. I could not cut through the liners without disrupting what order they had, either, so there was nothing for it but to come about on a beam wind, and sail on a reach. By then, however, 'round half past noon, Admiral Onslow was engaged over *here*, cuttin' through the Dutch line, and slicing off the last three ships. So I rather, um . . . stumbled my way to glory. If glory it was, gentlemen," he allowed with a wry expression.

Aye, come over all modest-like! he thought; *more becoming to a tale, than boasting. But,* he chid himself once more, *I was a damned fool!* And the after-action report he'd written Admiralty had been one of his rather more *creative* endeavours, to disguise idiocy!

"His usual custom, since boyhood," Sir Hugo supplied, though he wore a proud grin.

Lewrie reshuffled the order of the walnuts and such, recalling the smoke and haze, the low, scudding clouds of a raw, grey day, turned in an instant to a pea-soup fog, a reeking, hammered, echoing mist, as *Proteus* had reached West towards Onslow, just out of effective range of the Dutch liners in the middle, before putting about to sail back East towards Duncan, who by then (at a quarter 'til one) was also firing as fast as his gunners could load and run out.

"Now, the Dutch were sailing in two columns," Lewrie explained, indicating the hickories and filberts nearer the row of biscuits. "In their lee were some eighteen-gunned brigs or sloops, at least three twenty-four-gun ships or brigs, and four frigates, of varying metal. Not all were true warships, thank God . . . again, converted and armed merchantmen penned up in port, thanks to our blockade, and our cruising frigates hunting prizes. But, once we broke their line, those escort ships opened fire, though they were there to serve the same duties as ours . . . signals and salvage, and . . . well, sirs, once one fires on a larger ship, one turns into fair game!"

Duncan's *Venerable* had smashed her way through astern of their 74-

gun 3rd Rate *Staten-Generaal*, opening the way for *Triumph* and *Ardent* and threatening the Dutch Admiral de Wynter's flagship, *Vrijheid*. It was a wide, most tempting gap, and beyond it Lewrie could see the lee line of sloops, brigs, and frigates, now and then, turning up windward.

Gun-smoke, towering and blooming like cloud-heads from a summer thunderstorm, vision reduced to mast-tips, the quick-blossoming buds of cannon-shots . . . the staccato stutter of guns, by decks, by broadsides, making even more smoke and confusion, 'til the whole sky was blotted to grey gloom, the sea turned dull leaden for lack of reflecting sunlight; the Dutch ships, their own ships, so wreathed with sour, sulfurous mist that they became spectres.

He caught himself frowning, in a silent, fell musing, absently massaging the dull ache of his wounded arm. Not for show, this time, nor for approbation from his "audience" as he play-acted the pensive hero for their admiration or applause.

From dour remembrance, as he recalled that hideously glorious scene afresh, the scents and sounds, the rocking of his quarterdeck as *Proteus* swashed her way down the line, toward that gap. . . .

"They paid for their mistake, sirs . . . indeed," he told them.

CHAPTER TWO

*A*re they daft?" Lieutenant Langlie, the First Officer, commented as he lowered his telescope, after watching the nearest brace of Dutch sloops open fire on *Venerable* and *Triumph.*

"Perhaps more desperate than daft, Mister Langlie," Lewrie said as he stepped back towards the wheel and compass binnacle. "If they've waited so long for the winds to shift, so they can come out, maybe cooperate in some French intrigue based in the Channel ports . . . well, this fat Dutch *mynheer* de Wynter can't run back into harbour without being seen doing *something*!"

They watched as HMS *Triumph* yawed to show more of her starboard beam, opening the limited arcs of her guns, as she intersected the enemy's line. With a titanic roar, she opened with a full broadside, the first and the most carefully aimed and laid in any battle, at the next Dutch ship astern of the one already pummeled by *Venerable.* That was a death-blow of 32-pounder and upper gundeck 18-pounder iron shot that tore giant gouges and eruptions of side-timbers, that harvested upper yards and masts in an eyeblink! They could hear horrid thuds or howls of rivened wood, as scantlings and beams shattered.

"Do we sail on like this, we'll mask her guns," Lewrie decided aloud, to his quarterdeck officers. "Let's bear up to windward, three points or so, Mister Langlie, and pass upwind of her."

"Aye, sir."

"Deck, there!" a lookout, high aloft on the mainmast, shouted down to them. "Two Dutch brigs alee . . . four points off t'starboard bows!"

That gap was filling with a rolling wall of spent powder smoke, but even from the deck they could espy the spectral shapes of two light Dutch warships, hesitantly hovering under reduced sail, and firing at *Venerable*. *Venerable*, already busy with her larboard guns, replied to that harassing long-range fire with a starboard broadside. The Dutch brig was swatted away, much like a pesky midge; great chunks of timber were blown from her sides and bulwarks, while a sudden hurricane erupted 'round her hull and waterline, like massive breakers crashing on a rocky shoreline.

"And just how *does* one say 'oops' in Dutch?" Lewrie chortled in glee, as his crew cheered the sight of an enemy half-smashed to match-wood in a twinkling!

Venerable then swung back to larboard, abandoning the equally hurt *Staten-Generaal* to turn her left-hand artillery against the starboard side of the prominently flag-bedecked Dutch admiral's ship.

"Deck, there!" a lookout stationed atop the mizzenmast called. " 'Ware astern an' larboard! Our liners!"

Lewrie turned and frowned, for there were *Bedford* and *Director*, not a quarter-mile off, with about a cable's worth between them as they surged forward to the battle line. In the middle distance beyond was their consort *Lancaster*. They weren't steering directly for that gap, but seemed to want to sidle Eastward along the Dutch line, to the windward side of *Ardent*, *Venerable*, and *Triumph*.

"Avast, Mister Langlie," Lewrie said with a scowl. "Hold this course, instead. We're blocked." He peered aloft; yes, they still had Engage To Leeward and Close Action signals flying. *So why the Devil ain't they doin' it?* he groused to himself.

Did *Proteus* stand on much longer, though, she'd run afoul of *Venerable*'s group. As well, she couldn't stand sharp to windward, for fear of masking the *Bedford* group's guns, if not come nigh to a collision with one of them!

The wind? He shifted his gaze to the commissioning pendant at the mainmast truck. As in all sea-fights where heavy guns barked and boomed, the wind was getting flattened. The long pendant was curling and flagging limply. Not enough wind to work ahead of *Bedford*'s trio, nor was there enough wind to tack and pass astern of them, either. It would force them to fetch *Proteus* to, cocked up motionless to the wind, with her fragile stern bared to the foe, who had already proven to be eager to violate the old customs against firing at escorting frigates.

"Nothing for it but to haul our wind, Mister Langlie," Lewrie announced, with a sour note to his voice. "Let us wear ship over to starboard tack, swing 'round in a circle, then harden up and beat past our ships, to windward of 'em . . . where we should have been."

"Hmmm . . ." his darkly handsome First Lieutenant mused, unconsciously scratching at the side of his curly locks. "To leeward of our ships and their line for a bit, sir? Int'restin', if I may say so."

Naturally Lt. Langlie could *not* say "Are you barking mad?" or show any hint of disagreement with a captain; that was insubordination. It could also be taken for an inkling of fear and cowardice!

"We run into anything we can't handle, we duck right back out," Lewrie assured him. "P'raps even snuggle up to one of our liners and ask her t'shoo the big, bad bullies away. Aye, haul our wind, Mister Langlie. Five points alee, and prepare to wear ship."

"Aye aye, sir!" Langlie echoed, lifting his brass speaking trumpet to shout orders to the brace-tenders and landsmen.

A frenetic minute or two later, *Proteus* was off the wind, taking it large on her starboard quarters, her yards still groaning, her sails still clattering and slatting as they refilled.

"Mister Wyman?" Lewrie called from the quarterdeck nettings as he looked down into the ship's waist, searching for his Second Officer in charge of the main battery of guns. "Do you ready *both* batteries, just in case." Lt. Wyman was an angelic but eager young fellow, prone to a flushed, gingery complexion when excited, as he most certainly was at that moment. Lewrie could almost imagine he heard Wyman's wide-eyed gulp, and his customary "My goodness gracious!"

"I wish us to be the biter, today, sir . . . *not* the bit!"

"Aye aye, sir!" Wyman piped back, springing to redirect his gun-captains and quarter-gunners, his powder monkeys and excess crewmen on the run-out, train and breeching tackles over to larboard, then to run in the 12-pounders, remove their tompions and load with powder and shot, then open the gun-ports and run them out in-battery . . . just in case.

Proteus sloughed her way further alee toward the gap, the only clear and unimpeded water open to her, into that sour, towering pall of gunsmoke, coastal haze, and low cloud scud, with her bowsprit and jib-boom, forecastle and chase guns, then her foremast, becoming indistinct.

By sound, Lewrie tried to plot the dangers; astern, now, where *Venerable*, *Ardent*, and *Triumph* were hammering away, being answered with Dutch broadsides; to the West, where Vice-Admiral Onslow was breaking through the rear of the Dutch line, and a general cannonading roared.

Nothin' much in between, though, Lewrie thought; *yet!*

"Deck, there!" a lookout howled. "Ship o' the line, starboard and abeam! Dutch flag on 'er fore jack!"

"Bear away, Mister Langlie . . . make her head Sou'east, and run 'both sheets aft' off the wind!" Lewrie quickly snapped.

Boom! Boom! Two quick cannon barks from that ship's focs'le chase-guns, and six or nine pound round-shot went sizzling and moaning overhead and astern! As their blooms of powder smoke blossomed, the Dutch warship seemed to melt away, to grow fuzzier and less distinct in the fog. A moment later, it was as if she had never been!

"Gap's not as wide as I hoped," Lewrie confessed in a soft voice, as if loath to speak too loudly and be rediscovered . . . with a broad-side, next time! "Mister Langlie, a cast of the lead."

They were now running full off the wind, with the shifting and curling mists traveling with them, for *Proteus* could sail no faster than the wind could blow; Sou'east, toward a coast that ran Nor'east, shallow and filled with shoals and bars!

"Eight fathom! Eight fathom with this line!"

That's only thirty feet of water under our keel, Lewrie thought, in a quandary; *we draw about eighteen feet aft. Put about . . . soon!*

"Two points a'weather, Mister Langlie," Lewrie ordered. "We'll start circlin' back, anew. Hopefully, well clear of that . . . ."

"Deck, there! Two brigs . . . two points off t'larboard bows!"

"Ready the larboard battery!" Lewrie shouted, "Hop to it, sirs! Mister Wyman? Ready quarterdeck carronades, as well."

Spectral, grey-on-grey forms emerged, turning hard-edged, gaining colour. A two-masted brig o' war was cocked up to weather, motionless, with her stern towards *Proteus*, a perfectly helpless target for her guns! With none but stern-chasers able to fire back, her fragile stern timbers, transom, and galleries so easily shattered, turning her inner decks and gun-deck into bowling alleys for hurtling shot, it'd be a brutal buggering, a rape, and quick, wholesale murder!

"Stand by . . . on the up-roll!" Lt. Wyman yelled, brandishing his sword, eager to slice it down to release Hell.

"Avast, Mister Wyman!" Lewrie countermanded. "Hold your fire!"

Dutch officers were at the brig's taffrail, shouting and waving frantically; a white waistcoat was wig-wagged, in sign of surrender or an urgent truce.

For there was a second brig o' war a bit beyond the first, down by the head and canted far to larboard, sinking from the swatting that *Venerable* had given her earlier. Her yards and masts hung in shambles of torn rigging and sails, canted forward and nearly horizontal as she heeled over. Dozens of men thrashed and yelled in the water between the two brigs, some swimming to the over-crowded boats the first brig had lowered. Dozens more sailors clustered at her larboard bulwarks, now almost awash, tossing over hatch-gratings, anything that would buoy them up, whilst some tried to manhandle their own damaged boats off the crossdeck boat tier beams and into the water before she went under.

The near Dutch brig o' war fired one forward gun, to *leeward*, in a plea for gentlemanly conduct and mercy!

"Mister Wyman, one starboard gun to fire, to leeward."

"Aye, sir!"

God, but it would've been beautiful! Lewrie sadly thought, as *Proteus* ghosted past the brig's stern at close range; *one broadside up her stern, and she'd have sunk* before *her sister!*

But, as a 6-pounder from the forecastle fired, Lewrie only lifted his cocked hat to doff it in salute, and the Dutch captain and his officers solemnly doffed their fore-and-aft bicorne hats high over their heads in reply.

"A point more to starboard, Mister Langlie. Keep us circlin'."

"Aye aye, sir. Poor devils."

"Commissioner Proby at Chatham told me that the Dutch require all their sailors to learn to swim," Lewrie off-handedly informed him. "And *if* they drown, they roll them over a keg laid on its side, until the victim coughs and spews up what he's swallowed or inhaled, so they stand a decent chance . . . if they got off that other brig, unwounded."

"I see, sir," Langlie replied. "Damn' odd, though, sir. Never seen the like . . . not in a full-blown battle, that is, Captain."

"What, the bloody bicorne hats?" Lewrie shrugged it off. "You're right . . . I've never seen the like, either! They may be all the 'go,' but you'll never see a *British* officer in one! Too damn' Frenchified."

Proteus sailed on, bearing away, and the two Dutch brigs o' war were enveloped in the gloom and smoke once more. A quick peek into the compass bowl showed Lewrie that their frigate was now headed just a bit West of South, away from that treacherous coast, almost abeam what wind there was, and still turning up to weather, the hull beginning to heel, the sluice of water 'round her gurgling and sighing more urgently. It was a hopeful sound.

"Nine fathom! Nine fathom t'this line!"

That news was hopeful, too; as was the dimly perceptible thinning of the haze, smoke and mist, the sky ahead and North'rd brighter, as if within moments they could sail out into sunshine, and safety.

"Deck, there! Three-master, one point off t'starboard bows! I think she's a frigate! Dutch flags! Bearin' Easterly!"

"Dammit!" Lewrie spat, peering intently into the smoke to spot what the lookout could see from aloft. "This is worse than tryin' to cross the Strand in a thick Thames fog! Coaches to right and left . . ."

"There, sir!" Mr. Langlie all but yelped, pointing.

As if a stage curtain had been raised, a Dutch frigate appeared just off their starboard bows, crossing their course almost at right angles, her quarterdeck staff almost leaping with surprise as they also pointed and jabbered, now silhouetted against the mists.

"Ready, starboard battery, Mister Wyman! Helm hard alee, helmsmen! Lay her full and by! Brace in, Mister Langlie! We'll shoot *her* up the arse, 'stead of that poor brig! Stand by to fire as you bear! Mister Devereux?"

His elegant and aristocratic Officer of Marines stepped forward.

"Lay waste her quarterdeck . . . your best marksmen in the tops and along the starboard gangway!" Lewrie insisted, his words tumbling out in a rush, urgent from the closeness and quickness of the situation. "I want grenadoes, too . . . lashings of 'em!"

"Aye sir . . . two bags full!" Lt. Blase Devereux answered, saluting, but with a tongue-in-cheek joy. "Marksmen!" he bawled, turning away.

Long musket-shot, Lewrie speculated as the Dutch frigate sailed on Eastwards, opening the range, her brailed-up main course lashing as it was freed and hauled down to increase her speed; *'bout a third of a cable as our bows come abeam her transom?*

"As you bear!" Lt. Wyman was screeching, sword aloft again. "On the up-roll! *Fire!*"

First, a 6-pounder chase-gun, shrill and sharp; then one of the 24-pounder carronades, a "Smasher" that Lewrie had shifted forward to the forecastle shortly after taking command, for *Proteus* had the fullness of form under her bows to bear the weight. The first of the starboard 12-pounders, the long-barreled Blomefield Pattern guns, erupted, followed by a slow blasting as each of the remaining twelve guns along the starboard side came level. Lastly, the quarterdeck 6-pounders and the pair of 24-pounder carronades mounted there also belched and roared.

Muskets aloft and along the bulwarks spat and crackled, as well.

"Uuppp . . . *yours!*" Lewrie shouted in mad joy to see his round shot strike, one at a time, with the deadly, metronomic pace of a good gun salute! Quarter-galleries, the sash windows of the Dutch captain's great-cabins, the small ports of the officer's gun-room immediately below, the taffrail and the lanthorns and posts, her transom wood, along with her thick rudder post and rudder, were smashed in! Pieces of her double-wheel and compass binnacle went flying, her mizenmast shuddered and jerked, her lower spanker boom sagged, broken in three pieces, and guns run-out on her larboard side, facing the unseen British battle line, jerked, tilted, and slewed in their ports as they were struck and shifted by the howling weight of metal bowling down inside her at more than 1,200 feet per second!

"Too far for grenadoes, sir . . . sorry," Lt. Devereux said with a sorrowful expression. "Still . . . we gave them a good peppering."

"She's turning up, sir!" the Sailing Master, Mr. Winwood, noted.

"Can't see just how, with her rudder and helm shot up so thorough."

"To unmask her larboard battery . . . the one that was manned," Lewrie realised at once. "Mister Langlie, ready to tack! We'll fall below her on larboard tack, and use our ready-loaded larboard guns to serve her another stern rake!"

"*Give* her the wind-gauge sir?" Mister Winwood queried.

"If Admiral Duncan can fight from loo'rd, then so can we, sir," he replied. "Her starboard ports are closed, she ain't ready, and with any luck at all, they've got the wind up. Quick-around, lads! Hurry!"

"Ease helm, ease off jib sheets . . . haul weather mizen to windward . . . tend lee mizen sheet!" Langlie was babbling, too, urgently ordering what was usually a staid rite. "Let go foresheets, check the lee forebrace, check the fore topbowline . . . *rise*, tacks and sheets!"

"Be ready, Mister Wyman . . . as you bear!" Lewrie urged. He went to the nettings overlooking the waist to watch as each gun-captain put a fist in the air to indicate readiness, the trigger-lines to the flintlock strikers taut in their other hands.

Yards, blocks, and parrels crying, *Proteus* came up to the eye of the wind, hesitated for a dreadful second as if she'd miss stays and become a motionless victim, then slowly swung farther to starboard with a breeze beginning to tickle her sails. "Now, mains'l *haul*!"

"Yes, by God!" Lewrie exulted, now rapt with battle-fever, his usual state, with all thought of stoicism and the *sang-froid* of a true English captain quite flown his head.

"As you bear . . . *fire!*" Lt. Wyman shouted, slashing down his sword in a glittering arc as they crossed the Dutch frigate's stern once more, this time at an acute angle, left-to-right.

Timber shattered, side planking was ripped away and flung as if a tornado had struck her! Her mizen groaned and shook once more, yards turning and spiralling as the lower mast was shot through below decks, and shedding sailors and Dutch Marines from the fighting top in a tangle of rigging and upper spars, releasing aft tension to her mainmast, that groaned and canted forward, too.

At an angle, yes, but closer this time, at half a hundred yards, and they could hear the screams and howls as their roundshot tore down the gun-deck, open from end-to-end; hear the thuds and crashes of shot

tearing away carline posts and turning stout timbers to clouds of splinters
that flew about madly, swiftly, ripping into flesh, breaking bone, as mer-
ciless as Col. Shrapnel's case-shot shells that exploded in clouds of musket balls!

Her rudder and her transom post, with the pintles and gudgeons that
held it in place, were turned to kindling. And, without a rudder, and
with the loss of her balancing mizen sails to counter the pressure on her
foresails, the Dutch frigate sagged offwind, falling off to parallel *Proteus*
as she sailed past.

"Damme!" one of the helmsmen gasped as the enemy's gun-ports on
her starboard side opened, hinging upward, as here and there the dark
snouts of readied guns jerked into view! It would not be a complete or
ordered broadside, but at this close range, it would be a blow to the
bowels!

"Flat on the deck!" Lewrie shouted to his crew, though standing with
his hands behind his back, planting his feet to receive the blow with
courage . . . even if his innards had just turned to gurgly water!

B-b-*boom!*

The Dutch broadside stuttered, perhaps with only ten of her guns.
Lewrie had time to count gun-ports, now that she was abeam them.

Ten out of fourteen, he thought with a wince, as the thundrous roar
surrounded him, making his heart flutter with its nearness; *she's a thirty-
six, but thank God those ain't eighteen-pounders!*

Proteus sounded as if she was screaming, with those hideous parrot
squawks as roundshot tore clean through her sides; *Rwwwarrwwk!* then
thud and crash! She jumped and trembled, juddering enough to toss him
inches off the deck, then rise to meet him as he dropped with his knees
flexed. Hot gusts of wind pummeled at him as he opened one eye to see
if he, and his ship, were still in one piece, or among the living.

Shot his bolt, Lewrie thought, hot anger flushing him that he'd been
fooled into reach of the Dutch gunners; *now, it's our turn!*

"Everyone up! Man your guns! Load, load, load!" he shouted.

The Dutch had fired low, English fashion, "twixt wind and water"
instead of emulating the long-range firing of their allies the French, who
preferred firing high, to dis-mast and cripple enemy ships, so they could
be out-manoeuvred and taken . . . or fled, if things went against them.

He daren't even look over the side, to see damage done to his beautiful new frigate, how shattered she might be below! Someone would come run tell him, he was mortal-certain.

The Dutch frigate was close, sagging down against *Proteus*, and *Proteus* was slowing, with the light, gun-shot wind stolen from her by the sails and rigging of the Dutch, up to windward of her!

Damme for goin' under, too! he chastised himself; *now, we're to be hull to hull, with no chance of slippin' off!*

They would fight like line-of-battle ships, instead of dancing, weaving, and sparring; locked yardarm-to-yardarm, guns blasting with the muzzles almost touching the enemy, taking fire in like manner!

"Load and fire . . . point-blank! Mister Devereux?"

"Captain, sir?"

"Think it's close enough for grenadoes, *now*, do you?"

"I do indeed, sir," Devereux replied with a slight grin, drawing his smallsword and shouting at his Marines aloft to light fuses, to get their light swivel guns firing like one-inch bored shotguns, filled with langridge or bags of pistol balls. "Sir . . . pardon my suggesting it, but . . . were I you, Captain, I'd pace about. Don't give their marksmen a chance at you."

"If it gets thick, Mister Devereux, I'll lurk behind you. With that handsome red coat of yours, I'm sure you're the finer target."

Wyman got his guns going again, firing at will, as fast as the bores could be swabbed out, reloaded, and run out. Thirteen guns, first; then only twelve as one was up-ended, then eleven. The Dutch must have loaded and prepared that one, good broadside, though, and hadn't crew enough still on their feet to serve their pieces quite so quickly. The Dutch response was eight guns, then seven, then six.

It was deafening, howling chaos, loud enough to make sailors and Marines bleed from their ears and noses. Between the titanic blasts from heavy guns, the barks of swivels, the crack of muskets and pistols, and the dull bangs from flung grenadoes created a continual drumming. Ball spanged and caromed from gun barrels, *thonked* into timbers and tore out gouts of dust, splinters, and lead splatters. *Proteus*'s quarterdeck was quickly quilled with torn-up slivers of holystoned wood, making it hard to walk. The surgeon's mates, Mr. Hodson and the laconic French *emigré*

Mr. Maurice Durant, made continual trips up from below with the narrow, rope-strapped carrying boards borne by their loblollymen to haul shaken and wounded men below. The dead were piled about the bases of the masts!

"Yah pistols, sah," his Coxswain, Andrews, said, fetching him a brace of double-barreled Mantons. "I thought ya might like havin' yer Ferguson rifle, too."

Lewrie stuck the pistols in his waist-belt, slung the cartouche box over his shoulder, and accepted a horn of priming powder, quickly loading the deadly-accurate breechloader rifled musket. Shooting back, he decided, beat pacing about like a fart in a trance, all hollow! He took aim at an officer in a bicorne hat, swung slowly to follow him as he paced about, bellowing and waving a sword, and . . .

"Got you!" he exulted after the muzzle-smoke cleared, seeing his foeman fall into the arms of a pair of Dutch mates, then drop below the bulwarks and disappear. One turn of the screw-breech lever, below the trigger and lock assembly; lower the barrel, rip a cartouche open with his teeth, shove it ball-end forward into the barrel, then screw in the opposite direction to close the breech. Frizzen at half-cock, the pan open for a touch of priming powder; snap the frizzen shut; draw the lock to full cock, and search for another target . . . a thickset gunner's mate or something like that, up on the gangway and urging his crews to load . . . a careful aim, a pent breath . . .

"Got you!" he crowed again.

"Sir, their fire's slacking!" Langlie pointed out, coming over to his side. "We're shooting her to pieces, they don't have Smashers, and we're turnin' her into a sieve! They're gatherin' amidships, with pikes and pistols. I think they're about to board us!"

By then, Lewrie was half-deaf and it took concentration to heed Langlie's words, mostly by lip-reading. But the only cannon fire he could hear was now under his own feet. He lowered his gaze to see the damage done to the Dutch frigate's hull, and it did, indeed, resemble a sieve or colander—one could not find a stretch of her scantling more than ten feet long without a ragged, star-shaped hole punched in it! He saw sailors and Marines gathering, cutlasses waving, surviving officers, mates or midshipmen shoving them into order. . . .

"Mister Wyman! Last rounds, then take up arms!" Lewrie called down to the gun-deck. "Boarders! Mister Devereux, your Marines, down from the tops, and ready to re—"

Something went *Bang-splang-fwee!* off a quarterdeck 6-pounder, a blink before Lewrie felt as if someone had just hit his left arm with a waggon-tongue! He was spun about in a half-circle leftward, to trip over his own feet and tumble to the deck!

"Goddammit!" he meant to shout, but it came out rather weakly, even to his ears. *'Cause I'm gun-deaf?* he had to wonder. Suddenly, he was shivering cold, with only the cattle-brand heat in his arm to warm him. He looked up at Langlie and Devereux, as if from the bottom of a well, with the sides blotting out most of the sky, and . . .

"B-boarders!" he insisted, the ringing in his ears smothering his own words.

"Surgeon's Mate!" someone was keening.

"Never fear, sir . . . we'll take her for you," someone very like Langlie whispered, leaning down over his face as he was jostled by many hands, soaring aloft like a freed soul, with something hard and narrow under him as he was quickly bound with ropes like some *damned* soul for spitting and roasting on the Devil's *rotisserie*.

"Proteuses . . . away boarders! Away boarders!"

"No, *repel* boarders, not . . . !"

He was *sure* he'd said it, but no one paid him any mind but for Mr. Durant, who was making clucking noises and shaking his head sadly.

Daylight was gone; he was plunged into reeking, foetid darkness, feet-first into the "fug" of unwashed bodies, bilges, and stinks; below into glim-lit Hades. To the cockpit on the orlop, where the wailing and shrieking of the eternally damned soared and chorused in an atonal agony. Those saved, above, shouted Hosannas of blissful and eternal joy— though they were making a rather noisy, tinkery, metallic and *feu de joie* music along with their paeans!

"It must come off, at once," Mr. Thomas Shirley, the twentyish surgeon, lowed like a cow, spouting some dry, esoteric dog-Latin.

"Non, non . . . ze humerus is broken, not shattered, *m'sieur*," Durant (or *somebody* Froggish, anyway!) insisted. "See, ze axillary responds when I stick 'is palm, and . . ."

"Ow! Bloody . . . !"

"Ze blood loss suggest ze axillary artery is *non* torn, *aussi?* Cut eez coat and shirt off, *s'il vous plaît* . . . gently. Ze ball pass through complete, you see? *M'sieur Capitaine?* Drink zees, an' think ze pleasant thought." Followed by more "Ahumms" and Latin gibberish.

A large pewter cup of rum was shoved under Lewrie's nose and he drank it down, just before a leather gag was put between his teeth to bite on when the pain got severe . . . which it did!

They probed, retracting wool coat and silk shirt shards, taking out slivers of bone and tiny splashes of lead, Durant insisting that a watered tincture of brandy be splashed around inside the wound, over the instruments, before they squeezed, twisted, and pried at his arm to see how it lined up before getting shot . . . and re-set it!

"A simple fracture, after all, sir."

"SonofagoddamnbitchI'llbloodykillyourmiserableFrogass!"

"You are welcome, *M'sieur Capitaine.* Next?"

He was bound in linen, with lots of batting, also soaked in the French *emigré's* watered brandy, that stung like Blazes; over the bandages, two wooden belaying pins were bound taut with twine; some spare Number Eight sailcloth, the lightest aboard, was fashioned into a neat sling; and he was stowed forrud on a straw-filled mattress, armed with another hefty measure of rum, then ignored.

"We took her, sir! We took her!" Langlie was crowing about a quarter-hour later, coming to his side with flecks of blood (hopefully someone else's!) on his coat facings, his cheek, and shirt. "Oh, 'twas a hard fight, but we took her! You were right to call for boarders, Captain Lewrie. Had they formed and attempted to board *us*, well . . . ! But we beat them to it, and broke their spirit into the bargain."

Lewrie could but gawp at him (a trifle drunkenly by then) and wonder what the Blazes this idiot was babbling about!

"Very good, sir. Just get me out of this cess-pit and back to my roomin' house, 'fore the wife finds me, hey?"

"Sir?" Lt. Langlie gawped in puzzlement.

"Oh, never mind, I'm too sleepy t'care."

⚓

"And that, sirs, is how I conquered a Dutch frigate," Captain Alan Lewrie, RN, concluded with a blithe laugh. "Stood up shirtless, strapped to a carryin' board by the windward mizen shrouds, with a cup of rum in my hands, towin' out our prize! Speaking of . . . allow me to propose another toast. To Lieutenant Anthony Langlie, my able First Officer, and the true hero of the piece. He placed the Batavian Navy *Orangespruit*, a thirty-six gun Fifth Rate frigate, on a platter for me, and served her up . . . well done!"

His fellow diners gave out a loud, prolonged cheer, along with the curious onlookers who had gathered to peer over their shoulders as the tale was told, and they clapped and laughed, as well. Handsome women in the height of Fashion that season fanned and flushed, or made as if they'd swoon. They raised a rousing "For He's A Jolly Good Fellow," to which Lewrie nodded and smiled, raising his port glass in answering salute and acknowledgement.

Of *course*, it made a good tale, a 32-gun taking a 36-gun; what the public expected their Navy to accomplish. Of course, he did not tell them of his mistakes, of stumbling about in the smoke, damn near *lost*, of his sin of over-confidence, of yielding the wind-gauge to the Dutch so stupidly, being drawn like a lamb to the slaughter into the mouths of the guns of a doughty, wily, and desperate enemy captain, who had taken much the same precautions as he, to be the biter and not the bit, that day!

No, this crowd wouldn't appreciate unvarnished truth, *nor* would they tolerate another toast, this to the dead, the maimed and gutted, to those men now minus limbs or sight, and doomed to a lifetime of poverty ashore, with but a pittance of a pension to atone for a too-brief moment of glory.

Nineteen killed, listed with the simple "D-D" in ship's books for Discharged, Dead and interred at sea, out of sight and mind. And twenty-nine wounded, too, with fourteen of those merely Discharged . . . landed ashore at Sheerness and lumbered off to a naval hospital, never to return to duty, should they survive the ministrations.

For the Dutch, it had been a slaughter-pit, as well; over sixty dead and over an hundred cruelly wounded. That was the sort of harvest that England's public liked; the greater the number of enemy slain, the higher cost in British lives, well . . . the greater the honour! *Losing* captains had been knighted for bravery after such fights, since they'd run up a high "butcher's bill" of their own people before striking!

Perhaps he *should* tell them the cost, he speculated; they might get a vicarious thrill from so much *distant* blood! All due to his work, his cockiness, his famed "luck," and his "tradition of victory"!

While they cheered and clapped, his beloved *Proteus* languished in a Sheerness graving dock, her guns and stores warehoused ashore as the shipwrights repaired her many hurts. She was as nearly shattered as the captured *Orangespruit*! *Damn 'em all!* he thought; *no matter what face I put on it, 'twas a costly damn' victory. Something I could never say even to Caroline in strictest privacy. My father, well . . . he knows of it, he's a military man, I spilled my secret to him, but . . .* Caroline!

He almost felt like breaking down and blubbing in public, after all! And fearing that Dame Fortune had decided to turn on him and feed him to her wolves!

"A flutter of the cards, Captain Lewrie?" Mr. Lumsden asked.

"Ah, no," Lewrie soberly replied. "I feel as if I've stretched my luck far enough, lately. Haven't heard from the Prize-Court yet . . ."

"Our reckoning, I should think," his father quickly suggested as he spotted his son's wavering. "We should be gettin' home, son, gettin' *some* part of a good night's rest. Do you gentlemen excuse us? I keep at Willis's Rooms when in town. Do call upon me, and we could pursue the matter of a gentleman's club further, perhaps discover some backers who might also find the notion intriguing . . . ?"

They said their good-nights, gathered their hats and cloaks from the tiler, then stood chilled at the kerb outside whilst a young "daisy kicker" servant of The Cocoa Tree whistled them up a hired carriage to bear them home.

CHAPTER THREE

*I*t was "fashionably" well past midnight before they entered the lodging house, with but a yawning servant to unlock the door for them and offer candles so they could light their way abovestairs. Willis's was otherwise dark and broodingly silent, the cheery fires in the common and public rooms banked, the equally cheery bar now shuttered. Sir Hugo assured his son that, failing the publican's commerce, he had a bottle of good Frog brandy in his room.

Lewrie by then was exhausted, and not much in need of a drink; he'd had half-enough for a lifetime, thankee very much!

The spirit's willin', but the body's weak, he thought, in awe of the other diners' capacity, of his father's ability to put it away with nary even a slurred word. *Navy's ruined me, damn 'em,* he decided, as he fumbled out his key, peering about owlishly.

Lewrie hesitated before the door to his set of rooms, key finally in hand, wondering should he knock or scratch first. With a sorry curse, softly muttered, he rued again fleeing the park with his father, of coming back so late and so "in the barrel" and bedraggled, instead of rushing back to Willis's after merely an hour's pause to argue things out with Caroline, and defend himself, once she'd cooled down.

"Devil with it," he grumbled, inserting the large key; well, he tried to, but there was but one wee candle in the passageway, the key was perversely upside-down, then backwards, and the slot, though large, seemed to be queerly mobile!

At last he managed to unlock the door and enter the rooms, glad to see a fire in the hearth, low and orange, flickering scant light off the brass reflector plate. Only a single candle guttered on the tiny wine-table near the settee, upon which a form huddled.

"Bless me!" the form groaned, sitting up, half-scaring Lewrie out of a year's growth! "Oh, 'tis you, sir," his manservant Aspinall said, rubbing sleep from his eyes like a toddler. "*Meant* t'sit up an' wait for ya, Cap'um Lewrie, but . . ."

"No matter, me lad, no matter," Lewrie replied, waving overly wide, and unsteady on his "pins." "The wife's asleep, I trust?"

"Erm, uhh . . . no sir," Aspinall said with a wince. "She's gone, sir . . . her and the children, all. Packed up an' took the coach back to Anglesgreen, Lord . . . *hours* ago, sir. Not long after she come back by herself. Long 'fore dark, for certain."

Aspinall had tricked himself out in snowy white slop trousers, a clean new shirt, a red neckerchief, and a short sailor's jacket with a set of shiny brass buttons. He sloughed off a dark blue grogram greatcoat under which he had been napping, and felt about with his toes for his new shiny-blacked shoes, those with the real silver buckles that Lewrie had bought for him after coming ashore.

"Ah," Lewrie replied, after a long, deep sigh. "I see."

"Can I get ya anything, sir? Didn't know as how you'd dine, so I sent down for some . . ."

"No thankee, Aspinall," Lewrie said, removing his cocked hat and boat-cloak, which Aspinall rushed to gather in.

"Still some cold roast pork an' bread, sir. Make a good snack. There's some wine, and . . ."

"I dined, not so long ago, no," Lewrie replied, trying not to snap at his manservant; it wasn't *his* bloody fault. Though, from the half-empty carafe of wine, the skimpiness of the remaining slices of pork, and the half-loaf, Aspinall had dined well, he thought. And why not? Stuck in the middle of a domestic battle-royal, not knowing the details, and loath to step out to visit his ailing mother here in London, to go much beyond the public rooms belowstairs 'til his master returned. . . . Lewrie could picture poor Aspinall standing well out of the way, wringing his hands,

unsure whether he should help them pack, or scurry off and hide 'til the
thunder had subsided.

"Go get some rest, Aspinall. Turn in. I can mangage. I might even
discover my own bed, if my luck's in," Lewrie throatily said.

"I'll build up the fire, sir, an' heat a warmin' pan. Won't be a tick,"
Aspinall uneasily offered, overly anxious to please. Simply plain *anxious*,
Lewrie could imagine. *'What shall become of us?'* as Sophie had fretted
earlier today . . . was it yesterday, by now?

"Well, then . . ." Lewrie demurred, tearing at his neck-stock and col-
lapsing upright on the settee.

"Uhm, Missus Lewrie left that note, sir . . ."

How could he have missed it, leant against the carafe of wine. Was
that a not-so-subtle slur about his "beastly" nature?

Aspinall became even more cringingly unobtrusive as Lewrie took up
the note, broke the seal, and unfolded it. For being penned in the heat
of the moment, Lewrie decided, it was as forebodingly chilly as a hunk
of Arctic ice! Though *claiming* she'd never suspected a blessed thing *at
the time*, Caroline's worst suspicions had been confirmed, in the blink of
an eye. The gist of that accusing, anonymous letter she had gotten,
enumerating her husband's sins, was proved true! Back in their rooms
after the row, she'd dredged confirmation from poor Sophie de Maubeuge, their ward; yes, he'd had a mistress in the Mediterranean, Phoebe
Aretino, *kept* at Gibraltar 'til his return in '94, kept as well on her home
island of Corsica . . . the dread secret that Sophie had held all these years,
spilled at last! Phoebe Aretino, a conniving, mercenary Corsican whore
he'd met at Toulon, the damning letter had described her, Lewrie's *long-
term* mistress, so any dalliance could not be excused as a lone moment
of weakness, and even much worse than any passing idea Caroline had
had about Theoni Connor, whose appearance in the park had set all this
off! Though *confirmed* in Caroline's mind was his adultery with Theoni,
now, for the anonymous letter had spelled it all out for her . . . both the
first back in the spring, and the latest!

How he had cossetted Theoni Connor, perhaps the first night he'd
taken her aboard HMS *Jester* after rescuing her from Serbian pirates in
the Adriatic, how he'd schemed and finagled to have her and her actual
son Michael sail to Lisbon as his guests in his great-cabins, how he'd

paid court to her in that port before she'd taken the packet to Liverpool and the in-laws of her late husband! God above, but Caroline had an inkling of an attractive, *busty* Italian courtesan in Genoa, *and* in Leghorn, and . . . !

She'd be shootin' lava 'bout that'un! Lewrie told himself, with a sick and swoony feeling of doom as he dashed a hand cross his brows; *Theoni's more blessed in that department, too, and Caroline's more . . . petite! Damme, don't she know men don't* marry *teats . . . they just want t'sup on 'em a tad, now and then?*

Though how in Blazes anyone, much less the anonymous scribbler, knew that much was beyond him; Phoebe, for certain; Theoni, well maybe. But Claudia Mastandrea, too? No, *who* could've known that much, and who could despise him enough to write his wife and tell all?

He had suspected Commander William Fillebrowne, who had openly boasted of taking Phoebe's "saddle" after she and Lewrie had thrown in the towel with each other; he'd been in Venice, in their squadron, in the Adriatic when Theoni Connor turned up, but Claudia was *long* before his time, an actual, official "mission" handed him by that old Foreign Office spook, Zachariah Twigg . . . damn his blood! That was supposed to be very secret!

He'd also suspected Lucy Beauman, his first and frustratingly unrequited lust way back in the "early-earlies" of 1780. Now Lady Lucy Shockley, she'd been in Venice, too, also taken with that Fillebrowne; his lover, in point of fact, behind her decent (huge and filthy rich) husband's back not six months after they were wed, the filthy baggage! Lucy and Fillebrowne together, for mutual revenge?

He'd spurned her offer of a tumble or an affair, should handsome Fillebrowne go stale, or fail to clear all his "jumps"; perhaps at the same time, for all he knew or cared. So rich, spoiled, and pampered . . . Lucy was not a woman to cross, and Fillebrowne . . . !

His old schoolmates from his *short* term at Harrow—Lord Peter Rushton and Clotworthy Chute, ever the "Captain Sharp" without a pence to his own name—had been in Venice, too, and Clotworthy had diddled Fillebrowne over some "ancient" Roman bronze statues recently "dug" in the Balkans . . . about as old as the half-loaf of bread standing by the wine carafe!

The one letter his father'd seen had been written on fine paper, and done in an elegant copperplate hand, he'd said. Oh, but it was a bootless enterprise, to speculate *who'd* ruined him. The thing was done, and the fat was truly in the fire!

Caroline had borrowed sixty pounds from his sea chest, she wrote, to sustain their farm 'til his solicitor, Mr. Matthew Mountjoy, could make new arrangements for her and the children's upkeep . . . which she *firmly* intended to extract from him, no matter their estrangement. Income from their 160-acre rented farm should be hers alone, she wrote, since *he'd* never been a bit of help in that regard, and had never done a thing to learn it during his *idle* years ashore on half-pay, between the wars! He had to admit that that accusation was true.

Lewrie had been a city-raised London lad, only going down to the country on spring or summer jaunts, as a weekend house guest, and knew nothing of crops or livestock, didn't know one flower from another and could really only identify oak trees. Well, he knew good horseflesh if he saw it, and he *could* ride well . . . but Hell's Bells, was there any true English gentleman who couldn't, he'd eat his cocked hat!

Caroline then demanded that half his inheritance from his grandmother Lewrie's plate and paraphernalia be turned over to her; that *he* could live on his damned *Navy* pay, and the £150 *per annum* that Granny Lewrie had granted him long ago as an annual living, once she had rediscovered his existence during the Revolution.

Sewallis and Hugh must be schooled, she continued; their daughter Charlotte would soon require schooling *and* "finishing" in the arts, music, dance, and deportment necessary to a young lady to-be of her due station, then "dotted" when finally espoused.

The children, she accused, were already inured to his years-long absences on the King's Business, so they would treat his estrangement as just another extremely long active commission. And be the better for't!

"Damme, she's dotted all her I's, crossed all her T's," Lewrie sadly marvelled. "Minds her P's and Q's . . . pints an' quarts, pence'n shillings. Worse'n a publican . . . pick yer pockets for the reckonin', 'fore he tosses ye in the gutter."

Her note was, except for the occasional spiteful slur, of course, remarkably icy, as if she'd written a dry commercial contract to a complete stranger!

"Warmin' pan's in yer bed, sir, and yer covers turned down," his servant announced, padding stocking-footed back into the sitting room.

"Night, Aspinall," Lewrie said, slumped in defeat.

"Aye, sir," Aspinall said with a jerky bow, then departed for a bed of his own in what amounted to a large closet, though the children's beds in a proper, separate room were empty, and better-made.

Of a sudden, the carafe of wine was more than tempting. Lewrie poured himself a goodly measure, a brimming glass.

"Oof!" he was forced to exclaim, spilling a few drops on his new snow-white kerseymere breeches as his ram-cat Toulon jumped up into his lap. "Hallo, Toulon. 'Least you *ain't* abandoned me, pusslin'."

The black and white tom, now grown to nigh a stone-and-a-half in weight, and as firmly muscled as a well-fed basset hound—like petting a log with legs—made mouth-shut trills and grunts in welcome as he kneaded Lewrie's lap, rubbed his head against his chest, and slung his bulk against him, his thick, white-tipped ebony tail a brush that lazily twirled and tickled under Alan's nose.

Lewrie managed one sip, then set aside his glass to pet him and stroke him, else he'd be a pluperfect pest for a full half-hour. "Aye, I know, big baby, been gone too damn' long. Left you behind, did she? Been just you and Aspinall, hours and hours? Well, I'm back now, just you an' me, yyess. . . ."

An' by God, ain't it just! he sadly told himself; *me and a damn' cat, the rest o' my days, if Caroline don't come round . . . somehow.*

And how his wife could ever reconcile herself with such a faithless hound as he, he couldn't quite fathom . . . yet, anyway. She wasn't the sort to pine away; she'd proved that by running their farm as well as any man during his other commissions. Rearing the children, becoming such an astute woman of commerce, never given to the vapours, just coping deuced well, with her stillroom, jams, and jellies, the domestics they employed, neighbours, skin-flint horse-copers, homemade vinegars, wines, and spring ales, her sewing, knitting, and economies. . . .

She didn't *need* him, he realised with a start of revelation; he was a sometime amusement, like a visiting troupe of jugglers and acrobats! Caroline was complete unto herself, and had been for years; what ties of affection and custom there had been were now severed!

Caroline had kith and kin, the house, the village, and the church, and the long, predictable roll of the seasons in peaceful and settled country life, home and hearth, whilst he had the sea, and . . .

"Murff," Toulon muttered in his lap, strewing hair over the new breeches that he had bought for the celebration ball that they *should* have attended this evening, done up in their best finery, dancing with the great and near-great in glittering triumph and praise.

Toulon turned about in his own length and slunk inside the sling that bound Lewrie's left arm, stretching out once inside, feeling like a hairy 18-pounder shot, with but his whiskers, nose, and slitted eyes showing after he'd turned about once more. He gave out a long, happy yawn, stretched out his front paws and legs to dangle either side of his master's wrist, and began to purr, rattling like signal halliards and light blocks might clatter in a stiff breeze.

Lewrie was too tired to think anymore, too drunk and too numb for self-pity or a good, cleansing admission of guilt. He was certain those'd come, though, as he picked up his abandoned wineglass and took a melancholy sip. Now that he was alone, and still.

And it was goin' so bloody good this mornin', he mourned as he recalled how promising the day had started out . . .'til that encounter in Hyde Park. . . .

CHAPTER FOUR

*W*ell, *that came off well,* Lewrie thought for a hopeful moment, as Theoni bade them all a gracious goodby, took her sons and her maid-servant and new-fangled wheeled perambulator off down the pale grav-elled path. *Polite and innocent as anything! Whew!*

He had turned back to face his wife, after perhaps allowing his gaze to linger just a blink too long on the departing Mrs. Connor.

Ka-whap!

Caroline's stinging blow made his jaw feel as if it was broken!

"Oow!" he'd yelped in sudden pain and astonishment, face reddening. "What the bloody . . . !"

"You . . . beast!" Caroline fumed; her upraised hand—just used to slap him halfway into next week—now fisted, as if she'd contemplated boxing his ear, or making his nose spout claret! Her parasol, a flimsy thing good only for languid strolls, was held low and furled in her left hand, its pointy brass ferrule winking in the wan sunshine, putting Lewrie in mind of a sword-point.

"What was that for?" he'd demanded, though he knew damn' well.

"You . . . *faithless* . . . lying . . . *bastard!*" she'd accused.

"Caroline . . . dearest!" he'd assayed, hoping to cozen her from her pet. "You're sadly mistook! It's not . . . *oww!*"

The fragile parasol had swept up high on her right, then slashed downwards and leftwards, catching him on the scalp (proving harder than advertised) and sending his ornate new cocked hat flying over the dun December grass. He'd lifted his wounded left arm in its sling to ward her off, too late, making him grunt with sudden pain.

Christ, she'd hit a wounded man? he gawped as he'd skittered to the rear in retreat; *mean t'say, me . . . and a wounded bloody hero?*

And this was the gentle wife and mother who'd spank the unruly child, then go off and weep into her aprons, the most kindly and . . . ?

"Bastard!" Caroline had insisted, moving that parasol into her right hand, taking a swordsman's lunge at his offending groin, making him squeak in alarm and retreat a step or two more.

With a pang of chagrin, he had realized that he'd fired a hulling shot into *himself.* Caroline might have been chary, and less than sincere with cordiality when presented with the sight of the handsome Widow Theoni Kavares Connor and her youngest drooling "git" in the perambulator. Impossible to avoid on the park's pathway, since Theoni's party and their skirts took up so much of it, impossible to snub her when here came the bold captain who'd saved her in the Adriatic, here came his father, General Sir Hugo, who'd called upon her before; glorious in his best uniform, glittering with gold lace and chain gimp.

Caroline hadn't voiced the slightest cattiness when shown the pudgy little bastard, who, unfortunately, was enough grown a "crawler" for the *uncanny* resemblance to her loyal husband to begin to be evident, no! The vertical furrow in her brows that sprouted when she was wroth with him *hadn't* sprouted 'til Theoni was leaving. She *hadn't accused him* of that . . . yet.

And then he'd blurted out that she was mistaken, before she said a blessed thing, only confirming her deepest suspicion! *Idiot!* he had chid himself; *but if the mort had t'honour me for her salvation, why not call him James Alan Connor, 'stead o' Alan James, for all the damn' world t'wonder at?*

No time for rational thought or inventive lying, though, for his wife had begun to slash right-and-left like a trained cavalry trooper; forcing him to retreat and duck that gaily coloured parasol! *Him* of all people, the very picture of a British sea-dog, two medals jouncing on his chest, sporting an honourable wound taken in arduous Service for King and Country, the tasselled epaulet of a Post-Captain of less than three years' seniority on his right shoulder . . . retreating from a woman? Just about ready to cut and run?

There'd been a clutch of fashionable onlookers, tittering and hooting Caroline encouragement, guffawing at him; Royal Navy officers, midshipmen, and tars watching, too, ashore to share the day of celebration. *Gawkin' at me?* he'd quailed. But, what *could* he have done, in those circumstances . . . draw his sword in defence? Slug her senseless?

"Caroline, for God's sake!" he'd pled, instead. "I've not done anything, honest! Tongue-lash me in private if you like, but . . . !"

"Liar!" Caroline shrilled, loud enough to startle even the fat park pigeons to flight, slashing at him some more. "Liar, liar, liar!" she had howled, pleasant, familiar features pinched pale, but oddly dry-eyed, Lewrie had taken ominous note. That had been the very worst sign. Had she wept tears of rage, sadness, or betrayal, he *might* have held out hope.

"Madam!" he'd huffed, dredging up what shreds were left of his courage, and his husbandly dignity and authority—safely beyond her reach, it must here be noted!—"This is nought for the Mob's amusement. Your uncalled for rage is unseemly, and common!"

That'd stopped her in her tracks. Caroline had always put the greatest stock in their Public Image, her determination to appear as good as anyone of the squirearchy, no matter she and her kin had turned up as poor as church mice after fleeing the Lower Cape Fear settlements of the North Carolina colony after the Revolution, living on charity grudgingly given by her miserly Uncle Phineas Chiswick—thin as that was! 'And just you wait 'til I get you home!' Hadn't she regularly frozen the children stock-still, arrested in mid-stride, with that'un?

Caroline had hitched a deep breath, and had at last relented, lowering her "weapon" from High Third to rest the point on the ground, giving Lewrie space in which to look towards his family to see how the dispute was going down with them.

His eldest son, Sewallis, a lanky-lean eleven, looked as pale as death, hands pawed at midchest, ever the miniature parson, the one to shy like a whipped puppy at every start and alarum. His second, Hugh "the fearless," had gawped wide-eyed, glancing from mother to father, half-hidden and clinging to their ward Sophie, Vicomtesse de Maubeuge, and her skirts. Daughter Charlotte, now a brisk toddler and Caroline's duplicate, had glared at him as fiercely as his wife, face screwed up in tears, but mortal-certain it was his, a *man's* fault!

Sophie, who moments before had been lavishing in the grins and tipped hats, the admiring glances of single young gentlemen, now hid her face behind an ivory-and-lace fan that vibrated against her lips in rapid little wing-beats, standing close to his father Sir Hugo, as she always did, eyes full of more sadness than shock.

And his father . . . ! The fashionable old stick looked as if he had bitten into a tart lemon; e'en so, there was the tiniest glint of "told you so" in *his* eyes.

So much for sympathy from him! Lewrie had sadly sighed; *Oh, it ain't fair! None of 'em meant a fig t'me. Not now, when I've gotten a touch o' real fame!*

"Damn you, Alan . . . damn you!" Caroline had spat, voice lower at last. "All the years you were at sea, me thinking so trustingly, and now . . . !" She'd hiccoughed, on the edge of breaking—mellowing at last? No, for she'd hitched a breath, one hand on a hip, one hand on the handle of her parasol as if it was a walking stick. "You're right, *sir!*" she'd snapped, the cynicism dripping. "This is not a public . . . *affair*, nor shall it be a private one 'twixt us, either. I know you now for a lying, cheating, dissembling, adulterous hound . . . *sir*, and I tell you now that I have no more desire to speak with you, nor see your earnest fool's face . . . nor even hear your name, ever again!"

She'd been choking, but she'd managed to say all that.

"Caroline . . ." Lewrie had attempted to say, opening his arms to her and taking a tentative step forward.

"Back, Devil!" she'd cried, bringing her parasol up to Guard and freezing him in place; she was too bloody good with it, as good as a French grenadier with a bayonet-tipped musket! "You will consider yourself dead to me, sir . . . to us. For so I, and we, consider you!"

"Uhm, Caroline, m'dear, surely . . ." his father had at last attempted to placate, but she'd whipped about to glare him to silence, and aimed her parasol at *his* crutch, too!

"Blood *does* tell, does it *not* . . . Sir Hugo?" she'd purred, all scornful. Which threat and cutting comment forced a quick retreat on that worthy's part, Sir Hugo's drink-wizened "phyz" suffused as red as his tunic, as he coughed "courtly" into his fist.

"Come, children. . . . Sophie. We are going back to our lodgings, now!" Caroline had ordered.

"But, Mummy!" Hugh had objected, whilst Sewallis dithered as was his timid wont, and Charlotte had glared daggers at father and her brother both.

"Madame, I . . ." Sophie had squeaked, lowering her fan, turning to Sir Hugo, whom she adored as her racy, stand-in *grand-père*. "Oh . . . what shall become of us, if . . . ?"

"Go along and obey your mistress, Sophie, there's a good girl," Sir Hugo had said. "Worst comes t'worst, we'll arrange something. Is that not so, Alan?"

"Hey?" he'd contributed, in his usually "sharp" manner.

"Gawd!" Sir Hugo had muttered under his breath, despairing.

"I am so sorry, *M'sieur Alain*, I . . ." Sophie had whispered, patting his good shoulder with a lace-gloved hand. Looking scared . . . enough to blab what she knew of Phoebe Aretino, at long last, did his wife browbeat her long enough?

All the years since the dying Baron Charles Auguste de Crillart had forced him to swear to see his family cared for after their escape from Toulon as the city fell, not knowing that his brother and mother had died in the same fight that'd killed *him*, that Sophie his younger cousin was all that was left. Since Sophie had become their ward, he had feared what she might reveal about his nubile young concubine . . . yet all that time, he was safe as houses on that score . . . 'til now!

A *vicomtesse* or not, Sophie would have nowhere to go, and with all of her family's wealth and lands lost—along with their heads to the guillotine!—would be as "skint" as a day labourer without the Lewrie roof over her head. She was young, pretty, vivacious, "missish," and coy; Caroline might even suspect that he and she . . . !

"I will write, somehow," Sophie promised, before turning away, joining Caroline, who had taken hold of Charlotte's hand and laid one on Hugh's shoulders to steer him; Sewallis would *always* be dutifully obedient. Caroline marched away, head held high, nostrils pinched and eyes afire for anyone who might gainsay her; briskly and huffily. His sons did turn and look back, now and then, whilst being frog-marched, with Sophie half trotting to catch up, one hand holding up her skirts, the other plying a handkerchief to her nose or eyes, and the elegant egret feathers of her saucy bonnet a'dance.

"What shall become of us, indeed," Sir Hugo had intoned. "Or of poor Sophie, should Caroline turn on her?"

"Christ on a crutch, but I'm fucked!" Lewrie had groaned aloud, shuddery and awestruck, nigh to tears as he saw Hugh looking back and trying to dig in his heels.

"Fair-accurate assessment, yes," Sir Hugo had replied, and his cynical little chuckle had snapped Lewrie's head round to gawp at him.

"Think she'd divorce me?"

"Damned expensive, a Bill of Divorcement," his father had speculated, flicking stray lint from his tunic. "Years o' litigation in Parliament. More trouble than they're worth, 'less there's a mountain o' money ridin' on the outcome. The cost . . . money *and* the notoriety, too. *That'll* mostlike daunt her. I'll see she sees the consequence . . . assumin' she lets me on the property 'fore next Christmas! Worst might be total estrangement . . . more common than ye know, even considerin' the kiddies."

"Oh, God," Lewrie had gloomed, dashing a hand over his brow.

"She'd have t'hire a solicitor, lay a case with her own Member of Parliament," Sir Hugo had sensibly pointed out, not without one of his sly leers and almost a nudge in the ribs. "And that's Harry-bloody-Embleton. She just may despise *him* worse than she despises *you*, me lad! Wouldn't give him the satisfaction, after all these years!"

"That otter-faced whoreson hears of it, he'll offer, to get even with me!" Lewrie had fretted. "Get back in her good books. He *always* had his cap set for her, and now . . ."

"Sir Romney, the baronet, won't let him," Sir Hugo had scoffed. "What, his son, down for the baronetcy, wed to a tainted wife? With a brood o' children not his *own*, sir? A grass-widow 'thout a dot o' free hold land or anything beyond her paraphernalia? Embletons don't wed . . . tenants! No, Caroline's the sort to groan in her martyrdom, take solace in family sympathy, perhaps, but never that. Too righteous."

His father had shivered and made a "brrr!" sound at the idea of Righteousness. "Doubt she'd put cuckold's horn on ye, either, takin' any lover. Be tempted, p'raps, but that'd be too common, too much of *your* nature t'suit her primness."

"Damme!" Lewrie had fussed of a sudden. "Can't you say something, I don't know . . . charitable, or comforting, or . . . ? My entire life's just turned t'dung, and . . ."

"Ye know it's rainin', so why 'piss down yer back'?" Sir Hugo had snickered, relentlessly sarcastic. "Oh my, you'd prefer . . . ?"

He'd laid a hand on his heart, cocked back his head, one palm to his "fevered" forehead, and "emoted" like an overly dramatic thespian. "You *poor* misunderstood *fellow*, how *horrid* for you! It is just *so* unfair!" he'd declaimed. "None o' *your* doin', I'd vow! There," he said, leaving character. "Was that better?" he asked, reverting to a sardonic squint.

"Damme, you know it's not!" Lewrie had snapped.

"Why'd ye *ask*, then?" his father chirped back, with a shrug.

"Fair, I mean," Lewrie had stammered. "Mean t'say, a man in his prime, so long away from home . . . bloody years at sea! What must a woman expect, now the heirs are born, and healthy? The fashionable sort, they spare their wives the risk of more childbirth, it's what people *do*, for God's sake, and . . ."

"Oh aye . . . either of *us* become the fashionable sort, you just run come tell me," Sir Hugo had sneered. "Caroline ain't the fashionable sort, though, son. Farm-raised, Colonial pious. Not the sort to be thankful for you . . . sparin' her the terrors o' childbed fever."

"Damn!" Lewrie had sadly groaned, seeing a glum future ahead.

"Women simply *won't* see things in their proper perspective," the old fellow grumbled peevishly. "Still . . . a few months' absence might mellow her, once she thinks on her new situation."

"Do you really believe that?" Lewrie had said with a scowl, realising that his wife was not the sort to knuckle under merely for the sake of her financial security, nor her children's sake, either.

"No . . . but you *were* castin' for straws."

"Gawd, they never meant a thing to me!" Lewrie had carped. "A night or two o' comfort and pleasure, that's all. Not even Theoni, or Phoebe Aretino. Well, months in her case. Claudia, Lady Emma Hamilton—"

"Name me no names!" his father had cautioned. "Does Caroline know of 'em, I'd best *appear* clueless. Damme, our Ambassador to the Kingdom of Naples and the Two Sicilies's wife? Umm-*hmmm!* Impressive!"

"Whatever shall I do?" Lewrie had beseeched.

"Soldier on, buck up! The both of us. I just may've ridden a last time with the local hunt, too. Well, London's nice this time o' year . . . top o' the Season, and all. Stock in John Company's doing main-well. May run up a town house, after all. Though I will miss my new *bungalow*, and the stud . . ."

"Sorry I ruined *your* retirement years!" Lewrie had shot back.

An urchin came up with Lewrie's hat, hand out for reward, and Lewrie fumbled a copper from his coin-purse.

"A bluddy *pence?*" the urchin scowled. "Yer a cheap bashtid . . . *an'* a hen-peck!"

"Bugger off!" father and son chorused.

The very day of glory, Lewrie had groused as they'd begun a slow walk down the gravelled pathway; *a prize frigate sure t'be bought in, a king's ransom for her as my share, real financial security at last, 'stead o' dribs and drabs from corrupt overseas Prize Courts paid out years in arrears! What'll this cost me? All, most-like, with kiddies to rear, Sophie to dowry, Charlotte. . . .* It'd like to made him weep!

The onlookers had departed, bored with a lame show. His good name *might* survive the confrontation!

Lewrie had grown up not far from the Park in St. James's Square. He'd learned well the cynical lesson of Society, with all its charade and humbuggery. The world accepted what a man showed, believed an outward, public face. Did one *saunter* away from such a shaming, languid and unaffected, shrug it off as a minor domestic annoyance, even *jape* about it, well . . . ! People would even admire his blithe *persona!*

What Men thought—and when you got down to the nub, it was what Men thought that mattered, not women—would depend on his play-acting. Now, did he blub and boo-hoo, act cutty-eyed and overcome, he'd become known as a sentimental cully, one unable to rule his own house or wife, who confessed his affairs, and that would *invite* sneers and guffawings.

No, no matter how he *felt,* he'd have to play up bold, the merry rogue, rake-hell, and "damme-boy"; un-contrite and only a *tad* abashed! Cynical as Society was, how eager other men enjoyed to see another in their situation escape with a smile upon his lips (and by association be successful at their own failings!), Lewrie was mortal-certain that, did he stay in London long enough, there'd be more'n a few who'd dine him out on his disaster!

Hmmm . . . disaster, Lewrie had thought; *cat-as-tro-phe. Wonder why I don't hurt, bad as yer s'posed to? 'Coz I'm a callous bastard? No, that can't be it.* Knew *I'd trip over my own prick, sooner or later, but . . . two, three years gone, thousands of miles alee, what was I s'posed t'do, live like a hermit monk? This as bad as it gets? Not so bad . . . yet. Practice my strut? Grin? Put me a bounce on. . . .*

Making Easterly, they came to the end of the footpath, where it crossed a carriageway, where Lewrie had frozen in midstep, stumbling against his father's arm as he suddenly realised that Dame Fortune— that fickle whore—wasn't done with him!

"God Almighty!" Lewrie had gasped.

"What the Devil's come over ye?" his father had griped.

"Them . . . in the coach, yonder. Don't *look* at 'em, damn your eyes!" Lewrie had warned, which made Sir Hugo peer and glower, as if ready to yank the coach door open, drag 'em out, and challenge them to a duel, *instanter*, the truculent old bastard! Lewrie had tried to see how the clouds were shaping, count leaves on trees, take up the hobby of bird-watching, *anything*, looking anywhere but at the coach; as two pinched, high-nosed, top-lofty men had glared back before the coachee whipped up and rattled them away.

"*What?*" his father had demanded, petulant. "Who were they?"

"One was George John the Earl Spencer," Lewrie had informed him with a woozy sense of impending doom beyond what Caroline had in- stilled. "First Lord of The Admiralty. T'other was Mister Evan Nepean . . . the First Secretary. Them who tell me where t'go and what t'do. My damned . . . *employers!*"

"Ah!" Sir Hugo had answered, snapping his jaws turtle-like in as- perity. "Well damme, that's a bugger . . . ain't it."

"Christ, I am *fucked*, really, really, *really* fucked!"

"All's not lost. There's always strong drink," Sir Hugo said. "Have

I learned a blessed thing in this shitten world, 'tis that wine tends t'soften the blows. Brandy's even better. Aye, brandy's what's called for. What I'd prescribe. Shall we? Mind, you go all weepy in it, and I'll swear I don't know you from Adam."

"Lead on," Lewrie had numbly demurred. "I've *seen* Disaster in my life. I know how t'bear up."

"Topping!" Sir Hugo had chortled. "Forward, then! We'll need song, mirth, and glee, too. Here's one for ye. Irish. It'll make yer bog-trottin' sailors happy, d'ye learn it! Ahem!

> *"Oh, there's not a trade that's goin',*
> *wor-rth knowin' or showin',*
> *li-ike that from Glory growin',*
> *for a Bowld Soldier Boy!*
> *Whe-ere right or left we go,*
> *sure you know, friend or foe,*
> *we'll wave a hand or tow*
> *from the Bowld Soldier Boy!*
> *There's ain town that we march through,*
> *but the ladies look, and arch . . .*
> *through the window panes will sarch*
> *through the ranks to find their Joy!*
> *While up the street, each girl you meet*
> *with looks so sly will cry 'my* eyye'!
> *Oh, isn't he a dar-el-in',*
> *the Bowld Soldier Boy!"*

It had worked, Lewrie had to admit. They'd gathered prancing children, as a marching band might, the sight of a trim and elegant old general with the pace and spine of a younger man, with a brave captain by his side, voices raised in praise of Glory and Women. Even soberlookin', too! People clapped their approval as they paraded off for a public house.

And bedamned—for the nonce—to Dame Fortune!

CHAPTER FIVE

*W*illis's Rooms had seen its share of wastrels and rollickers in its time. While their common rooms began serving hearty breakfasts for the industrious sort 'round 7 A.M. the kitchen staff also was ready for those idle layabouts who rose much later or sent down for chocolate, rusks, or toast, too "headed" from a night of amusements to even leave their bedsteads . . . sitting upon plumped pillows, swinging to sit on the side of the mattress for a proffered chamber pot; and one breath of fresh air once the bed curtains had been pulled back, was about all they could manage.

Lewrie, unfortunately, felt about as "headed" as any man born, even after rising at a lordly 9 A.M. dousing and scrubbing with a tin of hot water, and receiving a fresh shave from Aspinall whilst he had himself a wee nap. Three gulped cups of coffee had only made him bilious and gassy, with a tearing need to "pump his bilges," much like a dairy cow on hard ground, at least thrice.

"Breakfast, sir?"

"Don't b'lieve I'd *manage* solids this morning, Aspinall," Alan replied with some asperity, "but thankee."

His father, Sir Hugo, came bustling into the set of rooms, done up in his regimentals, less his tunic, and draped in a tan nankeen and flower-sprigged embroidered dressing gown; face fresh-shaved and ruddy, eyes bright and clear, tail up, and bursting with *bonhomie*.

"Bloody *awful* mornin!" Sir Hugo rather loudly informed him. "It is rain, rain, rain. Urchins and mendicants'll drown in this, just you wait an' see!"

"Hush!" Lewrie begged, squinting one-eyed at that fell apparition, wondering why turning his head resulted in thick, swoony feelings.

"Dear Lord, still 'foxed,' are ye? Out o' practice, I expect. Takes work, d'ye know . . . years o' conditionin'," his father said with a faint sneer at Lewrie's lack of "training" as he swept back his gown, plucked a chair from the small card table, and plunked himself down . . . damn' near by the numbers like a military drill, with all the requisite "square-bashing" thumps and thuds of the steel-backed Redcoat.

"Christ," Lewrie grumbled, ready to cover his ears.

"Amateur," Sir Hugo scoffed with a twinkle. "Ah!" he cried, as his swarthy, one-eyed Sikh manservant, Trilochan Singh, entered. The pock-marked *baʒaari-badmash* with the swagger of a *raja* was the terror of half the goose-girls in Anglesgreen; all Surrey, too, for all Alan knew!

"*Namasté,** Leerie *sahib!*" Singh barked, at stiff attention with a stamp of his boots, damn near saluting in Guard-Mount fashion.

"Bloody Hell!" Lewrie groaned. "*Chalé jao . . . mulaayam!*"†

"Ah, ye *do* recall some Hindi!" his father noted, clapping his hands. "Pay him no mind, Singh. *Chaay, krem ké saath,* and *naashté ké li-ye* for *do.*"‡

"*Bahut achchaa,* Weeby *sahib! Ek dum!*"§ Stamp-Crash, About-Turn, *Crash-Crash-Crash,* Quick March, *Crash-Stamp* Salute, *Baroom,* Slam Door!

Lewrie put his head in his hands and laid his forehead on that small table, feeling that whimpering in pain might not go amiss.

"Here, for Christ's sake," Sir Hugo growled, producing a flask of brandy and pouring. "Never heard o' hair o' the dog that bit ye? Decent French guzzle, too. Thank God for smugglers. This'll put the spring back in your step, and clear the cobwebs. Aye . . . good lad."

Lewrie made "Bbrring" noises, grimaces and gags, but the brandy seemed liable to stay down, and his vision *did* slightly clear.

---

*Namasté = Good morning.
†*Chalé jao . . . mulaayam!* = Go away, soft(ly).
‡*Chaay, krem ké saath/naashté ké liye* for *do* = Tea with cream/breakfast for two.
§*Bahut achchaa/Ek dum* = Very Good! At once!

"Caroline scarpered, I take it?" Sir Hugo asked, gazing about the set of rooms, noting the lack of children, noise, clutter, and luggage.

"Aye, more's the pity . . . soon as they got back from the park," Lewrie mournfully informed him, giving him a *precis* of her letter, too.

"Well, damme," his father harumphed. "Thought she had more sense than that. Not that she didn't shew it, anent your finances. At least there's no mention of divorcement. Now, were it I who got such a note, I'd heave a great sigh, cry 'thank God for gettin' off so cheap' then dance off t'me bus'ness. Won't break you, after all . . . and, there's a sum of prize money still owin' that's yours alone."

"Damn!" was Lewrie's sour comment to that. "She's my *wife*, not a deal gone wrong, they're my children, not . . . oh, why bother trying to explain such to you!"

"Aye, I forgot, I'm a callous ol' bastard," Sir Hugo replied as casually as if he'd been told he had grey eyes. "Ah! Breakfast!"

Trilochan Singh entered astern the housemaid, who bore a large tray full of covered dishes, looking like to pinch or goose her, once the tray was safe. Boiling-hot tea was quickly poured, with cream in a small silver plate ewer, and a footed silver bowl of brown West Indies *turbinado* sugar, pre-pared from the loaf. Aspinall attempted to assist, but was outbustled by the maid and Singh as they removed the lids to reveal both fried and scrambled eggs, buttered hot rusks, and a choice of sizzly-crisp bacon or sliced roast beef.

Lewrie stared at the repast, pondering and massaging his belly, cautiously inhaling the savoury odours and steams; watching, as his father turned a brace of fried eggs into a soupy mess with knife and fork, spooned up some jam to slather on half a rusk, then dredged it in the eggs and took a bite.

"Only enemies of the Borgias died of eatin'," his father said, chewing and sighing most ecstatically. "Trust me . . . the greasier the better, in your condition."

Lewrie tentatively allowed his plate to be laden. Hot tea with cream and sugar, well . . . hmm, well, well! More cobwebs cleared. A taste of bacon . . . a forkful of eggs, which needed pepper and a *lot* of salt, he discovered. The roast beef was a tad dry and crusty, perhaps leftovers of last night's fare in the common rooms, but . . . my my, was that mango *chutney* in the jar with which to liven it up? Yum! Oh, even better, for here came a dab of fried, diced potatoes ... his favourite "tatty hash"!

The rusks were crunchy, but softened with good butter, and the jam was a tangy-sweet lime marmalade, and good God, was he out of tea so soon?

"Lazarus ... come forth!" Sir Hugo said with a snicker.

"Mmmmf ... something like that," Lewrie confessed, swallowing.

There was a knock at the door, which Aspinall answered, coming to the table a moment later. "There's a note come for ya, sir," he announced, setting it beside Lewrie's plate, sealed and folded shut, with no return address—local? A sudden pall fell over the table.

"Well?" his father pressed at last, as Alan studiously ignored it. "It can't be from Caroline, surely. She ain't *that* prolific!"

Lewrie opened it, wishing he had tongs, sure it'd scald. . . .

"Ah," Lewrie commented, after reading the salutation, with the *sang-froid* he rarely displayed aboard ship. "Of a sort ... it *regards* Caroline," he lied (main-well, he thought!) as he refolded it and stuck it in his waistcoat pocket. "From my solicitor, Mountjoy. She must have sent him a note before coachin' back to Anglesgreen. He asks me to come round."

Actually, he'd *meant* to call upon Mr. Matthew Mountjoy that day, to make an equitable arrangement—or one that wouldn't break him! ·

"I see," his father replied, going back to his breakfast, but with a leery cast to his eyes; too *blasé*-bland for comfort!

Not a total lie, Lewrie consoled himself; *but, damme, do I dare? All I can do with Theoni is accept her sorrow that she caused a mess in the park yesterday! Be a damn' fool t'go, but ... Gawd, what if she finally cries 'belly plea' to a court and takes what I've left to keep up her ... our son? No, surely not, not Theoni, she's rich as Croesus in her own right ... the currant trade, an' all? Hmmm ... still.*

And he thought it deuced odd that, far from having his breakfast turn to lead in his stomach from even more to worry about, he was digesting rather well, thankee very much!

Catastrophe *can* be stood, he decided!

CHAPTER SIX

South Montagu Mews was a very fashionable street, Nor'east of Oxford Street and its confluence with Park Lane and Hyde Park, within nonstrenuous walking distance, really. Though not quite as costly an address as the more stately Montagu Square, it was better than passing-fair as a place to hang one's hat.

Much like the Navy, London houses were under The Rates for tax purposes. A house that took up 900 square feet of footing, no matter how tall, was a First Rate—and Mistress Theoni Connor's was!

"Done herself proud," Lewrie muttered to himself as he climbed down from the back of the one-horse hack that was little better than a two-wheeled country dogcart with a canvas covering, and paid his cabman.

A sullen rain still fell, but nowhere near the morning's deluge, so, clad in a snugly impervious boat-cloak, and a cocked hat that had already seen its share of "heavy weather," he could take time to assay the street and the house before him.

It was a homey red-brown brick, set off with the white cornices and stone bands so popular in the '50s and '60s, with an elevated doorway at the left-hand side, redone Palladian, and trimmed with railings in ornate wrought iron filigree; two wide windows filled the right-hand side. Above, there was the ostentation of a wrought iron balcony across the whole of the first upper floor. It was a four-storey house, with three windows set in each level. Even with a typical two rooms per floor, it was a *lot* of house!

Up and down the street, Lewrie could see a mix of old brick and the more fashionable Italianate facades that people insisted on putting on lately.

He ascended the steps up from the sidewalk to the door, and lifted the knocker—a grinning Venetian lion's head shockingly similar to the one on his own door, back in Anglesgreen! For a second, he felt his resolve melt, feeling in his bones that seeing Theoni in person was a really bad idea, but . . . she had asked to see him, for him to call, and they *did* have a child in common—purportedly. Chiding himself for a coward, he began to rap the knocker.

A cherubic older fellow in a suit of plain, dark grey "ditto" opened the door and beamed at him with the smile of a well-fed prelate in a rich parish. "Sir?" he asked.

"Captain Lewrie, come to call . . . I believe your mistress expects me?" Lewrie replied, a bit more tentatively than he liked.

"Come into the front parlour, sir . . . Captain Lewrie, and I'll inform Mistress Connor of your arrival," the old fellow bade, bowing as he stepped aside to wave him in. "Just this way, sir . . . I do believe you are expected, though there was no reply to mistress's note . . . ?" he seemed to scold; obviously, the old catch-fart knew more of his employer's business than was good for him, though Theoni could only have hired him in the last year. He accepted Lewrie's hat and boat cloak, but only took them as far as the mirrored coat-stand; easily fetched if she shooed him off, or had no time for him.

The parlour was impressive; pale green walls were nicely set off with stark, gleaming white wood trim. Pastoral artwork was hung, along with gilt-framed mirrors. The massive fireplace was smokey-threaded white marble, and the furnishings were upholstered in pale yellow or in floral-patterned ecru, atop gleaming wood floors carpeted here and there with Turkey rugs. There were rather good books in the cases, and might even have been read once, though Lewrie suspected they'd been picked up at a secondhand auction by the lot, displayed mostly for the ornate gilt bindings—the way most new homeowners who aspired to Society did! Lots of brass and silver plate objects out for show . . .

"Alan . . . Captain Lewrie!" Theoni called, spinning him about.

"M-Mistress Connor," he barely had the wit to say, though in his heart, as deeply in trouble as he was, thinking "Yum!"

She wore one of those Frenchified concoctions, in an *un*-widowly azure with white trim, a high waist sash, and no underpinnings, so the gown hung straight, clinging as she walked toward him with her hands out in greeting; puffed upper sleeves, very tight lower sleeves, down to her wrists, and a very low neckline. Her russet-chestnut hair was long and loose, but gathered with matching ribbons.

So exotic-looking, with wide, high cheeks in a fairly lean face, a squareish jaw that tapered to a pert chin, a wide and generous mouth graced by such full, plump lips, eyes so amber-brown and slanted almond-shaped . . . those gently bobbing poonts!

Their hands met below waist-level, decorously keeping them apart for the servant's eyes, at least, though there was a glimmer of joy in her eyes. She gave his hands a shake, then frowned.

"Sorry, I forgot your noble wound," she said ruefully. "Not the first you've borne," she commented, releasing his left hand. "Captain Lewrie was my rescuer in the Adriatic, Mobley. He took a wound fighting for my life there, as well."

"Yes, madam," the old servant replied, bobbing, blinking, and nigh fawning, admiring the two medals twinkling on Lewrie's chest.

"We'll have coffee, Mobley."

"Right away, madam."

She led him to a settee, each taking one end, with a space apart; again, decorously. There followed some idle chit-chat 'til the coffee arrived, delivered by an older maidservant.

"That should do for now," Theoni said.

"Yes, ma'am," the maid replied, bobbing a curtsy and departing.

"Man and wife," Theoni announced after she had gone.

"Hey?" Lewrie could but gawp. *Gawd, what'd she mean by . . . !*

"Mobley and his wife . . . the maid," Theoni explained. "I took them both on, together. She also cooks. I try to run a small staff, now that the French have occupied the Ionian islands. The currant business is disrupted, you see. They now hold poor Zante, and the English House. My parents get a letter out, now and then. They say things are bad, though the French buy currants, as well. Even if they are tyrants. And tyrants never pay *well*, not like the days before, so . . ."

Right, she's out for blood and *money*, Lewrie thought, steeling himself for a "touch" on his savings!

"You are not in, uhm . . . financial distress, are you?" he asked, thinking he was getting to the point.

"Oh, no, Alan!" Theoni chuckled, with a generous grin. "What my in-laws sell is dearer than before, and you English *must* have jams and preserves for your puddings and duffs! I merely take sensible precautions against wasteful expenses. An annual trip to Bristol, so Michael knows his late father's kin . . . but I do not aspire to a country house or acres, and I do not quite follow London style. I stay in town the whole year round."

"Reassurin' for your servants, then," Lewrie said, feeling as if he would exhale with a loud *whoosh* if allowed. "No one laid off at the end of the Season, when most folks head for the country, and they end up broke and homeless 'til the Quality come back."

"Yes. It makes for a certain . . . loyalty," Theoni supposed as she poured coffee for them. "Should I have sent for tea, instead? I prefer coffee . . . strong and dark, the Turkish way. All *those* tyrants were ever good for, but . . ."

Lewrie sugared his and sipped; it was ambrosia! Strong, dark, and heady, indeed, quite unlike most of the coffee served in London.

"The Turkish way is perfect, thankee," he agreed most happily.

"Now," she intoned, setting down her cup, leaning back all prim and folding her hands in her lap. "The reason I asked you to call. I am so very sorry for what you suffered in the park, yesterday . . . at your hour of honour and triumph, after all! Alan, believe me, it was never my intention to . . . what we had . . . it was always my hope that it would remain only between us."

"Have," Lewrie added, turning glum, though able to look her in the eyes; and was puzzled to see her almost stiffen in response, those eyes of hers glittering too brightly, with the ghost of a grin upon her lips! "Father says he has my eyes. Mean t'say . . ."

"Yes, he does," Theoni cheerfully confessed. "More than your eyes. Barely a year old now, and I swear that he already has your . . . boldness.

I know the world would say that I should feel shame, but I do not. I never will," she vowed, slipping a tad closer to him on the settee, her voice gentle and cooey... loving! "Your wife... did she know, or...?"

"Suspected," Lewrie said with a sigh, outlining the anonymous letter and its results, despite his father's assurances back in the summer that he'd seen Alan Connor and saw no resemblance, how there were too many other affairs hinted at. Theoni nodded patiently, and sagely through it all, sipping coffee and pouring warm-ups, but with her gaze demurely averted.

Disappointed, 'cause she's findin' out I'm a total rake-hell? he asked himself as he took note of her seeming discomfort; *Christ, does she harbour some notion I'd leave Caroline for her, since we have that child, together, or...?*

"So... Caroline has left me, in essence," he confessed at last, feeling alien, inhuman, in that he could say it *without* screaming out loud in anguish. "No divorce, but..."

"Alan, you poor man! I never meant to cause you such a pain!" she vowed, shifting even closer and opening her arms into which he rather gladly sank.

"Didn't quite plan on it, myself!" he countered, trying for the light note and almost making it, though a tad shakily. "Oh, hell..."

"I must say, though," she mused as she stroked his hair, leant quite close, almost cheek to cheek, "the look she gave me, just as we were introduced, filled me with dread. If *only* we had taken another pathway in the park, begun our walk earlier, or..."

"Had to happen, sooner or later, I s'pose," Lewrie graveled. "I expect, did her curiosity get the better of her, she'd have called on you on her own. Just what you need, a plague of Lewries 'fronting you in the streets. My father, my bloody in-laws...!"

"Well, Alan," Theoni all but cooed, "some Lewries are more welcome than others. I was quite surprised by your father's arrival. A very droll old gentleman."

"He behaved himself, then?" Lewrie just *had* to ask; he knew his father too well to trust him around any available, and handsome, lass.

"Quite well." Theoni chuckled again. "Though he does have the..."

jaunty? Is that the right word? The jaunty leer in his eye?"

"Aye, jaunty," Lewrie said with a wry smile. " 'Tis the tamest way for what he had in his eye to be said in polite company."

"Imagine my surprise when he did call," Theoni said, sitting up and reaching for her cup once more. "Mobley announced a General Lewrie, and I thought he had gotten it wrong . . . that it was you! He told me about that letter. He apologised for intruding, for . . . probing about at your wife's request. Barging in upon a total stranger."

"What'd you tell him, then?"

"The truth," she said, bald-faced. "Though elderly, he is *far* too cynical to accept lies. He winced at that. Screwed up his face. But he nodded . . . as if he understood."

She heaved a wry little laugh, a hitching of her shoulders.

"I expect that *he* left more than a few offspring in his path in his younger days," she commented.

"Me, included. I'm the only one he owned up to, and took as his own. Not as a Willoughby, though. Trust me, 'tis a long, sad story, and there was a pot of money involved."

"He is wealthy, now?" Theoni suddenly asked.

"Aye, he is," Lewrie answered, suddenly on his guard, suddenly feeling a sinking in his innards. Of *jealousy?* he wondered. "Some."

"Then the world is no longer at risk," Theoni said, laughing at that news. "Well-fed sharks do not bite, usually. He might even turn mellow . . . into a safe supper guest who doesn't have to sing."

Lewrie burst into a side-aching peal of laughter.

"Oh, God! My father . . . *safe!*" He hooted. "He'd steal the coins from his *own* eyes on his deathbed . . . and pinch the chambermaid with the winding sheet!"

"Then I see where you got your spirit." Theoni tittered.

"Aye . . . blood will tell, they say," Lewrie replied, sobering, recalling just where, and how, that adage had most recently been used.

"So what will you do now?" Theoni enquired.

"God knows," Lewrie said with a frown, slouching back into the settee. "Saw my solicitor, made some arrangements . . . safeguarded some funds and such. . . . . Most-like, it's back down to Sheerness for me, to put *Proteus* back in the water and toddle off to sea. What I'm good at. Where I don't get in much trouble. Mostly."

"But that was where you got in trouble with me, Alan," Theoni pointed out with a becoming smirk. "At sea."

"Aye, it was," he agreed, enfired by the look in her eyes, as if she wouldn't mind a tad *more* "trouble," should he dare risk it. All of a sudden, the tension between them became as palpable, and as visible, as St. Elmo's Fire surging in the top-masts of a storm-cast ship!

"I ... uh," he croaked, groping for lucidity. "I'd best ..."

"How to say this?" she puzzled aloud, frowning. "Though I wish you no pain in your life, Alan ... and I certainly do not wish to complicate things even worse than they are, I will never regret being your lover ... even for such a short but blissful time. I will never regret having your son. I feel ... blessed! He will be the part of you that I will have, always. All the part of you that I *expected* to have in this life, knowing that your wife ... but now?"

"Theoni, I ..." Lewrie croaked again, sure now that coming was a bad idea, that yawning before him was a gaping abyss that could sear his soul in Hellfire, should he abandon all his vows, his ...

"I told your father the truth when he came, as I said," Theoni continued, sliding close once more and gazing at him with such an open and frank expression. "I told him that I loved you, Alan. That when I married my late husband, it was arranged ... for the business. After a time, I *came* to love him, I was comfortable and content, and I had Michael, but ... that's why I asked you to come call upon me today. To tell you that whatever happens, I am sorry for causing any rift. I did *not* pray that you and your wife would part, and that I *do* regret, now that I know it.

"But I want you to know that whatever happens, should you feel free, should you truly *be* free," she went on, stumbling a bit, waving a hand in haste, her words tumbling together, "that I will *always* be here for you. Not just as a 'dear friend,' Alan, but as someone who really loves you! Who would be yours completely, but for fortune!"

"Theoni ..." he said with a dry gulp.

"Oh, I know!" she almost whimpered, getting to her feet to dash away and hide her face with her long chestnut hair, as if ashamed of his seeming rejection. "I only make it worse! But if I wait to tell you in a letter, and you a thousand miles away at sea, you'd never see me as . . . !"

She turned to face him, though with eyes downcast at the floor, arms crossed tight below her bodice. Her eyes were wet with tears!

"If you ever come to me, no matter what your English Society has to say about it . . . about *us*," she vowed, chin up of a sudden, proudly and almost defiantly forlorn, "I will deny you nothing. Whatever we may make of stolen time together, *open* time together, it makes no difference. I *know* I'm not English, the sort one can take into the public, I *know* it's brazen and sinful of me, but I cannot help that, Alan. I love you so much, I have no shame!" she vowed, her face screwing up.

He'd risen, drawn by her retreat; he stood non-plussed, short of enfolding her in comfort, or lust, or *whatever* it was that he felt at that moment!

"Theoni, I had no idea, I . . ." he stammered. Now he knew that he really *should* go, *instanter*. But he couldn't, of course.

She raised one hand to dab at her eyes, and that tore it! Lewrie stepped forward and embraced her as best he could, and her arms went about his neck, her tears and muffled sobs trickled on his neck, and their loins pressed together *so* fiercely; almost grinding.

"There, there . . . there, there," he whispered, stroking her back. "I never knew! Theoni, I knew it was special, it felt so righteous, if one can use that word, so . . . holy, but I never thought . . . !"

Leave, leave, leave, and never a backward glance! he thought in agony; *be a man, for once!*

"You *did* care for me, Alan?" Theoni asked, hot breath searing him. "Really cared, not just for a little while?"

"Well, o' course I did! But, we both knew the circumstances of our lives. We took solace . . ."

"And pleasure," Theoni added, with a hiccoughy chuckle, and an easing of her fierce grip to something more . . . fond.

"Aye, that too. Lashings of pleasure!" he admitted, recalling all too well those stolen hours in his great-cabins, in that lodging she'd taken in Lisbon before her packet ship had departed. "I don't know what's to happen, though, Theoni, and I can't just walk away from Caroline so easily . . . mean t'say, I can't cause *you* pain, hanging by your thumbs with false hopes, and . . . I won't make you go through that, I won't!"

There, he thought, despite himself; that *felt right-righteous!*

"I *know* that, Alan, I trust you!" she declared, "But, even if your wife and you reconcile, I would *still* long to be near you as we are now . . . as we were then," she added, suggestively.

"I must go," he stated, far too late.

"I know," she acquiesced, easing her grip on him, yet loath to release him completely. "We must wait and see what happens. After all that has passed between us, though . . . I wanted you to know how I feel. Oh, that you were a bachelor when you fought the Serb pirates for me!"

"Saved a lot o' woe, all round," Alan sadly chuckled, forehead to forehead, and equally loath to let go of her flesh, enraptured by a heady aroma of clean hair, rosemary and thyme, commingled with a newer scent of light rosewater. They lifted their chins at the same time, their noses bumped—her artfully wee and sculptured nose!—then their lips. Searching, hungrily writhing, her breath already hot and musky with arousal!

"I must go," he repeated, after a *long* few moments of bliss.

"I know that, too, dearest Alan," she whispered back so fondly, toying with the back of his neck with her nails, sending chills down his spine, straight to his groin! "It is too soon, too shocking, atop the other shock you have taken. Too early. But before your ship puts back to sea, if you want me, I will come to you, I promise. And I will ask you for no promise in return, no matter how things stand. I truly do love you, so I could not do otherwise. Now, go! Be a hero!"

She turned playful, after a moment of shuddery truth, as if to shoo him away with a spank on the hindquarters.

"Theoni . . . no matter how things fall out, thankee," he said.

"I have your darling namesake son," she replied. "It is me who should be thankful."

She gave him one last parting kiss in gratitude.

"Now, go, before I become so tempted that . . . !" she gushed, now shoving him towards the hallway. "Be England's hero, Alan. You are already mine. Write me, for I will surely write you, and . . . oh, please go, before . . . !"

"I'll write," he promised her, fetching his own hat and cloak.

"I'll come to . . . Sheerness?" she suddenly proposed.

"Sheer-Nasty? You'll hate it! *Dreadful*-boresome hole!" he japed.

"With you, it will be Paradise," she swore with a smile.

Egads, what'd I just promise? he asked himself once by the kerb; *does Caroline despise me now, why make it worse? But . . . she can't loathe me more! In for the penny, in for the pound, oh God . . . !*

BOOK ONE

Longa exilias et vastum maris acquor arandum.

Long exile is thy lot, a vast stretch of sea thou must plow.

AENEID, BOOK II 780
PUBLIUS VERGILIUS MARO "VIRGIL"

CHAPTER SEVEN

C old, cold, cold! Faint skifts of snow littered the cobbles of the street
before the tavern and posting house, lay between the stones to make a
stark chequerboard, and skittered as dry as sand when a gust of icy wind
stirred. It was false dawn, the "iffy" time that outlined roofs and chim-
neypots with faint light, whilst the bulk of the street still lay in darkness,
here and there pinpricked by only a few faint lanthorns by the entrances
to homes or commercial establishments, and upon the quays, where false
dawn drew black-on-charcoal traceries of rigging and masts aboard the
ships that lay alongside.

Tiny, glim-like lights glowed at taffrails and entry-ports on those
docked vessels; a few more ghosted across the harbour waters as guard
boats rowed about to prevent desertion or smuggling. Hired boats and
ships' boats stroked or sailed to and fro, even at that ungodly hour,
bearing officers ashore, or taking officers or mates from a night of shore
comforts, perhaps even pleasure, in Sheerness.

Barely visible against the darkness, and a fine sea-haze off the North
Sea, fishermen were setting out, no matter the cold or the risk, to dredge,
rake, or net a meagre day's profit. Some sailed, a very good omen, with
tiny masthead lanthorns aglow that created eerie tan blots of lit, shivering
canvas—while the boats were invisibly dark—as if a plague of weary
Jack O'Lanterns were on the prowl.

There was a decent slant of wind, out of the Nor'Nor'east for once;
not enough to dissipate the cold sea mists, nor enough to toss the many

ships anchored in the Little Nore or Great Nore, but it'd do, for Lewrie's purposes; and after the night before . . .

Lewrie heaved a troubled but mostly contented sigh, recalling.

There had been a fine sunset, rare for winter, as red as any one could wish, that had lingered for an hour or more, much like a summer sunset; "Red Skies At Night, Sailor's Delight."

And wasn't it just! Lewrie told himself.

The glass barometer filled with coloured water by the door of his posting house had shown little rising in the narrow upper neck, a sign of higher pressure that had happily coincided with that sunset, and now a shift of wind, as well. HMS *Proteus* would not fight close-hauled to make her offing, then jog down-coast to The Downs or Goodwin Sands to re-anchor and wait for a good down-Channel slant, but could head out boldly, round Dover and bowl along like a Cambridge Coach, perhaps as far as Portsmouth, before the wind turned foul, as it always would in winter. Foul, and perilous!

The costly travelling clock on the mantel chimed five times, in civilian manner, as far-off ships' bells struck Two Bells of the predawn watch; a cacophonous tinkling disagreement 'twixt lieutenants' or mates' timepieces and sand-glasses, that put him in mind of the myriad of wind chimes he had heard in Canton, between the wars.

The night before, Gawd . . . !

A final round of shopping for last-minute cabin stores such as quills, ink, and paper, a new book or two, a chest of dried meats and hard-skinned sausages for Toulon's sustenance. They'd supped at a new and rather fine public house that featured large boiled lobsters aswim in drawn butter, some ham, boiled carrots, and winter potatoes, a green salad, a roast quail each, completed by cherry trifle. Then, as old Samuel Pepys had so often writ in his diary, ". . . and so to bed," most daringly nude for a few moments in the chilly room, no matter the big fireplace, the warming pans and enfolding bedstead curtains, the thick down-filled quilts and extra blankets. Bliss, strenuous bliss!

Unconscious of doing so, he had drawn out his pocket watch and opened it to compare its reckoning against her mantel clock and those ships' bells. With a firm-lipped sigh and a slight nod, he shut it up with a definite *clack* of finality.

"I must go," Lewrie softly pronounced.

"I know," Theoni Kavares Connor sadly replied, barely mouthing her words, her eyes already moistly aglitter. "I promised not to go on so, but . . . two years or more, so far away . . ."

She reached across the remains of their breakfast table to twine her fingers in his; slim, graceful, but incredibly strong and urgent.

"It's what sailors do," he told her. "We're not known for bein' a dependable lot." He strove to be winsome and Devil-I-Care, as well as noncommittal. Noncommittal won, with "winsome" a distant second.

" 'Absence makes the heart grow fonder'?" Theoni asked, citing an old adage, striving for a cheery note herself, forcing a smile.

" 'Early to bed, early to rise, makes a man healthy, wealthy and wise'," Lewrie countered, tongue-in-cheek.

"Quoting a revolutionary?" Theoni attempted to tease. "The American rebel, Benjamin Franklin . . . *Poor Richard's Almanack*, I believe?"

"Knew I'd heard it somewhere." Lewrie chuckled as he rose, with her hand still in his—leading and prompting his departure. Theoni sprang to her feet and rushed to embrace him, pressing her soft, sleek body tight to his in a twinkling, still toast-warm from the bed and their last "eye opener" bout, still redolent of perfume, musk, and sex.

"You're certainly healthy, dear Alan," she snickered against his cheek, as he stroked her back, so pliable and tender beneath the flimsy and revealing morning gown she wore, despite the chill. "Last night . . . it was heavenly!" Theoni sighed in recalled bliss.

"Don't know much about the 'wealthy' or the 'wise,' though," he pointed out, his voice deep and gravelly. "Nobody with a lick o' sense would get out o' bed so early, nor sail off to the West Indies, if . . ."

Nor take such a hellish risk as this! he chid himself, and not for the first time since the week before, when Theoni had breezed into Sheerness and announced her presence! Madness, sheer madness!

She rose on tip-toe to kiss him, as if to stifle any objections he might have voiced, her slim arms a vise about his neck, her breasts heavy and hot against his shirt and waistcoat.

"But you must," she said more soberly, after a long moment. "I will write you! I'll write daily . . . long *reams* of letters, what you call 'sea letters'!"

"As shall I," he found himself promising in return; such vows were easy at pre-dawn partings, though fulfilling them was a different story . . . depending on the excuses of Stern Duty once back aboard his ship, with its ocean of *minutiae.*

"Oh, I can hardly bear it!" she whimpered, going helpless and slack against him, forcing him to hold her tighter. "So *few* days we've had . . . *hours,* really!"

"But rather nice hours," Lewrie muttered in her hair.

"And when you return, there must be many, many more!" she vowed with some heat. "Nothing will keep us apart then. It would be unjust if . . . No matter how things fall out, I'll . . ."

"I know, Theoni," Lewrie cooed back, both hands now sliding up and down her slim back, from her hips and wee bottom to breast-level, to hoist and fondle. . . .

There came a rap upon the door.

"Damn!" Theoni fussed, stepping back and quickly gathering her dressing gown over her bed-gown and morning wrap, and scowling crosspatch for a second before vigourously brushing her hair into order.

"Enter?"

" 'Ere fer yer traps, sir," the manservant chearly said, bustling in with a boy servant in his wake. "Sailin' t'day, are we, Cap'um?"

"Aye," Lewrie replied, hands guiltily behind his back, quarterdeck fashion; as if to say, "I never touched her, honest!"

"Just th' one wee chest, an' these two soft bags, sir?"

"Aye, that's the lot," Lewrie answered.

"A fine mornin' t'set sail, Cap'um sir. Clear skies, an' fair winds," the manservant nattered on. "Does yer gig come t'fetch ya, or should I whistle ya up a boat, yer honour?"

"A hired boat would suit, thankee," Lewrie told him. "I'll be down, directly. T'settle the reckoning, and . . ."

"Rightee-ho, then, sir . . . Missuz Lewrie," the servant said as he doffed his battered tricorne to them and departed with the luggage.

Ouch! Lewrie thought with a wince; *salt in the wound, why don't ye, ye clueless bastard!*

When he turned red-faced to Theoni, though, he noted that she was amused, smiling to herself in the mantel mirror as she fiddled with the long reddish-chestnut curls at either side of her neck.

He slung his hanger through the sword-frog on his belt and took up his boat cloak to swirl about his shoulders, gathering his cocked hat and a pair of wool mittens . . . the ones that Caroline had knitted for him! His mouth made a tiny *tic* of ruefulness.

"There . . . think I'll pass muster?" he asked, once his hat was firmly clapped upon his head.

"Always, dear Alan," Theoni assured him, smiling even wider as she came to his side once more, flinging her warmth against him, kissing a'tip-toe. "The handsomest . . . most fetching . . . bravest . . . and cleverest . . . hungriest Sea Officer in all Creation!" She even managed to giggle between compliments and teasing, coy kisses.

"All my love goes with you," Theoni whispered at last, going all earnest, staring him directly in the eyes.

Crikey, what else can ye say t'that? he asked himself; *it's five thousand miles or so, two years at least . . . well, hmm.*

"And all of mine remains with you, my dear," he declared, though quickly burying his face in her lush hair and the hollow of her neck to nuzzle, savour and *groan* a semblance of agreement.

It ain't a total lie, he qualified to his conscience; *had I not wed so young, not met Caroline, before her, Theoni'd be . . .*

No matter her suspicion that he was lying like a rug, that made her seem to purr with contentment, to cuddle close and sigh happily.

"I am yours completely, Alan," Theoni softly swore. "Forever. Now go!" she suddenly ordered, playing at pushing him away. "Go beat the entire French Navy. Win the war all by yourself, then return to me . . . soon!"

"I'll work on that," Lewrie said with an *honest* laugh, letting her go as she played up brave for him, even essaying a playful pat on her rump, a love swat. No, his hand lingered; *so* soft and wee!

"I'll watch from the window. Blow me a last kiss, give me one last smile and wave," she demanded.

Dear God, it simply wouldn't do to saunter off with a last kiss, no matter it was all a sham! He swept her into his arms once more, to devour her mouth with his, to slither his hands beneath her gowns, for her warm flesh.

"Now that's a *proper* sailor's good-bye!" he cried, breaking away and all but sweeping his boat cloak 'round his body like an actor making a grand exit, stage left. "Good-bye, Theoni. Anything I can fetch you from the West Indies?"

"You!" she quickly announced, smiling and chuckling, even if she was again at the edge of hot tears. "As hungry for me as when you left me. Oh, perhaps a coconut or two. Well. Good-bye, my dearest Alan . . . safe voyages. . . ."

"*Adieu*," he declaimed by the door, ready to sweep out after his *congé*, hat on his chest, and the other hand on the doorknob. It need not be said that Captain Alan Lewrie, RN, knew a good moment for escape when he saw one!

"I've already paid the inn their week's reckoning," she said.

"Err . . . uhmm, well, then . . ." he flummoxed. "Thankee, for *all* you've done for me! *Encore, adieu, ma cherie amour!*"

"*Bonjour, mon amour . . . mon vie!*"

He tromped down to the public rooms, made a production of shivering at the cold, of studying the barometer, and japing with the two servants as he stepped outside into the dread chill, stamping his feet along with them as they trundled his chest and bags in a wheelbarrow toward the quays, and a hired rowing boat.

Once in the street, he turned and looked up at the front of the inn, to see Theoni framed in the windows of the room they had shared. She had fetched a four-arm candleholder to the sill, one that he didn't recall being lit when he'd departed, that illuminated her as well as the footlights of a Drury Lane theatre.

He waved widely, blew her that required kiss, which she played at catching and pressing to her own lips, then suggestively sliding it down to her heart, her face half-crumpled 'twixt glee and agony and so bravely bearing up. Her morning gown was parted, revealing amberish candlelit, and ample, bosoms. . . .

Damme, if I ain't ready t'cry off sailin' and go nuzzle 'twixt those beauties just one *more time!* Lewrie speculated, feeling the fork of his crotch tighten. *Gawd, she knows me too well, already, what sets me goose-brained* . . . witless *for it!*

One final wave, a doff of his hat and a "leg" made in *congé* and he *had* to turn away and tramp off quickly . . . before he was tempted to rush back and chuck his active commission!

CHAPTER EIGHT

"Hoy, the boat!"

"*Proteus!*" the bow-man called back, showing four fingers to indicate the size of the side-party for a Post-Captain, causing a scurry despite the fact that his return was known to the half-hour. Bosuns' calls shrilled, booted Marines thundered on cold oak decks, bare tars' feet pounded on the ladders, and icy hands slapped musket stocks, as a well-drilled ship's crew mustered to greet him.

As Four Bells struck, Lewrie took a moment to admire his ship, now that he was close-aboard her starboard side. Dawn had made her a shining jewel of fresh paint and linseed oil, of gilt trim and tarred rigging, her yards crossed to mathematical perfection, and fresh as a new-minted guinea. Even up close, she was just about perfection, now that she was out of the yards and back on her own bottom.

Lewrie stood, swept back his boat cloak, and tucked his sword behind his left hip so it wouldn't tangle between his legs, then clung to a side-stay of the hired boat as it nuzzled up to the ship's side by the main-chains, the boarding-battens and man-ropes of the entry-port. Judging the slight roll and toss of both boat and ship, he timed a leap and made it on the first try, nimbly ascending the side, with but only the merest twinge of weakness in his now-healed left arm as he gained the deck, fresh-scrubbed and holystoned nigh to parchment whiteness, and still damp from the crew's predawn labours, about the time he had drunk his last cup of coffee with Theoni, ashore.

Swords were flourished, boots stamped, muskets were presented, and the calls sang like eagles on high as he stepped in-board, safely on his own decks once more, and doffing his hat to the side-party and his gathered crew, who stood on gangways or in the waist with their hats in hand, their heads bared in their own salute. Some still chewing?

"The hands have eat, Mister Langlie?" he asked.

"In the process, sir," his First Lieutenant responded.

"My apologies for arriving in the middle of their meal, then, and pipe them back below, 'fore it goes cold on 'em. I take it that the galley is still hot?"

"Aye, sir."

"Then I'll have a pot of coffee," Lewrie briskly said, clapping his mittened hands together. "I've a chest and two bags to be got up."

"I'll see to it, directly, sir," Langlie vowed.

"Everything else in order for sailing, Mister Langlie?"

"Aye, sir. Last despatches came aboard just after you went off for shore, last afternoon," the darkly handsome Langlie said, smiling.

"Very well. Dismiss the hands back to their breakfasts, and I will be aft and below, 'til . . . Six Bells, at which time we'll get her underway. Carry on, Mister Langlie."

He went down the starboard ladder from the gangway to the waist, then aft into his great-cabins, past the Marine sentry; past the dining coach to larboard and the chart-space to starboard, the two dog-boxes where his clerk and his manservant slept, and into his day-cabin where an iron brazier/stove tried its best to banish the cold, its belly stoked with sea-coal and kindling.

Aspinall took his hat, cloak and sword, and his mittens, while Lewrie rubbed his hands over the brazier, thinking that if Admiralty were of a mind to punish him by shooing him off someplace very *far* overseas, he could at least be thankful that it would be someplace warm!

Riddled with malaria, cholera, and Yellow Jack, but warm! Lewrie chortled to himself. After a futile moment of trying to thaw out, he went aft to his desk, to survey the pile of official despatches bound in canvas and wax-sealed ribbons, his last personal correspondence. . . .

Nope, nothin' new, he thought with a tired sigh.

He had tried to call upon Lord Spencer and Mr. Nepean at Admiralty, but had been informed that those worthies had nothing *particular* to say to him, hence he had not been admitted. A letter *had* come from them, urging him ". . . should there be no pressing delay in your affairs, to repair at once to Sheerness to supervise the refit of your ship."

And once in Sheerness, the dockyard officials had been dilatory in supplying his wants, while other letters came down from London that urged a *quick* return to sea, and slyly asking "whyever not, *already?*"

Oh, it was harsh! Admiralty was miffed, not for his "affair" or morals; officialdom was miffed because he had had no control over his wife in public! On such things were careers unmade.

If he wished *Proteus* repainted, it would be at his own expense, though he had written one of those letters asking ". . . with the supply of paint on hand, Sirs, and the meagre budget allotted for the task, which *side* of the ship do you prefer that we paint?"

That had not warranted a reply, which was fortunate, for Admiralty was not known for its sense of humour, and any answer would have been a harsh censure, perhaps his relief and replacement as captain!

Finally, orders had come aboard, for the West Indies! Sealed orders, most intriguingly not to be opened 'til he had weathered Cape St. Vincent off Spain's Sou'west tip, had also accompanied them.

Since the war started in 1793, Prime Minister William Pitt and his coterie had shoved troops and ships into the Caribbean, eager for possession of every "sugar" island. It had cost the lives of 40,000 soldiers and seamen, so far. Once Fever Season struck, regiments and ships' companies could be reduced to pitiful handfuls in a trice!

No matter Lewrie had prospered there in his midshipman days, he *had* gone down with Yellow Jack in 1781, and had been damned lucky to survive it, even if every hair on his head had fallen out and he had turned the colour of a ripe quince! He was safe, therefore, unable to catch it again, but his hands . . . ?

Whilst *Proteus* was being re-rigged and re-armed, he had studied every anecdote, every official report he could lay his hands on anent service in the West Indies, looking for any clue as to why some ships hadn't suffered catastrophic loss, while others turned to ghost ships. He had spoken to Mr. Shirley the Surgeon and his mates, but even they were pretty much clueless.

It was "bad air"—*Mal-Aria*—the miasmas that rose from the soil of tropic lands at night, but they could not seal every port and hatchway, not without smothering or roasting the "people" in their own sweat and exhalations. They had requested *assefoetida* herbs to make sachets through which to breathe "bad air," but had been told that such would come from their own pockets, like much of a naval surgeon's stock of medicines, no matter the terms of the recent mutinies that required Admiralty to issue them free.

Empirically, fresh-boiled water was sometimes safer than water kept for weeks in-cask, and water taken aboard in the tropics was best if placed in fresh-scoured casks, and taken only from a clear-running stream. Mr. Durant had suggested going a bit more inland for water, to get above the usual wells or streams where cattle or horses drank, to avoid taking on the obvious turds, but even he didn't think that would aid in avoiding malaria or Yellow Jack. Cholera, perhaps, he had concluded, with a mystified Gallic shrug.

Lewrie had even queried his Coxswain, Andrews, once a slave in a rich Jamaican plantation house, about malaria and Yellow Jack as he had seen it when growing up.

"Wuss in mos'keeter time, sah," Andrews had puzzled, "when it's so hot an' still, an' th' air's full of 'em. I heered some ships don't get took so bad, do they stand off-and-on, nor anchor on a lee shore, but . . ." A mystified black man's shrug was nigh to a French one, one could safely deduce. For God's sake, *every* safe harbour in the Indies was in some island's lee!

Shovin' us off t'sea in February, Lewrie groused to himself, as he pawed through his pile of letters; *if that ain't a sign of their displeasure, I don't know what is. Lisbon first, despatches to Old Jarvy and his fleet . . . mid or late March, maybe early April before we fetch Antigua or Jamaica, hmmm . . . a safe month or so, 'fore it gets hot and the mosquitoes begin to swarm?*

He pondered Jesuit's Bark, *chinchona*, what was termed quinine; South American, probably cheaper and more available nearer its source. It was *reputed* to cure malaria, or ease its symptoms. Could he force the hands to drink *chinchona* bark tea as a preventative? Or would he have another mutiny on his hands, since it tasted like Satan's Piss?

Fresh fruit would be plenteous everywhere they went, and Mr. Shirley was certain that almost any fruit was anti-scorbutic to some degree, so they could avoid scurvy, if nothing else.

But one had to go ashore to get 'em, he thought; *Never anchor in a lee harbour or bay, near marshes and such, stand off-and-on after dark, well out to sea and up to windward of any land . . . ?*

"Yer coffee, sir," Aspinall announced, entering with an iron pot cradled in a dish-clout against its heat, to set on the brazier.

"Oh, good!" Lewrie replied, turning to smile at him, but seeing Caroline's portrait on the forward bulkhead of the dining coach; back when she was young and new-married, fresh and willowy, in a gauzy off-shoulder morning gown with a wide straw hat bound under her chin with a pale blue ribbon, East Bay of Nassau Harbour behind her, her light brown hair still worn long and loose and girlish, teased by the Nor'east Trades, painted smiling instead of the more common stern visage of most portraits, her merry eyes crinkling in delight, with the riant folds below those eyes . . . !

He averted his gaze.

He *had* considered taking her picture down, but had feared what gossip that would cause, worse. Busy ashore, and sleeping out of the ship nights, even when she was back in the water . . . God only knew what the gunroom, the bosun's mess, the midshipmens' cockpit on the orlop, and the forecastle hands had made of that! Already there were the averted eyes, the cautiously framed speech . . . !

Aspinall brought him a cup of coffee in his silvered tankard, from the HMS *Jester* days, with shore cream and pared *turbinado* sugar.

There *were* letters of a personal nature on his desk; one from his father Sir Hugo, one from Sophie, and a damned thick one from Theoni . . . already? He quickly shovelled that one into a drawer. Nothing from Caroline or the children, though.

All his official correspondence was up to date; his clerk Mr. Padgett had seen to that the past afternoon, all his bills paid. There was nothing to do but stew and fret and drink his coffee 'til Six Bells and 7 A.M. when it was time to sail, after the mists had burned off.

"Yer dunnage, sir," Aspinall said as two of his Irish sailors, the dim giant Furfy and his mate Liam Desmond, came traipsing in with his shore bags and the chest of last-minute stores.

"Mornin', men."

"Mornin', Cap'um, sor . . . top o' th' mornin', sor. That eager we be, t'see th' Indies . . . beggin' th' cap'um's pardon, sor."

"At least it'll be warmer, there's a blessin'," Lewrie replied, smiling in spite of himself. "Thankee, men. That'll be all."

Toulon bestirred himself after an impressive stretch or two and a gargantuan yawn, to come sniffing and pawing at the chest that held his "treats" for the coming months, mewing with expectant delight.

"Toulon . . . *look!*" Lewrie enticed, taking a new knit ball from his coat pocket. Theoni had made it, complete with a wee harness bell and some ribbons firmly sewn to it. "Tinkle, tinkle, see?"

"Murr-*errf!*" was the cat's glad cry. In a trice, he was hounding it from transom settee to forrud bulkhead, tail up and thundering.

"Up and down, sir!" Midshipman Grace, their youngest and newest, called from the forecastle.

"Heave and haul away!" Lt. Langlie shouted back. "Bosun . . . ! Pipe topmen aloft! Trice up, lay out, and make sail!"

Lewrie paced his quarterdeck, wondering if he would ever be warm again, gazing upward with his hands in the small of his back, watching as his well-drilled crew scrambled to free gaskets, take hold of clews, and begin to bare canvas.

"Atrip ... heave and awash!" The best bower anchor broke free of the sandy bottom and swayed above the surface.

HMS *Proteus* sidled a bit, swinging free of the ground, taken by the Nor'Nor'east winds, a quickly hoisted outer flying jib backed cross-deck up forrud to force her to fall off to larboard tack, taking the wind on the left-hand side of her bows, her square sails on her yards swinging about and luffing end-on, blocks clattering, canvas snapping and rustling.

Free!

Langlie was an able deck officer; Lewrie left it to him and his juniors to get way on her, as *Proteus*'s bows swung more Easterly, still not under control. He stepped over to the double-wheel and the compass binnacle, to stand by the quartermasters on the helm.

"Full and by on larboard tack, Mister Motte," Lewrie ordered as he looked out to weather. "Nothing to loo'rd. Make her head Due East . . . or as close as you may manage."

"Aye, sir . . . Due East, an' nothin' t'loo'rd," Motte echoed as he tentatively spun the wheel to find a "bite" to the rudder.

The forecourse and main course were now drawing, being braced in to cup the wind. Inner, outer, and flying jib were bellied alee, as were the middle stays'l and main topmast stays'l; the mizen tops'l and the main and fore tops'ls were stiffening with the wind's press, and their frigate began to heel a bit, beginning to make her sweet way, churning salt water to a slight froth close-aboard, chuckling and muttering back to the sea as she got a way on, and hardening up on the wind's eye, on larboard tack.

There! A first lift of the bows as the scend off the North Sea found her as she gained the Queen's Channel, the first burst of spray under her jib-boom!

Free! Lewrie exulted, taking a deep, cleansing breath of iodine tang; *Caroline, Theoni, rage, bills* . . . shore-*shite!*

He paced over to the windward railing, up the deck which was now slightly canted as more sail sprouted to gather free, willful winds. A faint chorus sang in the rigging, a faint applause rose from her wake as she laid the start of a wide bridal train astern, fought to make the "mustachio" of foam before her bows.

He felt like singing, at that moment!

"Do you wish more sail at the moment, sir?" Lt. Langlie asked, once the t'gallants were set and drawing.

"No, Mister Langlie, that'll do quite nicely," Lewrie said as he turned to face him, smiling, at ease at last. "Stand on as we are, 'til we make a long offing."

"Aye, sir."

"And I'll have a tune, Mister Langlie," Lewrie added. "Summon the fiddlers. *Spanish Ladies*, I should think."

"Er . . . aye aye, sir."

The hands were piped down from aloft, the last tug of a brace was tugged. Sheets and halliards were gathered on pin-rails and fife-rails, the hawsers were hosed down and stowed below in the cable tiers, the hawse bucklers fitted to block spray and sluices from high waves. Excess ropes were flemished down in neat piles. *Proteus* was ship-shape.

> *"Farewell and adieu, to you Spanish ladies,*
> *farewell and adieu, you ladies of Spain!*
> *For we've received orders t'sail from old England,*
> *and we hope in a short time t'see you again.*
> *We'll rant and we'll roll, like true British sailors,*
> *we'll rant and we'll roll, all across the salt seas!*
> *Until we strike soundings, in the channel of old England,*
> *from Ushant to Scilly is thirty-five leagues!"*

Fiddles, tin-whistles, the youngish Marine drummer, and Desmond on his *uillean* lap-pipes, made it sweetly longing.

" 'So let ev'ry man, raise up his full bumper,' " Lewrie joined in, bellowing (as was his wont when singing) the words out, " 'let ev'ry man drink up his full glass . . . for we'll laugh and be jolly, a-and chase melancholy . . . with a well-given toast to each true-hearted lass!' "

A few lances of sunshine broke through the dawn clouds, spearing HMS *Proteus*, making her glisten as bright as a new-minted coin, as she proudly made her way to sea, all bustle and swash, gleaming fresh canvas and giltwork flashing . . . out where she properly belonged.

No matter where those sealed orders took them.

CHAPTER NINE

*I*s he reading them?" Lieutenant Catterall, the sly and waggish rogue who had risen from senior Midshipman to Third Officer, asked.

"Aye, just now," Lieutenant Langlie answered as he paced along the windward side of the quarterdeck, stepping over the ring-bolts and tackles of the light 6-pounders and 24-pounder carronades.

"Opened 'em, sir?" Bosun Mr. Pendarves enquired.

"I do believe, Mister Pendarves," Lt. Lewis Wyman replied with an abrupt nod, as he stood at the top of the larboard gangway ladder.

"So we'll soon know our orders, won't we, Mister Pendarves?" Mr. Midshipman Sevier (the shy one) opined near the ladder's foot.

"Or, not," Mr. Midshipman Adair, a clever Scots lad, jeered at him. "He has no duty to tell us anything, if it's secret doings."

"Gracious!" little Midshipman Elwes gasped. "Secret work?"

"Work o' *some* sort's in order, young sirs," Bosun Pendarves told them, noting that all six "mids" were hanging about, ears cocked for a bit of gossip and doing nothing, which was sinful in boys, either nautical or civilian. "Go on, now . . . back t'yer duties, lads."

"Bloody Christ, this is lunacy," Lewrie muttered aloud once he had broken the seals on his canvas-bound supplemental "advisories."

"Sir?" Aspinall idly asked from his wee pantry.

"Someday I'd love t'meet a one-armed Admiralty clerk, Aspinall.

Someone who can never say 'but on the other hand'," Lewrie griped. At least Aspinall was amused.

The Royal Navy was infamous for over-vaunting orders. Sending a small brig o' war to patrol off Leith was too easy, too simple. No, additional tasks were always larded on, like sketching the headlands, taking new soundings when not chasing smugglers, amassing a new dictionary of Scots' slang, trawling for a 1588 wreck rumoured to contain Spanish Armada gold and silver, or fetching back some pregnant female sturgeons for the royal table!

His advisories did not require any new tasks of a secret or more perilous nature than usual, but . . .

On the other hand! Lewrie most snidely thought, snickering.

They were secret, nonetheless. Lewrie suspected that they had been so labeled because no one responsible for their issuance was willing to let himself be known as a complete lack-wit!

Lewrie got to his feet, shaking his head in wonder as he paced aft to the transom settee, to gaze out upon the ship's wake. It was a grey and blustery day, the horizon a bare two miles of visibility even from the mastheads, when *Proteus* was rolled and scended upwards atop a salty hillock. The ocean was a'heave, grey-green and spumed by white caps and white horses. *Proteus* groaned and creaked, then roared as she soared aloft on a wide, rising wave, her sails and masts, her standing rigging strained wind-full. Moments later, the sluicing roar was even louder as she coasted and surfed down into an equally wide, but deep, trough, where her courses were robbed of wind and slatted, whilst her tops'ls and t'gallants remained taut, and her stout bows thundered as they met a low hedge of water that ran a shudder through her timbers from stem to stern.

He unconsciously shifted his weight from foot to foot, as if he were riding a short seesaw atop a drum, as *Proteus* metronomically rolled about fifteen degrees either side of upright every thirty seconds or so—all the while soughing or rising, by turns, at least one every forty-five seconds, now that the weather had moderated, the seas had flattened a bit, and the space between great waves had increased.

The last cast of the log a half-hour before showed that *Proteus* was making about twelve knots, even under cautiously reduced sail, but the winds were finally out of the Nor'east on her starboard quarters, pre-saging the first of the Trades that would bear her slantwise for the West Indies. With a clean and newly coppered bottom, *Proteus* was always fastest on a quartering wind.

The rest of the voyage had been perfectly, miserably vile, but for a short break in the weather when they had met up with old Admiral Jervis's fleet to deliver despatches; day after day of reduced canvas, pouring icy rains and sleet pellets, of soaked and swelling rigging all going slacker by the hour, threatening the loss of spars and masts to every sickening heave, toss, or roll, with the bows smashing fist-like into every oncoming wave with a deep, echoing boom, as if they had run aground, an hundred miles out in the Bay of Biscay! Cold rations from an unlit galley, tepid soups and gruels when they *had* risked fires in the hearths under the steep-tubs, hatches mostly closed and everyone in a dim, foetid "fug" on the gun-deck, with bedding and every stitch of clothing sopping wet or only half-dry when re-donned, the drying salt crystals itching like mad, creating boils wherever flesh and wool had a chance to chafe, had made even the "chearly" hands grumble. Bedding was no dryer, and the hammocks, so tight-packed, had swayed and dipped and jerked to the ship's vicious motion, robbing everyone of sleep, and awake or a'nod, the cold and wet had set everyone coughing.

Even that brief spell of decent weather had been boisterous, he re-called, just nice enough to air and dry things out under a weak and watery winter Mediterranean sun, and being rowed over to "Old Jarvy's" flagship, Lewrie had nearly been pitched from out his gig as it rose and fell so swoopily that he'd had to hang on for dear life, or end up flipped arse-over-tits like a pancake!

Not the sort of activity for a man who could not swim; nor was scaling the tall sides of a heaving, rolling three-decker. At least Admiral Jervis, now Lord St. Vincent, had been appreciative, and had a welcome glass of claret whistled up once Lewrie'd gained her upper decks; all the while doffing his gilt-trimmed cocked hat in his eccentric manner, from the instant Lewrie had addressed him 'til the moment he had turned to depart.

Now, even here past 15 degrees West and 34 degrees North, where he had been at last allowed to open those intriguing additional advisories, the weather was foul; just better by matter of degree. It was no longer frigid ... now it could perhaps be described as only "cool and brisk." And he *had* finally thawed out!

He slapped his hands together behind his back and rocked on the balls of his feet as he swayed from side to side along with his ship, pondering.

No matter several expeditions sent out from France attempting to reclaim their prewar island colonies, the French had lost most of them, except for Guadeloupe, and the much smaller isles nestled close around Guadeloupe—Marie-Galante, La Desirade, the tiny Iles de Saintes and Iles de la Petite Terre. They had lost St. Barthelemy, Dominica, and Saint Martin, which they had shared with the Dutch; they had lost Martinique, its planters and settlers *welcoming* British occupation as salvation from the brutal Jacobin terrors of Parisian revolutionary officials who panted to behead or hang anyone suspected of less than total ardour for the Republic.

The French had also lost Tobago, Grenada, and Saint Vincent, and for a time had lost Saint Lucia, 'til the islanders had rebelled, driving British troops off the island three years before, in '95. Grenada was also "iffy," with British forces only holding Fort St. George, and the rest of the island in the hands of a slave rebellion led by a coloured planter, Julien Fédon.

Guadeloupe (so Lewrie was informed) was a hornet's nest of privateers, with everything from proper merchant ships to longboats outfitted and armed. French frigates, corvettes, and smaller National Ships sometimes called there for resupply. A particularly vicious and greedy bastard by name of Victor Hugues had landed with a small army in June of 1793, after Guadeloupe had been occupied by British regiments under General Sir Charles Grey, and had defeated them. Ever since, he had sent *agents provocateurs* to stir up revolution on the former French islands, among the French-speaking slaves and free coloureds on Dominica and Grenada, among the Black Caribs of Saint Vincent. A bloodthirsty fanatic, he had guillotined over 1,200 "disloyal" white settlers so far. But he was brutally effective, even getting agents, arms, and money to British-owned islands' slaves and freedmen.

Lewrie and *Proteus* were, therefore, to patrol vigorously, with an eye out for privateers, proper French warships, and anything suspicious, no matter how small, that might help foment more troubles.

Right, so far so good, he thought; *so's especial care to protect British merchantmen, and enforce the Navigation Acts. British goods in British bottoms, to and from British colonies . . . and everyone else can go sing for the scraps!*

Except for the Americans . . . *temporarily!*

The Spanish were still at war with England, but his "advisories" didn't make them sound up to much; Cuba had few ships, and was under a heavy blockade from Jamaica. The aforementioned Santo Domingo was not a real factor; neither was Puerto Rico, even if the locals had driven off a British expeditionary force. Should French ships not be able to use French ports, their privateers and warships *might* be found near a Spanish possession, or lurking among the Danish Virgin Islands. . . .

Then there was Saint Domingue . . . and the Americans, again.

Before the French Revolution in 1789 (so his "advisories" told him), Saint Domingue had been the richest prize in the West Indies, and its trade in sugar, molasses, rum and *arrack,* coffee and dye-woods had been worth more than all the British colonies put together. William Pitt the Younger, the Prime Minister, along with Lord Dundas and those worthies in Whitehall, had desired it above all.

Another British expeditionary force had invaded Saint Domingue from Jamaica in 1793, with eager help from white French planters and traders, the so-called *grands blancs,* those richest, with the most to lose . . . along with their heads; most were royalists who'd be first in line for the tumbrils to the guillotine. At present, British soldiers held most of the seaports in South Province and West Province, with the French Republicans pretty much in charge of North Province.

Tired of staring at the ocean, Lewrie turned and strode forrud to his chart-space for a peek at a map. Toulon woke from a nap and trotted beside him.

"Good puss," Lewrie cooed as Toulon rolled onto his back atop a map of the island of Hispaniola. "That's it . . . crush the Dons in Santo Domingo, not this half."

Saint Domingue was like the letter *U* laid on its side, the two long arms aimed Westerly. First settled and richest, North Province was the upper arm and long peninsula that thrust towards Cuba and the Windward Passage. British troops held the harbour of Mole St. Nicholas near its western tip, and Port de Paix; the Royal Navy blockaded the provincial and colonial capital, Cap Francois—he made a note to himself that the locals referred to it as "Le Cap"—and the port of Fort Dauphin, near the eastern border with Spanish Santo Domingo.

Between the two arms lay a vast bight, and West Province, with all its freshwater rivers running down from the high mountains, where the French had dug intricate irrigation canals to water their fields. British troops held the port of Gonaives, just above the river Ester and the port of Saint Marc.

In the south, the small island of Gonave was lightly garrisoned by British troops. The isle broke the Bay of Port Au Prince into two channels leading to the large harbour and town of the same name, down at the "elbow bend" where South Province's peninsula began. British troops had a firm grip on South Province, and the port towns of Grand Goave and Petit Goave, on the northern coast, and Jacmel on the southern shore. South Province had been last to be settled and farmed with slaves; it was much drier and less productive, since it lay in the lee of those storm-breaking mountains, in the "rain shadow." Most nourishing rainwater fell on West Province, therefore.

Such a rich place, so lush and green . . . and so deadly.

"*Murff?*" Toulon asked, sprawled on his belly, with his chin on the border, looking for "pets."

"Damn' bad place, aye . . . you're right, puss," Lewrie said, as he swept him up to cradle him and tickle his white belly.

It was no wonder to him that the British forces, now under General Maitland, had gone little farther inland. After all that *"Liberté, Fraternité, Egalité"* bumf of the revolutionary mobs, Saint Domingue had erupted in civil war between Royalists and Republicans, with the *grands blancs* and the *petits blancs*—which could mean any white settler from a modest tradesman or overseer to a drunken harbour layabout—up in arms, with the help of those aspiring *gens de coleur*, the free Blacks and mixed race Mulattoes. Until the Whites had made it plain that the colony wished freedom from France, but would keep the slave plantation system and the strict racial hierarchy, that is; then the "persons of colour" had made it a *three*-sided civil war. High-flown edicts written in Paris, granting full voting rights to *gens de coleur* born free, and of two free parents (maybe 400 in all the island!) had enraged the lower class *petits blancs*, who would die before being valued lower than a "Cuffy".

And, to top it all off, in 1791, the 450,000 darkly black slaves in the countryside had risen in revolt, murdering their masters, burning lush manor houses, raping white women, raiding and looting, before forming into loose battalions that used hoes, pitchforks, scythes, and cane knives to fight and defeat European-trained and armed soldiers and militias, as well as the countryside police, who were mostly Mulatto or half-coloured to begin with.

Paris had sent another slobbering fanatic, Léger Sonthonax, to Saint Domingue, with 7,000 European troops *and* some portable guillotines. More Free Blacks had arrived, too, fresh from the Terror to lead the cause of full equality. Sonthonax thought that *all* island whites, no matter their station, were Royalist or separatist, so his guillotines stayed busy, and as his home-bred troops died of malaria and the Yellow Jack, or got massacred in the back-country by slave rebels, he aligned with the Mulatto militias, who aspired to emulate their white parents rather than side with the darker, mostly illiterate plantation slaves.

Now the interior of the colony was controlled by the slaves in arms— well-armed, too, so Lewrie was informed—and led by a man who styled himself General Toussaint L'Ouverture, a former house slave himself. When the war began in '93, a Spanish army of 14,000 men had tried to invade Saint Domingue from Santo Domingo; now L'Ouverture was just about ready to invade the Spanish half of Hispaniola to free his fellow Spanish Blacks!

Such servile unrest, his orders firmly advised, was *not* to be allowed off that unhappy isle; he was to take, sink, or burn any ships of a "slave navy" departing Saint Domingue, before rebellion, along with arms and encouragement, could get to Jamaica and other colonies.

"But on the other hand, Toulon . . ." Lewrie wryly mused, as he stroked the ram-cat's silky belly, making Toulon rattle-purr and half shut his eyes in bliss.

He was to do nothing to *impede* the slaves, since they were good at making mincemeat of what troops the French still had ashore, or had a chance of fetching from Europe. As the orders subtly hinted, "arms and munitions imported by whatever means are not to be discouraged, so long as no hint of future export to British colonies is suspected."

It was hoped, the advisories stated, that this spring of '98, General Maitland could march inland and defeat the ill-fed, barefoot slaves, further isolate any remaining French garrisons, and finally conquer the damned place. Failing that, the *semblance* of amity, encouragement, and cooperation with the slaves' aspirations, to either delude them long enough to disarm them, or "bring them into the fold" as temporary allies would suit.

And speaking of temporary allies . . .

Those orders and advisories waxed eloquent about the Americans. They were back at sea with a real navy, after scrapping their last old Continental Navy ships in 1785, no longer dependent upon a tiny clutch of revenue cutters in the Treasury Department, or small customs vessels maintained in coastal waters by the several states.

Not that the Continental Navy had been worth all that much in those days, Lewrie recalled with a snort of derision. He'd only seen one real warship, and she'd gone down with her guns firing in a hopelessly one-sided fight with his old ship, HMS *Desperate*. The brig o' war . . . *Liberty*, had been her name?

No matter. The Royal Navy had taken, sunk or burned, or blockaded most of them 'til they'd rotted at their anchorages. No, it had been their adventurous privateers that had carried the fight, decimating British trade. Americans were an odd lot, Lewrie had gathered; if war came at sea, they'd prefer the lax discipline, and hope of profit-sharing, of a privateer to the regimented life of a *navy* vessel! Patriotism for flinty-eyed, avaricious "Yankee Doodles" went down better when sweetened by plunder, prize money, and the chance to gallivant in high adventure for a few months.

The Americans he'd met when a callow Midshipman during the Revolution had struck him as leery of a central government with too *much* power, of a large standing army at the beck and call of potential tyrants or despots . . . in that regard, at least, Americans and Englishmen were of one mind. They'd much prefer a sea-going batch of "Minutemen," what they called their casual, volunteer farmer-soldier militias, to the high cost of a formal fleet.

"Perhaps an American navy's more palatable, puss," Lewrie told his cat, now stretched nigh-boneless across his lap. "Out of sight and no threat ashore. 'Less they smash up the taverns."

American trade had grown like mildew in his dirty shirts, though. Merchant ships under their peculiar "gridiron" striped banner were seen on every sea these days, trading with anyone despite the war, belligerent or neutral, and admittedly bore a fair portion of British goods. As neutrals, they were raking in the "blunt" with both fists. He was advised that American merchantmen could be encountered in the Indies in large numbers, even entering Spanish ports on Cuba and Puerto Rico, and he was to follow a wary but "hands-off" policy unless he suspected any contraband going to French or Spanish ports.

Lately, though, their old friends, the French, had turned a new leaf in their dealings with America. French trade was practically nonexistent due to the Royal Navy, but even so, the Frogs were now stopping and searching American ships for "contraband," requiring them to produce not just passenger lists and manifests, but lists that showed the names and nationality of officers and crew, *rôles d'équipage* or else. America and Great Britain had recently signed a treaty that had settled some border disputes in the Pacific Northwest, and disputes at sea about exactly what "neutral" really meant, and that treaty had piqued the French even more. They had renounced the American notion that "free ships make free goods," a clause of their *own* Treaty of Amity and Commerce with America in force since 1778! France had stated that, henceforth, they would treat neutrals *in the same manner that England did* . . . whatever that meant. If American ships carried cargoes to or from England or her allies, and lately even if they carried goods to or from France and *her* allies, they were subject to search and seizure. The British ambassador to the United States had estimated that nearly 200 ships had been taken in the Caribbean alone since 1796!

It was all part of an ongoing plan to bully, threaten, cajole, coax, or bribe the United States into war on France's side. French agents had been tampering with American domestic politics for years, in point of fact, even after "neutral" American merchant ships had both fed and clothed them in the early days of their Revolution, when crops had failed year after year, and France was rocked by internal revolts against the Jacobin republic.

Now, the advisories said, France had declared that any American ships caught carrying *any* British goods were *"bonne prise"* and prey for their warships and privateers.

Worst thing t'do to a Yankee Doodle, Lewrie thought; *hit him in the coin-purse!*

Engraged at last, so the British ambassador had written, those Americans were rushing to finish six large 5th Rate frigates that had been started in '94 and '95, and patriotic public subscriptions were being solicited in every seaport from Maine to Georgia to buy and arm, or quickly build, a United States Navy.

The advisories hinted that America might even declare war upon the French, and ally themselves with Great Britain! So captains were warned to do nothing to discourage such a declaration, perhaps find a way to encourage such a move. They could always use another ally, and one with nautical experience and knacky skill—as shown by the privateers in the last war, at any rate—would be more than welcome. An ally that did not need vast bargeloads of silver to prop them up, like the Austrians and Prussians and Neapolitans did during the time of the so-called First Coalition in 1793, would be doubly welcome!

So American merchant ships must be protected from privateers or French cruisers, but on the other hand . . . !

British trade and the Navigation Acts were still in force, and American ships that overstepped the boundaries of their "cooperation" had to be stopped and searched, at the same time.

American vessels could still use their neutrality to trade with the Dons in Cuba, Puerto Rico, and Santo Domingo . . . but contraband and martial cargoes were not allowed, on the other hand?

Americans could trade with the French on Hispaniola, in Saint Domingue, if they wished to risk it, but on the other hand, the export of arms, monies, and agents to British colonies on American ships was to be stopped?

Good God, the newborn United States Navy (so said his orders) would share the private signals books with Royal Navy warships, and an American naval presence in the Caribbean was expected shortly, but . . . they're not *yet* allies, nor are they *yet* at war with France, so give all aid and assistance, but joint operation as co-belligerents, out in the open for all to see, was to be avoided, unless there was pressing need for quick action?

"Double-dealing hypocrisy!" Lewrie felt like shouting in anger, as he leaned over his sleeping cat to scan his orders once more.

And, to top all, he was to be on the lookout for Spithead and Nore Mutiny deserters, Royal Navy deserters, or British merchant tars who had taken service in American vessels to avoid the Impress Service, and their proper duty in the Royal Navy . . . even though American ships were already ready to fight over the demand for a *rôle d'équipage* by the French, listing crewmens' names and national identities?

Most especially, he was to seek out specific persons, listed by name and description, who had served in the *Hermione* frigate in these waters, those who'd mutinied against a Captain Pigot, murdered him in his bed, murdered officers, mates, and midshipmen, then sailed her off to a port on the Spanish Main and sold her as "prize" to support themselves . . . even were they aboard American merchantmen or *warships?*

Were any found, they were to be taken aboard, bound in chains on the orlop or in the bilges, thence to be taken ". . . with all despatch" to either English Harbour, Antigua, or Kingston, Jamaica for court-martial and later hanging . . . whichever was closer.

"Troll for pregnant, female sturgeons, too?" he whispered.

God, give me reasonable orders! he gravelled to himself; *fetch home the Golden Fleece, sweep out the Augean Stables . . . something like that. Somethin' do-able, for pity's sake!*

He lifted Toulon from his lap and deposited him on the desktop before him, the cat grumbling and arching as he turned to go aft for a whiff of fresh air. The transom sash-windows were open a touch, letting in brisk cool air, after weeks of tight-shut "fug."

Close-up, he now took note of how the panes were splattered with dried salt, and half-misted on the outside with a dull grey film of sea salt crystals . . . given his mood, he could almost mistake it for smears of congealed pork fat. He rubbed his hands together, disliking how the air felt so coolly humid and . . . greasy! Of how humid-oily-clammy his skin felt under his clothes.

"This cruise will turn t'shit," he muttered softly.

It would be more "war on the cheap," more sleaziness, one more hefty dollop of semi-covert underhandedness, where, he foully suspected, his every step must be circumspect . . . else he'd finally find the one "slick" one that tumbled career, repute, and income to Perdition!

"Aspinall?"

"Aye, sir?"

"A glass of claret, if ya will."

" 'Fore Noon Sights, sir?" Aspinall dared to query, surprised.

"Aye."

CHAPTER TEN

*T*he difference that a couple of weeks made was amazing, running before the Nor'east Trades, sometimes with the winds large on the starboard quarter, sometimes right up the stern, and "both sheets aft." In what seemed a twinkling, the horizon expanded, the scudding gloom overhead lifted, parted, and turned cerulean blue, swept by mares' tails in faint, cloudy tracings. The seas no longer churned like washtub suds, but rolled in majestically long periods, spattered with choppy smaller waves that broke and parted against the hull with the sounds of elated sighs, no longer hammering or threatening.

And the sunrises, and sunsets!

Magnificent orange suns, presaged by a faint streak of grey on the horizon, burst like bombshells, painting the eastern skies amber, shading to dusty rose-red or the palest yellow for a brief minute or so, and one could *feel* the day coming, racing across the ocean faster than any frigate could ever swim, or wing-churning sparrow fly, as the warmth spread outward, westward, as if the doors to a lush garden had been flung open, and hands and officers and mates standing Quarters to greet any nasty surprises at dawn could smile with relief for *Proteus* to be alone once more, and with a small measure of delight at Nature's glories.

And the sunsets, at the end of a long day of work or gun drill, late enough now to fall in the Second Dog Watch after the crew's mess, brought off-watch hands on deck to peer forward, westward, to savour a sight that most, in their coal-smoked, foggy, and rainy towns, hamlets, or villages had rarely seen. Great, towering cumuli, shading off to pearly-grey or charcoal, were speared by sword-blades of golden light, the sun golden-red, surrounded by roses ahead; and a soft, blue-grey gloom astern, in which first stars could be made out, swept closer by the minute to overtake their ship as it surged over the sea with a sibilant hissing, the tops'ls painted gilt, or a gleaming parchment hue.

Shoes had been dispensed with, suffocating blue wool jackets so welcome in March were stowed away except for Sunday Divisions. Shirt sleeves were now rolled above the elbow, loose slop trousers gathered above the knees, collars spread wide and placket buttons undone for a breath of cooling air, or a greater exposure to the healing rays of a benign sun. Shirts were rarely worn at all, for many doffed them despite the Surgeon Mr. Shirley's warnings about sunburn and the cost of butter-based salves that would be deducted from their pay if they appeared lobster-red at Sick Call.

Officers and senior warrants, now . . . some dignity was demanded, though Lewrie did allow them to dispense with cocked hats and uniform coats. Proper breeches, clean shirts, and neck-stocks were *de rigeur*. *And* stockings and shoes. It was only during the Second Dog that they could undo their stocks, roll up their sleeves, and savour the cooling winds 'til full sundown, before heading aft and below to the gun-room for their own suppers, at the change of watch.

Pipes would glow on the darkening deck, as the smokers had the last taste before heading below, off-watch, or taking station for the eight-til-midnight. Fiddles, fifes, penny-whistles, and the soft hums of Desmond's *uillean* pipes would sound every sunset, unless it rained, and crewmen would dance hornpipes or slip-jigs, sometimes for competition between eight-man messes, sometimes between larboard or starboard watches, to see who was the best. Country-dance tunes would jerk and tootle more urgent paces, more exuberant turns on the decking, and the men might pair off by twos to practice for future shore leaves in the islands, or perhaps to whimsically recall better times before they'd taken the King's Shilling and gone to sea.

Bedding was dry now; clothing did not have to be wrung out to be donned. Every third day or so, there would come a mildish squall, with lashings of warm, welcome rain, creating a scurry for all hands to rig canvas sluices to catch it in empty casks, to trap enough for a cask to be scrubbed clean of the slick, brownish growth that eventually would infest them, turning reputedly fresh water pale brown and semi-opaque. Stubs of soap would appear, along with salt-stiff, sweat-stiff shirts and trousers to be spread on the deck, scrubbed furiously while the rain lasted (sometimes only minutes), then thrashed or slapped or wrung out, then hung up to dry after the rain had passed. A bit more than a few might strip naked and pound the smuts from the slop clothing they wore at that moment, or merely stand wide-armed, mouths open and turned up like hatchling birds waiting to be fed, to be showered cooler and cleaner.

All in all, HMS *Proteus* was a happy ship. They had been *paid*, just before departing Sheerness, the usual six months of arrears made good, and the wonders of the West Indies were still to come, if they were allowed ashore to sample the foods, the ale-houses and taverns . . . and the women. Their days were filled from sunrise to sunset with the usual labours, such as re-roving the rigging, tautening the standing stays every other day, one side at a time after wearing from larboard to starboard tack off the wind, when the lee side would have a little more slack to work with; taking down the storm-canvas and stowing them below, after the sailmaker and his crew had patched, darned, and sewn frayed seams; hoisting aloft and bending on the lighter, everyday set of sails. And, of course, there were the unending drills during the Forenoon Watch; running-in, mock-loading, running-out, and firing the great-guns, carronades, and swivels, with a weekly live shoot at a jettisoned keg or chicken coop; cutlass drill and boarding pike drill to keep their skills sharp and give them some additional exercise; a turn at live musketry at over-side targets, even practice with horrid Sea Pattern pistols that were only considered accurate when jammed in a foeman's belly and triggered off; striking top-masts to the deck in quick order, then hoisting them back aloft, preparing for the day when a raging West Indies hurricane might overtake their ship, and the topmasts would *have* to be lowered for survival—or the day when enemy fire might dismast them, and victory or defeat might hinge upon how quickly spare top-masts and spars could be deployed.

And, when all that was done, there was grog, a turn at a water-butt, the galley funnel spuming a partly homesick aroma of wood smoke and boiling meat: the smells of soups or pease puddings as the sun declined, as a country cottage or town worker's humble lodgings smelled at sundown, when the day's pay had been collected, an ale or two had been drunk at one's favourite local pub among fellow workers and neighbourhood friends, at the end of the loose-hipped, mellow stroll on the high street or side lane that led to family, wife . . . and home.

Weary, aye . . . mostly satisfied with their lot for the moment, some a trifle "groggy" as usual, each dusk they still had the spirit to open their voices in rough tune, revive the sentimental, lachrymose airs that sailors liked best of all . . . and sing the sun down.

"Toulon, don't leave yer mark on the hammock nettings! Sailors have t'sleep on those things!" Lewrie admonished his ram-cat, perched on the canvas-covered bulwark of tightly rolled hammocks, overlooking the ship's waist. He gave him a neck-tousling pet, then strolled up to the windward side, plucking at his shirt. One more sign that they were in the tropics; the day's heat that had been welcome at first, was now nigh punishing, more glaring, and the prismatic flashes of sunlight off the sea were now more like a field of too-bright snow that gave everyone a perpetual squint.

Lewrie turned to face inward, once he had taken hold of a mizen stay and given it a tug to test its tautness, taking note of Dowe, one of the quartermaster's mates serving his "trick" at the wheel. He was an American, the son of a long-dead Loyalist who had fled to Nova Scotia at the Revolution's end. Dowe lowered his gaze from the draw of the sails and eased his own squint, raising his brows for a moment, which made Lewrie smile. With a face at ease, Dowe showed white, untanned streaks round his eyes and on his forehead that squinting kept as pale as a lady's thighs . . . "them raccoon eyes, sir," Dowe had termed them, Lewrie recalled, making him chuckle, too. He thought he had seen one when HMS *Desperate* had put into Charleston back in '81, and he was sure he had *eaten* a raccoon when besieged and half-starved at Yorktown with Lord Cornwallis's doomed army. Either way, Lewrie thought the description apt.

"Sail ho!" the main-mast lookout screeched from the cross-trees.

"Where away?" Lt. Wyman yelled back, his hands cupped about his mouth, though that was little help for his thinnish voice.

"One point off th' larboard bows! Hull down! A schooner!"

"Well, about time, too!" Lewrie muttered, pleased.

They had proved that the ocean was a huge, empty place on their voyage, for even though they had steered *Proteus* Sou'westerly nigh to the latitude of Dominica, and across the most-used track for any merchant ships, this would only be the second ship they had encountered. Most merchant masters bore on South from Cape St. Vincent to Dominica's latitude, then ran it due West—they only had to solve their slight variation in latitude, daily, and calculate longitude by adding up the 24-hour sums from their knot-logs, by Dead Reckoning. And if all else failed them, the cloud-swept peaks of Dominica were the tallest marks in the Caribbean, damned hard to miss for even the most lubberly, cack-handed navigator—like the master of the only other ship that they had "spoken," a reeking Portugee "blackbirder" laden with a cargo of three-hundred-odd slaves fresh from Dahomey, and so creaky and slow it appeared that at least a quarter of those forlorn souls would die before arrival; the damned fool had actually asked Lewrie where, exactly, they were!

Here though, within two days' sail of English Harbour, Antigua, the presence of local shipping could be expected. English Harbour was a Royal Navy station, a safe place for overseas trade, as well. This schooner, Lewrie surmised, was most-like a local. Schooners were popular craft in the West Indies, fore-and-aft rigged to go like a witch to windward, and "point" at least ten-to-twelve degrees closer to the winds, a desirable trait did one desire to beat back eastward against the unvarying Nor'east Trades. Some adventurous types sailed schooners from as far north as Maine, in the Americas. And schooners made hellish good privateers, too, due to their speed and agility!

"Mister Elwes, aloft with a glass, sir. Tell us what you see," Lieutenant Wyman snapped.

"Aye aye, sir!" the eager young midshipman piped back, dashing to the rack by the binnacle cabinet to seize a telescope, then scampering up the weather mizen shrouds as spryly as a monkey.

"Should we clear for action, sir?" Wyman asked.

"Not quite yet, Mister Wyman," Lewrie demurred. "Hull-down, on such a clear day, means she's ten miles off or more. Plenty of time to 'smoak' her. Unless she runs, of course."

"Hoy, the deck!" Midshipman Elwes cried down. "Schooner rigged, and flying no flag! Sailing abeam the wind, to the Nor'Nor'west!"

"I do, however, desire that we harden up to the wind, sir, and cut the angle on her. Make our course . . . West by North. Shake out those first reefs in the t'gallants, and stand by, should we need the royals," Lewrie said, after a peek at the compass.

Lewrie took a telescope of his own and ambled back to the windward rail, braced himself on the mizen stays, and eyed their stranger. The merest sliver of her uppermost hull sometimes loomed up above the horizon as a distant swell lifted her; in another moment, she would be swallowed, leaving only the upper part of her sails visible.

Damme, is she foreshortening? he asked himself with a frown.

"Deck, there!" Mr. Elwes called. "Chase is hauling her wind . . . turning West-Nor'west! Chase is hoisting gaff stays'ls!"

Foreshortening, aye; showing *Proteus* her sternquarters. Mr. Elwes might be presumptive in calling her a Chase, but that turn gave Lewrie a premonitory thrill.

"Has she shown any colours yet, Mister Elwes?" Lewrie queried.

"None, sir!"

Lewrie rubbed his unshaven chin, ideas percolating. Even were she British, or neutral and innocent as anything, fear of the French privateers *might* make a ship run from a strange vessel, one that looked lean and fast like a ship of war, but . . .

Did the schooner continue West-Nor'west, she could just shave by the northern coast of Antigua, and would be on a perfect course to duck into "neutral" waters in the Danish Virgins, near St. Croix, though by sunset *Proteus* could surely run her down, with her longer waterline and her much larger sail area.

Or the schooner might try to come about, rounding Antigua, and head Sutherly for St. Kitts. In Antigua's lee, schooners were two-a-penny, and by full dark she might hope to escape in the gloom, letting another similar schooner be the goat.

Proteus slowly swung onto her new course, her decks heeled over more to leeward as the press of wind on her reset sails made her start to race and surge. She was after a "Chase"; and like a staghound on a firm spoor, like a tiger pacing an Indian millet field after an addled goat, she strode out confidently, surely. Off-watch crewmen were drawn to the deck by the commotion, all but licking their chops in anticipation of a prize.

"This isn't a cockfight, lads!" Lewrie had to shout. "There's gundrill to perform. Keep yer eyes in-board, and your minds on your evolutions . . . 'fore the Bosun and Master Gunner pass among you, with their . . . reminders?"

Even so, Lewrie knew, the hands would whisper among themselves, try peeking over the gangways or out the windward gun-ports; men aloft would find a way to send the latest observations down to their mateys, no matter *what* the Bosun, the Master Gunner, the Master At Arms and his Ships' Corporals threatened—it was simply too much of a novelty!

"Deck, there!" Midshipman Elwes cried. "Chase is hull-up, sirs! She now shows a flag! *French* colours!"

A hundred horny paws slapped together and rubbed with a sound like dry grit; a hundred voices muttered "good prize!" together, and a palpable *frisson* of delight and greed swept the decks, making mates, sailors, and officers alike beam with joy, and ships' boys jig-dance.

Lewrie clapped his hands behind his back, and pondered. If he hoisted the French Tricolour, as well, there was a chance that he might reel this schooner in like a fish, relieved to meet a fellow Frenchman so far from home. *A privateer?* Lewrie silently mused, *more than glad t'see a National ship? Enough to haul her wind and fetch-to, waitin' on us?*

There was the possibility that a Frog privateer would know the few confirmed French ships of war sailing out of Guadeloupe by sight.

"Mister Wyman," Lewrie said, with a sly grin, "do you hoist a French flag on the foremast . . . and run up a 'who are you?' where she can see it. Does she answer with a private signal, she's confirmed, and ours."

"Oh!" Lt. Wyman gawped for a second. "My goodness gracious, I see, sir! Aye, sir! We know the Frog's *'qui va la'* signal."

Moments later it was done, and they waited to see what signal would be hoisted in return. Despite his best intentions (like most of those,

Lewrie could rarely keep 'em!) a smug grin creased his face, a "sly-boots" look of cocky satisfaction.

"Deck, there!" Midshipman Elwes cried. "French colour's *down* . . . she's hoisted *British!*"

"Hah! Liar!" Lieutenant Wyman commented, all but hooting to his fellow officers, who had also come up to share the excitement.

Well, damme, Lewrie thought, deflated in an instant; *Didn't think o' that! Could she really be?*

He cupped his hands and bellowed aloft, "Mister Elwes, has she changed course? Reduced sail? Hoisted any signal at all?"

"No, sir! Still running! Same course, and no private signal!"

"Damn!" Lewrie griped softly. "Mister Wyman, get that Frog rag and signal down, then. Hoist our own colours, and this month's recognition signal. And ready a forecastle gun to fire to leeward."

"Aye, sir."

The Red Ensign went up the foremast, a string of code flags was bent on and hoisted, followed a minute or two later by a single cannon shot. The schooner was closer now, not over four miles off as *Proteus* swiftly strode up to her with a bone in her teeth.

"Deck, there! Chase now bears Nor'west by West! I think I see stuns'ls! No reply to signals!"

"Dammit, make our heading Nor'west by North, Mister Wyman, and hoist royals," Lewrie snapped, now irritated. "And once that's done, we'll beat to Quarters, and ready the larboard battery!"

"Aye aye, sir!"

Proteus heeled a bit more, her wake and bustle growing louder and more insistent. Three-quarters of an hour, and the schooner grew larger as they closed the range to three miles, no matter how swiftly the schooner scudded along in flight. She had lowered British colours long before, seeing that the ruse was fruitless. Hands stood swaying behind the great-guns, already loaded with the smoothest and roundest solid iron balls, charged with powder, and the newfangled flintlock strikers primed.

"Ease that quoin out even more, there, lads," Lt. Catterall told his larboard gunners. "We're heeled, and shooting to leeward, so keep the barrels aimed high. We'll adjust once we're close and the ports are open, so you can mark your target and gauge the range."

"Mile and a half, I make it, sir," Lt. Langlie volunteered from his place near Lewrie on the lee rails. "Almost Range-to-Random-Shot, for the six-pounder chase gun."

"We'll wait 'til the larboard battery can bear, Mister Langlie," Lewrie countered, slowly pacing, now dressed in his second-best uniform, with his sword at his side, and the sweat trickling down his back and itching icily on his spine. "I doubt yon schooner mounts anything heavier than a four-pounder. Once we're near abeam, with the guns run out, perhaps this 'M'sieur' will gain some sense, and strike before we have to blow him out of the water."

"Antigua, to leeward, there . . . I think," Lewrie heard Lieutenant Devereux, their Marine officer, say. "And Barbuda, off our starboard bows?" he opined, jutting his chin towards a greyish hump on the horizon. "No, couldn't be . . . Sergeant Skipwith?"

"Sure I don't know, sir," Skipwith commented.

"Still an hundred miles to leeward, sir," Lt. Langlie took time to inform their senior "Lobsterback." "Well, a day's sail, by now. I expect you're mistaking squalls on the horizon for islands. Were Barbuda and Antigua this close, we'd see them plain. The channel between is only thirty-seven miles, d'ye see. . . ."

"Half a day, in chase," Lewrie muttered. And he still had not gotten his chin shaved! The galley fires had been doused and dinner had been delayed, the crew's hunger only slightly eased with hardtack biscuit, water, and dry, crumbly Navy Issue cheese. Of course, the rum ration had been doled out; some customs were observed no matter what.

"Three-quarters of a mile, now sir," Lt. Langlie pointed out.

"Mister Wyman!" Lewrie called down to the Second Lieutenant by the foremast, now in charge of the starboard guns. "One chase gun to windward! Let her know our intentions!"

"Aye, sir!"

A windward gun was a challenge to battle, and a threat. Strike your colours, haul up, and fetch-to . . . or else!

Bang! The foc'sle 6-pounder barked out a blank charge, billowing a sour cloud of maggot-pale gunsmoke that was quickly scudded off to larboard, across the forecastle, by the Trades that were now almost abeam Proteus's deck. Lewrie, along with every senior man allowed the liberty of the quarterdeck, lifted a telescope to see what answer was forthcoming.

Like most stern-chases, hours could pass before any noticeable progress was made, then all of a sudden, the Chase would *leap* within spitting distance in an eyeblink, no matter that her sails still drew, her wake still seethed, the mustachio under her bows still flung spray so busily about her ... as if she'd grown weary of it all, and meant to surrender to her fate.

"Quarter-mile, I make it, now, sir," Lt. Langlie observed.

"Open the larboard gun-ports and run out, Mister Langlie. Hull the bitch, when nicely abeam," Lewrie coldly replied, his eyes gone as grey as Arctic ice, as was his wont when angered or in action.

"Sir!"

There was a puff of smoke upon the schooner's bows, then a tinny, flat *bang* from a lee-side gun, the sound masked by her sails and hull, muffled by the wind's roar and the onward rushing *sshhuush* of *Proteus*'s hull. She had fired a leeward gun, in sign of peaceful intent ... or to signify her surrender?

A second or two later, down came her patently false British colours, as if she had indeed struck, but ... up went a "gridiron" flag, a busy banner of red and white horizontal stripes, with a canton of blue, splattered with stars, in one corner!

"An American? Mine arse on a band box!" Lewrie exclaimed.

"Another sham!" Lt. Langlie all but spluttered at their gall.

"No, sir, look!" Midshipman Adair cried, pointing. "Her hoist! That is this month's private signal, sir."

"You're *sure*, Mister Adair?" Lewrie gawped at those pennants, spinning to face the midshipman.

"Quite sure, sir. See, here in my copy book, it's ..."

"Dammit!"

"She's let fly her sheets, Captain," Lt. Langlie said, drawing Lewrie's attention back to the schooner.

She had freed her large gaff-hung fore and main sails, letting them flag and clatter almost abeam the wind, no longer cupping power from it, keeping the outer and inner flying jibs standing, but hauling down the foretopmast stays'l and those upper gaff stays'ls. Without those sails, she was now slowing like a bowling coach being reined in and braked!

"Well . . . hoist the proper damn' reply, Mister Adair," Lewrie snapped. "The gun crews to stand easy, Mister Langlie."

"Aye, sir."

"Half the damned day we've chased this silly clown, and it is only *now* he has wit t'recall he's a Yankee, that we're almost allies?"

Proteus would pass within an hundred yards of the schooner, and would spurt past her rapidly, with all her top-hamper still drawing, t'gallants, royals, and stuns'ls rigged on the windward yards; all that sail blanketing what wind the schooner could receive in her lee.

"Christ, it'll take an hour t'work *back* to her!" he growled.

He took Langlie's brass speaking-trumpet and crossed to the lee rails to speak her whilst he could, before they left her in their dust!

"Who the hell *are* you?" Lewrie ungraciously bellowed.

"United States Treasury Department cutter, the *Trumbull*!" came the thin reply. "Lieutenant Gordon, master! And you?"

"You bloody idiot! This is His Brittanic Majesty's frigate, *Proteus* . . . Captain Lewrie, commanding. You'd think you could've—"

But they were past by then, surging along at better than ten or eleven knots.

"Mister Langlie, get way off her," Lewrie snarled, turning inboard. "Strip us down to all plain sail. Then we'll wear down below her, tack and round up windward of her. I've a bone t'pick with that . . . that . . . ! Mister Wyman . . . Mister Catterall! Worm out your shot and charges, and secure from Quarters! Goddammit!"

He'd wasted most a day's sail chasing a pluperfect fool! Even worse, he'd been made to *look* the fool before his officers and men!

"And Mister Langlie?" Lewrie fumed, glowering.

"Aye, sir?"

"Whilst we perform all those evolutions in plain sight of that Yankee Doodle, I'll want everything done to a *very* salty Tee!"

"All hands! All hands!" Lieutenant Langlie bawled, accepting his trumpet back and turning away to hide in furious activity.

As topmen raced aloft to fist and fight canvas, to haul in and reduce sail, deflate the set of the stuns'ls, clew them to the booms and haul them in along the permanent yards, *Proteus* slowed and soughed into the brilliant tropic waters, sighing and groaning as her timbers resettled, like a racehorse taking a cool-down lap round the turf.

Minutes later, the royals were furled, gasketed, and the thin yards lowered to the cross-trees, the t'gallants two-reefed, and hands piped to Stations to Wear. The schooner was by then at least four or five miles astern, plodding along somewhat like an ignored hound under plain sail, as if unsure of following its master all the way to the end of the drive. She continued to plod while *Proteus* wore downwind, took the Trades on her larboard side for the first time in weeks, and began to "reach" back across the wind on an opposing course, about two cables below the schooner.

"Mister Adair, assumin' this slack-jawed Yankee can actually be able to *read*, do you hoist 'Take Station In My Lee,' " Lewrie sneered.

"Aye aye, sir."

"I'll put her off our larboard quarters before we tack, sir?" Lt. Langlie asked, hands behind his back, where, Lewrie strongly suspected, he still had his fingers crossed for luck.

"Too bad we can't shave his transom, Mister Langlie. By the by. A creditable showing for our erstwhile allies . . . so far, that is."

"Uhm, thankee kindly, sir," Langlie replied with a gladsome grin . . . though tempered with a First Officer's usual quick *moue* for all the things that could yet go "smash," and at the very worst possible time.

"At your discretion, Mister Langlie."

"She replies 'Affirmative,' sir," Midshipman Adair announced.

The schooner began to fall off the wind, all but pointing her bowsprit and jib-boom at *Proteus*'s midships!

"Damn him, I didn't mean come under my lee right bloody *now!*" Lewrie barked. "Wait 'til she she's *well* off our larboard quarters before we tack, Mister Langlie. A longer board close-hauled before the tack, as well. Mister Adair, haul that signal down. Hoist 'Hold Course.' "

"Aye, sir!"

The schooner dithered, swinging back to abeam the Trades, while *Proteus* surged past once more, rapidly falling astern.

"Safe enough, now, I should think, Mister Langlie."

"Aye, sir. All hands . . . Stations for Stays!"

Proteus swung up onto the wind, close-hauled and heading to East-

Sou'east, her hands freeing braces, tacks, and sheets. Langlie left it for a long moment, rocking upward on the balls of his booted feet before opening his mouth to shout through the speaking-trumpet.

"Quartermaster, ease down the helm. Ready, ready!" Lt. Langlie cried, waiting, turning and swivelling about, eyes everywhere for this maneuevre. "Helm's alee . . . rise, tacks and sheets!"

HMS *Proteus*, for all her length and tonnage, was a lively one, and she came up to the wind briskly, jibs clattering, the spanker aft eased amidships and driving, the foretops'l flat a'back, swinging easily until . . . "Haul taut! Now, mains'l haul!" and she was across the eye of the wind, the deck swaying upright, then canting leeward, yards swinging, blocks clanging, and canvas rattling like musketry.

"Stars above, if he hasn't come up close-hauled!" the Sailing Master Mr. Winwood exclaimed, coming as close to blasphemy as that good man might ever dare.

Lewrie spun about to glare at the Yankee schooner, chilling, as the thought struck him that, were she truly a French privateer that had captured a set of private signals, now would be the very best time to fire, with *Proteus* and her crew still all sixes-and-sevens, everything in the running rigging still free, her guns unloaded, run in, and bowsed snug to the bulwarks! Even a puny broadside of pop-guns could confuse the crew, turn their tack into a bloody shambles, whilst a bold French privateersman could swing up to windward—like the schooner *was doing!*—and scamper full-and-by to weather, pointing higher than ever a square-rigged frigate could attain, into the open, empty seas east of Barbuda, giving them a Gallic horselaugh, and with a tale to gasconade about the entire Caribbean!

No, Lewrie took note; *Proteus* had completed her tack, and would block this so-called Treasury Department cutter on her present course.

'Course, does she hold her course, she'll ram us! he thought; *I don't see more'n thirty hands, all told, and all o' them hangin' in her riggin' for a good look-see!*

"Very good, Mister Langlie. Now, stand aloof of that hen-head, 'til we may cock up into the wind and fetch-to. Mister Adair?" Lewrie bawled.

"Aye, sir?"

"A second hoist, young sir. Tell that aimless bastard to 'Fetch To.' Leave 'Come Under My Lee' flyin'. Is God merciful, even *he* might get our intent. Then, should he *actually* fetch-to in our lee, I will wish you to lower both of those, and hoist 'Captain Repair On Board.' Smartly, now ... go!"

Again, like a hound warned away from the promise of fresh meat when a hog was slaughtered in the barnyard, the schooner shied off the wind to roughly abeam, leaving a thankful gap between them and ending the imminent threat of collision, as *Proteus* began the evolution for fetching-to, with some sails still drawing on starboard tack, driving forward, and others backed to snub her progress.

"Gad, quite the quadrille we're dancin' with 'em, hey, Mister Winwood?" Lt. Catterall said as he ascended the lee ladder from below. "Thought we would do 'swing your lady,' the rest of the afternoon!"

"Mmmmmm!" Lewrie harumphed quite pointedly, though he felt like growling at him.

"Though, they aren't *quite* fetched-to, yet," Mr. Winwood noted.

"Save us a spot o' bother, that," Catterall breezed blithely on. "And give them a shorter row."

"And us with more rigging and sail aloft, with more freeboard, we'll drift right down aboard her, if this fellow don't . . ." Winwood began to fret.

"I'll *skin* the bastard, swear it! That cack-handed, whip-jack, cunny-thumbed sonofa . . . lubber! *Damn* him!" Lewrie swore, nigh to one of his rare foot-stomping rants or a helpless whimpering, flinging his arms up in appeal to Heaven at *Trumbull*'s captain, and his ignorance, his clueless disregard for side-timbers, paint-work, or seamanship!

"Do we get under way once he's aboard, sir, perhaps our loo'rd drift will not be so great, before we, uhm . . . ?" Lt. Langlie helpfully suggested, heaving a deep, speculative shrug.

"Ah, hummm . . . p'rhaps, Mister Langlie," Lewrie said. Helpless appeal to Heaven won over rage, as he sagged in philosphical defeat.

"Side-party for a mere lieutenant, or a putative captain, sir," Lt. Catterall casually enquired.

"Bu'ck?" Lewrie answered, with a "what can you do?" shrug, and an unintelligible little noise that sounded hellish-like a cluck.

"Very good, sir," Catterall replied, backing away with a wary look on his face.

CHAPTER ELEVEN

$\mathcal{T}$he crew of HMS *Proteus* had "oohed" and "aahed" over the sights of land they had encountered as the frigate continued on about Antigua and sailed near Nevis and St. Kitts before reaching English Harbour; a pack of mostly "Johnny Newcomes" to the bleak infinity of the sea, and starved for even a hint of green. Sere as those isles were, they *did* have trees and bushes, and plantations that reached down near the thin sand beaches. But those appreciative noises were nothing like the ones they made when once they sighted Jamaica!

Morant Point was barely above the horizon, but the Blue Mountains stood tall and cool and bold to the Nor'west, with Blue Mountain Peak spearing over 7,400 feet into the air; smoky and hazy blue-grey, cloud-draped as if it bore a magical snowcap even in the tropics, all above a descending, hilly swath of headland so lushly verdant, land so brightly green and welcoming that the hands could almost mistake it for Faeryland, or the Irishmen in the crew could conjure that they had discovered the legendary Happy Isles that always lay just beyond a sunset, somewhere across the wide western sea.

The officers and midshipmen—and Lewrie, too, it must be admitted—stood entranced at the starboard rails or bulwarks as *Proteus* cruised on under "all plain sail" nearer the coast, straight West and within a bare two miles of Morant Bay and bound for Kingston. For Alan Lewrie it was almost like coming home, for Jamaica had been the scene of many of his adventures, and misadventures, during the American Revolution, where he'd won and lost a very young and missish Lucy Beauman, had gotten orders to scout the Florida coast and march inland to the Muskogee Indians, where he'd learned the war was over in the summer of '83 and knew he'd lose his brief command of HMS *Shrike,* the old snowrigged brig o' war he had "inherited" from her former master, Lieutenant Lilycrop. Lewrie did not need a telescope to "see" the old headlands, the planter houses near the shore, the hints of coastal road between groves of trees, or the fringe of beaches where he had once gamboled nigh-nude in shallow surf with some hired strumpet.

"I do believe that is the Palisades before our bows, sir," Lt. Langlie announced. "Just above the horizon."

"And the ruins of old Port Royal at its western tip," Lewrie said with a slow, pleased grin. "Once the wickedest town in the whole wide world, or so 'twas said. And Kingston beyond . . . a 'comer' on the wicked roster, itself. Let's take two reefs in the courses and harbour gasket the royals, Mister Langlie. Slow but steady, on a 'tops'l breeze.' The harbour entrance is narrow, at the western tip of the Palisades, just by Fort Charles, and I'm damned if I wish to tangle with another frigate leaving port . . . and both of us with a 'dash' on."

"Aye, sir."

"Mister Wyman, once we're ship-shape aloft, you and the Master Gunner, Mister Carling, will have a salute ready for Admiral Sir Hyde Parker. Mister Catterall?"

"Sir?" the Third Lieutenant said, after a long moment.

"Ashore and with the Jamaican ladies already, were we, Mister Catterall?" Lewrie said with a smirk, twitting him.

"Natural philosophy, sir . . . the *flora* looks quite intriguing," Lt. Catterall quickly replied. "Why, I might discover a new orchid or a sprig of Captain Bligh's infamous breadfruit trees, or . . ."

"When we enter harbour, round up into wind and let go anchors. I'll be depending on *you,* sir, to make it presentable. With our new admiral and two-dozen post-captains watching. *Flora,* indeed. Ha!"

"Aye aye, sir," Catterall answered, the underlings' best reply in such situations. "Best performance." Catterall gave the middies who would serve at both forecastle and stern kedge anchor a glare, to warn them *and* pass the "mustard" on.

"Mister Winwood?"

"Aye, sir?" the Sailing Master said, presenting himself.

"I think we should steer a point more direct for the entrance," Lewrie said. "Do you concur?"

"Aye, sir . . . we can round up abeam once we're fair in the channel. Better than coming abeam a mile or more off the entrance, and get a veer in the wind off those mountains."

"Then make her head West-by-North, half North."

"Very good, sir. Quartermaster . . ."

"If I wer'nt a gunner, I wouldn't be here . . . number five gun, fire!" their new Master Gunner, Mr. Carling, droned, pacing aft from the forecastle belfry towards the stern, one arm swinging like a bandmaster's, now and then swinging in a larger arc to point to a waiting gun-captain in signal to trigger his fire-lock and discharge his piece. "I've left my wife, my home, and all that's dear . . . number six gun . . . fire! If I wer'nt a gunner, I wouldn't be here . . ."

Marines in full red-coated kit, pipe-clayed crossbelts, and hats of white-piped black felt for once, stood at the hammock nettings overlooking the waist, and along the starboard side facing Fort Charles, their muskets held at "Present Arms." Usually, they saved wear on expensive uniforms (for which they'd have to pay if faded, torn, or soiled) and wore sailors' slop-clothing when not standing guard duty by doors to the officer's gun-room, Lewrie's quarters, the spirits stores, or the ladders to the quarterdeck.

Proteus ghosted into harbour on tops'ls, jibs, and spanker, and wreathed in gunsmoke from her salute that only slowly drifted leeward on a mild breeze. There were several two-decker 74-gun 3rd Rates anchored near the north shore, but none flew an admiral's broad pendant or looked even close to being a flagship. Frigates, sloops of war, brigs, and hired or captured warships below the Rates were two-a-penny, though, presenting a pretty problem as to where Lewrie could find room for his ship to anchor, and swing.

Why so many in port? he wondered to himself: *don't they know I need room? Don't they know there's a war on?*

"There's a guard-boat, sir ... waving a jack at us," Lieutenant Langlie pointed out. "I do believe he's showing us an anchorage."

"Well, thank God for small favours. Come about onto the wind, and steer for him, Mister Langlie," Lewrie said with a well-concealed sigh of vast relief. "Do *not* run him over, sir. It's bad form."

"Ya gig's ready, sah," his Cox'n Andrews informed him from his left side. "Ya don' mind, sah ... I'll bring de boat off, oncet you step ashore, an' keep an eye skinned t'come fetch ya when ya done."

Lewrie frowned and turned to look at Andrews, who was "sulled up like a bullfrog," ducking his head and his eyes darting as cutty as a bag of nails—looking six ways from Sunday—in embarassment.

"Something *wrong* with a drink ashore, Andrews?" he teased.

"Be sumptin' *bad* wrong, do my old master see me, Cap'um, sah."

"Oh, that's right, you ran from Jamaica. But surely, so long ago ..."

"Woll, he allus liked Spanish Town more'n Kingston, true, sah, but him an' his neighbours, dey was a *hard* set, sah. Hold grudges as bad as dem Serbs an' Turks back in de Balkans. D'ya not mind, sah, I don't wanna take *no* chance o' gettin' took up, again."

"Remind me to have my clerk Padgett forge you a letter of manumission from a master ... in the Carolinas, Andrews," Lewrie decided. "For the other Black hands, too, just to be safe."

"Law, thankee, sah!" Andrews said with a wide grin of relief on his phyz. "Dot'd be hondsome-fine, sah!"

"After all, forging runs in the family." Lewrie chuckled. "But 'til we've proper, uhm ... 'certificates' ready, aye, bring the boat back to the ship, and I'll hire a bum-boat for my return."

"Aye aye, sah."

Proteus found her anchorage, rounded up to slither on windward for a piece, her fore-tops'l flat a'back to brake her progress, until the very last of her way fell off and the helm went helpless. At that moment, the best bower anchor dangling from the larboard cat-head was let go to splash into the water, and the hawser paid out then snubbed after a run of half a cable, to see if the anchor would hold. With a faint jerk and groan, *Proteus* came to a stop, her voyage over.

"Hello, the boat!" Lewrie called down to the guard-boat that had been so obliging. "Where am I to report to Admiral Parker?"

"His flagship's in the careenage, sir!" the midshipman in the boat's sternsheets called back. "His staff captain keeps office at Fort Charles, for now!" he added, pointing back at the tip of the Palisades, the natural breakwater mole that made Kingston such a calm anchorage in most weathers, with the Blue Mountains lying in the harsh Nor'east, where most hurricanes blew their fiercest early winds. Lewrie looked in that direction, using a telescope to see if anyone had hoisted the usual "Captain Repair On Board" code flags. No, nothing. For the main base of the West Indies Station, Kingston maintained what could only charitably be termed as "peacetime" activity.

"Very well, sir, thankee!" Lewrie shouted down.

"I'm going that way, sir!" the midshipman offered. "Would you care to be rowed over?"

"Aye, that'd suit admirably. Come alongside!" Lewrie agreed.

"Thank de Lord," he heard Andrews whisper *sotto voce*.

"Don't feel too relieved, Andrews . . . you may have to come and fetch me back, *then* take me ashore to the civilian part of town. You scamp, you."

"Mebbe you'd speak t'Mister Padgett afore ya go, then, sah? He get dem certificates started?" Andrews countered, still looking wary.

"Dear Lord, what a lack-wit!" Captain Sir Edward Charles said, after Lewrie had filled him in on his meeting with the hapless Lieutenant Gordon of the United States Treasury Department cutter *Trumbull*. "If he's an example of what we may expect to meet in the near future, then God help them. In such a small service as their Treasury, or the new navy of theirs, surely only their very best and most experienced officers would gain commands. Unless they simply *have* none, o' course."

"I gathered that most of their experienced naval officers by now are quite aged, sir," Lewrie informed him, "those who won fame back in the Revolution; and most of them were privateersmen, to begin with."

The interview was going quite nicely, Lewrie thought. Captain Charles was Admiral Sir Hyde Parker's staff captain, a most ebulliently friendly sort—big as a rum keg about the middle and twice as stout, with the rosy cheeks and nose of the serious toper. The first thing to be done was to fetch newcome Captain Lewrie a glass of claret, *and* take up a refill with him to be convivial. They sat in leather wing chairs to either side of a wine-table, not before and behind the massive desk as junior and superior might, like cater-cousins or fellow clubmen.

Lewrie was turned out in his newest and nattiest uniform, run up in London for the December *fête* to celebrate Camperdown. The dark blue wool coat was hard-finished and smooth, and perhaps a bit too hot for a tropic day, but a snowy-white silk shirt and equally pristine sailcloth cotton waistcoat and breeches somewhat eased any discomfort that Lewrie might have felt. The single gilt epaulet on his right shoulder, all the buttons, and gold-lace cuff trim was so new, and so well packed away so long, that he fair gleamed. And the two medals hung about his neck had gotten a polish, along with his new Hessian boots with the gilt tassels. Captain Sir Edward Charles's eyes had drifted to the medals several times, in an almost wistful way, since their introduction.

Ain't ev'ry one-winged captain that can boast one medal, Lewrie smugly told himself; *much less two! Poor old soul's jealous!*

"Within two day's sail of Antigua, was it?" Sir Edward asked as he topped up their half-filled glasses.

"Aye, sir. Mister Gordon told me that Saint Kitts would be one of their 'rondy's,' as would Dominica. American merchantmen will gather there and await escort for convoys, he said, to perhaps as far north as Savannah, in Georgia. He gave me the impression that what few French privateers or warships that had harried their coastal shipping were now scared off by their new frigates, and that the bulk of their losses now take place in the Caribbean. This new naval minister of theirs, termed a Secretary of the Navy, a man name of Benjamin Stoddert, gave Gordon the further impression that he's that eager to make a 'forward presence' . . . as soon as they have enough ships in commission, of course."

"Well, if Gordon's little cutter was the best they have to show the flag . . ." Sir Edward smirked over the rim of his glass. "How well-armed was she?"

"Four four-pounders, and a batch of swivels, Sir Edward, and all rough-cast," Lewrie said with a deprecating sneer of his own. "Not two from the same foundry. Old-style touch-holes with powder-filled quills for ignition. That, or port-fires. The muskets and pistols that I saw were a tad rough, as well. Copies of Tower muskets," he said, heaving a tiny shrug. "Though some mates and officers had purchased long-range Pennsylvania rifles, and those were quite well-made and very accurate. We had a little shoot-off, sir. I with my Ferguson breech-loader, and they with their muzzle-loaders."

"Who won?" Sir Edward snapped, "tetchy" of a sudden.

"Uhm . . . they did, sir. Though ramming the ball down a rifled barrel with a lubricated leather patch about it takes forever. I was told that their new Marine Corps will be issued rifles, not muskets. A squad of Marines in each top, with rifles, could decimate the officers of a foe at nearly two hundred yards, maybe even a full cable's range. Then, sir, God help the French, when they meet!"

"Don't hold with such doings, myself," Sir Edward scoffed, now growling with ill humour. "*My* Marines'll volley from the bulkwarks. Shooting officers, sir, is un-gentlemanly. Deliberately targeting an officer is abominable! Dishonourable! Might as well cut their throats in their beds! Piratical, barbaric! Just what I'd expect of *American* manners, morals, or 'honour!' Pack of Red Indians, near-like, sir, in all those deerskin clothes, with feathers—and dung!—in their hair so please you! We'll not have such in *this* fleet, sir, and I'll thank you to remember that!"

The feathers, deerskins . . . or snipin'? Lewrie had to ask himself.

"Never stood and fought in the open, Captain Lewrie, no! They skulked in the bushes and shot from *cover*, the coward's way! Armed to the teeth, e'en the women and children," Sir Edward querulously carped, in a "pet" over past experiences, Lewrie surmised. "Uncivilised thieves and highwaymen, riotous armed bullies, hah! But never the stomach for a proper battle, and I doubt they've improved, now they're on their own without English law to rein in their chaotic nature. Do we *really* see American warships down here, I'll lay you any odds you wish, they will skulk in port, fatten off our stores, but leave the hard work to a proper navy such as ours! The French'd eat 'em alive!"

"Well, sir, even as addle-pate as their Lieutenant Gordon was," Lewrie dared to point out, "they did run a taut enough ship, and they sounded quite eager to prove themselves against the Frogs."

"*Ev'ry* calf-headed innocent sings eager before his first fight, Captain Lewrie," Sir Edward countered. " 'cause he knows nothing about battle. Let idiots and fools like your Lieutenant Gordon cross hawse with a real French frigate, and *then* see what tune he sings, hah! No, sir . . . Americans are too disorganised, too stubbornly individualistic to achieve much. Put a dozen in a room, you'll hear fifteen different opinions! Lazy, idle; twiddlers, who'd rather get drunk on their corn whiskey—a *vile* concoction!—just enough bottom to 'em to plant more corn, so they can make more whiskey! As money-grubbing as Jews, too. But not a single gentleman, a single educated and civilised man in a thousand to boast of. Barbarians, sir! Ignorant . . . *peasants!*"

Does he really hate 'em that bad? Lewrie wondered. *Or is he just drunk, and ravin'? And how 'in-the-barrel' was he before I got here?*

"I s'pose we'll see, Sir Edward," Lewrie said, noncommittally. "This Gordon fellow expected their warships rather soon."

"In hurricane season?" Sir Edward responded, leaning far back in his chair to the point that it almost tipped off its front legs, agape with a mix of horror and amazement on his now-glowing phyz.

"Their Secretary of the Navy, that Mister Stoddert, is of the opinion that really bad storms occur more rarely than people think. I believe Gordon said perhaps no more than once a year, sometimes once in five years, sir. American merchantmen in the Caribbean keep records of weather, and their studies of those records—"

"*Told* you they were purblind fools!" the staff-captain said with an angry bark. "Well, let me tell you, Captain Lewrie, the Royal Navy has records, too, and vaster experience in the West Indies than anyone else, *hundreds* of years in these waters, and even *we* depart the Indies by June, and don't come back 'til late September. Why Sir Hyde's flagship *Queen* is in the careenage this very moment, sir . . . to ready her for her voyage to Halifax."

And here I thought it was 'cause the seaweed on her bottom had taken root in the harbour mud! Lewrie thought, hiding his smirk. He'd heard that Sir Hyde Parker was making a vast fortune in prize money in the West Indies, the richest plum assignment that Admiralty could bestow; and that he was doing it the classic way . . . trusting to others in frigates and sloops of war, to junior officers in hired brigs, cutters and tenders to reap the spoils, whilst the big ships languished at anchor, waiting for a French fleet that might never come, so tight was the British blockade of the French ports.

"Why the other Third Rates are in, outfitting, too," Sir Edward further informed him. He topped up his own glass, but made no offer to do the same for Lewrie's this time. "By no later than mid-June, this harbour will be nearly empty. Then it will be up to the lesser ships on the station to exert themselves in our stead. Tenders to the Third Rates, tenders to the flagship . . ."

Pets and toadies, Lewrie sneerfully told himself; *captains' favourites who can fatten their sea-daddy's purse, and their own. While better men twiddle their thumbs and never see tuppence.*

". . . hired brigs, captured schooners, and a few frigates, just to keep the French on the *qui vive.* What is your draught, sir?"

"Umh . . ." Lewrie said, coming back to the moment, "seventeen and a half feet aft, sir."

"Excellent! Though you'll want to purchase, or capture, a tender, or tow some additional single-masted boats for close inshore work," Sir Edward suggested. "Base out of Kingston, here, so the voyage over to Saint Domingue will be short, when you run low on stores. You may even contemplate landing some stores, sailing lighter, to reduce draught to seventeen feet, or slightly less."

"I see, sir. Most helpful advice," Lewrie replied, realising he was probably the lowest-ranking Post-Captain on-station, and would be staying after the *valuable* ships departed for hurricane season. Dull blockade work off some French-held port on Saint Domingue, off-and-on plodding back and forth, and nothing worth chasing but for island-built luggers and single-masted sloops. And reefs and shoals, aplenty!

"So *Proteus* is to patrol *close* to Saint Domingue, is she, sir?" he simply had to ask, in way of sly prompting for a wider liberty for action . . . and prize money! "Or shall she have leave to patrol more, uhm . . . aggressively?"

"Blockade work, Captain Lewrie," Sir Edward told him, sounding almost glad to grind it in, as if he had formed a low opinion of him, in a twinkling. "Get your sea legs in the West Indies, after all that derring-do of yours in European waters," the staff-captain sneered, with a dismissive gesture towards Lewrie's medals. Unfortunately, the hand that he employed was the one that held his wineglass, and he spilled a goodly dollop of it on his own breeches, the wine-table, and his carpet, which was a very fine—mostly pale—Turkey. "Goddammit!"

"Oh, what a pity, sir . . .'bout the rug," Lewrie said, making a charitable grimace, instead of the angry scowl he felt like showing.

"Best pair, dammit," Sir Edward seethed, trying to swipe at his drenched thigh, setting that dangerous glass down, at least . . . but he flung droplets from his hand with an idle shake that spattered Lewrie in turn. "Oh, bugger!"

"Actually, Sir Edward, I did a few years in the West Indies in the Revolution. Started out here, in '80. So I wonder if the *best* use of *Proteus* is . . ." Lewrie slyly attempted to wheedle.

"Damned puppy!" Sir Edward screeched of a sudden, glaring back at him. "Don't like your orders, do you? Presume to talk me out of 'em, will you? In debt, are you? *That* eager for prize money?"

"Never, sir!" Lewrie declared, with his best "righteous" face on. "*Proteus* is fast and nimble, and *does* draw seventeen feet, sir. I was merely wishing to point out that a shoal-draught brig or large schooner would better serve close-in, whilst a frigate might stand farther offshore, to better interdict ships attempting to smuggle arms into Saint Domingue. And be better placed to intercept the odd French warship. As you say, in a few weeks our strength in the Indies will be reduced 'til the end of hurricane season, and fewer ships will have to cover a vast area, so it struck me that the most, uhm . . . *efficient* use of all our vessels is necessary, so—"

"Teach your granny to suck eggs, would you, sir?" Captain Sir Edward Charles fumed back, still mopping himself with a pocket handkerchief. "Know better than your superiors, do you?"

"Absolutely *not*, sir, why—!"

"Specific orders will be draughted and aboard your ship by the end of tomorrow's Forenoon, Captain Lewrie. Good day, sir."

"Very good, sir," Lewrie answered, quickly quaffing the last of his claret and getting to his feet, his face now an inscrutable public mask. "Uhm . . . there is still my courtesy call upon the Admiral. Do you think . . . ?" he enquired in an innocent tone, trying to salvage his odour, thinking that, should he make a favourable impression upon Sir Hyde Parker, what harm he'd done himself with this quarrelsome drunk could be cancelled out. And those orders changed!

"Our admiral is a *most* busy man, Captain Lewrie," Sir Edward intoned, "engaged with weighty matters anent the war, and his additional duties as prime representative of the Crown in this part of the world. Most busy. Some other time, perhaps," he concluded, not without a malicious simper to his voice, and a top-lofty twitch to his lips. He did, at least, rise to his own feet to steer Lewrie out, though more than a trifle unsteadily.

"Thank you for receiving me, sir," Lewrie was forced by manners to say, just before the double doors closed in his face, and the muffled cry for a manservant to come swab up the mess reached his ears—ears that were burning with rage!

Damme, but I mucked it! he chid himself as he stomped down the corridor, all but leaving gouged hoofprints in the gleaming tropical mahoghany boards; *never argue with a drunk! One who holds powers over you, especially! If my luck's not out, mayhap he'll be half-seas-over by teatime, and so foxed he'll forget I was ever here!*

"Arrogant old bastard!" he muttered under his breath. "Must keep his manservants up all night, washin' the wine and the vomit from out his wardrobe! Not sayin' he's so ignorant, he doesn't know how to pee, but I'll wager there's more'n a time or two his breeches are yellow, and his shoe-buckles're rusty! God!" he spat aloud. Cautiously.

And it wasn't as if Sir Edward Charles was likely to stand tall in repute, either, he groused to himself; he was a *staff*-captain, not the flag-captain of the fleet. A drunken stumbler a pistol-shot shy of being "Yellow Squadroned," a jumped-up senior clerk left ashore by his superiors to shuffle papers for the real *fighting* captains!

He found a black servant tending to a laving bowl and a stack of towels just by the wide double doors that led out to the courtyard and coachway, a luxury for officers and civilian visitors who wished to swab off perspiration and cool themselves before reporting to superiors. Badly in need of a cooling-off, Lewrie set aside his hat and plunged his hands into the water, sluicing his face and neck several times, wishing that he could bury his head in the bowl until he blew bubbles, or just up-turn it over himself 'til his choler subsided.

"Thankee," he said to the well-liveried slave as he offered him a towel. "Needed that. Hot in there."

"Aye, sah," the slave replied, not *quite* rolling his eyes with long experience of officers who needed his ministrations *after* their interviews.

Damme, I know I saw a man in admiral's togs, standin' on a balcony as we sailed in. Was that Parker? Lewrie recalled.

Fort Charles had partially blocked his view, along with all of the gunsmoke, but Giddy House had been in clear sight for a little bit! It had been too far off to count buttonholes or cuff rings, but he *had* seen what looked to be a coloured sash and a star of knighthood!

"Uhm, is Admiral Parker ashore, today?" Lewrie asked the slave.

"Aye, sah," the servant said with a sly smirk. "But he's werry busy, sah," he told him in a distinctive Jamaican *patois*.

"And here I must still pay my courtesy call," Lewrie responded, retrieving his hat, and his hopes. Something about the servant's expression gave him a salacious clue. "And he'd be busy doing . . . ?"

The slave pointed a finger skyward to the upper floor above.

"His shore office?" Lewrie enquired.

"His chambers, sah," the servant replied with a wee grin.

"Napping, then?" Lewrie further pressed.

"Oh, *nossah*," the slave answered with a wider grin and high-pitched titter.

"With company, is he?" Lewrie puzzled out. "Well, that's good reason t'be busy, I s'pose. All the live-long day, I take it?"

"Mos' de night, too, sah," he was further informed. "Been ovah t'Saint Nicholas Mole, 'board ship so long . . . De Admerl, he got a *fine* eye fo' de ladies, Cap'um, sah."

Lewrie heaved a sigh of defeat. The staff-captain's impression of him would get to Sir Hyde first, and he and *Proteus* would be slighted. Attempting to gain admittance, mid-jollifications, would make his odour even worse! He clapped his hat on his head and strode out into the late morning glare, pausing in the shade of Giddy House to steel himself for the full brunt of the sun. And, merry and light as local birds, he could hear the tinkle of a harpsichord, and the soft chuckle of at least two people on the balcony above.

" 'Least *someone's* havin' a good mornin'," he growled.

CHAPTER TWELVE

*R*emind 'em again, about the Maroons," Lewrie told his officers. "All to be back aboard by midnight . . . with so many ships in port, it's impossible *not* t'hear the watch-bells chime it. *Plain* drunks and half-dead get slung below . . . fightin' drunks'll get the 'cat' *and* stoppage of rum and tobacco for a month. Remind 'em not t'take too much money ashore, too. That *should* do it . . . pray God."

"Aye, sir," the officers, senior mates, and midshipmen chorused as they doffed their hats in dismissal.

It was a hellish risk he was running. Lewrie knew that more men took "leg bail" from ships' companies that were fairly new together, whereas ships longer in commission, and shaken down together, had fewer hands who would end up marked as "Run." After a time, the ship became home, one's closest mates and supporters *almost* like family. A stake in future pay-outs of prize money could provide a leash, as well, and HMS *Proteus* still awaited the reward for the *Orangespruit* frigate. Maybe his luck was in. He uncrossed his fingers.

Lewrie had seen unhappy and happy ships both, and felt that *Proteus* had shaken down rather well, even after the Nore mutiny and Camperdown. The music, the dancing in the Dog Watches, showed him high spirits; he had a *somewhat* honest Purser, so the rations were not rotten "junk" and were issued to fair measurements. He had decimated the gunroom and midshipmens' mess of bullies and tyrants, by refusing to take back aboard those budding despots and brutes the *crew* had wished off during the mass mutiny of the year before. There were very few requests for a change of mess, these days. A constant reshuffling of who could not stand the others in an eight-man dining/sleeping group was a sure sign of unrest and trouble. And, lastly, he had called everyone aft and had spoken to them.

Of trust and honour . . . of shipmates, future pay, and the prize money; of how Marines and the Army garrison and local militia kept up a full patrol; that Jamaica was an island, after all; that did anyone run inland, there were venomous snakes released long before by plantation owners to frighten their slaves into staying put; that runaways in the hills and back country, the slave "Maroons," were just waiting to butcher lone whites . . . well, he'd stretched the truth on that one. The Maroons were mostly high up in the Blue Mountains, fortified in the inaccessible places, not on the very edge of Kingston town; but thank God for the naive gullibility of your average tar—they'd eaten it up like plum duff, and had goggled in horror.

"But, most of all, lads . . . I trust you. I trusted you when we almost lost the ship and her honour at the Nore," he had told them and meant every word of it. "And you proved yourselves worthy. And I will trust you with shore liberty, knowing that you will return to duty . . . with thick heads and a bruise or two, most-like. *Does* anyone run, the rest of the crew will lose their chance, 'cause you'll have proved me mistaken in my trust. Don't let your shipmates down. Don't toss away what you've earned. Don't let *Proteus* down. Prove me right in trusting you. That's all . . . dismiss. Larboard watch to go ashore."

In an English port, he would never have risked it; once ashore and with access to civilian "long clothing," a fair number would have scampered, no matter how happy the ship, but here . . .

And when one got right down to it, Lewrie thought that his men had earned something better than putting the ship "Out of Discipline" and hoisting the "Easy" pendant to summon the bum-boatmen and whores aboard. *He* would be going ashore, after all, as would his midshipmen and officers . . . and it didn't feel fair, that the men who might still have to die with him, *for* him and their ship, would be denied what he could enjoy as a captain, as a gentleman.

Damme, I'm become an imbecile in my dotage! he chid himself one

more time; *bad as a Frog . . . Republican! A "popularity Dick"?*
He found that he'd crossed his fingers all over again.

The seat of government on Jamaica was thirteen miles west, over a rough
road, at Spanish Town. Kingston was the principal commercial harbour
and naval base, so even without the presence of the great or near-great
who decided things, it was a lively place.

Lewrie landed just by The Grapes, the cheery red-brick Georgian
inn and public house hard by the foot of the landing stage, an inviting
establishment mostly frequented by ship captains, naval officers, and
chandlers, along with an admixture of importers and exporters looking
for a ship to haul their goods.

He strolled over to the chandleries and shops, at first with an eye for
novelty, of being on solid ground and presented with the many rich
goods displayed, nigh as varied and of as good a quality as could be
found in England. There were his wine-cabinet and lazarette stores to
be replenished, more paper, ink, and quills to be purchased, a book or
two to read—great, whacking thick ones to be rationed out at a chapter
per day. He was low on mustard, coffee, and tea, and eager for local-
made preserves, the mango chutneys, the exotic dry-rub spices he remembered from his early days that could enliven grilled shoe leather,
and, like Hindoo curry, make even rotten salt-beef or salt-pork worth
eating. More dried meat—"jerky"—for Toulon, and a fresh keg of low-
tide beach sand for his box in the quarter-gallery.

And, on the spur of the moment, cotton canvas uniforms! He sought
out a tailor's that he remembered, got measured, and ordered a brace of
dark blue undress breeches, another pair in white, and coats for undress,
at-sea, days.

"Bleed all over your shirts and waistcoats, sir, the first time in a
squall," the tailor cluck-clucked, just as he had back when Lewrie had
needed a new midshipman's uniform in '81.

"Well, wash the cloth a time or two first, then run 'em up. No
shrinkage then, either, right?" Lewrie countered.

"Cost extra, it would, sir," the old fellow contemplated.

"Hang the cost. Better a shilling or two than suffocate in a wool coat, with summer coming."

"Be ready in two days, sir."

"And, do we sail before then, I'm assured my ship will be back in harbour quite often. You could hold them for me, if I put half the sum down now?"

"Quite acceptable, sir. Unlike some, d'ye see. Why . . . here! I *recall* you, Captain Lewrie. Long before, oh years and years, but . . ."

"I do not *owe* you from then, do I, sir?" Lewrie teased.

"Not as I recall, sir. And I've a long mem'ry for debtors. In this line, such is ruin or salvation, don't ye know."

The tiny bell over the front door tinkled, and an Army officer entered, mopping his face with a handkerchief and fanning his hat.

"Ah, Colonel . . . all's ready for you, as promised!" the tailor chirped. A large-ish order, or another who paid his reckoning on the nail, Lewrie gathered.

"Well, stap me!" the officer said, with a goggle.

"Damn my eyes!" Lewrie rejoined quite happily. "Cashman!"

"Young Lewrie! Made 'post'! Hell's Bell's, who'd have dreamt you'd rise so high!"

They advanced on each other and clasped hands with warmth, all but pounding each other on the back and shoulders.

"And you, a Colonel," Lewrie marvelled.

"Well, Lieutenant-Colonel," Christopher Cashman allowed with a becoming modesty in one Lewrie remembered as so brash.

"But with your own regiment, I take it?"

"Aye, the Fifteenth West Indies, just raised last year. A one-battalion, wartime-only regiment, but all mine. Local volunteers, and funded by rich planters. We do have a Colonel of the regiment, but for the most part, he's too busy making money. The odd mess-night boredom, when he shows up to bask, d'ye see."

"So you may run things as you see fit, at long last!" Alan said.

"Mostly, and thank God for it!" Cashman said with a merry laugh.

"You must tell me all about it."

"We'll dine you in, and you can see 'em," Cashman vowed. "And you've a ship, I s'pose. What is she?"

"HMS *Proteus*, a Fifth Rate thirty-two gunner. Damn' near new!"

"And been busy, I see," Cashman said, eyeing Lewrie's medals.

"Tell you all about it over dinner. Is Baltasar's still open?"

"The old Frog's fancy *restaurant*?" Cashman asked. "He died of Yellow Jack, ages ago. A Free Black feller dared buy it, and kept the name. Frankly, the food's much better and his prices ain't so high."

"Let's make it my treat, then," Lewrie offered. "Feelin' a tad peckish? Have time for it?"

"Yes, and yes. Let me collect my new articles, and we're off!"

Baltasar's was much as Lewrie recalled it. There was a curtain-wall with a wrought iron gate in front, with a small brass plaque the only sign that it was a commercial establishment and not a residence. Within, there was a cool and shaded courtyard, with a small fountain that plashed and gurgled beneath a pergola, between trellises hanging heavy with fragrant tropical flowering vines. A second curtain-wall split the entry into two clean white gravel or oyster shell paths, by *jardiniers* filled with even more flowers.

Inside was a cool, open room with plaster walls and heavy wood beams, wainscotted to chair-height with gleaming local mahoghany, and the tables covered with clean white cloths. At the rear, there was a slightly raised dining area facing a back wall pierced by large windows and glazed double doors that led out to a back garden overlooking the harbour, where even more wrought iron tables sat under sailcloth awnings for shade, to dine *alfresco*. The decor was much simpler than what Lewrie remembered, more Caribbean than imitation Versailles or Tuilleries Palace ornate. Most tables were taken, and the intriguing aromas coming from the separate cooking shed told him why.

A fetching Creole or Mulatto wench came to take their orders, a young woman with whom Cashman joshed as though he was a more than regular diner . . . or an after-hours lover? Like Lewrie's Cox'n Andrews, she was light-skinned and her features were finer and handsomer, than brutish.

"A mere touch o' the tar-brush," Cashman explained once she had headed for the kitchen shed and had spoken to the barman.

"Fair handsome," Lewrie amiably agreed. "A *particular* friend?"

"Almost pass for white, a fair number of 'em," Cashman told him, ignoring the query, "but what may one expect, with so many sailors and soldiers runnin' off and takin' up with the first decent-lookin' wench they see? Planters and overseers, married or no, who can't resist the Cuffie housemaid's charms? Some free girls who turn to whorin' and out pops a mulatto git. And their dialect, did ya hear it? Damn' near an Irish brogue, or a Cockney twang that takes ya back to Bow Bells, with a Creole lilt. Jamaica could be a fine country."

"Same as India, or Canton in China, anywhere Europeans go," Alan said, as their wine arrived, taking Cashman's evasion as confirmation.

"Same as Saint Domingue," Cashman pointed out with a frown. "If you think Jamaica's a hodgepodge, wait'll you get ashore, over there."

"Wasn't plannin' on it, Christopher," Lewrie scoffed after tasting the hock. "From all I've heard, a mile or two safe offshore'll do me fine. Do they *ice* this, by God? Marvelous!"

"Massachusetts ice, packed in straw and wood chips, down in the storm cellars," Cashman informed him, beaming. "Americans can even turn shite t'money, s'truth! Whole shiploads of dried manure to dung thin island soils. Saint Domingue, though . . . you know the French. Put the leg over a monkey did someone shave the face first. Saint Domingue's a bloody pot-mess when it comes t'race. Dozens of terms for how black or white a person is . . . mulatto, *quadron*, octoroon, *griffe*, dependin' on whether the father or mother was black or white, and what *shade*, if the mother was slave or free, house-servant or field hand, how rich or important the sire. Most confusin' bloody war ever ya did see, and I doubt if the Blacks over there can sort it out. They're comin' to call it the 'War of The Skin.' Everybody's terrified of the real dark Blacks, the half-castes with nothing side with this fella L'Ouverture, the half-castes with anything t'lose side with Rigaud, or the whites."

"The *petits blancs* side with the *grande blancs* . . ." Lewrie added.

"Someone fill you in, then?"

"Written advisories," Lewrie told him, scowling. "But you must know how little those're worth, and how out of date by now."

"We're going there, soon," Cashman said. "General Maitland has been run pretty-much ragged, whenever he sends battalions out into the countryside. Lucky he hasn't been butchered and hung up by his heels, suffered total massacres, so far. Like the Frogs. Poor bastards."

"So what is this, the Last Supper?" Lewrie asked. "Eat, drink, and be merry, for tomorrow we shall die?"

"Been there, before. Call it a preventive dose of civilisation, so I don't go mad *quite* as quickly," Cashman snickered.

"How *did* you get your own regiment?" Lewrie enquired. "Last we saw of each other back in '83, you were a brevet-captain in a fusilier regiment."

"Ah, well . . . long story," Christopher said, winking.

"We'll take a long dinner," Lewrie assured him.

"Well, once the Revolution ended, what was left of us were sent back to England. Recall, I told you how much I despise cold climates? Damn-all raw and rainy, and damn-all dreary, too . . . peacetime soldiering. I had picked up a little loot, here and there. Lots of officers in the regiment were selling up their commissions, but I still couldn't afford t'be more than a lieutenant, with a fifteen-year-old over me as captain, damn his eyes! Cost of a commission *always* goes up in peacetime, in regiments that won't get sent overseas for a long spell. But I found a daddy, needed a place for his slack-jawed young imbecile, so I sold up and resigned. *Then* turned round and bought a captaincy in a *kutch-pultan** with the bad luck t'be ordered to India. Could've bought it for the price of coach fare, with so many young fools worried about their thin, pale skins, of a sudden! And I'd been there before, as ye knew, and it hadn't killed me yet, so . . ."

Cashman sketched a neck-or-nothing career of heat and flies, of bad water and food, nigh-poisonous native "guzzle," surely poisonous serpents, spiders, and scorpions for bed companions, the sun murderous.

"To a bloody war, or a sickly season," Lewrie proposed, raising his glass with one of the Royal Navy's toasts. "Ah, India, the land of loot and lust! I take it you were fortunate in both, hmm?"

"Brevet-major in six months, as officers keeled over like nine-pins. Some kerfuffles with a native prince or two, and I'd amassed me enough t'buy a permanent majority," Cashman boasted, "*and* laid enough aside

*_kutch-pultan_=a poor, undistinguished regiment.

t'come home a chicken-*nabob*, and then I had me a think. Never in this life would I make lieutenant-colonel, not even in a shoddy battalion such as mine. Home depot in England picks those who suit the Colonel of the Regiment, or Horse Guards, when there's no war, and they've no need of *my* harum-scarum sort. Things got quiet after a few years, so I sold up and took passage here. Not quite as hot, a *tad* less dangerous, and a *tad* less unhealthy. Got into sugar cane, cotton and such, in a small way. Ran up a rather nice house, ran about twenty slaves, my own cane-mill, press and pans. Down southwest of Spanish Town, on Portland Bight. Milled for neighbours who didn't get the wind to run their own mills proper . . . done main-well raisin' horses and cattle as well. Takes less labour and fewer slaves. Oh, I played ship's husband for a while, backin' cargoes on the Triangle Trade, but after a time or two, I got out of that. A drib here, a drab there, and it all added up, somehow."

"But your regiment," Lewrie pressed as their soup arrived, a hot and spicy pepperpot. "Sounds as if you had a fine retirement or second career. But then, you . . . ?"

"Boredom, Lewrie!" Christopher told him with an outburst of too-bright laughter. "I was bored silly! Like most things, one claws and schemes t'get Life's treasures, but once in hand, they lose lustre, and you find it was the *chase* that was the real fun."

"I think I see your point," Lewrie replied, thinking of his own tenant farm in Anglesgreen, the mark of a landed gentleman that *should* have been satisfaction enough, and the mark of success.

"And . . . there's the slaves," Cashman admitted, turning sombre. "Recall, do ya, we once had a schemin' session on a riverbank in Spanish Florida, when we got sent up the Apalachicola t'deal with the Muskogee Indians? How it'd be a great land for crops like cotton, did I fetch in some Bengalis, 'stead o' the Indians? Grow it, pick it, and card it, wash it, bale it, and ship. Or spin it and loom it on the spot, usin' the river for power. Even build a manufactory, and sell made clothin' all over this part of the world?"

"Aye, I do recall. How close did you come?" Lewrie smiled.

"You *pay* a Hindoo *ryot* for his work, Lewrie," Cashman confessed in a much lower voice, one that would not carry to his contemporaries and fellow planters. "You hire him. Aye, he slacks off and acts lazy and ya thrash him, and he'll take it and shrug it off, then get back to work proper. But the Cuffies, Alan ... the Samboes. With them, all we *have* is the lash. Die off in droves from snake bites, diseases, worked t'death or starved halfway there—have t'buy more of 'em, and start all over again. We've thirty-thousand whites on Jamaica, but there're over three hundred *thousand* slaves, and barely ten thousand Free Black people. And there might be a total turnover every generation, do you see? And ya *can't* do anything t'ease the misery. Cosset your slaves, and your neighbours'll think you're weak ... a 'Merry Andrew.' Go too harsh, like most of 'em do, and you get rebellion. *And* start fearin' what yer house slaves serve ya, do they slip poison in your food and drink! That's no way t'live, Lewrie, believe me. I thought I knew what I was gettin' into when I bought land and slaves t'work it. Knew my way round *natives*, d'ye see ... Bengalis, Mahrattas. Muskogee or Cherokee. Hell ... Irish?" he added with a grin and a shrug.

"But it didn't work that way," Lewrie said for him, though yet mystified. It was a *given*, that slaves and acreage were the marks of colonial gentlemen, of success and prosperity! Yet Cashman sounded as if he'd turned his back on everything except honourable soldiering.

"May've been the worst mistake I ever made, Lewrie, to settle out here," Cashman confessed in a mutter. "I considered America, but even with over-mountain land goin' for ten pence an acre, it requires slaves t'work it, too, 'less you settle far north, among those stiff-necked, hymn-singin' Yankees, with all their 'shalt nots.' And it's a *cold* damn' place, to boot! Oh, I plunged in with a will at first, and thought things were goin' hellish fine, doin' what everyone else about me did, but ... first thing I did was get out of the Triangle Trade."

Lewrie knew about that; sugar and molasses, coffee and cotton, dye-woods and indigo to American ports. Sell cargoes and invest some of the profit into rum, tobacco, hemp ropes, tar, pitch and turpentine, resin and naval stores; ship that to England and make another profit, which was partly invested in cheap trade goods, trinkets and gew-gaws, cast-off muskets and cutlasses, bolts of gaudy cloth and such to sell or trade in West Africa, where the Black chieftains and Arab traders would fetch you thousands of their own people, or those captured from other tribes, then ship "Black Ivory" on the Middle Passage to a Caribbean port to be auctioned off. Three legs of trade, three profits in one, and five hundred pounds could end up fetching four thousand!

"Saw the wretches landed, sold off at the Vendue House," Cashman said so softly that Lewrie had to lean over his soup to hear him. "I felt . . . sick. Smelt the stink of a 'blackbirder,' have you? Once is enough for a lifetime. Fed me own slaves a touch better after that, I did. Shoes and new slop-clothing more'n once a year. Let 'em have an hour 'or two more on their vegetable plots, bought more salt meats and such? Felt I was doin' right, no matter what the neighbours thought. Salved my conscience a little, but that was all I was doin'. What my overseers did in my name, though . . . What's the difference?"

"So you got more into livestock?" Alan asked.

"Yes. Less cane, where the real misery lies, the killin' work."

Lewrie studied Christopher Cashman—the "Kit" of his early derring-do—as he returned to spooning up his pepperpot soup before it got cold. He *looked* much the same as the old Cashman of his remembrance, but for more crinkles 'round his eyes and mouth, his hair now sprinkled with more salt than pepper. He was still the lean, fit, and hungry-looking rogue from the '80s, and had not battened as most men would, once success and a semblance of riches got within their grasp. His wardrobe had improved, of a certainty; Lewrie could recall shabby uniforms so faded from red to pink that one could conjure that he had bought his regimentals off a ragpicker's barrow. Now he was prosperous, tailored as natty as anything, well shod in popular Hessian boots, his sword of good quality and gleaming, his tunic heavy with real gilt lace and embroidery, his breeches, waistcoat, and shirt snowy-white and well cared for, his hair dressed neatly.

But, Lewrie wondered, where was that "fly," sardonic rogue from those days, the one with the wry, sarcastic, or flippant comment in the face of danger or disaster?

"You know about the Second Maroon War, I take it?" Cashman asked of a sudden, as if all that had passed between them moments before had never occurred.

"Yes. Started in '91, didn't it?"

"Prompted by the slave revolt in Saint Domingue," Cashman said. "Got beaten back, but broke out again in '95. I retook colours then, as a major once more. Nothing near so big or widespread as our Frogs suffer, but bad enough. 'Twas a great slaughter, e'en so. Eye for an eye, tooth for a tooth, and not a jot o' mercy. Ambush for ambush, massacre for massacre. Shut 'em down by '96, but there's still many skulkin' about. Then along comes General Maitland, who asks me to be on his staff at Port-Au-Prince. Spent a year at that, then the people here suggested raisin' another local regiment. Maitland put in a word for me, and I had the support of my neighbours, who put up the money."

"But Kit . . . whyever agree t'fight rebellious French slaves, if you didn't care for fightin' your own?" Lewrie puzzled aloud.

"In any society, Alan my old," Cashman said, leaning closer to mutter even softer, with a sardonic gleam in his eyes, "you're either on the side of the angels or you're a *pariah* dog. You have to sing along with the choir, nod and say 'amen' in the right places. My good name was on the line. And I didn't say I *don't* like fightin' slaves. They'd slaughter white folk like so many hogs in November, given the chance. They despise us, d'ye see. They despise *me*! Act harsh, and they despise you . . . be soft, and they take advantage. Treat 'em well, gift 'em on the holidays, and they'll fawn and slobber on yer boots to yer face, all grateful-like, then roll their eyes and snicker behind yer back, and despise you for your weakness! I'd much rather kill 'em than own 'em . . . any day."

Lewrie's jaw dropped open in surprise. *Is he daft?* he queried himself, *No, he looks and sounds as sane as . . . as me!*

"Servile, obsequious cringers, liars, and frauds, all of 'em," Cashman rather calmly went on, between sips of his soup and a dabbing at his mouth with a fine linen napkin. "I've an overseer runnin' things for me, for now. Once this war on Saint Domingue's done, I'll sell up, lock, stock, and barrel, and get free of this pestilential place. Sham a lingerin' fever, invent a troublin' wound . . . grief? Any excuse to placate my neighbours and peers. I'll have done my bit by then, and there'll be no shame in it. *Something* that took too much outta me . . . and d'ye know what I'll do then?"

Lewrie shook his head in the negative.

"I'll sell off my slaves with the greatest of glee," he said, with a nasty smirk, "to the harshest masters I know, and I know most of 'em, believe you me. Those *few* I think were straight with me, I'll manumit and give 'em a small sum for a fresh start. But the rest . . . I'll see 'em all in a livin' hell. Then I'm shot o' this place, and off to the *East* Indies again, where a man with 'chink' can live like a *rajah*, and stuff ev'ry wench in the *bibikhana* ev'ry night, do I get the itch. And never have t'buy folk, ever again!"

"Surely, you knew, goin' in . . ." Lewrie countered. "You were out here for years, and saw how a slave society . . ."

"Ah, but it looks so *dev'lish* easy, goin' in, Alan," Cashman scoffed. "Sit on your balcony and watch the money grow? Play cards and dance in the parlour, with everything at yer beck and call, with nary a thought for *how* it's fetched. Damned beguilin' life, from the outside lookin' in, when it's *other* people's slaves doin' the bowin' and scrapin' to ya. Once in, though . . . it's a hell on *all* sides."

At that moment, the pretty young mulatto serving wench arrived with a tray heaped with platters; split crab claws and legs, lobsters split and steaming, with fresh-caught pompano grilled in key-lime rob and crisp with breading; removes of fresh chickpeas and diced scallions; plump boiled carrots topped with brown sugar; and a basket piled high with piping hot yeast rolls made with imported fine wheat flour!

"Ah, Paradise!" Lewrie extolled, after his first taste of every dish, rolling his eyes in ecstasy. "And damn all Navy rations!"

"Another thing, Alan," Cashman said after a bite of fried fish and a sip of their chilled hock, with a blissful smile on his own face. "When the time comes t'sell, a hero's lands go higher than a poltroon who didn't serve . . . or those of a secret Abolitionist. Ever hear of William Wilburforce or Hannah More?"

"Aye, damn 'em," Lewrie sourly replied.

William Wilburforce was in Parliament, Hannah More was one of those Society Women with more energy than wit; both were determined to "reform" English Society in their own mould, to tame it, gentle it, and "improve" it. And they were Church of England, not Dissenters!

"Church of England, but they talk more like the Wesley brothers and all their leapin' Methodists," Lewrie went on, after a cleansing slosh of wine. "Spendin' all their time, and half their money, along with lots of other fools, 'bout Sunday schools, so please you, so our children don't grow up wild. Or pick up Republican ideas, and rebel like the Fleet did."

"Somethin' t'be said for that, at least," Cashman commented.

"Ending bear-baiting, dogfights, cockfightin', all sorts of country customs. Hell, it'll be fox huntin', next! Bad as Cromwell and his Roundhead Puritans, out t'take all joy from life. Marketin' fairs, gamblin', even morris dancin' . . . the heart and soul of us!"

"I'll send them a contribution . . . to their Abolitionist Society," Cashman secretly whispered. "And damn the neighbours. Now, do you imagine the reception Wilburforce and More would get, did they ever dare come out here to preach, well . . . they'd be strung up and hung."

"And pray God for it!" Lewrie quickly vowed.

"Same'd happen t'me, Alan. Or get pence to the pound when I sell up," Cashman assured him. "Did they know my true feelings on the matter. I'm not gettin' any younger, and all I have is tied up in my lands and such. I'd never have the time t'pile up the 'blunt' all over again from scratch. I was lookin' for an out, and by God, here came a chance to take colours once more and get away from the problem."

"And so well-timed it felt dropped from Heaven?" Lewrie asked with a chuckle as he split and buttered one of those luscious rolls. "I see . . . '*turne, quod optanti divum promittere nemo auderet, volvenda dies en attulit ultro*' . . . 'ey wot?"

"Why, you pretentious . . . *hound*, sir!" Cashman erupted in an outburst of hearty laughter, much his old self once more. "That's about all the Latin that ever got lashed into you, isn't it? I'll lay it is!"

"Sir, I hold commission in the King's Navy," Lewrie replied in a false haughtiness, his nose lifted top-lofty. "I am a Post-Captain, therefore *eminently* superior to any Redcoat. Now, how else may I make you assume the proper humility, was I *not* pretentious?"

"One with crumbs on his shirt front," Cashman drolly rejoined. "Aye, by God. What the gods couldn't promise, rollin' time brought, unasked. An apt quote, I'll grant ye. Never saw that side of you up the Apalachicola. Which reminds me . . . how *is* your Muskogee 'wife,' Soft Rabbit was her name? And that bastard son she whelped?"

"Ah, uhm!" was Lewrie's witty response.

"I take it you're married by now, bein' a captain and all?" Cashman went on, casually enquiring. "And married well, I trust."

"Aye, with three 'gits,' now."

"Capital! But I wager you haven't said word one to *her* about your first 'wife,' now have you." Cashman most evilly grinned.

"I *like* breathin'," Lewrie retorted, a tad sharpish, wondering if word of his troubles had gotten to the islands ahead of him somehow. "And what about you? Did *you* ever wed, Kit?" he countered.

"The once," Cashman admitted, quickly losing his jaunty, japing air. "Out here, in '91. No children, sorry t'say, before she passed over ... back in '95, just about the time the Maroon War began."

Another reason to quit his lands? Lewrie wondered in sympathy. *Another reason to take a commission?*

"I'm sorry to hear that, Kit, I ..."

"Oh, don't be," Cashman brushed off, swirling his wine aloft as if squinting at it for lees. "Prettier than the morning, she was, aye. But meaner than a snake. Raised out here, d'ye see, used to managing slaves from her cradle, and her kinfolk some of the harshest. She ran through three or four riding quirts a year, slashin' and layin' about at any servant who crossed her. Bought 'em by the half dozen, she did! Fascinatin' girl, but a beast at heart. Horse threw her, one morning. Broke her neck ... snap!"

"Dear God, but ..." Lewrie gawped, appalled.

"Towards the end, I couldn't abide the sight or sound of her," Cashman admitted with a rueful *moue* and shrug. "Happened whilst I was off in the Blue Mountains, start of the Maroon War. Took colours just t'be shot o' *her*, too. Mean as she was, I always suspected one of our stable boys *made* her horse shy, perhaps some of the field hands. Left her t'die? Snapped her neck themselves, so it looked accidental? Who knows. Did me a great favour, if they did. You get used to lordin' it over slaves, you simply *have* to turn mean and callous. Her, I mean to say. Perhaps me, as well, but ..." Be shrugged off once more, smiling disarmingly.

"I heard such once before, I think," Lewrie said, after wiping his mouth with the napkin following a dollop of lobster and drawn butter. "Out here, come t'think on it, oh ... ages ago, when I was fresh-commisioned, here in Kingston. Lady of my acquaintance ... sister of a girl I was wooing? God, they were *hellish* rich! Anne Beauman, do you know of her? Her youngest sister, Lucy, was the one I was after. Anne

said that a slave society gets callous and hard on everyone, once you
get used to wallopin' the Blacks, so why not wallop every . . . what?"

"The Beaumans, Alan?" Cashman told him, in answer to the gawpy
look on Lewrie's face, once he'd seen the smirk on Christopher's. "Who
hold great swaths of land . . . on Portland Bight, do they?"

"They're your neighbours, of course! You do know 'em!"

"Hugh Beauman and his wife Anne are my patrons in the regiment,"
Cashman delighted in informing him. "Made up his mind I was the man
for him, and he's used to gettin' his way."

"Aye, just as they were back in '82," Lewrie recalled. "So how is
Anne? At the time, she was the most exotic-lookin' woman."

"Ah, well . . . faded, sorry t'say. Island women mostly do. The cli-
mate and the sun, I expect. Shrivel up and go sour and grey much too
soon. Do they not perish o' childbed fever, malaria, or the Yellow Jack."

"There was another sister, Floss, I think?"

"Died," Cashman coolly told him.

"Ah, pity. Poor old thing," Lewrie said. "But Lucy! Now . . ."

"Mmmmmm!" Cashman agreed most heartily.

"My first *real* love. On my part, at least," Lewrie confessed. "Ran
into her in Venice two years ago. She'd remarried a Sir Malcolm Shockley, baronet. Richer than God. Why, richer than the Beaumans!"

"She was still here when I bought my lands, in her first marriage,"
Cashman reminisced. "Aye, one of the great beauties of her time."

"Unfortunately, dumber than dirt, too," Lewrie pointed out.

"My dear Alan," Christopher Cashman leered back at him, "I never
asked her to *recite!*"

"You never!" Lewrie chortled, catching the sly meaning.

Always did *have the most Philistine of tastes, she did!* Lewrie assured
himself, trying to picture Lucy taking up with Cashman.

"Ah, but I did," Cashman slyly boasted. "Along with half the young
swains in Jamaica, I suspect. You?"

"Uhm . . . no, actually," Lewrie had to admit, "but not for want of
trying, mind. She was only seventeen, back then, and chaperoned as
close as a Spanish convent girl."

"Watched like a hawk, aye," Christopher said with a knowing nod.

" 'Twas after she wed that she took up her own household, with a young husband on the land, and her here in town. Got a ragin' hunger for it, and then *no* man was safe. And too rich to be scandalised, don't you know. Small world, ain't it."

"Bad as old Mistress Betty Hillwood. My, uhm . . . replacement," Lewrie said with a sly boast of his own, "for when I couldn't get the leg over Lucy. Used to keep rooms uphill, the fountained court . . ."

"Oh, my yes!" Cashman said with another knowing purr. "It *is* a damn' small world. Been there, too, Alan. She died, though, in '86."

"And a hard'un," Lewrie said, sighing, and returned to a crab claw with his name on it.

"Want to guess who the Colonel of the Regiment is, then?"

"Hugh Beauman?" Lewrie supposed aloud.

"Lord, no! *Much* too rich and involved t'be playing soldier."

"Hold on, there was another brother . . ." Lewrie said, frowning as he tried to recall a name to place on a braying horse's ass.

"Ledyard Beauman, that's the one," Cashman said with distaste.

"Lord, *that* fool? That hoorawin' jackanapes?" Lewrie cried in utter surprise. "When I met him, he was still limp-wristed 'Macaroni' fashion, *years* after the style'd passed. 'Bout as sharp-witted as his sister Lucy, God help us. Couldn't pour pee from his boot without a footman's help!"

"He's lost ground, since," Cashman sombrely assured him.

"Ledyard Beauman, by God! And *he's* your Colonel? Is he actually capable of anything?"

"He's been . . . studying, d'ye see. Tactics and such," Cashman grimly said. "Out of books, so please you. Marchin' wee lead troops 'cross his dinin' table, rattlin' on about Cannae, Hadrianopolis, and double envelopments. Caesar in Gaul, Scipio Africanus, and Hannibal? Turnin' into a perfect pest."

"Well, I'd allow he might look crackin' fine on a charger, at a parade," Lewrie snickered some more. "Just so long as he knows his limitations . . . and his place."

"Well, that's the rub, Alan," Cashman said, sighing a tad more and wriggling uneasily in his chair as if ants were inside his breeches. He unconsciously crossed his legs as if to protect his "nutmegs" from harm.

"Lately, he's of a mind—a fervid mind—t'go over t'Saint Domingue with us, when we sail. Bring us his . . . insights, or so he says. How best to employ and manouevre troops and such?"

"God help your poor arse, you *must* be joking!" Lewrie gawped. But he wasn't, of course.

CHAPTER THIRTEEN

*E*ager to show off his command, Christopher Cashman insisted that Lewrie accompany him a mile or two towards Spanish Town, to the encampment, and would not take no for an answer. After a quick row out to *Proteus* to see if orders had come aboard, or if members of the liberty party had created some havoc—the orders had not, and only a few of the hands had been returned "paralytic-drunk" by the shore provosts—Lewrie felt sanguine enough to go along.

"Kit" laid on a fine equipage, a silk-topped coach-and-four of gleaming wood and fragrant leather, bright coral-red wheel spokes that raised the faintest cloud of dust from the sandy track, and drawn by a team of matched roans of fairly impressive conformation; horses raised on Cashman's lands, he was smugly informed.

There was a florid letter *B* on the doors, though, encircled by oak wreaths. "Well, o' course, Alan old son," Cashman crowed, "this is a Beauman coach. Nothin' but the best for their 'hired' colonel!"

The 15th West Indies Regiment was under canvas, their company tents pitched in neat streets, with duckboards between in case of rain and mud, laid out to mathematical perfection, as laid down in the infantry manuals. Across a wide parade ground, still "stobby" with sugar cane stubble (for a cane field it had been 'til lately) stood a giant green-and-white striped pavillion tent large enough to shelter them all if stood shoulder-to-shoulder. Assuming anyone would allow any of the 435 rankers inside, that is; it had been erected for a special occasion, and was now filled with preening officers from the island garrison, with uniformed visitors from both Army and Navy, and with civilians in their finest, come to watch a parade. The ground above the pavillion teemed with carriages just as sumptuous as the one in which Lewrie and Cashman arrived, with nodding teams of horses being tended by slave grooms, and a long roped row of saddled riding horses in the shade of the trees.

"Think of graduation day, Alan," Cashman said as a black coachman came to fold down the metal steps and open the door for them, "and all the beamin' parents come t'see their sprogs pass out into Life."

"And you took yourself into town, 'stead of sittin' on 'em like a broody hen?" Lewrie wondered as he alit. "Good God, I can see three generals from where I stand! A hellish risk, Kit."

"I *know* they can drill, Alan," Cashman confidently boasted, "so what's the point of actin' like I don't trust 'em? Have to, sooner or later, won't I? Let the officers find their feet, too, 'thout 'mother' standin' over 'em and makin' 'em so nervous they wouldn't trust their own arses with their farts. That's the problem with your typical Army regiments . . . either too rich and casual, hopin' to muddle through, or they're lashed, drilled, and browbeat so bad, no one from majors down to corporals *dare* have a thought in their heads 'til a colonel puts it there. Same aboard yer ships, I expect . . . the way a captain can ruin a good ship, and make her officers spend all their time lookin' over a shoulder, too scared t'put a foot wrong."

"Well, there is that," Lewrie allowed.

"Not much to work with, I'll tell ya true," Cashman said as they strolled the short distance to the pavillion, and its wide, welcoming flies and awnings, "the dregs of the island, the scrapin's from Home regiments gone down from fevers . . . rich boy-officers, who had a mind t'soldier 'cause the uniform pleased the young ladies. Educated men who clerked, or finished their apprenticeships, but aren't from rich or even squire families—oh, a dense lot in the beginnin', but we set 'em straight. Sent 'em off on company marches and skirmish drill, all by themselves for two, three days, with no one t'wipe their arses for 'em. Shed a few, promoted a few, hang their pedigrees . . . and ya *know* I'd teach 'em t'shoot, Alan! By line, by platoon, by regimental volley . . . and in teams of four, two loadin' and watchin' whilst two deliver *aimed* fire out in the bushes. Nothin' like your classic set-piece battle, nossir, all flags and gallopers, and such."

"Like we were, in Spanish Florida," Lewrie said with a smile of reverie, twinging to what Cashman had been driving at, "fighting Red Indian fashion. Like Yankee Doodle skulkers, with rifles."

"Hunters," Cashman amended. " 'Cept here, we hunt men. Half the regiment'll be in skirmish order all the time, able to fall back upon the rest if they get in trouble. Can't parade battalion-front in three lines in a jungle. Saint Domingue ain't like Europe, all orderly and neat. Crops gone wild, grown horse-eye tall, wild shrubs grown back up as thick as dog-hair . . . aah, General Lazenby, and your lovely lady!"

Lewrie got introduced, then tipped Cashman the wink and wandered off to fetch himself a glass of something, leaving Kit to play host to his "guests." It didn't take long; a liveried slave in a white tie-wig produced a silver tray bearing long flutes of champagne—again iced—and Lewrie took a brace of them. It was a hot day for April, dash it all!

He then wandered, circulating and bowing, or doffing his hat to the other guests as he encountered them; as they encountered *him*, really. His was a new face in a rather insular society, he suspected (and forgave himself for the pun!) much like Anglesgreen of a Sunday, with nought but the usual neighbours to see 'til the London Season ended and absentee landowners came down to their properties, fetching along a raft of houseguests for a week or two in the country or the coach that brought the mails also brought in a clutch of passengers. Every day, folk would gather before the Olde Ploughman or the Red Swan Inn, just for a sight of them, even were they merely alighting for a shot at the "jakes," a quick half-pint of ale with a cold beef pie before "Whip Up And Away." And certainly, he smugly grinned to himself, the sight of two gold medals dangling on his chest didn't hurt when it came to a lure for the curious, either!

As men shook his hand with almost an admiring briskness, and the ladies curtsied or inclined their heads, with fans rustling faster in what he took for approval, he was pumped dry for information about the doings "at home" in England, the latest titillating scandals at Court, the prices of goods, the progress of the war. He also got a chance to enquire about people he had met in Jamaica in his early days.

"Mistress Margaret Haymer and her husband . . . name escapes me?"

"Dead, oh years ago, alas!"

"The Hillwoods?"

"Both passed over, unfortunatly."

"Feller who invited my commanding officer and several of us from the midshipmens' mess to a supper and ball once . . . Sir Richard Slade?"

"Joined the Great Majority in '86," was the shifty-eyed reply. "And good riddance, frankly. A *back-gammoner*, sir, d'ye get my . . ."

"*Thought* there was somethin' a tad . . . off about him, myself," Lewrie could say with a frown of pleasure. "A man o' the 'windward passage,' ey? Hid it well, he did, but . . . his house servants *were* a young bunch, and all boys. Well, well . . ."

"Alan Lewrie, is it you, sir?"

"Ma'am?" he replied, turning in the direction of the query. "I say! Mistress Beauman, a great pleasure after all these . . . after all this time."

Years, ye gods! he chid himself, *don't remind her of her years!*

Cashman had the right of it; Anne Beauman *had* aged badly. Only her lively brown eyes reminded him of the lass she used to be. She had shriveled like one of those apple-headed dolls the Rebels made that he had seen in Charleston or Wilmington; stout as a salt-beef cask, as well. Though still done up in the best apparel money could buy—and Beaumans could afford the best—she more resembled a weary harridan who had not been blessed by Life, the sort of shop-woman one could see in London, out on a Sunday stroll since that was better than desponding up in an airless garret lodging.

"Congratulations, sir," she said as if recalling maidenly coos and styles. "Lucy wrote us, once she was safely back in England. But she told us you were merely a Commander, at the time."

"She and Sir Malcolm keep well, I trust, Mistress Anne?"

"Oh, indeed! With you to thank for their lives."

"I did nothing more than warn them to flee Venice and get home, before the French took the place, ma'am, nothing like . . ." Lewrie said with his brow creased in confusion, wondering what spindrift the minx had invented to improve her tale.

"Oh, but was there not some adventure at some island along the Dalmatian coast, with pirates and . . . ?" Anne frowned in turn.

"We put in there for a bit, once she and Sir Malcolm took passage with us, but that was after we'd—"

"Ah, there ye be," a gruff voice interrupted; most thankfully, to Alan's lights—how *did* one disabuse someone of their kin's veracity?

"Ah!" Lewrie said, feigning joy. "Mister Hugh Beauman!"

He offered his hand, recalling that at one time this side of beef, this breeding bull—and his father—had threatened to thrash him in the streets of Kingston and finally *had* shown him the door, quite firmly assuring him he'd never darken their lives again! Surprisingly, Hugh Beauman took it and gave it a powerful shake of welcome; with a vise-like, crunching squeeze, though—just to remind him of his "place!"

"Lewrie, ah de do!" Beauman bellowed. "Years, wot? All grown up, I see. Stap me, a Post-Captain now!"

"Last year, sir, after the battle of—"

"On yer own bottom. Have a frigate, I'd expect? Yes? Good!"

Like all the Beauman men, Lewrie sadly told himself; *they talk in fragments . . . too busy for polite conversation. Prob'ly begrudge the time wasted, too!* The father Beauman he'd dealt with had been the same way, when Lewrie was courting Lucy. For all their wealth, they were "chaw-bacon" with not a jot of *ton* or style; tenant-tramplin', fox-huntin', beer-swillin' country-puts—the very epitome of that newspaper artist Cruikshank's droll cartoons of "John Bull" as a testy, drink-veined tub of ale, with the temper of a rutting steer, a poorly educated "squire" to the soles of his top-boots!

"How'd ye get out here? What fetched ye?" Hugh Beauman asked, sounding a bit suspicious, even after all these years.

Lewrie was *sorely* tempted to answer, "By frigate, then by coach," but wisely forebore. Hugh Beauman, for all his business acumen, didn't have what one could call an "ear" for waggish wit.

"Colonel Cashman and I are old compatriots, sir. We met in town and dined together. He invited me to see his regiment."

"Ah, ah?" Hugh Beauman said as he took that in, still looking like a man offered a dubious deal. "Never heard that. Must ask, I s'pose."

"In Spanish Florida," Lewrie informed him, with a secretive grin.

"Covert doin's with Red Indians, during the last war, d'ye see. Neck-or-nothin' in places, it was. Doubt a man of us got away with a whole skin, once the Dons found us," he boasted, to discomfit Hugh Beauman.

"You've risen so quickly, Captain Lewrie," Anne Beauman quickly said, to fill the gaps—and no longer using his Christian name, Lewrie noted, as if to distance herself, or haul their converse back to a politer plane. "And been decorated twice. And is that a wedding ring that I see on your left hand? You must tell us all about it!"

"Ah!" her husband exclaimed, as a trumpet sang out. "Parade's on! Later, Lewrie. Come, dear."

" 'Til later, sir . . . ma'am," Lewrie said, doffing his hat, and bowing them away as they ploughed their way through the throng to the raised platform before the pavillion that would serve as the reviewing stand. Lewrie snagged himself another pair of champagnes, in relief, then drifted over to where he could see.

Sure enough, Ledyard Beauman made a splendid sight on a charger. The horse was a sleek dapple-grey, with the conformation of an Arabian, its saddlery and reins polished, its showy sheepskin pad as white as new-fallen mountain snow, and the stiff under-pad so large that it fell almost as low as the flashing silver-plate stirrups; blue, trimmed in real gilt embroidery border, real gilt-lace regimental badge, Roman numerals, and oak leaves. Even silver bit and chains!

Ledyard, however. . . .

"Look! A uniform . . . wearin' a *man*!" some girl said in a very soft snicker behind her fan, before being shushed by the man at her side; it didn't do to sneer a Beauman . . . not and be heard!

Ledyard rode well enough, with his heels well down, as he cantered his charger out and drew his sword to take the salute of officers standing in a rigid row before the troops, now arrayed by companies on the far side of the field. The pace did put his hat—a cocked one as large as a ripe watermelon, all adrip with egret feathers and trimmed with gilt-lace cockade and vane—askew, though. Like leftover style from the '70s, Ledyard bought them too small to fit over his wigs! A hand that held his sword hilt snuck up to right it as he drew reins to return the salute, eliciting the faintest titter, despite the setting.

Always was a vain little cox-comb, Lewrie uncharitably thought.

After a bit of martial palaver, Ledyard spun his horse about on the off-hand foot, and walked it back to the front of the review stand. A small band of fifes and drums struck up "British Grenadiers," and at a command from Cashman, the first company on the right, the grenadier company, began to wheel about in lines four ranks deep.

"Shape main-well," a grudging commentator allowed.

For all the little that Lewrie knew of drill and marching, they did, indeed, seem to know what they were doing, as good or better than the Anglesgreen yeomanry that his father drilled on the village commons on Muster Days. For a mob of the usual drunks, failures, ne'er-do-wells, and no-hopers that armies tended to recruit, and given the smaller and "scummier" pool of volunteers to be found in the islands, they marched in straight lines, with no one staggering; all in step, and all their muskets sloped at the same exact angle.

They wore ankle-high shoes, well blacked, with tan cloth gaiters, or "spatterdashes," buttoned up to mid-thigh over dark tan breeches, not the usual white, with matching waistcoats beneath the usual red tunics, though Lewrie thought their red was more wine-red than scarlet; with buff turn-backs at the rear hems, and buff coat facings, trimmed with yellow-outlined buttonholes of red and blue. And their hats were not cocked hats, newfangled shakoes, or narrow-brim civilian hats, but were wide-brimmed, soft slouch hats, turned up on one side.

He grinned in recognition; hats like those had adorned the Loyalist Volunteer North Carolina regiment in which his future brothers-in-law, Burgess and Governour Chiswick, had served in the Revolution. He had discovered the practicality of slouch hats for keeping off both sun and rain at Yorktown, during the Franco-American siege.

Lewrie also suspected that hats like those were much easier to "sneak" through brush and jungle, making less noise, did Cashman really mean to "hunt men" on Saint Domingue in bushwhacking fashion, matching stealth-for-stealth with the rebel slave soldiers under L'Ouverture.

And their arms; a private soldier stood guard near the rope line by the reviewing stand, and Lewrie sidled over to study it and enquire, in a whisper, from the soldier's right-hand side.

"Fusil, sir . . . fifty-four-caliber ball," the man muttered back from the corner of his mouth, eyes still rigidly to the front. "They's acc'rate, they is. Colonel Cashman, 'e h'insisted on 'em."

"I would expect nothing less than the best from Colonel Cashman," Lewrie told him, making the soldier stiffen his back a bit more in his pride, and dare to grin, despite the solemnities.

More accurate than Brown Bess, aye, Lewrie thought. *I used one, and I liked it. More range than a plain musket, too. I still have one hangin' on the wall in . . .*

He cringed, wondering how long it had taken Caroline to remove any sign that the smaller side parlour had once been his, and his alone. The captured swords, the ship model that his Jesters had made for him?

The regimental pipes, fife, and drum band struck up a tune, "The Black Bear," and swung out from the far right of the formed companies, with the King's Colour and the Regimental Colour party behind them, to troop the colours before the men, an ancient custom of recognition, so that they would know their colonel's place, and their own, in any battle's confusion. Once the band returned to its place, some orders of the day were posted by the adjutant, before the call came to "Pass In Review" . . . *without* the mass mutter of "Up yours, too" that sometimes could be heard from British troops on parade, Lewrie noted.

Company by company, the regiment marched past the reviewing stand, with Ledyard Beauman swiping his sword to his chin in salute to each; band, the grenadier company, then eight line companies, lastly the official light company of skirmishers, though Cashman had trained them all for skirmish order. Finally, a two-gun battery of light horse-drawn artillery pieces, no better than 4-pounders, trotted past, and it was done. The companies drew up at their starting points across that stubbly field, to the cheers and applause of the assembled guests.

"Men!" Ledyard cried, rising in his stirrups. "Men o' the Fifteenth West Indies!" It came out rather thin, and probably didn't carry far, not like a "quarterdeck" bellow, Lewrie could sneer, as he tipped his champagne glass to them. "Creditable showin', I say! Day or two more, and we're off to Saint Domingue! Bash those murderous rebels, haw! Colonel

Cashman, dismiss the troops, sir! And a tot of rum for all! All, d'ye hear, hey?"

" 'Talion . . ." Cashman said, in a proper baritone roar.

"Comp'ny!" the captains chorused the preparatory order.

" 'Talion, *right* wheel to column of companies, *at* the halt!"

Ledyard Beauman did not wait for his troops to wheel about and march off to their tent lines; he tossed his reins, assuming that some orderly or groom would be there to take them, being the sort who went through life having things there when he needed them. He took several tries at stabbing the tip of his expensive "hundred guinea" sword into its elegantly trimmed scabbard before getting it right, then swung one leg over and sprang down . . . not without a rub at his fundament, from spending time in the saddle. Rather claw-like, that was.

Maybe his arse itches, Lewrie thought, draining one of his champagne flutes. Making an experiment, Lewrie tossed the glass over his shoulder, and was amazed to see a liveried servant catch it in mid-air.

Hell's Bells, it works! he marvelled.

As if those murderous rebel slaves on Saint Domingue had already been crushed, Ledyard was swarmed by his rich neighbours, hangers-on, toadies, and those who most-like owed him money or favours, and Lewrie had himself another covert sneer, then toddled off for a "reload" of champagne.

Now there was a long set of tables set up as a buffet, inside that vast pavillion, laden with dainties, so far covered with a gauzy material, or fanned to keep the flies off by slave women behind it, all done up in wildly colourful sack-gowns and head cloths, marked by snow-white bib aprons. Once the fawning was done, and the regiment's officers returned, there would be a minor feed, and despite his earlier meal, Lewrie found himself looking forward to "grazing" on fresh and spicy shore food. He was deterred from an anticipatory stroll to see what was to be offered, though.

"Surely you recall Mister Lewrie, Ledyard," he heard Anne gush as she led her brother-in-law over, "just a boy of a lieutenant, then. Captain Lewrie . . . you remember Ledyard."

"But of course I do, Mistress Beauman," Lewrie answered, having a "gush" of his own of false pleasure. "Ledyard, so good to see you! My

congratulations on your regiment, and its performance. Good as the
Guards Brigade in London." He extended his hand, forcing Ledyard to
take it, though with an involuntary wince. "I'm certain that General
Maitland will be pleased to be re-enforced by such a unit . . . and that
jumped-up *poseur*, General L'Ouverture, will have cause to run away
and hide!"

"Well! Yes, haw haw!" Ledyard brayed, after giving it a rather *longish*
think, blinking in un-looked-for delight. "Damn' white o' ye I must say,
Lewrie, damn' white. *Maul* those murd'rin' scum! Go right through 'em
like a dose o' salts. Lose their cocky airs, up against *British* infantry,
wot?"

"And pray God soon, sir," Lewrie replied, giving Ledyard his due
as his putative senior officer.

"Well, then! Hum . . . uhm," Ledyard hemmed, having run out of
polite conversation, and with his eyes cutting towards the food and
drinks. Anne Beauman tossed Lewrie her sympathy, with a weary arching
of her brows, and Lewrie responded in like sympathy for her having to
tolerate such a boorish clan for so many years.

"The best of fortune attend you and your troops, then, sir," Lewrie
said, preparing to free himself. "I'll just look up old Cashman, then."

"*Know* him, do ye?" Ledyard asked, engaged by Lewrie's presence
again, and looking a touch more leery than pleased by that news.

"Oh, for years, sir. Here at his invitation, in fact."

"Talented feller . . . organised, uhm . . ." Ledyard Beauman said,
musing aloud as if pacing behind an office desk, weighing the benefits
and disadvantages of a pending deal. "Unorthodox, o' course, but just
what we need, hey? Aggressive, uhm . . . a fighter, wot?"

He squinted at Lewrie, as if trying to convince himself of Cashman's
suitability to lead *his* regiment anew; or re-convincing himself in the face
of disquieting new evidence to the contrary.

"The very best, sir," Lewrie assured him.

"Mmm-hmm!" Ledyard answered, as if tasting a tangy dessert.

"Take my leave, then. Colonel Beauman . . . Mistress Anne," he said,
bowing his way off, and wondering why it was that every encounter
with Beaumans made him begin to chop his sentences to the bare bones
in the same *pidgin* that they used.

Lewrie snagged two more champagnes, then sidled his way through the throng of guests entering the tent, against the current, 'til he stood outside, beyond the rope-line, waiting for Christopher Cashman as he rode up on a fine chestnut gelding, trailed by his two mounted majors and the pack of company captains, lieutenants, and ensigns who were on foot, but eager for the party to begin.

He walked out to meet Cashman, offering up the freshest glass, sure that Kit was going to need it.

"Well, how'd you enjoy the parade?" Cashman beamed down at him as he drew rein and accepted his reward.

"Capital. On your part, at least. They look splendid," Lewrie truthfully told him,

"Aye, they're a grand bunch," Cashman gruffly agreed, showing pleasure over his "good show," and with a hint of "rough love" for his troops. "Though they're the usual scum who'd go for a soldier. Gutter sweepin's and harbour trash, e'en poorer a lot than you'd find in England, mind. Hard men, though. Tough enough to stick it, no matter what comes."

"Met Ledyard," Lewrie casually told him. "Had a word or two."

"Aye, and?" Cashman asked, one brow up.

"Kit, old son . . . I do b'lieve you're fucked."

BOOK TWO

Quod genus hoc hominum? Quaeve hunc tam barbara morem permittit patria? Hospitio prohibemur harenae; bella cient primaque vetant consistere terra.

What race of men is this? What land is so barbarous as to allow this custom? We are debarred the welcome of the beach; they stir up war and forbid us to set foot on the border of their land.

AENEID, BOOK I 538-541

PUBLIUS VERGILIUS MARO "VIRGIL"

CHAPTER FOURTEEN

*O*h, for God's sake, quiet! Still!" the luckless Lieutenant Wyman shouted to the arriving boats, bare minutes before Eight Bells.

> *"Nottingham Ale, boys, Nottingham Ale,*
> *no liquor on earth is like Nottingham Ale.*
> *Nottingham Ale, boys, Nottingham Ale,*
> *no liquor on earth is like Nottingham Ale!"*

That was the starboard watch's answer to his demands. They had commandeered the poor bum-boatmen who had rowed them offshore from town, had made the oars beat like birds' wings, raising bow waves and leaving creamy wakes. But once close-aboard *Proteus,* they had commenced rowing *round* her, bound and determined to savour their last bottles of wine or beer, and not end their precious shore liberty 'til the last watch bell had struck Midnight!

> *"You lovers who talk of your flames, darts and daggers,*
> *with Nottingham Ale ply your woman but hard,*
> *for the girl that once tasted will hopelessly stagger,*
> *and all your past suff'rings and hardships reward!*
> *You may bend her and twist her, and do what you list her.*
> *You've found the right way o'er her heart to prevail . . ."*

"Sounds very much like that bastard Irishman, Desmond," Midshipman Adair commented.

"Aye, he's a fine voice, that 'fly' lad," Lieutenant Catterall said.

"Let her take a glass often, there's nothing will soften
the heart of a woman like Nottingham Ale! Ohhhh . . .
Nottingham Ale, boys, Nottingham Ale . . . !"

"Desmond!" Lewrie barked, leaning over the quarterdeck bulwarks in nothing more than breeches and a shirt, hastily pulled over but not stuffed in. "You sing the *last* bloody verse, and you'll be late reportin' back aboard, me lad! The lot of you! Now pipe down and fetch-to alongside the larboard entry-port! You've five minutes, by my watch!"

"Muster the Marines, sir?" Lt. Catterall asked.

"Lord, no, Mister Catterall," Lewrie demurred, looking up from his pocket watch. "Though from the look of 'em, a cargo sling'd suit. I doubt there's a full dozen who can still keep their feet."

"Can you not keep order with your crew, sir?" an aggrieved postcaptain aboard a two-decker moored nearby bellowed through a speaking-trumpet. "Can you not, I will! You'll stop all that cater-wauling, or I'll send over my Marines and deem it a mutiny t'be suppressed!"

The larboard watch, wakened from their innocent slumbers below, had come up on deck to jeer and hoot from the gangways, some with glee, and some sounder sleepers with anger and threats.

Lewrie could make out a spectral figure on the stern gallery of the 74-gun Third Rate, someone in a white nightshirt bearing a shiny brass speaking-trumpet that also caught the glinting moonlight.

"Damme, the man's even wearin' a tasselled nightcap," Lewrie muttered with a groan, turning for his own speaking-trumpet. "No need, sir! They'll be aboard, and quiet, shortly!" he shouted across.

"You doctors, who more executions have done,
with powder and potion, with bolus and pill,
than hangman with noose, or soldier with gun . . ."

Desmond was rushing the last verse, but the first bum-boat was alongside the entry-port, and those who could among them were scrambling up the man-ropes and battens, calling for rope slings or bosun's chairs to be rigged for the rest. The second and third boats stroked in close, in a shower of flung "dead soldiers" that peppered the harbour waters like a "short" broadside of roundshot; to bump into the first, the safety of the hired oars between bedamned, to use it as a landing stage over which they crawled or staggered, dragging the less sober from boat to boat.

> "... than miser with famine, or lawyer with quill,
> to despatch us the quicker, more beerless malt liquor,
> our bodies consume, and our faces grow pale.
> But, mind you, it pleases, it cures all diseases,
> a comforting bottle of Nottingham Ale! Ohhhh ..."

Now the idle larboard watch had taken up the chorus! Bosuns' calls across the water were shrieking urgently, and the two-decker's timbers drummed with bare feet as her crew was called out.

Proteus's people were gathered in, some sprawled insensible on the deck, once they were hauled up and in by the larboard watch. Men reeled, staggered, and went to their knees, still babbling song.

"Cast your accounts to Father Neptune overside, *not* on the deck, you drunken louts! Gawd, Halfacre, you'll clean that up this minute if you have to use your tongue!" Bosun Pendarves roared.

Lewrie looked at his watch once more, sharing a glance with Midshipman Grace at the timing glasses. The sands in the half-hour and five-minute glasses were almost run out.

"*One* minute, you noisy bastards!" Lewrie shouted. "Up you get, smartly now! A 'mast' and rum stoppage for the last man in-board!"

Even the paralytic were spurred by that threat; larboard hands were over the side in a twinkling to grab hold of the final "corpses" and fling them upward from hand-to-hand, not waiting for the slings. A moment later and not one Proteus was left in the bum-boats; nothing remained but vomit, broken bottles, snapped oars, and the glowers from the Free Black boatmen.

"Officers, muster your divisions. Take the roll to see if any have run," Lewrie told his lieutenants. "Aspinall, are you here?"

"Aye, sir," his manservant piped up, still wrapped in a blanket.

"Go fetch three shillings for each of the bum-boats from my desk, Aspinall," Lewrie softly bade him. "To pay for any damage or loss."

"Aye aye, sir."

Lewrie snapped his watch shut and pocketed it as the first bells ending the Evening Watch pealed. He paced the quarterdeck as the roll was called, silently fretting. Many a dead-drunk's face was raised by a slightly soberer messmate to be recognised in the lanthorn's light; many a name was answered with "Here, sort of, sir" by another's voice.

"Bless me, sir," Lieutenant Langlie reported several minutes "they've *all* returned. All accounted for, and not a man has run."

There was a rather loud *thud* on the larboard gangway as Lewrie uncrossed his fingers in relief. Furfy, manfully striving to stand, had finally succumbed to rum and gravity, going face-first to the deck.

"Well, in their condition, Mister Langlie, I doubt they could!" Lewrie japed. "We'll rig an extra canvas hose in the mornin'. Use it on their thick heads. Hose 'em out of their hammocks, if needed."

"Ah, aye sir," Langlie rejoined, stifling a jaded snicker.

"Right then, you lot!" Lewrie called from the hammock nettings overlooking his swaying crew. "Everyone had a good run ashore? Fine. But tomorrow's another day. We're sailing . . . just in time to outrun the bailiffs and the damage bills, you lucky dogs. We'll also rise and scrub *all* decks, as per usual, so I trust you'll use your whole four hours of peace and quiet for 'caulking,' not yarning. Or more of your off-key singing! Now, lay below . . . quietly. Remember to puke in the buckets," he concluded, "not in yer hammocks."

Those who could began to shamble to the companionway ladders, snickering and snorting now and again as they whispered and chortled over their shore doings, despite others shushing them, or the gripes from the Master-At-Arms and Ship's Corporals, from Bosun Pendarves and his mates. Bodies were sluiced with water from the fire buckets, or the slow-match tubs between the guns. Those who woke were helped to their feet and half-dragged below; those who didn't were attended by the Surgeon Mr. Shirley and his mates, Hodson and Durant, with "volunteers" grudgingly 'pressed into loblolly duty with carrying boards.

"Just leave 'em on the deck, don't even try to sling 'em in a hammock," Mr. Shirley could be heard saying. "Near a bucket, mind."

Five minutes later, nary a man from either watch other than the men in the skeletal Harbour and Anchor Watch were on deck. Lewrie got his shillings and paid off the disgruntled bum-boatmen, just as other boats neared the entry-port.

"Hoy, the boats!" Mister Adair called into the night.

"First officer of HMS *Halifax*!" came the reply from a cutter filled with armed Marines, hurriedly dressed, catch-as-catch-can.

"Side-party, sir?" Mister Adair asked, looking for aid.

"There's not enough sober hands t'make a proper showing, no," Lewrie told him, striding to the entry-port. "Help you, sir?"

"My captain has sent me to put down your disturbance, sir. Are you the officer of the watch?" the officer said, all top-lofty.

"I'm the bloody captain, and I'll thank you to remember that!" Lewrie shouted back. "D'ye *hear* a disturbance, sir? Hark ye to the quiet, why don't you?"

"Well . . . your pardons, Captain, uhm . . . ?" the lieutenant stammered, after a short span of silence to listen.

"Lewrie . . . Alan Lewrie."

"Uhm, ah," the lieutenant from *Halifax* said, disconcerted to be in the unfortunate position between two Post-Captains. "You would be the one some call the 'Ram-Cat', sir? A pleasure to meet you, sir, I am sure. Permission to come aboard, and ascertain for myself—"

"Permission denied, sir," Lewrie uncharitably growled. "We do not allow visiting 'tween ships after the First Dog. Hell's Bells, we are *sleeping* here, sir! There was no mutiny, there was no riot, there was no disturbance. Just high feelings and good cheer, but it's over, and everyone's below."

"But . . . but what am I to tell my captain, sir?"

"My sincerest respects to your captain, and tell him to get some sleep, sir. There'll be a busy day tomorrow," Lewrie concluded, and turned away to go aft to his own bed-cot, leaving the poor lieutenant stewing in his own juices.

Poor shit, his captain'll have a strip off his hide, but that's his own lookout, Lewrie smugly thought as he kicked off his shoes and breeches, then rolled back into his bedding. Aspinall snuffed a lone candle, and the great-cabins were plunged into darkness once more.

Toulon leaped onto the bed, padded about, and grunted for attention, as Lewrie cocked an ear for the night. All he could hear were the creakings and squeaks of oars in thole-pins as the *Halifax*'s boats were rowed away; the usual slow groans of timbers, the faint flutters as the night winds jangled the running rigging and a myriad of blocks.

If anyone aboard was making noise, it was the officers in the gunroom one deck below as they settled back in, japing and sniggering among themselves after the return of the liberty parties. From forrud, there wasn't a peep out of the normal; just the discordant, chorusing snores, whines, and grunts from a now-sleeping crew.

The staff-captain *had* quite forgotten his interview with Lewrie; those threatened orders had not arrived 'til days later, and then they dealt with *Proteus* preparing to escort a small convoy of hired or converted troop ships over to Saint Domingue, to carry Cashman's regiment and other re-enforcements for General Maitland's command.

That delay had allowed Lewrie to award both watches with spells of shore liberty, twice for each, which had gone a long way to create good cheer; time enough in port, too, for the ship's people's letters to be put aboard a mail-packet bound for home.

And time enough in port for another packet brig to come in and land mail for distribution throughout the fleet.

But nothing from Caroline—nothing for Lewrie, this time.

"At least they had some good drunks, hey?" Lewrie whispered to his ram-cat, as he ruffled his fur and stroked him to a purring sack of limp contentment. " 'Fore we go over to that pest-hole. Bound to be more'n a few of 'em never survive the fevers that are comin', hey sweetlin'? Their last joy."

Maybe mine, too, Lewrie grimly thought.

Officers and gentlemen were not immune. Even so, he had comported himself rather primly, he thought; some grand suppers, more than one overfill of good wines, a rather good session with a surprisingly tasty island-brewed ale, a ball for the 15th West Indies regiment one night, a jaunt out toward Portland Bight to a country house, where he had mounted up and ridden himself half-exhausted—sight-seeing, of all things! And a fine, head-splitting drunk with Cashman one night, just the two of them, reminiscing over a stone crock of American corn whiskey that Cashman liked so much, and of which the staff-captain so strongly disapproved. Oh, there had been some *mild* flirtations, here and there, but nothing had come of them. He knew that he still cut a slim and elegant figure, and could shine on a dance floor, as old Marine Captain Osmonde had advised so long ago. He'd *seen* the fans and lashes in full flutters of admiration, and that had cheered him immensely, to be welcome should he dare make the offer, but . . .

One-and-a-half stone of ram-cat slung against his stomach as he shifted to his left side, with one arm under his head and the scrunched pillows, as Toulon settled in for the night. Lewrie gave him one last, long stroking that set him purring again. Toulon raised his head and let out a long, stretching yawn. In the faint moonlight coming through the stern windows, the cat's eyes glowed as brightly light green as a lensed fire on the Eddystone Lighthouse, in startling *chatoyance*, before they slitted in slumber.

" 'Night, puss. Love you, too."

Murrff was the shut-mouthed, grunted reply.

CHAPTER FIFTEEN

*S*o near, yet so far away.

From Kingston to Saint Domingue was only a little over two hundred miles as the albatross flies, but a real bugger to attain against the Nor'east Trades, forcing *Proteus* to stand out far to the Sou'east once past the Palisades, tack and jog back as close to the eye of the wind as she could bear, which was Nor'Nor'west! Even a conservative estimation had not allowed enough sea-room in which to weather Morant Point, so there was nothing for it but to tack again to the Sou'east and stand out at least sixty miles to make a goodly offing, before one more try Nor'Nor'west. That one, at least, had put them in the middle of the Jamaica Channel, and out of sight of land, steering as if for a landfall at Santiago de Cuba, or Guantanamo Bay!

And with the mountains of Spanish Cuba almost in sight from the mast-tops, they had tacked once more Sou'easterly, and had jogged along close-hauled, in showers of spray. Saint Domingue had come in sight at last—the heights of the Massif de la Hotte that rose 7,700 feet in the sky, on the jutting southern arm that encompassed Golfe de Gonave.

Another tack Nor'Nor'west, out to sea again, took them over 100 miles north of the *northern* peninsula, into the Windward Passage before they could at last turn Sou'east for the last time and "beat" into the Golfe de Gonave, north of the peanut-shaped isle of the same name, and attain Port-Au-Prince.

"Would've done better on our own, sir," Lt. Langlie complained as

HMS *Proteus* ghosted shoreward on a "tops'l" breeze, sails reduced to avoid disaster. Two hands swung the leads from the foremast chains up forrud to plumb the uncertain depths, and even stolid Mr. Winwood, the Sailing Master, harumpphed, hemmed, and fretted over Admiralty charts of the harbour and approaches, that were conspicuously littered with a myriad of reefs, wrecks, and rocks—and those charts sure to be out of date, if not complete fictions, taken from French charts long ago, which might have been lying fabrications to protect their secrets, and those taken from ancient Spanish charts, from when they had owned all of Hispaniola!

"I know, Mister Langlie," Lewrie sottly agreed, "and damn all hired merchant masters. And ships of the line . . . and *their* captains. Go to loo'rd like so many wood chips."

Two merchant vessels had been their charge, filled with soldiers and their supplies, the casked meats and bagged biscuit, the ammunition and powder for their muskets and field pieces; ungainly barges slovenly handled and thinly manned, that wore about off the wind instead of tacking, ceding even more hard-won ground to windward at each maneuver at each "corner" of their voyage. It had been all that *Proteus* could do to stay with them half the time, since the merchantmen crawled along at a snail's pace, and *Proteus*, like a thoroughbred racehorse, had been forced to fetch-to and wait on them at times; if not, she would have sailed them under the horizon within a four-hour watch.

And then there was HMS *Halifax*, the two-decker 74, in charge of their little convoy. She, too, had borne troops and supplies, rendered *en flute* with half her guns landed ashore to make room for them. With her weather decks and gangways crowded with ignorant soldiery, and her own slow handling in comparison with a frigate, their short sail had become a frustrating Hell. Not the least of which was her captain, who had spent nigh on a week of "getting his own back" against Lewrie and his impertinence!

He'd known he was for it when the convoy sailing orders had come aboard at the last minute; he should have known from the first, had he been aboard *Proteus* to witness *Halifax*'s guns being removed, and boats ferrying troops aboard her. But no, he had been ashore, sporting too much, imbibing a tad too much, then sleeping later than was his custom—rather the Navy's custom, to which he thought he'd become inured, after all these years of enforced activity.

Aye, give me a chance and I'll sleep 'til noon every time, he chid himself anew; *but . . . damn the man!*

Proteus led the way into Port-Au-Prince harbour, with the merchantmen strung out astern of her, and the two-decker last of all; just in case there were uncharted reefs or shallows in store, then let it be that saucy jackanapes Lewrie, and his toy frigate, to suffer first!

"Pretty place, though . . . in a way, sir," Marine Lieutenant Devereux pointed out, after sharing a "fetch 'em close" with the other officers.

Lewrie raised his own telescope at that comment, as they slowly sailed down the passage denoted as the Canal de Saint Marc, towards the port at the very end of the long "sack" of the gulf.

To the left of Port-Au-Prince was a coastal plain, backed by a massive and steep mountain range that began at the port of St. Marc up north, and ran sou'east, then east, all the way to the Spanish part of Hispaniola. South of the town, the Massif de la Selle brooded over the gulf, over 8,700 feet high. Both ranges were densely wooded, and impossibly green and lush on the lower slopes, turning stonier, bluer, and cloud-wreathed near the peaks.

The town, though . . . it *was* quite pretty, Lewrie decided, after a long look. Or it had been, in the past. The streets were as wide as Parisian *boulevards*, lined with a few imposing and rather impressive civic buildings, and hundreds of pastel-painted residences in a riot of sky blues, pale mint greens, pinks, and yellows.

But beyond the town proper were entrenchments, batteries, redans, and small fortifications, all lazily fuming with cooking smoke or the smoke from armourers', farriers', or blacksmiths' forges. The town, too, fumed, and Lewrie caught the sweet-sour aroma of burning garbage as the hazy pall overlying Port-Au-Prince was wafted to them on a fickle wind off the eastern mountains, that blunted and toyed with the Trades.

"Trust the Army t'muck pretty things up," Lieutenant Catterall quipped, all but elbowing Devereux in jest. "Makes you glad you're a Marine, I shouldn't wonder . . . not one of those dirty-faced soldiers yonder."

"Ah, but you'll note, Mister Catterall," Devereux drolly gibed back, "how pristine the waters of this gulf were . . .'til we sent all those ships in there."

Sure enough, the Golfe de Gonave, which had been so clear and so sparkling just a few miles astern, was now nigh the colour of mud and tobacco, from the plantation runoff of a certainty—but also dotted with refuse and floating *excreta* from the many ships' "heads."

"Very well, Mister Langlie . . . gentlemen," Lewrie announced as he lowered his glass, "hands to stations for anchoring. Pick us a spot, Mister Winwood. Not *too* near shore, mind. Does malaria come from bad night airs, then these smell sickly enough, even from out here."

"Aye, sir."

"And we'll depend on our own water-casks, long as we're able," Lewrie decided. "As Mister Shirley suggested. With so much ordure in the local streams, dumped by our own troops . . . no working parties to fetch water, either."

"Aye, sir," the glum Purser, Mr. Coote, sadly had to agree.

"All hands . . . all hands! Ready to bring ship to anchor!"

"Neatly done, sirs," Lewrie could quite happily congratulate his officers and mates several minutes later. They had come into harbour in "man-o-war" fashion, rounding up into the wind, firing their salute to the highest-ranking naval officer present, and taking in all sails at the same time, whilst dropping the best bower, rigging out the booms, and beginning to lower their boats even as the smoke cleared!

"Our number, sir . . . 'Captain Repair On Board,' " Midshipman Elwes called out. "From *Halifax*, sir."

"And why am I not surprised?" Lewrie muttered under his breath.

"Gig's in de watuh, sah . . . crew's mustered," Andrews reported, sharing a weary grin of foreknowledge with his captain. "Dot mon got it in fo' ya, Cap'um."

"Has a tin ear . . . can't appreciate good music," Lewrie quipped.

He squared away his hanger, the set of his waistcoat, and shot the cuffs of his best broadcloth uniform. In the lee of the mountains, Port-

Au-Prince was a stifling place, even at mid-morning; humid, steaming, and the air wet dish-clout close.

"Right, then . . . let's be doin' it."

"Ah, Captain Lewrie, so good of you to join us," Captain George Blaylock said with a patently false purr of welcome, though peering at his watch rather pointedly before snapping it shut with a tiny smile of satisfaction.

Halifax had still been under way, the two merchantmen had nigh run down his gig as they had swanned about seeking anchorages close to shore, where they could still have room to swing—and a much shorter row for their boats to ferry troops and supplies to land. At the last, Andrews's boat-crew had had to row like the Devil was at the transom to catch her up, shortly after she had anchored and fired her own salute.

"A glass of something, Captain Lewrie?" Blaylock offered, waving a hand at a wine-table.

"Bit early in the day for me, sir, thankee," Lewrie replied.

It was not too early for Colonel Ledyard Beauman and his staff, who had travelled on *Halifax,* it being the most spacious. Christopher Cashman was the only one of them who sipped cold breakfast tea from a china cup, looking impatient to get his troops ashore, whilst the two majors, and the adjutant, a young sprog of a Captain by name of Sellers, and a nephew of Ledyard's, Lewrie had learned, indulged in a decanter of claret.

"My word, what sort of 'sneakers' the Navy takes in, these days," Captain Blaylock tittered, turning his head to share the laugh with the others.

Lewrie's neck began to burn; to be compared to a "sneak," one of a carousing crew who didn't keep up his alcoholic intake at the same rate as the rest, and feigned his participation! When, by God, he had kept up with the best of 'em in his youth! Still *could*, he was sure.

Blaylock was a sour little stick of a man, a greying minnikin, as spare and reedy as Commodore Horatio Nelson, though possessed of a much deeper voice from one so lean. He wore a short, tightly curled tie-wig even in this heat, his face and hands tanned woody-brown from thirty

years of sea duty, and a complexion flushed with *rosacea* or some such
rash; perhaps *too* much drink, Lewrie uncharitably thought, asking himself if the entire West Indies Fleet was solely and utterly peopled by
hard drinkers.

"We've sent ashore for orders, Lewrie," Captain Blaylock said, as he
waved—no, shooed!—Lewrie to a wing-back chair. "Asking when and
where General Maitland wishes us landed, and in what order."

"Can't clutter up the piers," Ledyard Beauman commented. "Make
all sorts of confusion. Take our time, hey? Not 'til needed."

"What poor excuses for quays this harbour boasts are too busy al-
ready," Captain Blaylock added. "But what can one expect from the idle
French. Good enough for *them*, I s'pose. You'll hold all of your boats,
Lewrie, 'til we tell you when and where to come fetch and land."

"Tell Maitland what we've brung," Ledyard opined, legs stretched
out, and all but resting on his spine in his chair, his glossy boots that
rose above his knees, dragoon fashion, gleaming. "Know best what he
needs, first. Artillery or shot . . . loose powder . . . cartridges?"

Lewrie caught Cashman's frown of disapproval, no matter it was
carefully veiled in the presence of his "betters."

"In my experience at Toulon, sirs, I'd imagine that cartridges for the
troops already here would best suit," Lewrie blandly stated. "If not at
the quays, then there are several stretches of beach, would serve the
purpose. Cartridges, pre-bagged powder for his artillery . . . one company could be employed to pile and tote, then guard—"

"At *that* debacle, were you?" Captain Blaylock snapped. "What a
bloody muddle, it was."

"Aye, I was, sir. Were you, as well?" Lewrie asked.

"No, I was not, sir," Blaylock said with a petulant little *moue*. "Utterly ruined by the timidity of our so-called allies, the Spanish, by putting
too much trust in the French Royalists. Admiral Hood was . . . hah!
Hood-winked!"

"Good'un, sir! Capital!" Ledyard Beauman haw-hawed.

"Hood-winked," Captain Blaylock repeated, so taken with his jape
that he could not resist, "by gasconading boasts of fealty from French
anti-Jacobins, was the way I heard tell it. The Dons' admiral, ready to
trade fire with Hood over who held the right to command? Lost out and

sailed away. And not six months later took hands with the Frogs, against us! Pah!"

"Out-gunned, out-manned, and under-*supplied*, though, sir," Alan Lewrie pointed out after the growls of past betrayal and prejudice had subsided. "Generals Dugommier and Bonaparte held the high ground and all the cards."

"Oh, tosh!"

"Much the same terrain, when you look at it," Cashman piped up, in a cagey sort of voice. "A seaport with a small perimeter of level ground . . . surrounded by heights. Too few troops to push out into the countryside 'thout getting cut to ribbons, and outnumbered nearly ten to one. Too few troops to defend a larger perimeter. Too few guns, at the *moment*, to break a determined assault, sirs?"

Lewrie allowed himself a tiny grin of agreement at the stress that Cashman used; were he this General Maitland, he was certain that ammunition and more field guns would be his greatest demands. Now!

And yes, now that Kit had brought it up, Lewrie realised that a strong comparison could be made between Toulon and Port-Au-Prince; it explained the fey feeling he had experienced whilst ghosting shoreward, that prickle of wariness and uncertainty. The situation was much the same, too, with a British force surrounded, almost besieged, by enemy troops in much greater numbers. Did it turn out the same, was there to be a massacre of the innocents, as had happened when Hood had quit the place, and the Republican French soldiers had waded out into the water to shoot and bayonet the thousands who could not find room aboard the departing ships . . . ?

He gave himself an involuntary shake, wishing he had taken the offer of a drop of something, after all. For certain, he was suddenly glad that he would be shot of the place, once the stores were landed, and *Proteus* could get out to sea to serve in the blockade.

"Samboes don't *have* guns!" Ledyard quibbled. "Most of 'em are armed with cane-knives. Few muskets . . . few *shoes*, wot?"

"Our artillery will cut them down in waves, like reapin' cane," Captain Sellers chortled.

"Never even get in musket range," Major Porter added, "when the grape and cannister'll lay 'em out long before."

"Why we brought along caltrops," Ledyard Beauman boasted. "It was Cashman's suggestion, wasn't it?"

"Caltrops?" Captain Blaylock enquired, peering at Cashman.

"Scrap metal, ten pence nails and such, sir," Colonel Cashman explained with a shrug of modesty. "Colonel Beauman has the right of it . . . very few of 'em are shod. Take two and bend 'em together, so however it lands, a couple of points always face up, sirs. Strew 'em by the hundreds in the long grass before a position, even if a clear field of fire's been cut, and they'll tramp right over 'em before they see 'em. Even a Cuffy's horny hoof can't take that. Lame 'em, take 'em out of the fight . . . die of lockjaw days later, and take even more t'tend 'em. Brought enough for our own use, and I know that General Maitland had his quartermasters on Jamaica scour the countryside for scrap iron. Sure t'be umpteen thousands of 'em, cased up and waitin' to be landed, soonest. Slows 'em up somethin' wondrous, sirs."

"E'en through flimsy, worn-out shoes!" Ledyard hooted. "Gad! Think o' L'Ouverture, hoppin' about in his fancy boots after that!"

"Ooh, *merci*, ooh *sacre bleu*, ooh *massah*!" Captain Sellers playacted in a slurred slave accent, dancing his feet on Blaylock's fancy rugs and shrilling in "pain," which made all but Lewrie and Cashman double over with laughter. "Tak' eet out, I be a *goood* niggah!"

"You do not find it amusing, Captain Lewrie?" Blaylock asked, once the impersonation had paled.

"L'Ouverture and his tag-rag troops have defeated everyone on the island, sir . . . or so my advisories from Admiralty inform me. I doubt things'll be quite so easy. They never are, unfortunately.

"And, long as L'Ouverture fights *us*, he's supported by France, recognised by the Directory in Paris as a patriot, sir. To them, and to a great many people in Saint Domingue. They're better equipped and armed than we suspect, too, sir. From Hugues, down on Guadeloupe, and from the Americans. They're beginning to make decent muskets and—"

"Oh, rot, sir!" Captain Blaylock said with a sniff of humour. "We've the whole coast bottled up, with the cork hammered home! Not a rowboat could land supplies. No, the Samboes are fighting with what little they've gleaned from the pre-war garrisons, and there's little mineral

wealth here, not enough to make iron or steel, nor the ingredients for
even halfway decent powder . . . lead for shot . . . Before this war began,
the rich merchant traders at Rochefort, L'Orient, and Brest preferred
selling manufactured goods here, and blocked any attempt to make none
but the simplest things, locally."

"Good rap, and they crack," Ledyard Beauman said, nodding with
as much sagacity as he could muster. "Nought t'fall back on."

"Then how have they maintained their army this long, sir?" Kit
Cashman had to ask him. "How has Rigaud and his faction done so,
and the *grands blancs* up at Cape Francois? Good reason for my troops
t'be landed as soon as possible, Captain Blaylock . . . and for old Lewrie
to get back out to sea to add to your blockade, soon as we're ashore."

God bless the man! Lewrie thought in soaring thankfulness; *like he
read my bloody mind! Have to gift him for't . . . handsomely!*

"Welll . . ." Captain Blaylock said, after a long pondering, during
which a sly smile had crept upon his phyz. "Perhaps, are we so thin on
the ground hereabouts, Colonel Cashman . . . even more re-enforcments
may be needed to hold the perimeter. Long six-pounders, from a quarterdeck or forecastle, might be a welcome addition. Carronades? Easily
handled by a small team of gunners, and capable of large loads of grape
or cannister, too. Experienced naval gunners, along with some Marines?"

He turned his head away from the rest, who were nodding along in
rote agreement, and cast his lidded gaze upon Lewrie, who plumbed,
with a sinking feeling in his innards, exactly *where* such 6-pounders,
carronades, and warm bodies would be found.

Damn you, ya can't *be that big a bastard!* he silently yelped. *I best
think fast and hard!*

"To the contrary, Captain Blaylock," Lewrie rejoined, as calmly as
he could, "it would seem to me that *Halifax* has the larger Marine com-
plement, commanded by a Captain of Marines, with two lieutenants as
aides. And since she *is* a very deep-draught ship of the line, surely she
could be no assistance in the blockade. You are already *en flute,* and
therefore should hardly miss *your* quarterdeck and foc'sle guns."

"You do, do you." Blaylock smiled back, his lips and voice as thin
as winter ice. "Might remind you, Captain Lewrie"—his gaze fell pointedly upon the single epaulet on Lewrie's uniform, compared to his pair—

"that I am senior officer of our convoy. I will decide."

"Just pointing out the most efficient use of what we have at present, sir," Lewrie said, having to swallow his bile and eat bitter "shite," though wondering if there was another naval officer ashore, on one of those ships he'd saluted, who could countermand this idea.

And how quickly he could get to him to complain!

Before the confrontation could get more serious, there came a discrete rapping upon the great-cabin door and the stamp of a Marine boot. "First Awf'cer . . . sah!"

"Enter!" Captain Blaylock testily barked.

In came the unfortunate lieutenant that Lewrie had spurned at *Proteus*'s entry-port just nights before. With his hat under his arm, he looked a thin-haired, half-bald, and long-suffering sort, frazzled by his onerous duties and, Lewrie suspected, just about done in by a constant diet of Blaylock's dung on his plate. A short session with the man was bad enough, but to serve under him, day after day, watch-and-watch . . . ?

"I've a reply from General Maitland, sir," the lieutenant said.

"Well, out with it, man. God's sake!" Blaylock "tsk-tsked."

"The general's compliments, sir, and he desires that we begin to land troops and supplies, at once, sir. He adverted me to use the word 'urgent,' Captain."

"Well, then! But Mister Duncan . . . in which *order*, hah?"

"The, ah . . ." Lieutenant Duncan stammered, consulting a list, "newly arrived troops, under long arms, and with full field packs and ammunition issue, at once, sir. Musket ammunition and 'specials,' that'd be what he called caltrops, sir, second . . . with field artillery and teams, caissons and limbers, and munitions, third. Rations are to be last, Captain."

"Well, then," Blaylock said, stroking at the top of his wig. "There it is, then, gentlemen. To horse. Or rather to boat, haw!"

"Uhm . . . there is also a note from Captain Nicely, sir," the lieutenant added as Blaylock rose to his feet.

"Indeed!" Captain Blaylock rejoined with an offended snort.

"Here, sir," Duncan said, shoving the folded note at him and acting hangdog, but eager to get away, sure there would be reason to flee. All this intrigued Lewrie's curiosity, who stood with his hat under his arm, shamming respectful deference, but aquiver to escape as well—just as soon as Blaylock's sudden dyspepsia was explained. A Post-Captain senior to Blaylock, this Nicely . . . and from the sound of it, no friend of his; some rivalry, he wondered?

Blaylock's *rosacea* bloomed like Caroline's spring gardens, and the man actually growled like a wakened bear!

Oh, this must be good! Lewrie told himself; *Some 'dirty' passed on, from one vengeful bastard to another.*

Blaylock crumpled the note into a tight wad, so hard his fingers turned white, and his mouth and eyes pinched in rage; he could ram the note down a musket barrel for wadding, so fiercely did he work it.

"Captain Lewrie, I'll thank you to return to your ship and get your boats back here, *instanter*," Captain Blaylock snapped. "I will brook no delay, no dawdling or sky-larking, hear me? You are to land Colonel Beauman's regiment on the town beach, north of the quays, and God help you do you shilly-shally."

"Aye aye, sir, directly," Lewrie parroted off from long usage; bowing from the waist like a German and stalking for the door. The unfortunate Lieutenant Duncan took the opportunity to flee, as well, using the excuse of mustering the side party to render him honours.

"Bad blood, is there?" Lewrie casually asked, once on deck.

"Of long standing. They were once midshipmen together."

"Oh, good as a Scottish feud, then. Campbells and MacDonalds," Lewrie tossed off with a grin of sudden understanding. "There's more than a few still eager for *my* liver. Those compatriots of my youth?"

"Well, sir, success has a way of attracting the envious," Lieutenant Duncan told him with a shy smile, one almost of open adoration!

Damme, is my name that *well known?* Lewrie asked himself: *Am I some sort of paragon to emulate? Mine arse on a band-box!*

"I wish to apologise for being short with you the other night," Lewrie told Duncan, feeling the need to sound "noble" of a sudden. "It put you in a bad patch. But then . . . I suspect you already know what that feels like, hmmm?"

"Oh aye, Captain Lewrie," Duncan had the sudden temerity to agree, in a faint whisper. "I, uhm . . . gather that Captain Nicely should have fresh orders for you as well, soon as you're done, sir."

"Ah . . . any hint you may share with me, Mister Duncan?" Lewrie cajoled, hoping against hope that this Nicely hadn't had the same idea about using *Proteus* as an armory or reserve barracks.

"Out to sea, where you're the best use, sir," Duncan said, with a tired but wistful expression, "but, you didn't hear it from me!"

"I quite understand, and thankee, Mister Duncan. For not saying a bloody word," Lewrie beamed, offering his hand.

"T'will be *Halifax*, I was told, that will be stripped for guns and gunners, our Marines and . . ." Duncan continued, eagerly taking the offered hand and shaking it with joy; though with a sad and disappointed look on his face. "The curse of old 'liners', I fear, sir. Never so exciting as being appointed to a frigate."

Of course, every aspiring young officer yearned for place aboard frigates and sloops of war, where the independent adventures happened; though Lewrie *did* wonder if Duncan was as guileless as he looked, and whether he was slyly wangling for a berth aboard *Proteus*, should any of his present officers die of battle or fever. Given the joylessness of life aboard *Halifax* under Captain Blaylock, though, Lewrie decided that Stroke-Oar on Tom Turdman's Dung Barge would be a distinct improvement!

Hell, leave him something, he's been helpful, Lewrie decided.

"So many men sent ashore, though, Mister Duncan," Lewrie continued, "they'll need a capable officer. As I was, at the siege of Toulon in '93. A grand opportunity for an aspiring man to make his name."

"There is that, though, isn't there, sir?" Duncan said, his mood brightening in an instant. "I *am* senior . . ." he mused, all a'scheme.

And Blaylock despises you, Lewrie thought; *much like old Captain Braxton on* Cockerel *hated me. That's how I got my 'chance' ashore, at Toulon—he wanted t'see the back o' me.*

"A grand chance for glory, and official notice," Lewrie encouraged. It was the honourable, the courageous thing one *had* to say when a man like Duncan was seconded to command a neck-or-nothing endeavour;

instead of "Gawd help yer mis'rable arse." *That* simply wasn't done! *Grand chance o' dyin' with a pitchfork in yer belly, more like,* Lewrie imagined; *if things ashore have gotten that desperate.*

"It will be, won't it, sir?" Duncan decided aloud, putting the good face on it, despite his own qualms—and if he didn't have any qualms, Lewrie would have considered him daft. "Why," Duncan joshed, "a few more chances like this'un, and I could end as famed as you, sir!"

"Oh, don't do *that*, Mister Duncan." Lewrie pooh-poohed the idea, breezing it off, as a properly modest "hero" was supposed to do. "The hours are horrid, you *can't* keep clean, and it's damn-all hard work! Far too much for a lazy-bones like me. But . . . the very best of good fortune go with you, if you have the honour to be appointed ashore."

"Thankee, Captain Lewrie, thankee indeed." Duncan chortled, now in high fettle, his saggy hound-dog eyes alight and crinkled in joy.

The bosuns' calls were twittering, Marines were stamping boots and slapping muskets about, so Lewrie doffed his hat to them all and turned his back out-board to descend the man-ropes and boarding battens, gazing at Duncan's face and wondering if he should have thrown in more than a trifling note of caution.

For Lewrie had the queasy, fey suspicion that he had just shaken hands with a dead man, who would dare too much in pursuit of fame.

Just as long as it ain't me! he gratefully told himself.

CHAPTER FIFTEEN

$\mathcal{B}$loody chimera," Christopher Cashman said with a growl of disappointment. "Always looks better from a distance. Gotten worse, since last I was here, too."

Before the French Revolution had begun in 1791, Port-Au-Prince had been the second richest town in Saint Domingue, trailing the main port of Cape Francois—"Le Cap"—by only a few *livres*. Now it was sadly fallen, no longer the lively and cultured town of music and arts, of operas and farces, and grand balls. Frankly, it was a cesspit. The few stores still open sold only the barest necessities, with most shelves bare and the prices exorbitant. There were too many refugees down from the countryside, and many of those closed stores were now converted to housing, if they hadn't been commandeered for Army use. Even the grand pastel-stuccoed mansions that Lewrie had seen out at sea resembled tumble-down, long-neglected hovels in the worst stews of London's East End; centuries-old manses turned to anthills of tiny rental lodgings, some going for a penny a night for a pallet on a bare wood floor. And many bore chalk marks denoting that a certain company of a certain regiment lodged there, with the smaller houses bearing a number around 8 or 10, showing how many troops could be barracked.

The reek of garbage, of human wastes, was even stronger ashore, and the kerbside gutters were stained with it, the channels down the middle of those faeryland *boulevards* could run brown with ordure when it rained. And it rained a lot in Saint Domingue.

"Like Venice," Lewrie supplied to their conversation, "pretty to look at, but Dung Wharf once you get into the canals."

"Oh for the sailor's life," Cashman drolly sing-songed, "why, th' places I been, an' th' things I seen, cor blimey! Tyke New South Wales, f'rinstance . . . kangaroos as big'z dray 'orses . . . eat men up whole, an' spits h'out th' bones, 'ey does!"

"You sound in better takings this evening," Lewrie pointed out.

" 'Course I do, Alan." Cashman chuckled as they strolled along. "I've all my troops ashore, all my field guns, with five day's rations and cartridges, and something t'do with 'em. Our heroic Colonel's off swillin' in the staff officer's mess, and if God's just, he'll find it so agreeable, the Second Coming couldn't stir him out of it. A chance t'preen with General Maitland, and play dashin' hanger-on with the real soldiers . . . damn 'is eyes."

"I don't know _why_ I let you lure me ashore," Lewrie said for the third time, puzzling, as he peered into a converted shopfront that was filled with refugee families in stained finery. "The way they're talking, it's the last place I care t'be. Besides, I always get in trouble ashore, d'ye know that?"

"I promised you a grand supper," Cashman rejoined quite merrily. "And bein' a curious Corinthian, tales of mystery and gluttony won you over."

"The staff mess'd be safer than traipsing about like this, would it not?" Lewrie asked, noting how dark the night was, and how dimly and spottily Port-Au-Prince was lit, and its formerly grand Parisian system of illumination badly maintained . . . if at all, anymore.

"Ah, but only swill served, Alan." Cashman laughed at his reticence. "Most of the officers are English-raised, so they have no idea of good food, no sense of adventure. It's all John Bull, boiled beef and puddin's, and 'Wot's 'is here tripe? _Pâté de foie gras?_ Wouldn't feed that foreign trash t'me hounds!' You know the sort. Not like us. We have worldly palates."

"Just so long as I'll have a whole neck down which to swallow," Lewrie said, taking comfort in the two small double-barreled "barkers" in his coat pockets, and the heft of the hanger on his left hip. Just in case, he had secreted a wavy-bladed *krees* Mindanao pirate dagger inside the left sleeve of his coat, to boot.

"Been here before," Cashman promised, "and it can't have changed all that much in a year. 'Tis a *hard* man and wife, runs it. Once you taste their dishes, you'll slit yer own throat . . . just t'prolong your pleasure. As the Yankee slaves say, it's 'slap yo' mama good.' "

"Good God," Lewrie had wit to jape, "never have I heard such a 'back-handed' compliment. *Back*-handed . . . d'ye see?"

"God'll forgive you." Cashman snickered. "Ah, here we are."

He had directed them to one of those imposing pastel mansions, at the intersection of two *boulevards*, where a roundabout and fountain stood, though the fountain barely burbled these days, and was mostly green and brown with moss, mildew, and scum. The house was fitted with a rounded wraparound set of balconies on the two upper floors, and the overhangs formed a wrought iron collonade above the ground floor doors and windows, which were barred with more intricate wrought iron grills. Heavy draperies were pulled over the windows, but from within Lewrie could espy the faintest hint of candlelight, though the place seemed to be abandoned.

Cashman lifted the hilt of his smallsword to rap on the heavy iron-strapped doors, a particular *tap—tap-tap—tap-tap-tap-tap*. After a moment, the Judas hole swung aside and a glint of light showed from within, quickly covered by a man's eye. A moment later, though, those doors were flung open and they were hurriedly welcomed in.

"Jean-Pierre . . . *Maman!*" Cashman cried in joy, flinging himself upon the swarthy man and woman who stood guard in the tiled foyer with pistols, cutlasses, and a brace of muskets.

"Ah! *Commandant* Keet, *bienvenu!* Has been so long we see you!"

"A Colonel, now," Cashman preened, twirling about to show off.

"*La, mon dieu . . . felicitations!*" the wife of the establishment cried, hands to her cheeks with joy. "You hunger, *oui*, you wish wine, as before? Come, you and your frien'. Nossing but ze best *pour vous.*"

Swarthier manservants in livery came to take their swords and hats; servants who also bulged here and there with weapons discreetly hidden. They didn't seem to share the joy of *rencontre* with Cashman, or the sight of Lewrie, either; they wore permanent wary scowls. The swords, Lewrie carefully noted as they were led to a table in a back parlour, were stood against a sideboard, within easy reach should he or Cashman need to grasp them.

Once seated, the pocket doors were slid half shut on the hall, and he and Cashman had the entire parlour to themselves. From without Lewrie could hear the low hum-um of other conversations in other chambers, a piercing laugh now and then, some boisterous shouts as a toast was made and drunk. Hmmm, some rather high-pitched laughs and words . . . some women? Things might just be looking up, he thought.

A waiter in livery and a white bib apron entered, and chatted quite gaily with Cashman for a piece; in *patois* French, of course, so Lewrie hadn't a clue what was being said, though it looked quite jovial and innocent . . . innocuous, rather.

As the waiter departed, Cashman tipped Lewrie the wink.

"Old Jacques . . . wonderful old fellow, he'll take care of us," Cashman informed him. "Took the liberty of orderin' for us, do you not object. *Specialité de la hôte*. You'll love it, I assure you."

"So what are we havin', then?" Lewrie asked as the waiter came back with a magnum of champagne and two crystal flutes. Though it was too much to expect that Port-Au-Prince might run to Massachusetts ice, the champagne was velvety smooth and spritely, from a famous vineyard in France, and much finer than Lewrie might have expected.

"Grand, ain't it," Cashman said, once he'd had a taste. "Jean-Pierre and Maman always have the best of ev'rything. Before the Revolution sent things Tom O'Bedlam, this was the most exclusive place in town. They're the best smugglers and speculators, too. No one knows how or where they get things, or cache 'em 'til needed, but you won't eat or drink better, were you in Paris itself."

"Are those smugglers and speculators we hear, then?" Lewrie had to ask, savouring the dry mellowness of the wine. It was miles above any vintage he'd tasted lately, even better than the Beaumans' cellar!

"Cut-throats, pimps, courtesans . . . mistresses and their men, or the odd profiteer," Cashman quite cheerfully catalogued, "rogues from the canting crews, successful pickpockets and thieves, rich rake-hells who haven't fled yet. A shifty lot, but they pay well and they're always flush with 'chink.' B'lieve it or not, Alan, with all o' their hired beef watchin' their backs, this just *may* be the safest place in Port-Au-Prince, and I doubt things'd change, did L'Ouverture march in tonight! Give 'em a week, and *he'll* be dinin' here, him and his generals. May make more of a mess, stain more napery, but . . .

"As to supper," Cashman enthused, changing the subject and refilling their glasses, "we start with shrimp *remoulade,* followed by an *omelette au bacon et frommage,* followed by spinach salads, before the goat *ragout,* which is bloody marvellous, by the way, and the roasted *coq au vin,* with asparagus and other removes. Burgundy, hock, or Saint Emilion Bordeaux, p'raps a Beaujolais with the *omelettes,* if you like? The sideboard'll groan with bottles. And for dessert, a *crème fraîche* over strawberries and cut fruit. You should *see* the berries they can grow in this soil!"

"Thought most of the folk here in town were starvin'," Lewrie said in wonder as the waiter bustled in once more, this time trailed by a brace of serving wenches in fresh-pressed and sweet-smelling sack gowns; one with light brown hair, the other a striking redhead, and wearing their own hair, not wigs, artfully done up in ribbons.

"They are, but that don't signify if you have the 'blunt' and know your way about," Cashman said dismissively. "There's some that'll always prosper. Ooh-la, Vivienne, you darlin'! Still here, are ya?" Cashman said, turning his attention to the striking wee light-haired wench, drawing her even closer as she sidled her hip against him and served his *remoulade.* Fine coin-silver utensils magically appeared from a pocket of Jacques's bib apron; more spoons, knives, and forks than an English household might display all at once, prissily set out in bewildering order, either side of their plates.

"M'sieur," the redhead purred as she served Lewrie, pressing her hip against his shoulder, too.

"Mademoiselle . . . enchanté," Lewrie instinctively responded with a welcoming purr of his own, and a slow, sly smile. *"Comment vous appelez-vous?"* he asked.

"Henriette, *m'sieur. Et vous,* brave Englis' *capitaine?"*

He told her, took her hand and kissed it for good measure, and tipped her a wink before turning to face Cashman.

"You're going to get me in trouble, aren't you, Kit?" he asked, with a wry grin.

"Hope you fetched off your best cundums," Cashman muttered back with a smile of his own, this one of beatific innocence.

"God, this is good!" Lewrie had to exclaim after the maids had departed in a swirl of skirts and hips, and had closed the pocket doors completely so they could dine in peace.

"Reminds me," Cashman said, daubing at his mouth and sipping at his wine, " 'fore we depart, we'll ask Jean-Pierre for some coffee and cocoa beans. Saint Domingue coffee is as good as anything from Brazil, and their cocoa's sweeter an' mellower, too. Mix it with what ya have already—one-to-two—and you'll think you're in Heaven. It may be dear, what with the crops not bein' tended much since their slaves rose up, but worth it, if they have any."

"Dearer than what Jamaican chandlers ask?" Lewrie frowned.

" 'Bout half, I'd think," Cashman told him, pausing to savour a bite. "Hard to believe they're Samboes . . . ain't it?"

"Who? Our hostlers?" Lewrie asked.

"Them . . . and our servin' girls," Cashman told him, winking.

"They are?" Lewrie said, amazed. "But they look so . . ."

"*Petits blancs* need love, too, Alan," Cashman drolly snickered. "Most real Whites've fled to Havana or Charleston, even New Orleans." He seemed delighted by Lewrie's surprised look. "Those who stayed are mostly half-castes . . . brights, fancies, *quadrons* or octoroons, what are lumped into the catchall term Mulatto, hereabouts. Some of them owned *plantations*, sent their children to school in Paris before the war. Rich as the *grands blancs* . . . richer! But that don't signify, either. 'Tis pure White blood, the guinea-stamp round here. Remember I told you how the French divided folk by grades of White or Black? There're one hundred and twenty-eight diff'rent gradations—s'truth! Get into *marabous* and *sacatras*, maybe three-quarters or more White, and you couldn't say one way or t'other, even in broad daylight. But even a *sang-mélé*, with *one* part Black blood to a hundred-twenty-*seven* White, is still a Sambo to them. Vivienne an' Henriette, they're high *marabous*, maybe low *sacatras*. And still get the short end of the stick, 'cause their folks weren't rich, or landed, or much of anything, 'cept imitation *petits blancs*. And the worst part for them is . . ."

Cashman paused for dramatic effect, and a sip of his wine.

"The real darkies off the fields, the ones in L'Ouverture's regiments, think the same way about 'em, d'ye see," Cashman said, with an air of grim foreboding. "They look *too* White for one camp, but they're too . . . *tainted* with the tar-brush for t'other. *Lovely* place, Saint Domingue, ain't it," he sarcastically drawled.

"So what happens to 'em, if Port-Au-Prince falls to L'Ouverture and his laddies?" Lewrie asked.

"World turned upside down," Cashman tossed off, as if it were no worry of his. "The *too* White'll get knackered, and all the rest'll be allowed to kowtow and join up with L'Ouverture. Make their *salaams*, bang their heads on the floor, and live—on the bottom of Society, mind. And a poor'un it'll be, you mark my words. Take 'em a century t'turn this island back to a payin' proposition. Jean-Pierre, well . . . by God, but this is a marvelous *remoulade*, don't ya think, Alan?"

"Aye, 'tis," Lewrie agreed, a trifle impatient for Cashman to complete his statements, though. "But what about 'im?"

"Oh, he'll most-like have a schooner lined up for a quick getaway," Cashman speculated with another blasé shrug. "Does he stay, he might do alright . . . 'less they scrag him for profiteerin', when other folks were starvin'. God knows which side'll do that . . . L'Ouverture's as an example, or them that starved, for revenge. Now, does he cut an' run with all his goods and money, he could set up fresh in the United States. Savannah, Charleston, New Orleans . . . they all have so-called Creole citizens . . . under 'Polite' Society, o'course. Take the lightest girls along, and reopen a bordello? *Some* o' them could lie like Blazes, and swear they were *grands blancs* all the way back to Adam . . . pass for White, d'ye see. Ah, our *omelettes*!"

In came Jacques and the girls to remove the now-empty plates, recharge wineglasses, and deliver steaming "piss-runny" French style egg dishes—with more subtle bumping and lingering touches.

Lewrie studied Henriette more closely. The only hints of difference he could discern were a slightly olive cast to her flawless complexion, and very full lips. Her dark red hair, though curlier, did not appear to be hennaed, and her green-hazel eyes would not have been out of place in the Germanies.

"Somezing is wrong, *M'sieur Capitaine* Lewrie?" she asked, feeling the intensity of his scrutiny; perhaps resenting it as a prejudice on his part, he wondered?

"In no way, *Mademoiselle* Henriette," he answered, smiling more broadly, adding a touch of "leer" to dispel her wariness. "I was just captivated . . . utterly dumbstruck . . . by how lovely you are."

"You are too kind, *m'sieur*," Henriette purred back, her lashes fluttering most fetchingly as she leaned down a bit, allowing a promisingly soft breast to compress against his epaulet. "But delightful to hear."

"You do not object?" he dared to tease.

"*Mais non, Capitaine* Lewrie,*"* Henriette replied, lowering her eyelids. "A poor girl always enjoy the compliments."

"And you, Henriette," Lewrie muttered, leaning back in his seat to look up at her from even closer. "Are *you* kind?"

"La, I can be *très* kind, *Capitaine* Lewrie," she whispered, all but in his ear, letting her loosely gathered hair brush his shoulder. "If you wish, that is," she added, with that secret smile that women make when being sultrily coy. "You would like, *n'est-ce pas?*"

Hell's Bells, we're doin' it on the table? Lewrie wondered to himself, as he caught sight of Cashman and Vivienne from the corner of his eye; Kit already had his wench in his lap, one hand groping about up her skirt, and sharing a soul kiss with her.

He turned back to Henriette, who wore a leer of her own after seeing what was transpiring across the table. Lewrie gently reached up and took hold of her chin to steer her lips to his, enfired by her warmth and the womanly aromas beneath her exotic, flowery perfume.

"Very much . . . very bloody much." Lewrie chuckled deep in his throat, feeling her lips grinning against his mouth in agreement.

"Later, *mon cher?*" Henriette silently sounded against him.

"Later, *cherie* . . . *plus. tard?*"

"*Certainement, cher* Alain," she breathed against his cheek, a moment before Vivienne gave out a yip as Cashman play-spanked her on the bottom and shooed them out.

How long's it been since I've had a whore? he asked himself; *Phoebe Aretino? No, don't count. She was a mistress. Gawd, Calcutta and Canton . . . way back in '84?*

Cashman, smugly stuffing himself with a huge smile of anticipation, and slurping lustily at his wines, made Lewrie wonder if their dining chamber would have to serve *amour's* purpose. It was dimly lit with only a few candles, the drapes heavy and drawn, the windows iron-barred, the wainscoting and overhead beams made of dark wood that ate what little light the candles threw. There were several settees, and a pair of chaise longues along the walls. It could have been a seraglio in a sultan's harem—one of his oldest and most enduring fantasies—but it was a rather *seedy*, close and stuffy seraglio, with not a breath of air stirring. Much as he liked Kit, this was. . . .

"They have rooms t'let, I s'pose?" Lewrie asked, finally.

"Nice'uns, too," Cashman said with an enigmatic leer. "There's *some* don't wait, but I never thought of it as a spectator sport. Bad as mountin' yer filly in the middle o' Lord's cricket grounds. Try a glass o' hock with your eggs. There's a touch o' cinnamon to it that goes main-tasty with 'em, even better than champagne, t'my thinkin'."

"I think I will, at that!" Lewrie exclaimed, reaching for one of the bottles on the sideboard, now enthused and inflamed by thoughts of pleasures to come, and filled with a boisterous, expectant *bonhomie*. He was relieved, too, that his sport would be the private sort and not a public spectacle, with Cashman or Vivienne deducting points for awkwardness. Fond as he was of that harem fantasy, it had always been him and a round dozen wenches, with not even a *sleeping* eunuch as witness.

"God . . . ain't it grand?" Cashman snickered with delight as he hoisted his glass to be refilled.

"Not too much, though, good as the wines are," Lewrie cautioned.

"Ah, *plus tard*, hey? Can't take yer jumps if foxed blind."

"It did come to mind," Lewrie happily rejoined.

"Yoicks . . . tallyho!" Cashman crowed.

CHAPTER SIXTEEN

H enriette was *incredibly* kind, upstairs in an airy room lined with
wide-shuttered doors and window coverings that let in a blissful breeze
of much cooler air, down off the high mountains to the east.

A lone trio of finger-narrow candles lit the chamber, barely illumi-
nating anything beyond the bedstead, yet throwing mesmerising shadows
against the walls and shutters with each mild gust. Up that high above
the fouled and littered streets of Port-Au-Prince, it was refreshing to
escape the miasma of too much garbage, and the reek of too many
people. And those gently flickering candles threw such enchanting high-
lights and shadows over Henriette's fine body, too, limning a *chiaroscuro*
portrait in ambers and black hollows, making her even more exotic than
she already was.

The sheets were clean, if "wormed" with small seams of repairs, and
were redolent of soap and sunlight. The candles were local-made, scented
with flowers, almost as sharp on the nose as Chinee joss-sticks or very
High Church incense. Henriette had dabbed on fresh scent, too, after
they'd locked and barred the door, and that was all over the bedstead,
the pillows, and him, by then; for, cool as was that breeze, it was still a
warm and humid tropic night, and they had perspired . . . oh, *how* they
had perspired, in the throes of lust! The more common term of "sweated"
came to Lewrie's mind; sweated like *coolie* labourers loading cargo on
Jackass Point in Canton, or Hindoos up the Hooghly River! But more
than worth it, he smugly decided, stifling a yawn as he sprawled beside

her, getting his breath back, and watching the candle patterns dance on the overhead canopy of the bedstead.

There came a stronger gust of wind, a cooler and welcome zephyr. "It rains," Henriette whispered. Sure enough, the zephyrs were followed by the faintest plashing of raindrops on the balcony. There was a *basso* rumble of faraway thunder, and an eyeblink's flicker upon the shutters from a fork of distant lightning, the wide wood shutters thrown in blue relief for a second. *"Mon, Dieu, merci."*

Lewrie sat up and groped to the foot of the bed for a discarded sheet, to fan it and lift it to trap the cooler air, to let it fall slowly and drape over them, then fan it to soar and hang, again.

"Merci to you, too, *cher* Alain." She smiled, getting up on one elbow to face him and reward him with another token of kindness on his lips. "I have the basin . . . you wish me to sponge you? You are *très* hot? I cool you?"

"Better I get to sponge you, Henriette," he chuckled, reclining once more with his hands under his head and the pillow. "I don't wish t'get *too* cool. A certain . . . heat . . . is required, ain't it? Uhm, *l'ardour? La passion?"*

"But you were *born* with the passion, *mon amour,*" she told him. *"Mon Dieu* . . . so *formidable!"*

Whores' lies, he thought; *but . . . . so pleasin'!*

She slid out of bed on the window side, all those delectably shadowed hollows and sweat-sheened bright spots awakening his interest anew. Lean waist, long slim neck and arms, with entrancing hollows at throat and collarbones . . . firm, round and jutting young breasts that nearly defied Newton's laws of gravity, a bouncy round and firm bottom, strong-thewed thighs . . . with such a seductive dark hollow between.

She peeked flirtatiously over her shoulder as she walked to the windows, rolling her hips, chuckling over the effect she knew she had on him. At the nearest window she posed herself, drew open the shutters and stood silhouetted, feet apart and arms widespread. With a theatric sigh of contentment, she threw back her head to savour that cooler wind, began to run her hands over her body as if smoothing in a lotion made of raindrops, or the night's magic, with her back to him.

Well, he wasn't having any of that! Lewrie sprang from the bed and crossed the room to snuggle in against her from behind, to "help" her enjoyment. His hands roamed, and made Henriette softly groan deep in her throat; over her waist and belly, the tops of her thighs, then up to cup her bounteous breasts and circle her large, dark nipples and areolae with his thumbs. Up to the tops of her shoulders, then butterflying downward over her breasts again, and she stiffened with delight and parted her feet more widely as he softly traced down either side of her stomach, down to her prominent mons and the pouty lips of her vagina. She leaned her head back on his shoulder, raised her arms over her head, and juddered her luscious bottom against his groin.

A moment more, a groan more, and she stepped quickly away, over to the wash-hand-stand for the sponges and the basin of cool water, so she could return and do the same for him. Working her way down, down, 'til she knelt before him, teasing her hair over his member, now hard as a marling-spike. A look up into his eyes, a teasing smile upon her face, then she half-lidded her eyes, took hold of his manhood, and put her lips over the cap.

"Pour vous, mon amour formidable," she whispered, pausing for a moment before lowering her head once more to her ministrations.

The distant thunder seemed to rumble 'twixt his ears, steady as the excited pulse of his heart. He threw his own head back and let out a low moan, put one hand on the back of her head and gripped a shutter with the other.

Whores, by God! he exulted to himself, looking down at last to watch her, and him, work together. *Wives never know this, now and then maybe a mistress, but . . . go it, darlin'. Tonight you're mine t'do ev'rything I want . . . bought an' paid for, and by God, it feels* fine!

The novelty of having a woman so casually, of using her as much as he wanted, any *way* he wanted, then discarding her without a backward glance—though with a japing, teasing friendliness, a "fond" parting kiss, and extra shilling or two—it was *so* damned beguiling, so alluring, that he wondered why he'd eschewed whores all these years!

Wasn't for the Navy, I'd've most-like become a pimp! he recalled from his early days, the chuckle in his throat higher this time, almost a cackle of mirth.

Thud-thud-thud-thud, went the far-off thunder; *thud-thud. . . .*

No, it wasn't thunder, he decided after a moment of coherency in the grip of mindless pleasure. And it wasn't his heart, either, those regular thuds, for they were in counterpoint to the beat in his chest.

Henriette stopped and sat back on her heels, suddenly looking forlorn and frightened, clamping her arms over her breasts.

"Here, now . . ." he began to say, irked that she'd quit before the "melting moments."

"L'Ouverture!" Henriette squeaked. "The drums!"

"Drums? Oh!" Lewrie gawped, going to the window. "So that's what that sound is. Like . . . like Muskogee Indian drumming. Sort of."

"Is *voudoun!*" Henriette gasped, beginning to shiver in dread.

"Cuffy mumbo-jumbo?" Lewrie scoffed.

"Is *vrais* . . . is true! Very powerful!" Henriette insisted, at the verge of teeth-chattering terror. "*Voudoun* priests bless rebels, and curse town peoples. We hear the drums, it mean L'Ouverture and his armies 'ave come! In the hills now! Oh, *Mon Dieu,* zey kill us all!"

"They'll not get the town, *cherie,*" Lewrie told her, following her round the room as she dithered, thinking of packing, thinking about hiding the next moment, picking things up and then throwing them down. "There's a British army out there, with dozens of field guns. Redans and fortifications, lashings of ammunition. There's ships in harbour, just stiff with artillery, too. Nothing to worry about. Now, let us get back to our pleasures. Where were we, hmmm?"

He took hold of her arms and brought her to a halt by the bed, urging her to get back into it. She'd raised his desires, had brought him close to joy, and damned if he was going to quit now.

"British keep us safe?" she asked, sounding leery about it.

"Safe as houses, I assure you," he lied, embracing her and kissing her neck and shoulders, her hollows, but with a bit of a spraddle-legged dance to the edge of the mattress, a bit of pressure to topple her back to her duties. "Can't let a pretty young thing like you get in their clutches, now can we, Henriette . . . *ma cherie?*" he coaxed.

She submitted, and sat on the edge of the bed to re-engage her mouth over him. Sulkily, at first, but quickly warming to her work.

"Ah, that's me girl," Lewrie sighed, rock-hard again.

She quit, again! But this time, it was merely to reach over to the nightstand to retrieve a fresh, unused cundum and sheath him with the tanned sheep-gut, to tie off the ribbons around his waist and under his crutch, then award him a brave smile as she lay back and opened her limbs to him.

Lewrie slid in, kissing his way up her body, lingering over her groin for a long minute or two, 'til she began to grind her hips and make whimpery little groaning sounds. Up to kiss and lick her belly, that actually shuddered under his feathery touch, her hands now eagerly drawing him higher. Tonguing and suckling on her marvelous poonts and even play-nipping, that made her squeak and bounce and chuckle. Then her thighs raised and he was atop her and in her, and the Mongol Horde or all the Imps of Hell could have been howling for blood below-stairs, for all that Lewrie cared. Henriette, too, it seemed to Lewrie; this time was not artful or coy, but furious and mindless, as if sex could silence those drums and drive the bad'uns away.

Rap-rap-rap on the door. "I say, Alan old son? Time t'be out and doin'," Cashman muttered.

"Go . . . away! Later! *Plus tard!*" Lewrie gasped back, amid a skirl of squeaking bed-ropes and slats, and Henriette panting into his mouth as if trying to suck a *long* life from him. *Whining* in ecstacy!

"Heard the drums? I really think—"

"Bugger . . . *off*! Drake had time t'bowl . . . I've time for a romp! Whoo! Darlin'!"

Henriette was *keening*, grasping, clawing, nigh to a scream!

"*Oui oui oui, mon Dieu,* oh *oui* . . . *!*" Henriette shrieked. "I am going . . . *eeeehhhh!*"

"Aarrhhh!" Lewrie chimed in a moment later. "Rule, Brittania, by Jesus, *yes!*"

He collapsed on her, aswim in perspiration once more, gasping like a pair of landed fish, aslither to press close and grasp to keep the mind-lessness in hand as long as possible.

"Happy now?" came the sardonic, muffled voice beyond the door.

"Ain't Paradise yet, but damn close," Lewrie called back as he rolled off the bed, groaning with exhaustion and lingering joy, as he stood bare-arsed naked and stripped off the cundum for a quick washing and later use. "Quick sponge, and I'll be out in two shakes of a wee lamb's tail . . . and the first's already been shook. Uhm, Henriette, me darlin' . . . know where I dropped my shirt?"

Though it was hours before dawn, and still raining in a light, desultory way, the streets of Port-Au-Prince teemed with people. Some refugees were up and packing, or trundling two-wheeled handcarts down to the harbour, in hopes of a departing ship. There was more light at last, with almost every window or porchway illuminated by the curious and the fearful. Citizens stood on their stoops or balconies to stare out towards the countryside, or shout questions at passersby and their neighbours, who were also up and peering in their nightshirts or gowns.

British troops, and those handfuls of persecuted Saint Domingue Royalists who had taken arms with them, mustered and marched to drums of their own, and the thin tootle of fifes, in the opposite direction, forcing Lewrie and Cashman to shoulder and sidle aside on their way to the port.

And those far-off drums still thrummed, regular as a metronome, seemingly from every inland point of the compass, as if Port-Au-Prince was already surrounded and under a fell siege. There were some out on the streets who seemed glad of it, though it was far too early to show enthusiasm or loyalty. The guillotines set up by the original Jacobins still stood, waiting for their next victims; terrified *petits blancs* or Mulattoes could still turn into a mob and tear people asunder, if they had no other weapons than their hands.

Toussaint L'Ouverture's secret allies, those supposedly "happy" personal servants and household slaves fetched in from the country, had turned on their masters before. It was no wonder everyone went about as cutty-eyed as a bag of nails, with one hand near a pocketed pistol or the hilt of a sword. At present, all they could do was glare, maybe smirk with delight of a future victory, their chins high and their eyes alight, as Lewrie and Cashman passed—two officers alone, with no escort, easily taken by a quickly gathered gang?

Lewrie could feel their speculation, as if he were a yearling calf under the gaze of the farmer with a knife hidden from view.

"Yorktown . . . Toulon," Lewrie snarled, keeping his eyes moving and a firm grip on his sword hilt. "Looks and smells the same, of a sudden. Defeat and . . . disaster." He was still short of breath, and their rapid pace wasn't helping.

"Oh, rot!" Cashman snapped, still out of sorts for being kept waiting, when he was afire to dash off to join his troops. "What we built 'round this place, we can hold for months, if need be. Break 'em on our guns and ramparts."

"Certain you can, Kit," Lewrie replied, "but the rot's set *in*! Those drums . . . tales of *voudoun* and past massacres. British troops might hold but . . . whole town's against you. Ready t'roll over and quit. Can't you feel it, already?"

"They're scared, I'll grant you," Cashman answered. "But, let 'em see us shred the first assaults, and they'll buck up. *Let* some of the faint-hearts run! No use, anyway, and that'll be fewer mouths to feed. A week'r two of slaughter, and the slaveys'll melt back into the hills, lickin' their wounds. We'll hold, count on it," he said, firmer of resolve, as if saying it would make it so, though Lewrie doubted that it might make a real difference on the rest of the island.

What would be gained, with another Fever Season coming, Lewrie wondered? The slave armies decimated, for sure, but not defeated, as his advisories had boasted, free to recruit and re-arm, strike another place less well defended; another year of campaigning that would eat European troops, ammunition, and money like a glutton's box of sweets! To what end, after all the lives lost?

"Well, here we are," Cashman said, clomping to a halt. "Camp's that way, the quays t'other. Good luck out at sea, Alan. I do think you'll have more joy of it than I, the next few weeks."

"Pile 'em up in heaps, Kit," Lewrie said, offering his hand to his longtime friend. "And thankee for a hellish-good run ashore!"

"That I will, and you're welcome," Cashman said with a smile, easier and more relaxed now. "Though what a staid family man such's yerself is doin', makin' a right meal o' things, is beyond me. Or . . . p'raps 'tis been too *long*, as a family man and all?"

"You're corrupting," Lewrie assured him.

"You're corruptible." Cashman hooted. "Why I like you so well. *Damn* those drums! You'd think even *they'd* like some peace and quiet, a bit o' shut-eye. Fare ye well, ye tarry ol' whoreson."

"You, too, you old rogue!" Lewrie bade in hearty return, and then they became formal, doffed their hats and bowed away in *congé* to their separate commands.

Lewrie made the last cable or so to the quays, where he could whoosh out his relief to still be living; the warehouses and houses had seemed more than usually ominous. He stood in the dull rain and peered about for a boat, suddenly distrusting himself alone aboard an island bum-boat, with a Black crew who just might favour L'Ouverture's party. Finally, a Navy guard-boat ghosted past, and he whistled and waved 'til they steered towards him.

"Going my way?" Lewrie called to the young midshipman in the sternsheets, who held a blazing torch by which to see. "Lewrie, from the *Proteus* frigate."

"Oh, aye sir! Come aboard. Curlow, help the captain aboard, there!" the boy cried, seeming relieved, and snapping at a Jamaican sailor who served as bow-man. "Uhm, those drums, sir . . . started up 'bout an hour ago. My pardons for asking, sir, but . . . what does it mean?"

"It means," Lewrie intoned, once he had gotten settled upon a thwart, "that a whole hurricane of shit is about t'come down on this place, younker. And thank your lucky stars you're in the Navy and not ashore when it does."

And the Jamaican bow-man chimed "Amen, sah!" to that.

CHAPTER SEVENTEEN

*T*he coffee was rich and savoury, hot as the hinges of Hell, and laced with first-pressing sugar, lacking only milk to make it perfect; but then HMS *Proteus* did not run to nursing cows, and Lewrie had never cared for sheep or goat's milk, and that was all they had up forrud in the manger. One lean bullock, due for slaughter in a day or two for a taste of fresh beef; a sow with six piglets, one bedraggled and shorn sheep, and a nanny goat, along with about a dozen egg-laying chickens and their few hatchlings were all the ship could boast.

It was a grand morning to lean against the after-most windward bulwarks of the quarterdeck, right aft near the taff-rail and the flag lockers, and greet the day with the first pewter mug of coffee, relishing the brisk coolness of post-dawn, the beginning of what promised to be another of those sparkling days at sea. There was just enough wind to make the ship lively, and bedew even the quarterdeck with bursts of spray, with the slightly choppy wavetops curling and creaming with cats-paws and seahorses.

Frankly, every morning since *Proteus* had departed Port-Au-Prince had been delightful; the coffee and cocoa beans, and sugar bought from Cashman's friends was a piquant spice to early rising. *Not* one of Lewrie's favourite things about being in the Navy, this standing to dawn Quarters, but the habit had been drilled into him long before as a prudent precaution in peace or war, no matter which sea one sailed, or how rare the encounter with an enemy warship was reputed to be.

"Beg to report, sir," little Midshipman Grace piped up, doffing his hat, "the First Lieutenant's duty, and there are no sails within sight, sir."

"Very well, Mister Grace," Lewrie said with a nod and a final sip of his strong coffee, "my compliments to Mister Langlie, and he's free to stand the hands down from Quarters and pipe them to breakfast."

"Aye aye, sir," little Grace replied, eager to be the conduit between Commission Officers. Lewrie thought he was shaping well, for a lad who'd come aboard with his father and grandfather "before the mast" at Sheerness, just before the Nore Mutiny. Though small, he was lithe, quick-witted, and eager to learn, to excel at the rare opportunity for a shoeless lad from the fisheries and mud-bank dredgings of the Nore to become a midshipman, some day a Royal Navy officer with a commission of his own. Lewrie *had* been shorthanded after he had to cull the crew of mutineers, was grateful for the Graces' support while re-taking the ship, and there *had* been a mid's berth open. The Graces had lost their own fishing boat, and had scraped by on charity and the odd day-labourer berth aboard a friend's boat before taking the King's Shilling out of penury and desperation. So far, Lewrie had no reason to doubt his hasty decision.

He idled over to the helm, sat his mug down on the binnacle cabinet, and studied the chart with the Sailing Master, Mr. Winwood. The Sailing Master squinted, muttered under his breath as he counted, then bent over to place a tiny *X* on the chart.

" 'Bout mid-way 'twixt Cuba, Great Inagua island in the Bahamas, and Mole Saint Nicholas on Saint Domingue, sir," Winwood speculated in an offhanded way. "Two hour's run off-wind, and we'll be well in the Windward Passage. Isle of Tortuga is about six hours Sou'Sou'east, on this morning's wind, Captain."

"Once the hands have eat, Mister Winwood, we'll tack and charge down toward Tortuga, 'til midday, say," Lewrie decided. "The wind's a touch more Northing to it, today. Does it hold, we may tack again, and reach almost North towards Great Inagua. Cover a goodly portion of the area, and take a peek into the Caicos Passage, as well. And I am of the mind to see into the Mouchoir and Silver Bank Passages, too. 'Tis one thing, to stand off-and-on on close blockade, but it may be more productive to roam a tad farther afield."

"Aye, sir . . . leave the small craft to our luggers and cutters, but the large ships will be ours," Mr. Winwood said, the brightness of his eyes the only sign of amusement or joy the laconic older man ever evinced to others. "Fair winds and deep water, then, for most of the day, sir. I will, for the space of it, breathe much easier."

"Perhaps even caulk a bit, Mister Winwood?" Lewrie pretended to scoff. "Heavens, where is your famed industry flown, then?"

"Held in reserve, sir, for more trying circumstances," Winwood insisted. "I assure you, sir, I do not flag in my zeal for accuracy or—"

"Never mind, Mister Winwood," Lewrie said with a sigh, expecting that, should they be in active commission together for ten years, "jest" and Winwood would *never* be mentioned in the same breath.

"Mister Catterall, you have the deck," Lewrie said, turning to their Third Lieutenant. He took one last look 'at the gun-deck as the artillery was tompioned and bowsed snug to the bulwarks, a final peek aloft at the commissioning pendant for the wind direction, then went aft and below to his own breakfast.

Shore bread, butter and jam, a proper two-egg *omelette* with two strips of bacon and some grated cheese—done firmer and fluffier to *his* liking, not the runny Frog fashion—and Lewrie was sated. Once the tack to the Sou'Sou'east was completed, he thought, there would be bags of time to idle, with a cup of hot chocolate, and a new chapter in one of his books. Perhaps even one of Mr. Winwood's naps, he speculated, 'twixt then and "Clear Decks And Up-Spirits" at Seven Bells of the Forenoon, then Noon Sights?

"Deck, there!" the faint cry came wafting down. "Sail ho! Off th' larboard quarters!"

Boxing the compass in his mind, Lewrie frowned in puzzlement at that news, only slowly rising from the table to don one of his cotton coats; the wind was more Nor'east by North, and *Proteus* was now close-hauled on the starboard tack, steering Nor'west by North. For a ship to be sighted astern of her, off the larboard quarter, would put her down to the Sou'west of them.

How could they have missed her earlier, unless she was bound North from the Windward Passage, astern of them at dawn? Or, he also supposed, beginning to smile in anticipation, she had rounded Cuba by way of the Old Bahama Passage, south of Great Inagua, and was sailing Sutherly.

"Deck, there! *Two* sail off th' larboard quarters!"

Thud went the Marine sentry's musket butt on the deck. "Midshipman o' th' watch, *sah!*"

"Come."

"Mister Catterall's duty, sir, and..." Midshipman Grace began to say.

"I heard it, too, Mister Grace. Run tell Mister Catterall that I'll be on deck directly, and he is to ready the ship about."

"Aye *aye*, sir!" Grace yelped with excitement, scuttling out in a twinkling to scamper up to the quarterdeck and relay his orders.

Before Lewrie could get to the quarterdeck, the bosun's calls were shrilling, and *Proteus* thundered to the drum of feet as the crew came up from below. Officers and mates were calling for order, readying them to wear off the wind and head Sou'west.

Leaving the evolution in capable hands, Lewrie took a telescope from the binnacle rack and went aloft, up the larboard mizen shrouds to just below the cat-harpings to "weave" his limbs about the stays and rat-lines for a quick peek.

He saw what he thought were two schooner-rigged vessels, close together, the rake of their masts and the slant of their bat-wing fore and aft sails putting him in mind of American-built schooners; heading Sutherly, for certain, according to the "arrow" of their jibs and main sails pointing in that direction. They were well hull-down, with only the upper parts of their sails showing, so far. Schooners were wicked-fast, but...

He grinned once more. Off the wind, though, unless they hoisted crossed yards, a frigate with its acres of sail and a long waterline could run them down, once it got a bone in its teeth. Placed as they were, with *Proteus* to windward, the schooners had nowhere to run, or beam-reach, where they could use their famous speed. Beating up near the eye of the wind was out, for *Proteus* was already there!

He shut the glass and scampered down as Lt. Langlie issued the final orders to wear. The after-guard who tended the mizen had little need of an officer in the rigging, to daunt their work.

"It *couldn't* be that Yankee Doodle revenue clown, d'ye think?" Lt. Catterall whispered, once they had fetched the schooners hull-up, after a hard hour of sailing off-wind. "One schooner, chasing another? He might've gotten lucky. Sooner or later, anyone may."

"All cats are grey in the dark, old son," Lt. Wyman softly replied. "Diff'rent colour scheme to these . . . I think."

"Do they part . . ." Catterall continued.

"Don't go borrowing trouble," Wyman countered, looking shocked at the notion of two disparate Chases to run down.

Lewrie paced away from them, out of earshot. The dread of the schooners haring off on widely different courses had already occurred to him, and he didn't wish to hear such, either; the word was the sire to the deed . . . like causing the worst to happen just by saying it out loud. Or wishing on the wrong star!

The schooners had hardened up on the wind a bit, to use all the power of it they could; now they bore just a bit East of South, but on that course, they'd ram aground near Mole Saint Nicholas on the north arm of Saint Domingue's bay, did they stand on. That, or run into one more British blockader, and have to shy away.

Were they smart, Lewrie fretted, one might bear away Sou'west, angling for the Jamaica Channel, and the other, to put about and sail for Cuba's eastern tip. *Why* they were still together, he could not fathom, for it was the obvious ploy. He could only catch one of them, and had already determined that the Cuba-bound one would be the easier prey; he could cut the corner on her and fetch her up, whilst the other stood a poor chance of sailing past Saint Domingue without being taken by another Royal Navy patroller. But here they both were, clinging to each other as if glued or chained, the one astern slightly slower than her consort. There were about two miles between them now, and *Proteus* was within two miles of the nearest.

And God help 'em, if they're more Yankees, Lewrie thought, still rankled by the wild goose chase that *Trumbull* had run them. The idea of wasting an entire day in pursuit of a brace of idiots would be galling. *Maybe I'll flog me one,* Lewrie imagined, rather happily; *for an example to the others!*

He began to pace, head down and his hands clutched in the small of his back, unable to stand and wait any longer. Forrud along the larboard gangway, all the way to the forecastle and back, as if by pacing he could *walk Proteus* closer to them.

"Floggin'!" a seaman called, making Lewrie wonder if they were of the same mind, did these schooners turn out to be callow Americans.

"Summat carried away, there! 'Er mains'l's floggin'!"

Lewrie raised his head and peered at the far Chase; sure enough, her mains'l was now winged out and flapping like laundry, and she sat flatter on her bottom, instead of being heeled over so far, and in his quickly hoisted telescope he could barely espy a scurry of activity on her small quarterdeck, even a pair of ant-like figures ascending the shrouds to re-rove either her throat or peak halliard. He swung to see what the trailing schooner was doing, and found her standing on, still on course—no, by God! She was falling off the wind a bit, to run nearer her consort, as if she would come alongside and aid her!

"What in the world?" he muttered, puzzled even more.

Proteus now loped nearer the pair of them, almost within a long gun-range, and Lewrie quickly strode aft to his proper place among his officers on the quarterdeck.

"Mister Langlie, we'll try a ranging shot from the fore chases," he snapped, once there, at the centre of the hammock nettings. "If anything else, we'll put the wind up 'em."

"Aye, sir! Mister Catterall . . . a ranging shot!"

"Aye aye!"

Moments later, after much fiddling, the starboard 6-pounder gave out a sharp bark, flinging a ball with the quoin completely out from underneath the breach to stretch the gun's reach. Lewrie could see that roundshot as it slowed at the apogee of its flight, then dash into invisibility once more as it descended. There was a splash, a slim tower of water that rose from the waves as the shot struck about two cables short of the trailing schooner.

"Oh, damme," Lt. Langlie cried, "not *again.!*"

The schooner had hoisted an American flag!

"I'll not believe it 'til I stand on his damned decks!" Lewrie vowed.

"Stand on, and reload."

"Aye, sir!"

"Mis'rable, pus-gutted, poxy sonofa—" Lewrie grumbled.

The 6-pounder yapped again, and this time the roundshot struck within a cable of the trailing schooner. A third try, with the quoin in this time, and six pounds of iron struck short and skipped several times, like a flat rock being shied across a pond, to slam home with a thud, flinging a small burst of dust, paint chips, and splinters!

"Huzzah! Pound her 'til she strikes, no matter who she is!"

The far schooner was still sloughing along, her mains'l bagged out and flogging, even with the mainsheet drawn snug. She, too, hoisted an American flag, making Lewrie wonder if he should continue firing into them; surely, this would be a nasty diplomatic incident, if they truly were Yankee Doodle ships, but . . . why had they run so long, even after *Proteus* had hoisted her own colours an hour before? Could an entire people, a whole *race*, be quite *that* stupid?

There came a fourth shot from the bow chaser, and another strike 'twixt wind and water, smashing in part of her low larboard bulwarks, and caroming through a rowboat stowed amidships in a cloud of splinters. Lewrie eyed her through the telescope once more.

"Mine arse on a band-box . . . they're havin' a melee, yonder!" he gasped. "Take a look . . . they're fighting 'mongst themselves."

"Those that'd strike, and those that'd fight, sir?" Lt. Langlie wondered aloud. "Ah! There go her main and fore sheets . . . and their flag halliard! She's struck!"

"Cease fire, there! Cease fire!" Lewrie bellowed. "Sir, do you close on the far one, and take her under fire when in range. Chasers only. Rest of the gun crews are to ready a boat for lowering."

"Aye, sir," Langlie responded. "Mister Sevier, keep your eyes on this'un. Sing out, does she renege and try to escape."

The near schooner quickly flashed down the starboard side, and the far one, still not repaired, quickly neared. The bow chaser fired once more, finding the range almost at once, and dropping a ball close-aboard her waterline. And down came her American flag, too! Briefly replaced with the French Tricolour that had barely been two-blocked at the peak of the halliard before being quickly lowered, and allowed to trail over the schooner's taffrails in sign of surrender!

"We'll definitely lower boats for this'un, Mister Langlie. And a Marine boarding party," Lewrie instructed, feeling his chest swell in triumph. Still puzzled, it must be said, but triumphant.

"The schooner astern is underway again, Mister Langlie, sir!" Midshipman Sevier cried, attracting their attention. "She's following us, with her flag re-hoisted."

"Curiouser and curiouser," Lewrie muttered, rubbing his chin. "Fetch us to, Mister Langlie . . .'fore we end up in Port-de-Paix. Do you keep this'un under our quarterdeck six-pounders and carronades . . . just t'keep 'em honest."

"Aye, sir."

For long minutes, the frigate and schooner wallowed together, a cable's distance between them, as the labourious process of hoisting up, swinging out, and lowering ship's boats off the cross-deck timbers was carried out. Men from the larboard guns and gangways were ticked off for a boarding party, along with half the Marines, all under arms.

"Hoy!" Lewrie called across with speaking-trumpet. "What ship are you?"

"*Comment?*" was the reply; and a rather snippy one, too.

"Oh . . . Frog," Lewrie groused. "*Quel navire!*"

"*Ici c'est L'Oiseau! Un marchand!*"

"The *Songbird*," Lewrie translated aloud. "But a merchant ship, mine arse! There must be an hundred crew aboard her. Her sides are pierced for at least eight guns! *Vous êtes le menteur sanglant! Vous êtes un privateer!*" he bellowed across. "*Vous êtes le prix, à moi!*"

He could *feel* the Surgeon's Mate, the French exile Mr. Durant, wince near his side.

"Your French is . . . remarkable, *Capitaine*," Durant all but tittered.

"Good enough t'call *him* a bloody liar," Lewrie said with a grin and a shrug of haplessness outside his native English. "What's 'privateer' in French?"

"Privateer, sir," Durant informed him, unable to hide his mirth. "I believe zat is where it came from, ze French."

"Capital! He caught my drift, then." Lewrie chuckled before he turned back to watch more warily as his boats thumped into the *Songbird* and his boarding party began to clamber over her rails.

"Yankee schooner's passing to windward of us, sir!" Midshipman Sevier pointed out, drawing Lewrie to larboard with his trumpet.

"Hoy, the frigate! Thankee, sir!" a man in a master's coat said as the schooner let fly her sheets to slow and luff up. "This is the *Bantam* ... ten days outta Savannah. Yon French bastard took us off the Berry Islands two days ago. Who do I owe thanks to?"

"End vis ze preposition, tsk tsk," Durant muttered.

"HMS *Proteus* ... Captain Lewrie, commanding!" Lewrie shouted over, then turned to Durant. "My French, his English, it seems. But, what can you expect from our recently departed Colonials?"

"Stood up to us, bold as a dog in a doublet, he did!" *Bantam*'s master was shouting. "Flyin' our flag, with an American doin' all the talking for 'em! I'm Machias Wilder, by the by! Soon as you can hog-tie or chain up yon French bastards, I'd be that proud to stand ye to a stiff drink, Captain Lewrie!"

"And I would be more than happy to accept, Captain Wilder!"

"Probably has no palate, eizzer," Durant lamented. "No cognac. Only raw corn whiskey, I mus' warn you, *Capitaine*."

"Oh, don't poor-mouth corn whiskey, Mister Durant," Lewrie said, throwing his head back to laugh. "It has its own charm, once you get accustomed."

"I wish to thank you, as well, *Capitaine*. For ze extract of ze *chichona*," Durant went on. "Vis God's help, ze four bottle will suffice. I wish to ask, Zo ... will we be back in Port-Au-Prince, so I may purchase more from your mysterious source?"

"Can't guarantee anything, Mister Durant, but, does fever break out among us, we'll make every effort."

"Zat is all I may ask, sir. Forgive my intrusion," Durant said, doffing his hat and leaving the quarterdeck.

Odd damn' feller, Lewrie thought as he watched him go; *gloomy as anything. Competent, though. We can only hope.*

The captured American trading schooner snugged her sheets once more and began to ghost away upwind, out of *Proteus*'s business, for the nonce.

The Royal Navy didn't put much stock in capturing a privateer, Lewrie told himself as he paced along the lee rails facing his prize. Taking a National ship, a warship, counted for more, and the pay-out from a Prize Court was much higher, because a warship was usually purchased into the Navy for re-use. Privateers, though, well . . . worth a pittance for each gun aboard, along with the "head money" for every crewman noted in her muster-book before capture. There might be more if the privateer had transferred cargo from earlier prizes into her own holds, and that got sold at auction, but most of the time taking one was hardly worth the trouble.

Which way why, he decided, privateering thrived so openly. Most Navy officers didn't want to risk their precious bottoms inshore to chase them back to their lairs, and would let *three* privateers sail past if there was a chance of taking a rich-laden merchantman, or of winning an honourable fight with an enemy man o' war.

That was one explanation for why French privateers operated so boldly in the Caribbean, and why it seemed that the dozens and dozens of British warships had such abysmal luck in catching them.

But! This *L'Oiseau*, or *Songbird*, would fetch them *something* to show for their efforts, he could greedily speculate; the return of an American merchantman to their control might just result in a reward of some kind, too! Something beyond this Captain Wilder's generosity for restoring his livelihood to him, something official from the United States government, once they found a Consul at Kingston, or . . . ?

"Deck, there!" the lookout called down from his rolling, swirling perch high atop the mainmast as *Proteus* lay fetched-to. "Sail ho! Full-rigged ship, four points off th' larboard quarter! A frigate!"

"Oh, no!" Lewrie muttered, climbing up the mizen shrouds once more, his telescope slung rifle-fashion over one shoulder. "You're *not* 'in sight,' ya can't have a *penny* of 'em. Whoever you are. Not enough t'share, as it is."

Once settled securely, he unslung his glass and extended it 'til he had a shaky view of the new arrival. Sure enough, it was a three-masted, full-rigged ship, heading almost bows-on towards them. From the proud cant of her jib-boom and bow-sprit that hobby-horsed closer and closer, from the thickness of her crossed yards and lower masts, she *did* look like a frigate! But whose?

He slung his glass again and scampered back to the deck with a bit less decorum than a proper captain ought to display, trying to hide his anxiety as he peered over at the French schooner.

"Mister Langlie, is that prize of ours well in hand yet?" he snapped.

"Her crew's been disarmed and fettered, sir, and is now under guard by a file of Marines," the efficient Lt. Langlie replied. "I've placed Mister Catterall aboard her as prize-master, with Towpenny, the Bosun's Mate, as his second, and Midshipman Adair and twelve hands to get her under way, sir. If those choices meet your approval, that is, Captain."

"Perfectly. Then let's get under way ourselves, and ready the ship to meet yon frigate. They may have sent a man o' war north, with a clutch of privateers, t'keep an eye on them and their prizes. Once under way, sir, we'll return to Quarters. And someone tell that Captain Wilder over there t'stand well aloof of us, if things go wrong."

"Aye, sir," Langlie replied, without a qualm at the thought of impending combat.

"Deck, there!" the lookout shouted anew. " 'At strange sail *is* a frigate! She's hoistin' colours . . . American!"

"Well, whyever not?" Lewrie said, making it a humourous gripe to disguise his own qualms, and ease his crew's, as well. "Everyone *else* has, hey? But it may be a common ruse in these waters. We will still get under way . . . just t'be sure."

"All hands . . . !" Langlie began to cry.

Another hour, with the sun beginning to lower in the west, and HMS *Proteus* was nearing the stranger, boldly standing towards her with gun-ports open and all national flags hoisted; ready for battle if the strange frigate was lying, but with a query in that month's private signals also flying aloft.

The frigate stood on towards them, as well, with her ports shut, and angling a bit below her bows, to the Westward, as if to cede them the wind gauge and the traditional advantage.

"Pacific of 'em, sir," Lt. Langlie commented. "To sail alee."

"Mmm-hmm," was Lewrie's chary opinion of that.

"Rather a big'un, ain't she," Lieutenant Wyman noted. "My goodness gracious, she must be a forty-four gunner."

"Over-sparred, though, Mister Wyman," Sailing Master Winwood pointed out, "with much too much aloft. You midshipmen take note. Under all plain sail, her masts are as tall as ours when flying royals. Mark the length of her yards, as well. Under a sudden hard press of wind, she'd not get *those* reefed in safely. She may very well *be* an American frigate. 'Tis a common mistake I've seen from Yankee yards."

"My word, perhaps she's a fifty-gun Fourth Rate," Wyman opined, finally spotting the second, upper row of closed gun-ports, painted black to match her bulwarks, instead of the white of her lower gunwale.

"The Yankee Doodles built *some* two-deckers during the Revolution but I never heard of them serving," Lewrie felt prodded to contribute, dredging up so-called intelligence from his advisories. "Most-like, I believe they rotted on the stocks before launch. Their new construction plans may call for two-deckers, but did they need hulls on short notice, they might have razeed one before completion, and outfitted her as a large frigate."

By God, but she is big, though! he thought, daunted by the idea of having to fight her. With a two-decker's much stouter lower timbers and deck beams, she might be able to carry 24-pounders below, and even 12-pounders on the upper gun-deck.

"Razeed ships are rarely suceessful; though," Mr. Winwood droned on, "for they tend to 'hog' at both ends from the weight of their guns. And without the thick upperworks of a proper ship of the line, there's not enough linear support to prevent it. A long cruise or two is about all one may expect before they're due a serious, and prolonged, refit. In our own Navy, we've experienced such failures as—"

"Signal hoist, sir!" Midshipman Nicholas interrupted. "I make out this month's private signal!"

"So she *is* a Yankee," Lieutenant Langlie said, managing not to sound much relieved at that news. "Shall we stand down from Quarters, sir?"

"Close the ports, but I'll reserve judgement 'til I hear them speak us, Mister Langlie," Lewrie demurred. "Not 'til I hear a nasal Yankee twang. We will let her close us, though."

"Aye, sir."

And there goes any government reward for re-takin' Bantam, he sourly imagined; *not with a Yankee frigate to escort her away. My God . . . damn!*

The big American frigate sailed past, alee of them, taking advantage of the "wind-shadow" from *Proteus*'s sails to reef in and reduce canvas; then rounded up and tacked, once in clearer air. She was well drilled and handled, belying any slurs on Yankee seamanship, and seemed "handy" despite her great length, and the greater freeboard exposed to the wind from her higher sides. Under mostly tops'ls and jibs, as if accomodating the smaller British ship, she angled up to within a cable alee and abeam, at last.

"This is his Brittanic Majesty's frigate *Proteus*!" Lewrie called first, through a speaking-trumpet. "Captain Lewrie! And whom do I have the honour to address, sir?"

"The United States ship *Hancock* . . . Captain Joshua Kershaw! How-de-do, Captain Lewrie. I see you been busy!"

Hancock? *Lewrie thought, smirking despite the occasion; sounds like masturbation! Aye, he's a Yankee, right enough. Not Downeast . . . more like the Carolinas, or Virginia.*

Which connexion reminded him too much of his wife, making him hunch his shoulders and wince to dismiss such idle interruptions.

"Buy me a drink, Captain Kershaw, and I'll boast most immoderate on it!" Lewrie shouted over.

"Done, sir! Well met, and let's fetch to!"

CHAPTER EIGHTEEN

*C*aptain Joshua Kershaw, U.S. Navy, was a hearty older fellow, a tall, bluff, and stout man in his fifties, and in his youth might have been a most handsome and impressive physical specimen. His waistcoat strained over a rounded abdomen, and his thighs were as thick as standing rib roasts. His jowls were round, and he wore a white side-curled wig that was much too small for a head that large, yet he appeared elegant, and well turned out. Though Lewrie did find the American Navy uniform a bit too like the French to suit him.

The turn-backs, lapels, collar, and cuffs of Kershaw's dark blue coat were French-style red, as was his waistcoat, nicely trimmed with gold lace and gilt buttons. His breeches were dark blue, though, not French red, or the usual white.

"Such a *fine* ship, sir!" Captain Machias Wilder off the *Bantam*, Kershaw's other supper guest, exclaimed for at least the tenth time in as many minutes on their abbreviated tour of the *Hancock*, as he looked over the sumptuous decor of the great-cabins. "Aye, ye're fortunate, sir, t'be appointed into her."

"You are, indeed, Captain Kershaw," Lewrie agreed, keeping professional appreciation—nigh awe!—to a minimum.

"Just goes t'show what American know-how can do, Cap'um Lewrie," Wilder boasted as a cabin servant took their hats and swords. "I pity the French frigate that tries t'cross hawse with her."

Wilder, by contrast, was a wizened little fellow dressed in somber black "ditto," a civilian suiting, and eschewed a cocked hat for a narrow-brimmed "thimble" of a thing, much like what Lewrie's Marines of late were issued. Wilder was a Downeaster, a very brisk, older, classic Yankee from Connecticut, with the stereotypical nasal twang and fast speech that the London stages so delighted in twitting.

Unlike most folk, he wore grizzled grey whiskers and—from the way he had pranced about, all but stamping his feet and clapping hands in paroxyms of wonder on their abbreviated tour of the ship—had made Lewrie think of him as a short-haired terrier puppy, like to soil the deck if he got any *more* excited.

"For a poor old man from South Carolina, I s'pose I am lucky at that, Captain Wilder," Kershaw said with a proud and pleased simper. "Sit, gentlemen, sit. We'll have us a pre-prandial, before our supper is ready."

He steered them to some wingback chairs done up in red leather and nailheads, and puttered about at his cherry-wood and brass-trimmed wine cabinet.

Lewrie shot his cuffs, settled the tail of his handsome new cotton dress coat, and crossed his legs at the knee, surreptitiously eying the great-cabins, measuring worth; again, he was impressed. There were good figured carpets on the deck, atop a painted canvas covering of a solid colour. Despite the artillery bowsed to the ports, it was an elegant place, agleam with wax on the overhead deck beams and wainscotting. The furniture was mostly cherry or oddly pale washed oak, and was awash in brass, coin-silver, or gilded fittings. On one bulkhead in the dining-coach was a portrait of the ship's namesake, the Hancock of Revolutionary patriot fame. Lewrie dimly recalled that he had done, or said, something in the *large* way, but the circumstance escaped him.

This Kershaw was obviously not so poor as he bemoaned, he decided. This was the baronial suite of a rich shipowner or merchant trader.

"In honour of our guest, Captain Wilder, we'll partake of a good Englishman's favourite claret," Kershaw announced, turning back to them with a decanter in one hand and three stemmed glasses nested together in the other. He did the honours of pouring them all a brimming glass.

Wilder went along, though a little irked that stronger spirits such as corn-whiskey or neat rum were not served.

"To your rescuer, Captain Lewrie," Kershaw proposed.

"Cap'um Lewrie!" Wilder enthused, before tossing his wine back in one neat slug. Lewrie hoped, for his sake, that it would be a short night!

"Captain Wilder is right, ya know, Captain Lewrie," Kershaw said as he topped them up once more. "I *was* fortunate in getting orders to *Hancock*. All our major seaports raised subscription money to build or buy suitable ships for this French fracas. Had I depended on waiting for the Charleston, Georgetown, or Beaufort ships t'be built, I'd still be running up and down the banks of the Ashley or the Cooper. Like the joke that's told back home . . . 'bout the old boy who's flat-broke. If Indiamen went for a shilling, he'd *still* be running up and down the bank cryin', 'why ain't that cheap'!"

"Man of your reputation, though, Cap'um Kershaw," Wilder scoffed, "t'be left on the beach when the United States needs ev'ry experienced man o' war man, why . . ."

"It helps that most of the really experienced men were of age in the Revolution," Kershaw chuckled, "Too old now to strap back on the harness. I was only a midshipman in '78. Only served in our old Continental Navy 'til '80, and then resigned my commission to be first mate aboard a privateer."

"That would have paid better, for certain," Lewrie said after a sip of his wine. Kershaw's claret was of a piece with Jean-Pierre's wines at Port-Au-Prince . . . hellish-good! "And more exciting, too."

"Made my fortune by '83, true, sir!" Kershaw replied, booming for a moment with a burst of laughter. "Your Royal Navy tied us up in knots. Fifty ships in the old Navy, and I doubt more than three were in our hands, in any shape to sail, by the end of the war. Burned or took, or blockaded the rest so long, they rotted at their moorings. In our ports, or in France. Privateers, though . . . we could *always* get to sea. And have a high old time of it."

"Always find hands, when no one'd go aboard a ship o' war."

"Quite true, too, Captain Wilder," Kershaw allowed.

"Diff'rent now, I take it?" Lewrie asked. "Now that your nation is all but at war with France?"

"Can't beat 'em off with a stick, sir," Kershaw boasted. "Down below New Hampsire, of course. Our Southern states are a *bit* more hot for it than others. Like some of your neighbours, Captain Wilder?"

"It's our ships the French are takin' . . . like mine a few days ago, Captain Kershaw," Wilder grumbled, squirming a bit in his chair as if mildly stung or twitted. "It's our trade and livelihood they're harmin'. We're all in it together, North and South, the coasts and the over-mountain folk."

"Most of our skilled officers come from above Virginia, do you see, Captain Lewrie," Kershaw explained, "though Georgia and the Carolinas have thriving ports and build a fair number of good ships. That far from the centre of power, though . . . this new swamp they bought up on the sly, then turned into our new capital, what they've named Washington City? Oh, a *power* of money made on that transaction, by people in government who knew about it beforehand, or had a hand in enacting the placement! We poor Southerners feel a bit . . . overlooked."

"Worse, when the capital was in New York or Philadelphia," the terrier-like Capt. Wilder all but bristled. "Even further away. And wasn't it a whole pack o' Marylanders and Virginians who profited from it?" he slyly asked, laughing to prove that he meant nothing by it, all of which mystified Lewrie. It sounded like a visit to a country house for a weekend, and gossip about neighbours one had never laid eyes on, or a family spat only slightly alluded to before strangers.

Damme, do they dislike each other that much? he had to ask himself, though; *North against South, Middle against both, backwoods versus the Low Country interests? And is that exploitable, should we be at war with 'em in future? Their states don't sound that 'united'!*

"Never saw much of your part of the Americas, Captain Wilder," Lewrie assayed. "Sandy Hook a time or two, perhaps a stroll ashore in New York. I'm more familiar with Savannah and Charleston. In fact, my wife is from the Cape Fear country."

"Well I never!" Captain Kershaw boomed out, which prompted one of those pleasant interludes wherein family names and places were exchanged, a sport in which this Captain Kershaw took particular delight. He had dealings with some Chiswicks who still were seated around Wilmington, and surely they were Caroline's kinfolk!

By then, Kershaw's steward appeared and announced that supper was ready, so they repaired to the dining-coach and sat down to a fine meal of fresh turtle soup, a roast chicken pan-fried in corn meal, grilled turtle steaks, and air-dryed "leather-britches" pod beans for a remove, washed down with a decent hock or a Bordeaux.

Kershaw apologised for the lack of a fish course, but there was little chance of catching anything fresh, with his frigate bowling along at twelve knots or better most of the time. The catch would have been jerked to flinders by the time they got it on deck!

"Caught us a shark, t'other day," Wilder hooted. "Didn't mean to, really. Hopin' for sea bass, dolphin, or snapper, but a shark makes *good* chops. My first mate calls it 'sweet revenge,' ha ha! And d'ye know, the very first thing those French sonsabitches did once we struck, was turn up their noses and heave it overside!"

"Perhaps they had no *crème fraîche* in which to poach it, Captain Wilder," Lewrie snickered. "B'sides, the French may boast of being a maritime nation, but they aren't all that bold at sea. Maybe they thought the shark had dined on their poor, sunken cousins!"

"Way they go after poor, helpless merchantmen, maybe they are *kin* t'sharks, but too proud and arrogant t'turn cannibal!" Wilder rejoined quickly, raising his glass to clink against Lewrie's.

"You've seen no French warships, as yet, Captain Lewrie?" his host enquired.

"No, sir. My advisories tell me that there are very few true warships about," Lewrie answered, "though hundreds of privateers. I wonder, sir . . . perhaps we might break the old strictures, and share some, uhm . . . 'shop-talk?' After all, I'll be cruising north of Saint Domingue, and I gather that your frigate will be going south after we part?"

"That's so, sir . . . and an excellent idea." Kershaw agreed.

"Keepin' a close eye on me for the rest o' my voyage?" Captain Wilder hoped aloud.

"You may count on my support, sir," Kershaw assured him,

"I wonder, sir . . ." Lewrie said, putting down his glass. "Do you have any qualms about acting in concert, you and I, should we meet with a French warship?"

"I, uhm . . ." Kershaw waffled. "We are ordered to cooperate, in *certain* circumstances. America is not *officially* at war with France, not yet. I am not even certain that outright war is desirable. If a change in their policy towards neutral shipping—returning to the *status quo ante,* without boarding and demanding manifests and muster rolls—were to result from a show of determination, with the *threat* of force to make them change their minds, well . . ." He trailed off and waved one hand in a flaccid, "iffy" gesture, before busying his hands with a wine decanter.

"But, do you encounter one of their privateers, in the act of pillaging an American merchant vessel, a merchantman sailing alone as a prize," Lewrie pressed, irked by the man's sudden diffidence, "or if you met one of their privateers or warships in these waters, alone . . . ?"

"Then I would have a free hand to engage at all hazards, and I would, at once, sir," Kershaw told him, a bit more formally and stiffly than moments before. "But before we assemble a proper squadron in the Caribbean, my *initial* orders are to cruise, to escort convoys down as far as Dominica or Antigua . . . make a show of force off Guadeloupe and the other French isles, then pick up a convoy and escort them back as far as the Bahamas before returning to Boston."

"Yet," Lewrie said with a faint frown, steepling his fingers to his lips, "were we to be 'in sight' of each other, and I, unhindered by any strictures, engage a French National ship . . . would that allow you to co-operate in her taking? Would that be one of your 'certain' circumstances, Captain Kershaw?"

"None but a poltroon would reject a chance for action, Captain Lewrie," Kershaw intoned, making Lewrie suspect that he had in some way stung Kershaw "below" his personal sense of honour. "I doubt I'm al-lowed to *cruise* in concert with you. We may both blockade Guadeloupe, for one instance . . . but you run yours, and I would run mine. Our areas *may* overlap at times, but that would be all, since my country is not officially allied with yours. But . . . does the chance of a fight arise, then that's a different story. In that instance, I can see no limits on my coming to your aid . . . or, conversely, refuse any aid you render, should you heave up over the horizon and find my ship yardarm-to-yardarm with *Monsieur.*"

Lewrie could but nod at that cautious circumlocution, and reach for his wineglass to bury his nose in it and slurp, thinking it over.

"Now, that's not to say that when we have more ships down here, a proper squadron, my orders won't get expanded to closer cooperation," Kershaw continued, hemming and trimming as if speaking for himself and not his government this time. "Or, with enough ships, we might wish to go it alone. Either way, I doubt the French will back down and let our ships alone, without they get their noses bloody first. There is always a chance your frigate and mine could fight side-by-side . . ."

"Against the French, pray God," Lewrie chuckled. "After seeing her, I wouldn't wish to test my metal against the weight of yours."

Kershaw and Wilder both chuckled along with him, thankful for a jest to lighten the mood.

"Then you'll be thankful t'see the good ol' *John Hancock* stand up alongside ye," Captain Wilder boasted. "She'll save your bacon *and* beat the French so hard, they'll wet their britches at mention of her name! Ol' John'll write somethin' *else* large, ha ha!"

Oh, so that's what Hancock did! Lewrie suddenly recalled; *wrote his name on their Declaration of Independence so bloody big and bold.*

"Though a ship so well armed and well manned may never fear for her honour against the Frogs, sir," Lewrie offered, extending his hand across the table to Kershaw. "Do we meet again in such a circumstance, you may count on me to wade in and help you."

Kershaw pondered that but for a moment before reaching out, as well, and seizing hands with Lewrie, to pump away enthusiastically in agreement. "*Hancock* and I shall back you, as well, Captain Lewrie . . . any British ship that we encounter in need of assistance! And damn any fool in Washington City who'd dare say I exceeded my brief!"

"Then, gentlemen, a toast," Lewrie proposed, once he had gotten his hand back in usable condition. "To the United States Navy!"

"Huzzah!" Captain Wilder cheered, hurriedly pouring for all.

"Good supper, sir?" Aspinall asked, once Lewrie was back aboard *Proteus* and flinging hat and shoes to the wide in his great-cabins.

"Passin' fair," Lewrie told him with a grin, "though I'd admire a brandy. The Yankees didn't much run to it, it bein' French, and all. Prob'ly swore off for the duration outta patriotism. And find a place for this, would you?"

Aspinall took the large gallon stone crock of corn-whiskey and set it inside the wine cabinet, down at the bottom where it would not tip or overweight an upper shelf.

"A monstrous frigate, I tell you . . . hellish-powerful. Built as stout as a Norman castle, back home," Lewrie sleepily enthused.

And what wouldn't I give t'have a ship like her someday? he asked himself as he unclipped his hanger and stood it in the arms rack near his desk in the day-cabin. *Though I'd change some things.*

Hancock was massive, as solid as any towering ship of the line, and she did mount 24-pounders on her lower gun-deck, as he had suspected, with an odd mix of 18-pounders and 12-pounders on her upper decks. He put that down to the uncertain supply available in the States' seaports, arsenals, or yards when the war came, and the "iffy" condition of American foundries and their reliability at producing ordnance in the required numbers . . . or ordnance of decent quality.

With a patriotic smirk of his own, he recalled how many of the artillery pieces he'd seen on his brief tour had borne stamps or proof marks from British manufacturers! Though not officially allied, those Yankee Doodles were not averse to buying arms from their late enemies.

What had amazed him even more was the first sight of her upper deck, once he had been piped aboard. It was built *flush,* what junior American officers had boastfully termed the "spar deck," and that deck was simply *stiff* with guns!

His own frigate, and every Royal Navy warship he had ever seen, had open "waists" 'twixt the raised quarterdecks and forecastles, with narrow gangways meant only for sail-tending and Marine musketry, spanned by cross-beams between them, fit only for binding the ship's sides together, and as a place to rest ship's boats, as boat-tier beams.

The Americans, though, had widened those gangways, made hatches for companionways smaller, and reduced the size of the "waist" open to the sky to long and narrow openings much like a merchant vessel's cargo hatches; and stiffened that "spar deck" with thicker cross-deck beams, and longitudinal timbers, supported by stout carline posts, until that deck could bear heavy artillery, as well.

Too damn' much artillery, Lewrie silently groused, stifling one more weary yawn; *everything but carronades, and thank God we don't sell 'em those!*

Captain Kershaw had seemed very proud of the fact that *Hancock,* while officially "rated" a forty-four gun frigate, bore nearly fifty-eight guns of various calibers and weights; right down to 9-pounders on the quarterdeck! At that boast, Lewrie could have almost sworn he heard *Hancock* groan like Atlas under the burden. At first glance, the Sailing Master's suspicion that the frigate would "hog" at both ends, and eventually break her back, seemed an accurate premonition. But . . .

Down below, Lewrie had espied the massive knees, futtocks, and beams that made up her hull, as thick as anything aboard a First Rate flagship, and the other beams, those oddly *angled* timbers that curved up from below and continued upwards past the overhead deck, like some diagonal strapping inside a well-made wicker basket. Could *they* stiffen her enough to make her as rigid as an iron cauldron, a ship immune to the eternal flexings and groanings, as stresses made her abrade and weaken herself with every pitch, roll, or toss?

Despite being more than sated with supper and all that wine, he felt driven to sketch his impressions that moment, before they faded from his mind. If the Royal Navy could attempt some construction along similar lines, with those diagonal thingamajigs . . . !

He sat down at his desk and fumbled open a drawer for paper and pencils, suddenly aware that his brandy was sitting on it, with Toulon lurking over it, one curious paw raised and his nose at the edge, mouth hanging open the way it did when he found a new scent.

"Mine!" Lewrie hissed, dragging it to him. He took a sip, then stood briefly to strip off his coat before beginning to draw. Toulon was intrigued by that, too, following the pencil end wide-eyed.

Happy the officer who brought Admiralty an innovation, Lewrie told himself. Happy, too, the officer who provided a hint that Americans were divided by sectional differences, that their burgeoning new Navy was rent by jealousies 'twixt the rich maritime states closer to the seat of

power and interest, and the rest who dwelled too far away to north or
south. Even as he drew, a part of his mind was composing a report that
he would pen in the morning . . . once his head cleared.

They have an elite, an aristocracy just like us, Lewrie thought; *New
York, Boston, and Philadelphia . . . all of 'em related and schooled together.
Yale and Harvard, Wilder mentioned, just like our Cambridge or Oxford.
Fine republicans they are . . . what a sham!*

"Oh dear Lord, sir," Aspinall softly gasped.

"What?" Lewrie snapped, impatient to be interrupted. He looked up
to see Aspinall staring at him, as wide-eyed as Toulon. "Come down
with the pox, have I? What is it, man?"

"Yer shirt an' waistcoat, sir," Aspinall mournfully told him. "That
new cotton dress coat o' yours has bled blue all over 'em."

"What?" Lewrie yelped, jumping to his feet and trying to crane
around his own body, arms raised, to see how much damage had been
done. He pawed at his sides, trying to drag his shirt 'round to the front.
He quickly undid the buttons of his waistcoat and stripped it off to hold
it up to the light.

"Well, damme!"

The thin white satin back of the waistcoat was *very* blue, and so were
the armholes, shading outwards almost in a ripple pattern, like a trout-
splash down the sides to a paler sky-blue! Even the front of the garment,
originally pristine bleached white #8 sailcloth, was now faintly stained
where his coat had overlain it.

"Shirt's worse, sir," Aspinall meekly informed him.

Kershaw's great-cabins had been close, airless and humid, without
canvas ventilation scoops; even the overhead skylights in the coach-top
had been closed. Obviously, Kershaw, from already muggish Charleston,
was *used* to perspiration; perhaps even had a Froggish fear of night airs
and their miasmas . . . especially in the tropics, since Yellow Jack and
malaria were no strangers to the Carolinas.

"Well . . ." Lewrie said at last, lowering the garment in defeat. "It
seemed like a good idea. In broadcloth wool, I'd have turned to soggy
gruel hours ago. Live and learn, I s'pose. Try and wash 'em, but . . .
damme." Lewrie began to strip off his shirt, too.

"I'll give it a go, sir, but I ain't promisin' much." Aspinall said.

"Uhm . . . yer breeches're in the same shape, sir."

"Still have white *stockings*, do I?" Lewrie asked, feeling the need to laugh the tiniest beaten snort of sour amusement. It was that or scream to high heaven!

"I'll fetch yer nightshirt, sir."

"And a basin of water, Aspinall. Before I show up on deck tomorrow, as blue as an old Druid."

"Aye, sir . . . lots o' soap, too."

Once coolly bathed and clad in his thin nightshirt, Lewrie bent once more to his drawing, adding curved diagonal lines atop the crosshatchings of a ship's skeleton, thinking that even if the matter of his cotton uniform coat hadn't exactly worked out, the evening hadn't been a total loss. He had learned more than he had expected, had elicited *some* sort of promise of cooperation from a Yankee captain that could in future apply to the others as they assembled a squadron.

He eyed the small wash-leather purse of coins that *Bantam*'s captain had given him; £100 in various English, French, Spanish, and Dutch *specie* that, so far, took the place of a trustworthy United States currency.

It was what some—should they ever come to know of it, and he would be damned if they did!—might call a bribe. Taking *Bantam* and restoring her to her owner would involve reams of paperwork at the nearest Prize Court, at Kingston; placing a value on ship, fittings, cargo, and such to determine *Proteus*'s official reward, with poor Wilder paying court fees and demurrages for swinging at anchor for weeks in that port, 'til the matter was adjudicated and his ship returned to him.

Easier all 'round, really, for Lewrie to write his report, saying that in the spirit of "cooperation" he had surrendered precedence and possession to the arriving American frigate.

They had, after all, the value of *L'Oiseau* to reckon with, with eight great-guns and over one hundred privateers brought to book, with "head money" for each, along with the schooner's worth as a tender to a larger ship; why, with any luck, they'd buy her in, perhaps even let *Proteus* claim her as a tender, and if they did . . . !

Lewrie leaned back from his artwork with a satisfied smile, in full "scheme." With *L'Oiseau,* he could run the same subterfuge he had in the Mediterranean when captain of *Jester,* with a captured lugger on the Genoese and Savoian coasts; as an "innocent" harbour raider to cut out merchantmen who thought themselves safe in a friendly port, or as a tempting piece of "cut bait" trolled before a privateersmen, flying a French Tricolour flag, looking for "rescue" from those horrible English "Bloodies"!

He hefted the coin purse, calculating in his head; two-eighths of £100 was £25, a captain's share of the bribe. Who knows, it might just cover the cost of the ruin of his wardrobe!

CHAPTER NINETEEN

$\mathcal{B}$y noon of the next day, *Hancock* and *Bantam* were out of sight in the South, and *L'Oiseau* was hull-under on her way to Port-Au-Prince to report her capture . . . and dump her hundred-odd prisoners on somebody else. And with any luck at all, Lewrie imagined that HMS *Halifax* and her irascible Captain Blaylock would become their gaolers, now that she was stripped of even more guns and would have bags of room below. It was piquant to picture Blaylock's phyz turning purple at that news . . . and, Lewrie further surmised, that Captain Nicely, who already despised Blaylock worse than cold, boiled mutton, would be more than happy for a chance to "slip him a bit of the dirty" one more time. And perhaps even think fondly of the officer who'd made it possible! Again, with any luck, Proteus might have *L'Oiseau* back as her "unofficial" tender within the week; and then they could really hit their stride!

The winds had backed a full point from Nor'eastly to Nor'east-by-East, as well. *Proteus* had loafed Sou'easterly after their meeting with *Hancock* during the night, closer to Cape St. Nicholas, so a "beat" close-hauled to the North-by-West could take them up to Matthew Town at the western tip of Great Inagua, where *Proteus* could once more keep an eye on both the Windward Passage and the Old Bahama Passage, before tacking and heading Sou'east for Tortuga. Then she could slowly zig-zag her way Easterly between Turk's Island and Saint Domingue towards the tempting Mouchoir and Silver Bank passages, where arriving French merchantmen and privateers *must* appear, sooner or later.

"Mister Langlie, we'll stand in as close as we may to the Cape of Saint Nicholas before tacking," Lewrie announced. "Claw us out all the ground you can to weather, before we come about to North-by-West."

"Aye aye, sir."

"Ah, now that is Monte Cristi, sir," Mr. Winwood pointed out as he fiddled with his charts at the binnacle cabinet, "bearing, uhm . . . Sou'west-by-West. And to the East'rd . . ."

"Cape Isabella," Lewrie supplied, "which now bears, ah . . . Sou'east-by-East, or thereabouts. I make it . . . eleven miles, if the chart is correct as to its height." He lowered his sextant and fiddled with it for a moment.

"Then we are here, sir . . . nine miles offshore of Spanish Santo Domingo, 'twixt Monte Cristi and Cabo Isabella," Winwood opined. "And the depths shown are still abyssal. First *real* soundings with a deep-sea lead don't begin 'til we're within the three-mile limit, Captain."

"Three miles, hmm," Lewrie muttered. "Mister Wyman, we'll haul our wind and stand due South, for a piece . . .'til Mister Winwood says we're near 'soundings.' After that, we will wear and reduce sail, to scud back along the coast towards Cape Francois and see what's stirring."

"Aye aye, sir," Wyman said, reaching for a speaking-trumpet with which to relay orders to the watch.

"And let's hope *something* is out of harbour, Mister Winwood."

"Indeed, sir."

Lewrie's familiar old stomping grounds about the Turks Islands had been nearly empty of all but local fishing boats and small traders, the Caicos, Turk's, Mouchoir, and Silver Bank passages glittering but barren, and conversations with local boats had revealed that it was a rare day when they'd seen any sail at all. Such stops had allowed the Purser, Mr. Coote, to purchase a bonanza of fresh fish and sea turtles, now trussed with their flippers threaded together, and all for a song, but useful intelligence was nil.

"Once we take a good, long look into Cape Francois, we'll head back to the Old Bahama Passage," Lewrie decided aloud. "Yankee merchantmen'll be floodin' South this time of year, and most-like that will be where the Frog privateers'll be thickest, too. So many of 'em tradin' at

Havana, and other Spanish Cuban ports . . . before heading further South to the Leewards, ey, Mister Winwood?"

"Always a wrench, to cede the windward station, sir, but in the circumstances . . ." the Sailing Master said with a noncommittal shrug, as he carefully, almost lovingly, stowed away his own precious sextant in its velvet-lined rosewood box.

"Shortest distance, we might've been better off in the Gulf of Gonave, if they're comin' from Havana," Lewrie griped, "most-like sailing right past us. Or passing *far* to the East'rd of the Bahamas and Puerto Rico."

"Well, sir, there's great risk in that," Winwood replied, digging out another chart and spreading it on the traverse board. "There are reefs and shoals aplenty near Puerto Rico, and the Danish Virgins, and our own. Anegada and Virgin Gorda are infamous wrecking grounds, and the north shore of Saint Thomas? A rocky maze, sir!"

Mr. Winwood used a closed divider as a pointer as he indicated the dangers, sketching courses from America.

"Do they leave New York, Boston, or Philadelphia, the Chesapeake, or even the Carolinas or Georgia, their best course would be *very* far Easterly, out to beyond Bermuda, before taking a slant across, abeam the Nor'east Trades, with hopes to fetch Anguilla or Saint Martin just a touch alee of them, and close to all those lee-side harbours."

"Which'd put them in our Antigua squadron's bailiwick, then," Lewrie said, nodding, "and we'd never see 'em . . .'til on their way back home, through *these* waters."

"Aye, sir."

"But they can't *all* sail that far East and South first. There must be *some* who trade closer to home," Lewrie griped. "Witness those Yankee men o' war and Treasury cutters convoying merchantmen here. Or are you saying we've been handed a bill of goods, Mister Winwood?"

Winwood winced and sucked his teeth; it was a cold day in Hades when he ventured an opinion outside his own expertise.

"It might *not* have been the most productive area to patrol, sir. How else may one explain why, with over seventy or eighty men o' war on the West Indies Station, we've been so unsuccessful in eliminating the many French privateers?"

"Sloth and indolence," Lewrie scoffed, with a sour laugh. "So little profit in it, such hard work . . . when it's more exciting, more profitable, to hunt enemy merchant ships and warships! Prowling about for such— even if it's fruitless—holds the greater honour, and a chance t'get your name in the papers back home. Make a great show, with all the huffing and puffing? 'By God, we almost had 'em but for a slant o' wind, but we'll do better next time, wot?' Surely you know their sort by now, Mister Winwood."

"Indeed, sir," Winwood said in response, very even and flat.

And by God, was he lookin' at me *cutty-eyed when he said that?* Lewrie thought, trying to recall six months of bombast or excuses.

"Sail ho!"

Lewrie's head snapped upward to the mainmast lookout's perch.

"Where away?"

"Four points orf th' starb'd bows!" the spry young topman wailed back. "Three . . . *four* sail! They'm sloops and luggers, there!"

"And we're inshore of them!" Lewrie exulted. "Where bound?" he shouted aloft through cupped hands.

"Standin' North, sir!"

"North, hmmm . . ." Lewrie mused, riffling through the charts for one of Saint Domingue and Santo Domingo. "Fishing boats, perhaps. Out of a French or Spanish port. Either sort, they're fair game."

He traced the reciprocal course back to the coast, but found no point of origin, other than a few coves or inlets, and those were two-a-penny. He glanced at the commissioning pendant high aloft, which was flowing to the wind, now steady out of the Nor'east once more.

"A point higher than we could manage, goin' close-hauled. That fits," he muttered. "Now, Mister Winwood. Were you wishin' to coast to the East, you'd have to zig-zag, wouldn't you?"

"Aye, sir. A short board along the coast, but a long one, out to sea, to make *any* ground to weather," Winwood agreed. "Even with a sloop or lugger rig, it would be an all-day chore to make twenty miles to the good."

"Sooner, sooner or later, they'll have to come about onto larboard tack and head Sou'east, would they not? Right into our range, so to speak, sir?" Lewrie snickered.

"Aye, sir . . . do they not see us first."

"And if they do, their best hope'd be to come about Sou'west, and run back into whichever little harbour or inlet they left," Lewrie crowed. "And . . . we're *still* inshore of 'em, and can run 'em down; do they put about this instant!"

Lewrie went to the larboard bulwarks and looked out at the land, now that *Proteus* was within three miles or so of it and scudding along almost due West. Fingers drumming on the cap-rails, thinking, evaluating. . . . With a jump, he was at the binnacle rack and snatching a glass, then up into the starboard mizen shrouds, clambering aloft, up past the cat-harpings and onto the futtock shrouds, dangling dangerously for a second or two before gaining the mizen top platform, where he felt the need to pant for a bit before scrambling onto the stays and rat-lines to the upper masts and cross-trees above the mizen tops'l.

Stupid, stupid, stupid, he chid himself; *ya impatient sod! That left arm still don't feel right. Must've hurt it worse than I thought at Camperdown. Send a midshipman, next time, or Wyman. He's a well fed look about him, lately.*

Once he'd levelled his glass, there they were. Two two-masted luggers, and a brace of single-masted local sloops or cutters, flying large jibs forrud, and all four of them fairly big boats, perhaps over forty or fifty feet, overall. And crammed with people!

Incredibly tiny dark exclamation points were crammed shoulder-to-shoulder over there, he realised, braced up against their weather rails—perhaps as human "ballast" to keep them sailing flatter on their bottoms, making them faster.

"Deck, there! They'm hull-up, now! Four points orf th' starb'd bows!" the lookout atop the mainmast, forward of his perch, cried.

"Deck, there!" Lewrie shouted down. "Cast of the log! Now!"

Those luggers and sloops might just be about forty feet or so in length; Lewrie compromised at fourty-five feet. Their masts should be a third again longer, did they follow Caribbean custom of tall masts to catch more wind in larger sails, as opposed to European custom using shorter masts with longer booms, and the centres of effort of the sails lower to the deck. With sixty-foot masts, he could estimate that they were at least four miles out to sea. Did they turn and run before the wind, he guessed that they could make five or six knots, with the sail they already flew.

"Captain, sir!" Midshipman Elwes squeaked. "We make nine knots!"

"Thankee, Mister Elwes! Good lad! Mister Wyman . . . hands aloft and set the fore t'gallant, the main t'gallant stays'l, the middle stays'l, and main topmast stays'l! Smartly, now!"

"Aye aye, sir! Smartly t'will be!"

He looked aloft to the commissioning pendant once more. It was a decent wind this morning, a dependable, clear day Tradewind. With a bit more sail aloft, *Proteus* could make ten or eleven knots with it on their starboard quarters . . . as it now stood. Sailing almost due West, they'd intersect those small craft within the hour!

Now, t'get my puckered arse down from here, he told himself in a silent grimace. Clambering down to the lubber's hole was not manly or nautical, and after those uneasy twinges in his left arm, he didn't quite trust himself on the shrouds and rat-lines. He slung his glass and took hold of a standing backstay, using his right hand and leg to swing out and wrap himself around it, to slide-clamber hand-over-hand to the deck, the greasy, slushed stay grating 'twixt his knees, scissored calves, and along his groin.

With a thump against the bulwarks that he felt through the soles of his shoes, he reached the deck and jumped down to the quarterdeck, with an evident *whoosh* of relief, flexing his singed fingers despite a career of callouses.

"Damme," he sighed, looking at his breeches and shirt, now greasy with the skimmed fat from the steep-tubs used to lubricate the rigging to keep it supple, and the tar used to keep it waterproof. "At least they're the pale blue'uns. No great loss."

No amount of scrubbing could improve that condition, as Aspinall had proved the last few days, whenever they had caught some rainwater from the brief daily squalls. They were now hopeless.

"Perhaps sky-blue will become fashionable, sir," wee Midshipman Grace tittered; being the youngest, he was the only one who'd dare.

"You're no bigger than *bait*, Mister Grace," Lewrie told him with mock severity, "and I dearly love fresh fish. I'd keep that in *mind*, were

I you, younker," making the other midshipmen snigger.

He reached out and tipped Grace's cocked hat over his eyes, to prove that he wasn't upset, then stalked over to the helm to stow his telescope.

"Mister Wyman, once you've everything 'Bristol fashion' I wish the ship beat to Quarters."

"Aye aye, sir."

"Whoever yon bastards are, we'll have them for dinner."

"Deck, there! Puttin' about! Haulin' 'eir wind, and wearin'!"

"Ah, Mister Langlie," Lewrie said quite gaily, as the First Officer came to the quarterdeck, noting that Langlie already had his pair of single-barrel pistols hung on his belt, along with his smallsword. "I see you've come full-dressed for the ball. Good. The first dance is just begun."

After a quick look about, Langlie got a sly look on his face as he said, "From the look and sound of it, Captain, sir, I'd say they've gone past the quadrilles, right to the *galop* and country dances. Or rather . . . off to the races?"

"Captain, sir . . . Mister Langlie, sir," Lieutenant Wyman reported. "I am ready to call for Quarters."

"I'll take the deck, Mister Wyman," Langlie asserted his right.

"I yield with pleasure, sir," Wyman grinned back, with delight of the chase and the hunt in his eyes.

"Mister Sevier to stand as acting lieutenant in lieu of Mister Catterall, sir?" Langlie asked. "He can oversee the forecastle guns."

"Very good, Mister Langlie. And call on Desmond and his lads to give us a tune, once we're at Quarters. Something lively. I will be below, getting presentable . . . and armed."

"Dear Lord, sir, but I suspect that'un was 'The Battle of Aughrim,' " Lt. Langlie, who had a good ear for music, exclaimed. "An old fight from back in King William's days. Just *like* our Irish, to cock a snook at us."

"Lively, though, you must admit," Lewrie replied, beating one hand along in time as Desmond, the ship's fiddler, a Marine drummer, and a brace of fifers held forth in the middle of the waist.

"The Pipe on the Hob," "The Bride's Favourite," and old double jigs were mixed with "The Derry Hornpipe" and "Fisher's Hornpipe" as music for sailing into battle, followed by "Jenny's Wedding" and "Lord MacDonald," a pair of reels. Now, within a mile of the sloops and luggers, Desmond and the band were well into a lively, merry tune named "Planxty Browne," with the fiddler and fifers prancing the deck in impromptu dancing.

"I prefer hornpipes," Langlie groused, "Jigs, reels, and all are too . . . toodly. All over the shop, and too many flutt'ry notes."

"Well, so was Bach, and that little Mozart fellow," Lewrie said with a chuckle. "Might've killed him, in fact. Too many notes in his head, and 'Pop!' Hmmm . . . d'ye think we're in good range, sir?"

"I do, indeed, Captain," Langlie soberly agreed.

"Then please run out the starboard battery and give them a try, Mister Langlie," Lewrie bade, turning formal.

"Aye aye, sir. Mister Wyman! Make ready! Thank you for the music lads, but now belay! Run out the starboard battery!"

Creaks and groans, squeals and screeches sounded as tackle was run through wooden blocks, as wood trucks and axles turned under gun-carriages as they were trundled up to butt against the port-sills, and ports were opened. Tacklemen stood aside, overhauling their run-out, as gun-captains fussed at elevating quoins, ordering crow-levers for a shift in point of aim. The train-tackles were tautened, and breeching ropes adjusted so the guns would recoil smoothly, without a kink that would jerk their deadly weight aside and maim their minders. One at a time, gun-captains put up a fist to show readiness, and their Number Twos leaned away from their pieces, holding the trigger lines that led to the flintlock strikers over the touch-holes, taut and cocked.

"On the up-roll . . . fire!"

A second's pause as *Proteus* surfed and wallowed off the winds, slowly rocking upright and hanging still for a moment or two, her deck level to the horizon . . . then her 12-pounders erupted in ear-ringing power, almost as one! Great thunderclaps, huge jetting clouds of hot gases and smoke, reeking of rotten eggs and coal, as the guns lurched in-board to the limits of their breeching ropes, snubbing with a shock that seemed like to jerk the stout bulwarks apart, and made the frigate shudder as if she'd run aground!

The smoke was quickly whisked away by the Trades, to scud downwind off her larboard bows, to the shore which was now only two miles away, so the officers could spot the fall of shot among those boats.

Another long second's pause, and geysers erupted from the sea, tall and slender feathery plumes that hung in the sky like suddenly frozen icicles, that only slowly collapsed downward upon themselves in matching circles of frothing spume, drenching the targets like a torrential summer squall, and making them heel and rock, their winged-out sails sluiced and drowned with seawater.

"Damn' good shooting," Lewrie commented. "Now, serve 'em another," he ordered, raising his telescope.

"Sir?" Mr. Winwood whispered from his right side. "Sir, we are getting rather close inshore, and we *do* have them abeam. Perhaps one point abaft of abeam."

"You wish to harden up and stand out from the shore?" Lewrie asked, the glass still to his eye.

"I would, sir. The best we have are century-old Spanish charts."

"Mister Langlie, a point to windward," Lewrie called. "And put some spare hands in the larboard fore-chains to sound with the lead."

"Aye, sir."

"As you bear . . . on the up-roll . . . fire!"

Under a mile now, Lt. Wyman was letting gun-captains aim for themselves, picking their own targets. *Proteus* shuddered and jerked, anew, as the 12-pounders exploded in a stutter that ran from her bow to her stern. Wyman paced the waist of the ship between the starboard and the idle larboard batteries, betwen the foremast and main, urging gun-captains and more experienced senior quarter-gunners for a steady pace to keep the guns firing two rounds every three minutes.

"Hit!" Lt. Devereux the Marine officer cried from among his men on the starboard gangway above the guns. "Well shot, you lads! You've hammered one of the luggers, and shot a mast clean away!"

The gun crews cheered, even as they tugged and hauled, even as ship's boys scampered along the deck with their leather cases holding sewn powder cartridges from the risk of premature explosion, even as barrels were swabbed out by the rammer men, as Number Twos held leather thumb-stalls over the touch-holes to prevent backblast from the lingering shards of cartridge bags and smouldering powder embers.

Cartridges were rammed down, roundshot was thumped firm against the charges, as vent-pricks were inserted into the touch-holes, piercing the bags to spill powder, so the jets of fire from the flintlock strikers and the priming powder in their pans could ignite the charges in the blink of an eye when the trigger lanyards were jerked.

Up the deck to the ports the guns were rolled one more time, as *Proteus* swung her bows seaward one point, not only to flee the risk of hidden rocks and shoals, but to close the range on the small craft and cut them off from running any longer to the Sou'west. With the wind more on the starboard beam, it was harder to run the guns out, but the fire-blackened muzzles jutted through the ports and began to wave and elevate in small jerks, 'til the gun-captains were satisfied.

"As you bear . . . on the up-roll . . . fire!"

The damaged lugger was struck again, a heavy ball smashing into her larboard side and spilling people into the sea. A one-masted sloop in the lead of their gaggle was hit near her sternquarters and jerked to the impact, rolling half on her starboard beam-ends before rocking slowly upright, but beginning to settle as she started to fill, stern down but still sailing, like a wounded goose.

"Too good to last, sir . . . the other two are breaking free from their partners," Lt. Langlie pointed out, his arm outstretched to the right and a bit aft. "Ducking astern of us."

Lewrie took a long look at the damaged sloop, and found it low in the water, aft, its transom almost level with the sea. It wouldn't last long, in his estimation; nor would the crippled lugger whose lone surviving foremast could not drag her to freedom fast enough.

"Two points more a'weather, Mister Langlie, and engage the two off the starboard quarters," Lewrie decided. "Those two'll be there, when we've dealt with these. Damme! Right plucky of 'em, to tack and cross our stern! They'll be within carronade shot in a minute. We'll open with the stern chasers and carronades! Ready, the after-guard!"

"Perhaps there's more fight in the Frogs than we thought, sir," Lt. Langlie commented.

Lewrie raised his telescope once more and eyed the boats that were aiming to beat Sou'easterly and run aground where they might on the Spanish shore of Santo Domingo . . . before *Proteus* could kill them.

"Whatever they are, Mister Langlie, they ain't French," Lewrie said, after he had gotten a closer look at their foe. "They're Black! Ev'ry man jack of 'em, from what I can see."

The surviving sloop and lugger were within four cables as they completed crossing the wind's eye and began to gather speed for their run to safety, and Lewrie could pick out details. The men aboard them were armed, and wore a semblance of uniforms; cocked hats, military or civilian, but all decorated with the red-white-blue cockade of revolutionary French Jacobins . . . white breeches and colourful sashes, into which pistols, swords, or cutlasses were jammed. Some wore shirts and dark blue French uniform coats, or coats with no shirts; some had to make do in waistcoats and no shirts, but with crossbelts and brass breastplates in the middle of their chests. There were a few in full uniforms and plumed hats, wearing officer's swords, and dragoon boots, or breeches without stockings or any footwear. But all bore muskets with their bayonets already affixed.

Closer still, and Lewrie could see kegs of what could only be taken for gunpowder, kegs at which some rebel slave soldiers chopped with hand axes and tomahawks, while others worked at flints and lint to kindle sparks and flames, whilst others held oiled-rag torches to be . . . !

"Damn my eyes, Mister Langlie, I do believe those bastards mean to blow themselves to Kingdom Come, and us with 'em!" he shouted as the two small craft fell off the wind even more and, gathering speed, began to turn toward *Proteus*'s stern quarters . . . attacking the frigate!

"Marines to the quarterdeck, Mister Devereux! Man the swivels and the carronades, smartly now!" Lewrie urged, feeling a bit of panic. "Mister Winwood, a bit more speed t'get clear of 'em. Mister Wyman? A *broadside* would do right nicely, 'bout now!"

"Coming, sir, directly!"

"So's bloody Christmas!" Lewrie muttered under his breath, too fearful of the suicidal slaveys to care about "captainly" behaviour.

"Dem fools got de 'nutmegs,' sah," Cox'n Andrews breathed in awe as he appeared unbidden but welcome at Lewrie's side, with a brace of pistols and Lewrie's trusty Ferguson rifle and its accoutrements. "Dey Law', dey's *laughin*'!"

About two cables' distance now, the small boats surging up to carronade range, and Lewrie could hear a chant that nigh-shriveled his "stones" above the rumble of gun-trucks and the drum of running feet.

"Eh Eh! Heu! Canga, bafio té!
Canga, moune de le! Canga, do ki la!
Canga, li!"

"What the Devil's all that?" Lewrie demanded to know.

"Don' know, sah . . . *Obeah* stuff, maybe," Andrews replied, crossing himself for luck and blanching a touch pale. "Some sorta witchie workin'. Voodoo . . . *voudoun*. Deir Creole tongue."

"On the up-roll . . . *fire!*" Wyman screeched, at long last.

Not a full second after the guns erupted, before the spent gunpowder could even begin to wing alee, there came a huge tongue of yellow flame off the starboard side amid a titanic gust of wind that flung a pea-soup fog of reeking, blue-white smoke at them, stinging hot, and shot through with splinters, chunks, and burning embers! In that stentorian blasting roar, shrieks and screams could be heard. Things went wetly *Plop!* against the deck where they stood!

"Aah . . . that's part of a hand," Lt. Langlie said in a shuddery voice as he recognised the object.

"Get it overside, and let's sink the other one," Lewrie snapped, nauseated by the sight. The smoke of the broadside, and the blast, was clearing very slowly, and the second one still lived . . . somewhere out there.

"There, sir!" Marine Lt. Devereux shouted, pointing at a vague outline. It was the one-masted sloop, rounding up within a cable off *Proteus*'s starboard quarter . . . chasing her!

"Six pounders and swivels, aim aft!" Lewrie shouted, gathering up his rifle. "Marines, put 'em down!"

"Eh! Eh! Heu! Heu! Canga, bafio té!"

"Marines, cock your locks! Level . . . by volley . . . *fire!*"

"Canga, moune de le! Canga, do ki la!"

Lewrie took aim, the action at full cock, and squeezed the trigger of his Ferguson. The butt slammed back into his shoulder with an emphatic reassuring thump. His target, an "officer" in a blue coat over ebony skin and ragged field workers' trousers, clapped both hands to his face as the bullet took him in the left cheek, knocking his ornate cocked hat off as he left his feet and *flew* backwards into the tillerman and some sheet-tenders. The stutter of a volley of Brown Bess muskets followed a second later, and half a dozen Blacks were cut down, their cheering and shouting stopped. Swivel guns mounted in the metal forks atop the taff-rail and after starboard bulwarks barked and yapped, spewing handfuls of grape-shot or .75 caliber musket balls in a deadly hail that chopped down even more. Then the 6-pounders, loaded with roundshot and stands of grape-shot, began to fire, slamming so hard that chunks of hull and bodies were flung skyward, almost burying the sloop's bow in its own wave as it was *bludgeoned* to a stop.

"Canga, li!"

A torch was lowered to an open powder keg, the bearer bleeding from a dozen wounds, but still chanting and screaming at them. Before more musketry could bring him down, he smiled and shoved the fire into the keg—*"Canga, li!"* his dying comrades gleefully urged him!

"Duck!" Lewrie shouted, along with twenty others.

Not one hundred yards astern in *Proteus*'s wake, the sloop went up in a boil of flame-shot smoke, smashing in every transom window and taff-rail lanthorn glass pane. A huge, feathery pillar of water arose, bearing up planks and oars, bits of mast, seared ropes, and gobbets of flesh . . . to patter down amid a foetid shower of seawater!

The people on the quarterdeck got back to their feet, mumbling and working their jaws, tugging at their ears from the assault on eardrums and sinuses. A few even bled from their ears and noses.

Astern, there were now two roiled circles of white spume, with only a few identifiable bits of wreckage to be seen

"Don't s'pose there's much point in looking for survivors, is there, sir," Lieutenant Langlie said; it wasn't a question. He looked stunned.

"No . . . I doubt there is, Mister Langlie," Lewrie replied, his own ears ringing like Bow Bells. With an outward calm he did not feel, he cranked the breech of the Ferguson open, bit off a cartridge, then shoved it ball-first into the breech and cranked it shut. He primed the pan and closed the frizzen. "Now, let's come about and see to the other two boats, sir. Place us up to windward of them, and we'll use the larboard battery. No closer than two cables to 'em."

"*Quite*, sir," Langlie enthusiastically agreed.

"Carpenter to sound the well, and inspect the transom from the bilges up. Water carries the power of explosives better than air, I'm told," Lewrie prosed on, slinging the rifle, and turning to Andrews to take his double-barreled pistols to load and prime them, too. "We may have a plank stove in below the waterline from . . . that."

"Aye aye, sir."

"Anyone hurt?" Lewrie called out. "Yer bowels still work?"

His still shaken crew began to chuckle; even if more than a few were shifting their slop-trousers and clawing at their fundaments, as if their bowels had worked just hellish-fine, thankee.

"Ah, still living, Mister Winwood?" Lewrie chirped.

"Aye, sir. Never *seen* the like, sir," Winwood marvelled, about as much as Winwood could sound surprised by anything. "Why, they must be mad as a hatter to immolate themselves like that! Drunk as swine!"

"Anything t'kill oppressors, more-like, Mister Winwood," Lewrie speculated, still working his jaw, popping his mouth open like a fish to fully restore his hearing. "*They* tried t'sink *us*. Or die tryin'."

"They came out here deliberately then, do you think, sir?"

"Runnin' arms and powder along the coast," Lewrie said, shrugging in perplexity. "The roads must be horrid, with all those mountain ranges ashore, as bad as Italy. We were *told* that this L'Ouverture was out to invade Spanish Santo Domingo. We might have put a spoke in his wheel for a few weeks by intercepting these . . . madmen. Perhaps the other two boats'll tell us more. Do we take a prisoner or two?"

Wouldn't put it past 'em, Lewrie imagined, though; *sent 'em out to sink a blockading ship? Lured us in? Was it deliberate? Jesus!*

⚓

Proteus wore off the wind again to due West, well clear of her previous encounter, reduced sail, and ghosted down on the two crippled boats. In the short space of time since they had maimed them, one of them, the smaller sloop, had sunk, and only her bow bobbed upright in the sea, with a few wailing survivors clinging to it. The lugger was low in the water, and people were bailing with hats, pails, and their hands, others trying to rig a jury-mast from a pair of oars atop her planked-over forepeak, attempting to spread the leach and foot of her after lugsail to the wind by extending the oars out like cat's whiskers, with the tack of the sail shinnied up the foremast. As the frigate neared the lugger, wailing could be heard, and her crew, augmented by survivors from the sunken sloop, took up arms and stood trembling but game, some levelling their muskets at an impossible range.

"Pass the word for Surgeon's Mate Mister Durant," Lewrie said. "He speaks good French. Those slaves once got their work orders in it."

The larboard 12-pounders were run out and ready, the carronades and 6-pounders manned, as were the swivels. Devereux's Marines stood along the larboard gangway with their muskets, and a boarding party in Wyman's charge had cutlasses slung in baldrics over their shoulders, more muskets and pistols in their hands, and boarding pikes ready to deter any more suicidal charges.

"A point more alee, Mister Langlie," Lewrie ordered. And their frigate veered even closer to the lugger.

"Less than a cable, sir," Winwood warned.

"Mister Sevier . . . a shot from the bow-chaser! No shot across the bows . . . hull her if you can!"

The 6-pounder on the forecastle yapped, and its ball hit short but in line with the lugger, to carom off the sea and bound across her deck at head-height, scattering the close-packed Blacks, and killing a couple of the taller or slower ones.

"Ah, Mister Durant," Lewrie said, turning to the Surgeon's Mate. "Since my French is so execrable, perhaps you might try to make them see reason, and surrender. No one'll be harmed, tell 'em. I'll even let them go, once we've inspected their boat, and had a chance to interrogate them. They don't stand a mouse's chance, else. I'll set 'em ashore, un-

armed, and I'll sink the boat, but they'll live. We're not *grands blancs* . . .
we're British."

"I will try, *Capitaine*," Durant vowed, stepping to the bulkwark.
"Bonjour, mes amis!" he began, and slanged a long palaver in Frog.

"Reddition?" came a defiant shout at the end of that. *"Jamais!"*

"Zey do not believe us, *Capitaine*. He say, we are all *blancs*, French
or British, it is no matter. Zey die before zey surrender."

"Do they have powder aboard, like the others, sir . . ." Langlie cautioned.

"Mister Wyman? You may open upon the lugger," Lewrie ordered.
"One broadside only . . . from the main battery guns. *Damn* the fools!"

"As you bear . . . on the up-roll . . . fire!"

Proteus roared and shook, flinging defiance for defiance, and a new
chorus of screams erupted as the lugger was shredded at such short range.
As the smoke of the broadside drifted down alee and past that lugger,
she was revealed as a total wreck. Her mast was gone, and the jury-rig
up forrud was wiped away, along with the men who had tended it. The
lugger's starboard side was shot through like a colander and she heeled
with her rails awash to the sea. Of her crew . . .

There might have been fifty or sixty men crammed aboard, before
that broadside. Now her decks were piled with offal, with the dying and
dead wallowing in their own life's blood, in a coiling mass of entrails
and body parts! There were some in the water, splashing about and trying
to swim or grab some flotsam on which to gasp and keen.

"Now we'll close-her," Lewrie snapped, "before she goes under. Mister Wyman, a boarding party to search her for papers, anything. Mister
Langlie, lower a boat for Mister Wyman's party."

"Aye, sir," Langlie parroted, though not sounding happy.

"Fetch to, sir. Stand down the larboard battery, but keep the swivels
and six-pounders manned. About a cable's distance, hmmm?"

Lieutenant Wyman's boat had barely reached the stricken lugger, he'd
barely had time for a very quick snatch-and-grab from her decks, before
she slipped under in a welter of bubbles and foam, and sank, forcing
those few members of the boarding party who'd gained her rivened deck

to scramble for their lives. As she rolled over and sank stern-first, Lewrie could see that the lugger had been big enough for a coach-top and some accommodations below her main deck, with a canvas spread over a cargo hatch between the stumps of her masts. Lieutenant Wyman waved, then smiled, showing that everyone in his boat was uninjured and returning safely. Wyman steered well clear of the Blacks swimming near his boat, though, with some of his hands levelling their muskets or pistols at the bobbing heads.

"Ho, here's one, sir!" Able Seaman Inman cried from the entry-port, pointing down over the starboard side, which was now alee of the winds. Lewrie peered over to see the muscular, mahoghany-skinned man in the water below the boarding-battens and man-ropes, treading water and bleeding from the mouth, and a scalp wound upon his shaven pate. In the water, his skin was as shiny as a seal pelt.

"Don't got a fuse and powder keg wif 'im, does 'e?" Yeoman of the Powder Foster cracked.

"Mister Devereux, have your Marines fetch him here. He might talk to us," Lewrie decided. "I'll have more need of your services, Mister Durant. Now we've gotten this'un into a more amenable mood." From Lewrie's vantage point high above, the man did seem shattered, a pathetic, pleading half-grin on his features. He even raised his hands upwards in supplication.

Inman waved him up, leaning out the entry-port. "Come on, you son of a whore. Up ye get. Come *on*, we won't eat ye! Safe, see?"

The man nodded, querying, as if he could not believe his luck, pointing to his chest as if to say "Who, me?" before thrusting upward from the water and grabbing the lowermost wooden batten in one hand, then a man-rope in the other, slithering and scraping along the barnacles at the waterline, wincing with the pain, but scaling the side as *Proteus* rolled and wallowed, the boarding-battens first vertical, then easier to climb.

"That's th' way, mate, up ye get. There'll be a cup o' grog in yer gullet in no time, laddy," Inman encouraged, reaching down as the man got near the lip of the entry-port.

" 'Ware! 'Ware!" Lt. Wyman shouted from the boat as it neared, a pistol in his hand, awkwardly dragged from his waist belt. "Knife!"

"*Canga! Heu!*" the survivor screamed, whipping out a long cane knife secreted in the back of his ragged trousers, and slicing Inman's throat almost to the spine with a single backward slash!

Wyman's pistol barked and the Black stiffened, back arched and blood spouting from his mouth as he was lung-shot, before letting go and falling back into the sea with a large splash . . . followed not a moment later by Inman's body, that fell into the same target of roiled water! Fresh-killed, their lungs still full of air, after a deep, dead plunge they both wafted to the surface, almost arm-in-arm.

"God Almighty damn!" Lewrie breathed, shuddery and faint from surprise and shock. "Get him aboard, get Inman back aboard, now!"

"No use, *Capitaine,*" Mr. Durant sadly said. "What ze *noir* did to him . . ." Durant sucked his teeth and shook his head.

"I don't give a damn, I won't have him in the water with that treacherous, murderin' bastard!" Lewrie raved.

Sheets and halliards and braces were flung overside, safely belayed about the pin-rails, and a dozen hands sprang down to the chain platforms with quickly fashioned loops of line to snag Inman and bring him alongside, then coil them about his body and haul him back up to where others could take hold of his arms and lay him out on the gangway.

Lewrie went forward, his head like to burst with rage, but his feet as benumbed as if he were walking on pillows, until he stood over the body, removing his hat in reverence, as the people parted and made way. *My fault, my fault, my bloody goddamned fault!* he thought, full of hate for himself. Inman leaked a great puddle of water from soggy slopclothing, leaked from that huge, ghastly rent in his throat. . . .

"My fault," he croaked, having to swallow hard and cough before he could talk further. "Wanted prisoners . . . information! *Damn* 'em! Should've known . . . my fault."

"Nossir, *couldn't* a known!" Bosun Pendarves countered, raising an agreeing chorus from the hands nearby.

"Savages!" someone else spat. "Ya *can't* show mercy, 'coz they don't know what it is!"

"Ain't Christians, like us'uns," another growled.

"They sunk us wif 'at powder, they'da slit *our* throats, quick enough," Mr. Neale, the Master-At-Arms supposed aloud. "Let's kill 'em all, all that still tread water!"

"No!" Lewrie shouted. "We'll leave 'em. Let 'em sink, swim, or be taken by sharks, as God wills. 'Twas my fault that Inman died, our only casualty. We'll give him a proper shipmate's burial tonight, at sunset. And I'll not have his welcome to Heaven ruined by *more* murder."

"Amen, sor," Landsman Furfy said, teary-eyed and sniffling, hat in hand and leaning on his mate, the leaner and shorter Liam Desmond.

"We know the rules, now," Lewrie announced, close to tears himself, irritably dashing at his eyes with a coat sleeve. "We know how they mean to fight . . . and how much they hate us. We . . . *I'll* not be mistaken the next time. Next time, we'll stand off and shoot 'em to kindling. Survivors, bedamned!"

That elicited a guttural growl of agreement.

"Mister Durant, sir . . . would you and Mister Shirley be so good as to prepare Able Seaman Inman for burial?"

"But of course, *Capitaine*. We will see to him," Durant vowed. "Wiz as much tender care as his own mother. Men? Assist me, please?"

Lewrie turned and stalked aft to the quarterdeck, cramming his hat back on any-old-how, and slamming his fists together, his rage no longer quite so aflame, but still scouring himself for a fool.

"Er, Captain Lewrie, sir?" Lieutenant Wyman called, scampering after him. "Excuse me, sir, but . . . thought you should see this. Sorry if I shot too late, sir. Never killed a man before, not . . . up close? Artillery, aye, but never with a pistol. *Tried* to warn him, I . . ."

"I know, Mister Wyman," Lewrie said. "Don't blame yourself. I was at fault for letting him aboard, when I should've known better."

"Uhm . . . this musket, sir," Wyman said, getting back to point. "And this cutlass, and this sword? Look at the proof-mark, and these maker's marks stamped into the blades, sir."

"Bloody hell . . . *American?*" Lewrie barked, utterly nonplussed by this evidence. "They'd sell arms to rebellious slaves? Surely, if they succeed, their *own* plantations'll go up in flames . . . *their* slave owners'll be massacred."

"Musket's a copy of a French Charleville Arsenal. Poor made, sir. Perhaps surplus from their own army's armories? The blades . . . who knows about those, sir," Wyman said, shaking his head in disgust.

"Northern foundries," Lewrie noted.

"Not so many slave-owners in their northeastern states, sir," Wyman spat. "So perhaps what happens after they're sold don't signify to them. As long as a . . . *profit's* made!"

"Most of their ironworks *are* in the northeastern states, but . . ." Lewrie trailed off with a sigh. "God, this is hellish business Mister Wyman! I know it hurts the French in Saint Domingue, for rebel slaves to obtain arms. And later, our enemy the Dons in Santo Domingo, but the massacres that follow . . . !"

"We could tell someone, sir?" Wyman suggested in a soft voice. "An American consul, a senior officer? Let them lay an official protest, perhaps?"

"We could, Mister Wyman. Rather, we *should* and we will, just as soon as dammit!" Lewrie vowed. "Someone will pay for this!"

CHAPTER TWENTY

*M*orning found HMS *Proteus* ten miles Nor'west of Cape St. Nicholas, with her crew in a sombre mood following Seaman Inman's funeral two days before. Even a run close inshore of Cape Francois, the port still held by the surviving Whites of North Province on Saint Domingue, and a lively exchange with a harbour fort, had not lightened the mens' gloom. Inman had been popular, a cheerful and hearty worker, and one of the best voices in the foc'sle's off-duty chorus, a dab-hand at the hornpipe competitions between larboard and starboard watch, and a wag of no mean skill when imitating ship's officers, midshipmen, and mates behind their back, or below in the privacy of the mess-deck.

Lewrie was up early, before dawn, to watch the hands at their labours at the change of watch at 4 A.M. Today was the day that the "bears" were broken out and dragged across the weather decks; the heavy and rough-surfaced weighted sledges that sanded the planks harder than the small "bibles" men on hands and knees normally used to keep them new-wood pale.

Especially round the larboard entry-port, where Inman's blood had fountained, and the rebel slave's blood had erupted. Some vinegar poured on the stains before using the "bear" might even completely erase them . . . someday.

It was predawn, with only the palest streak of lighter sky to the East, astern, and everything else buried in a hazy blue-grey, just enough light to see from bow to stern, with a gibbous moon still low on the horizon, a few bright stars still aglow, aloft. The galley chimney fumed lazily, as the men's oatmeal gruel was boiled up, and coffee for the officers was kept warm, and shore bread was toasted for them.

Lewrie sipped at his mug of coffee, savouring the stoutness of Saint Domingue beans; savouring the blessed, windy coolness before the tropic sun burst over the edge of the sea to fry and roast them for another day. Hat off, clad only in breeches and shirt, he could almost feel a faint chill as the Trades whisked up the frigate's stern to waft her Westward towards Cuba once more.

Good pickings round Cienfuego in the last war, he thought; *why not just stand on, both sheets aft? Old Captain Lilycrop and I took more than one prize there, in '82. On West . . . round-about Jamaica's west cape and into Kingston to wood and water. The people need a joyful diversion, God knows, and . . .*

"Deck, there!" a lookout shouted down. "Lights ashore, on the larboard quarter! Looks like signals!"

Lewrie set his mug down on the binnacle and returned to the aft rails with a telescope, hearing the scrubba-dub and hiss of the bibles and bears cease as he spied out the mysterious light.

Proteus was enough West of Cape St. Nicholas to see into a long inlet that led to the British-held harbour of Mole St. Nicholas. High hills on either side of the inlet, the island that formed the northern shore, were blue-black and forbidding at predawn; only a tiny lighter shade were the waters leading inward. There were the usual wee winks of lanthorns ashore in windows, but there was also a brighter light . . . no, a pair! Wheeling about each other, first in one position, then another.

"Mister Wyman," Lewrie called, his glass still to his eye. "I think you said you were familiar with those new semaphore towers back home, did you not?"

"Aye, sir," the Second Officer replied, sounding unsure.

"Know how to read them?"

"Well, just a bit, sir," Wyman admitted. "But I've a book below in my cabins," he more-hopefully concluded.

"Do you please have it fetched, then, sir. In the meantime, lay us on larboard tack, abeam the wind."

"Aye aye, sir!"

"Ahem . . . excuse me, Captain," Marine Lt. Devereux said, clearing his throat.

"Ah, Mister Devereux!" Lewrie brightened, turning to face him. "Didn't know you were on deck, sir. An early rising, for one who gets 'all night in' and doesn't stand watch."

"The freshest coffee, and the coolest part of the day, sir," the Marine said with a modest shrug, and a wave of his own mug of steaming coffee. He, too, was dressed in only breeches, shirt, and waistcoat at that early hour. " 'Twas originally an Army signal system, Captain, to alert the coastal garrisons, should the French invade cross Channel."

"One that our local Army leaders didn't deem fit to share with us, I gather?" Lewrie posed, a touch sarcastically. "What a surprise."

"I know a bit of it, though, sir. If I may?"

Lewrie gave Devereux the telescope, and ambled back over to the double-wheel and binnacle to retrieve his coffee before it got cold. A moment later, up came Midshipman Elwes with Lieutenant Wyman's book, and both officers began to confer; with a deal of "What the Devil?" and "Goodness gracious" commentary, a deal more page-turning, and some scribbling on a slate.

"They're not signalling to us, sir," Lt. Wyman reported at last. "Can't even see us way out here, I expect. From what I, and Lieutenant Devereux, may construe, all that waving is meant for vessels still in port. The nubbin, Captain, is an order for all ships to begin loading supplies, and prepare to extricate our garrison."

"To pull out?" Lewrie puzzled.

"They seem to be hard-pressed by a slave army, sir, and things are going against them. The signals say that the troops ashore are at the outskirts of the town, that they've been driven back from the outer entrenchments. And Mole Saint Nicholas ain't that big, sir. More like a hamlet than a thriving seaport."

Lewrie nodded and pursed his lips, turned away and took another sip of coffee, pondering his options. He turned back to them at last.

"Mister Wyman . . . ah, Mister Langlie, there you are! Stow away the holystones, and 'vast scrubbing. We'll let the deck go hang, just this once. There's a problem ashore. Fetch the ship to, for now, and pipe the hands to their breakfast. Once they've eat, we'll short-tack our way inshore to the port."

"Aye, sir."

"Aspinall, just some toast for me," Lewrie bade.

The long inlet leading to Mole St. Nicholas was frustrating in the extreme. The first part ran roughly Sou'east, an easy sail across the wind for the first few miles . . . until the hills and the taller inland mountains blocked the Trades and created one contrary zephyr after another, leaving *Proteus* chasing patches of sea that were still cat's-pawed by wind, and each weakly wafting from the opposite direction of the last one.

Then came the Nor'east leg, directly into the Trades, meaning a short board to either larboard or starboard, no closer to the wind than sixty degrees, the channel narrowing and shoaling, so that each attempt at making ground to the East'rd was measured in mere hundreds of yards to the good after each pair of tacks.

And the worst part were the sounds coming from shore; the faint, echoing sputter of musketry now and then, and the thin *Crump!* of field artillery that tolled like minute-guns at a steady pace. Someone needed them . . . soonest! But it took forever to get there. And as the day progressed, and the land and sea warmed, the thin skeins of smoke from ashore, drifting upwards through the jungley tree line went vertical, and the winds died away to nothing.

"Damme, we'll *row* her into range!" Lewrie snapped, pounding his fist on the cap-rails overlooking the waist. "Mister Langlie, do you lower the ship's boats and pay out towing cables!"

"Sir, there's a rowing boat coming offshore for us!" Midshipman Grace cried. "I can make out Army officers . . . I think!"

Through his glass, Lewrie could see at least two dozen rowboats already working 'round the few ships in harbour. There was a brig, and at least three large schooners, a small and dowdy three-master swinging at single anchors . . . hired ships, and lightly armed, thinly manned by civilian seamen with little experience—and even smaller will—to turn their pop-guns ashore. It was all they could do to stow supplies belowdecks, as fast as they could be stripped from the canvas-covered piles near the piers and the beaches.

"Topmen aloft! Hand all sail! We'll row her in, bare-poled!" Lewrie shouted to his crew.

"Uhm . . . the depth, sir," Mr. Winwood pointed out, coughing in his fist.

"How shoal does it get, sir?" Lewrie growled, turning on him.

"I'd not get closer than two cables from the docks, sir, else we run her into the mud. Mole Saint Nicholas can't *dock* deep-draught ships. They anchor out in the roads. I've hands in the chains, heaving the lead already, sir. Just wished you to keep it in mind, Captain."

"Damn!" Lewrie spat, making Winwood wince at the profanity. He was a *sober* hymn-singer. "Very well, Mister Winwood . . . two cables, no more. Our guns can range a mile inland. And, from the look of things, what targets we engage'll be a lot closer than that. Just beyond the town, more-like. Keep me apprised."

"I will, sir."

The rowboats were hoisted off the mid-ships tiers, then swayed out with the main-course yard as a crane, and slowly lowered into the water, with snub-lines to check the swing and sway. It took forever, it seemed! By the time even his own gig had been wetted, and the boat crews began to scramble over the side to man them, Bosun Pendarves had gone hoarse from shouts and curses.

"Pass the word for the Master Gunner, Mister Carling," Lewrie ordered. And once the Master Gunner had come up from the magazines to the rare privilege of the quarterdeck, Lewrie pressed him at once.

"We may have to fire over the heads of our own troops, Mister Carling."

"Dear Lord, sir," Carling said, grimacing and glancing ashore.

"I know," Lewrie said, in sympathy for the great risk of killing British soldiers with a graze or a short round. "Quoins full out, breeches resting on the carriages, for more loft. But with the foe so close to the town . . . what about reduced charges, perhaps saluting charges? So we don't throw iron half a mile beyond?"

"Could do that, sir, but . . . that'd be *indirect* fire, Captain," Mr. Carling countered, rubbing at his close-shorn scalp, "and no way to know the fall of shot. Could waste a deal of shot and powder and not ever hit a Godd—. A *blessed* thing, sir. Like firing mortars!"

He had stammered, noting that the prim Mr. Winwood was nearby.

"It worked for a Frenchman who sank my ship at Toulon, back in '93," Lewrie said with a snort, and his first real moment of humour of the morning. "Bastard spotted fire for his guns from a bluff. If the Army could signal us, were we long or short, on target or not . . . ?"

So it's their responsibility, not mine! Lewrie could not help but conjure.

"Towing cables are ready, sir, and we're prepared to haul away."

"Thankee, Mister Langlie, carry on. Smartly, now. So if they could signal us . . . would it work, Mister Carling?"

"Aye, sir . . . I s'pose, but . . ." Carling answered, rubbing his scalp more vigourously. "The six-pounders on the forecastle and here on the quarterdeck. Main battery twelves'd not be able to elevate in the ports high enough."

"The carronades!" Lewrie insisted. "*They'd* elevate. Even with a full charge, they don't throw much more than four hundred yards. If we loaded with reduced charges, but with star-shot, bar-shot, and chain-shot . . . grape or cannister atop those . . . !"

"Excuse me, sir, but the rowing boat with those Army officers is now close-aboard," Lt. Wyman interrupted.

"Very *well*, Mister Wyman!" Lewrie snapped, exasperated with all the demands upon him. "Pipe 'em aboard! Dust 'em off, and trot out a tot o' rum for 'em, I don't bloody care!"

"Uhm . . . aye, sir!"

Proteus began to move as the pair of Army officers appeared at the larboard entry-port, and took the hastily gathered salute from a much-reduced side-party. Lewrie hoped that they were unfamiliar with proper naval custom, and wouldn't know that they'd been slighted. He was more concerned with the helm, and the gelatinously slow creeping pace that the towing boats could generate. A fiddler and fifer atop the roundhouse overlooking the beak-head began to give them a tune to slave by, as the hands dipped their oars and strained red-faced for a yard-by-yard advance.

"Captain Lewrie," Lewrie said, announcing himself.

"Major James, sir . . . Captain Ward," the older officer replied, doffing his hat. "Damn' fortunate you were bound here, sir. We need a bit of help."

"Wasn't bound here, just saw your signalling in passing. Once in range, I intend to swing abeam the town and anchor with springs on the cables, so I can throw shot."

"That'd be most welcome, Captain Lewrie, most welcome, indeed. Though . . .'tis a hellish risk, d'ye see," Major James told him. "We are now entrenched not an hundred paces beyond the farthest houses on shore, and the Blacks are perhaps one or two hundred paces beyond."

Now that *Proteus* did not make her usual noises under way, nor had the wind-rush to mask sounds, Lewrie could hear the *boom-boom-boom-b-boom* of *voudoun* drums, far back in the forests. Much louder and closer than any he'd heard at Port-Au-Prince.

"Do your artillerists signal me, it could be done," Lewrie said.

"Well now, sir . . . I doubt my brigadier'd wish to risk our men in such a way," Major James objected.

"I'm to wait 'til the Cuffies are running down the piers, then? To keep them off you as you row away?" Lewrie said with a snort. "You say you need my support, but . . . how bad *are* things ashore?"

"Lord, sir!" Major James said with a sigh, fanning himself with his hat. "Two days ago, we held a perimeter nigh a mile inland. Only have the three regiments, d'ye see, and we thought most of the Blacks were off near Cape Francois, or down south near Port-Au-Prince, so we had no worries. But, they hit us at dawn, just popped up in front of the trenchworks . . ."

"Spent all night, crawling up to us in the grass, sir," Captain Ward supplied, looking as shaken as if it had happened *this* morning. "Quiet and slow as mice, they were."

"Drove us back . . . damn' near overran us," Major James admitted, casting a leery scowl at his junior officer for sounding as if he "had the wind up."

"Lost nigh on two whole *companies*, sir," Capt. Ward continued, despite his superior's look of distaste. But he was one of those boy captains, not a day over sixteen, whose parents had bought him a set of colours early enough in life so he could live long enough to make a full colonelcy, if not become a general, before retirement, or inheriting some share of the estate back home in England.

"Field pieces overrun as well, I suppose," Lewrie commented.

"We *are* short of artillery, yes, but . . ." Major James objected some more.

"You wish my help or not, sir?" Lewrie snapped. "Then let's be about it. An artillery officer aboard *Proteus* here, another ashore to relay the fall-of-shot . . . using your signal flags, or whatever it is that you do, so there's no errors in communication. Perhaps a chain of signallers from your trenchworks right back to the docks."

"I suppose we *could,* Captain Lewrie," Major James said, frowning. "Don't know much about artillery myself, all that Woolwich bang-bangin'? I'm infantry, d'ye see."

He drew himself up with a touch of pride; wounded pride, Lewrie suspected, that he was forced to reveal himself as just another drone who knew how to shout, square-bash on parade, and look good in scarlet, and hadn't learned a thing in his climb from subaltern rank outside of his own narrow interests. And his promotions *bought,* not earned!

"But you could arrange . . . ?" Lewrie prompted, flexing his fingers on his sword hilt in frustration.

"Might be best, did you have *your* people do the signalling and use your own system, Captain Lewrie," Major James said at last. "Your guns . . . your fall-of-shot?" He tossed off a helpless shrug.

"Don't *have* a system for such as this!" Lewrie quickly growled. "I can send a midshipman or two ashore, but only to aid *your* people."

"Well, uhm . . ."

"Damme, sir, you wish help? I didn't short-tack in here, six hours' worth o' hard labour, then put my people rowin' so hard they'd herniate, just t'watch a raree-show. You refuse, I'll put about and stand back out to sea, and bedamned to ya!"

And naval captains outrank Army majors, Lewrie told himself: *I am almost sure of it!*

"On your head be it, Captain Lewrie," Major James demurred.

"No . . . on some over-educated *Woolwich* graduate be it," Lewrie countered, knowing how Redcoat officers demeaned the blue-coated artillery corps, "tradesmen," who could not buy a commission, but had to learn, work and *think*, before the Woolwich Arsenal passed them for field duty.

Sure enough, Major James treated Lewrie to an smirk of sudden understanding, and began to bow himself away.

Now, who do I send ashore? Lewrie wondered, after doffing his hat to the soldiers, and turning away to see to his ship's snail-like progress.

Midshipmen Sevier and Nicholas were the oldest and smartest, the rest aboard too young, too impressionable, and not yet challenged by independent command away from the ship; none of them were, really.

And who do I stand to lose? Who dies . . . at my command?

CHAPTER TWENTY-ONE

I think we're ready for a try, sir," the scruffy, and worried, Royal Artillery officer, a Captain Wandsworth, announced at last, after several minutes of arcane scribbling and muttering over a slate with his assistant, a younger lieutenant; arcs, windage, elevation, range, charge to be used *et al* had been figured and refigured.

"Very well, Captain Wandsworth. Carry on, if you please, and Devil take the hindmost," Lewrie said, hands in the small of his back and his fingers crossed for luck; hands well clear of actual responsibility! Then Lewrie nodded to Mr. Carling on the forecastle; the man stiffened and winced so openly that Lewrie could almost feel the fellow's lips stretch as he stepped clear of a 6-pounder chase-gun and yanked the trigger lanyard.

The 6-pounder yapped, spewing a great cloud of smoke from a barrel elevated higher than normal, and rolled back on its truck-carriage, slewing a bit out of true as it recoiled. The solid shot soared into the sky, visible for a split-second as it slowed at its peak of apogee and dashed downward.

"May work, after all," Captain Wandsworth muttered, taking off his cocked hat and running his fingers through his sweaty hair. "Did we fire direct, well . . . your decks are only twenty feet above the sea, and our trenches are about fifty. At ten degrees elevation, as high as one'd risk an iron barrel with a full charge without bursting . . . hope no one's standing up, over there, else he'll have his head took off."

Lewrie wasn't *quite* sure that Wandsworth had addressed him directly, so he raised one eyebrow and said "Hmmm?"

"Not to mind, just nattering," Wandsworth said, waving him off. "Ah! There! Fifty yards beyond our lines . . . no effect. Still . . ."

"Shame we don't have Colonel Shrapnel's bursting case-shot, sir," the lieutenant told his superior. "Timed fuses . . . spread some grief?"

"No way to graze solid shot, true," Wandsworth responded, lost in his arcane work, whilst he scribbled some more on a slate. "Can't lay 'em waste like a game o' bowls, this way. What guns we have on the line'll have to see to that. Droppin' heavy things on their heads . . . *wheee* . . . plop. Cow-pats. Won't even bounce, I'll warrant."

"This won't do any good, after all?" Lewrie asked.

"Put the wind up 'em, Captain Lewrie, t'be sure," Wandsworth replied with a fiendish little grin. "Who knows? You hammer away at a wall for days, before you effect a breach. I'm thinking grape-shot or cannister might get a rise out of 'em. Saturate an area, 'stead of an aimed shot at high angle, where a miss is as good as a mile. Try one of your carronades?"

"Lovely things," the lieutenant said in praise and envy. "We *never* get to play with such. Now, do we increase the charge by a dram or two, sir . . . stand of grape on its wooden wad base . . . uhm, that's eighteen and one-half pounds total shot, with *one* cannister atop . . . ?"

Lewrie shared a look with his lieutenants, Langlie and Wyman.

Like watchin' witches stir their pot, Lewrie thought; *one more eye o' newt, or no? Two wolf teeth, or was it three?*

"No no, four drams, at the least, but . . . !" Wandsworth quibbled.

They fussed with one of the quarterdeck carronades, pushing the regular crew out of the way, whose members looked to Lewrie for a clue as to whether they should submit or not. All he could do was toss them a shrug and let the Army piddle.

"Now, then!" Wandsworth announced. "Would you be so good as to let fly, my man? What's your name? Harper? Blaze away, Gun-Captain Harper, blaze away!"

The 24-pounder carronade, never meant to be fired at such high elevation, lurched backwards on its slide-carriage, wood rails groaning and smoking despite the grease and slush slathered on to prevent too much friction, and slammed into the cross-timber at the rear that stopped the recoil.

"You know, sir," the Royal Artillery Lieutenant said, "was it up to me, I'd come up with some sort of snubbers, some screw-jack compressors to increase friction, and reduce recoil."

"Well, it's a thought . . . ah!" Wandsworth mused, before raising his telescope to peer shoreward for the signalmen. "Well, damme! One hundred paces beyond our troops, and roughly on target! Well, well! I make out . . . saturation. Twenty . . . yards . . . *wide,* oh how wondrous!"

"Did it do any good?" Lewrie asked once more.

"A fall of hail, twenty yards wide and perhaps twenty deep, sir? Grape and cannister shot?" Wandsworth crowed. "I should imagine that'd take down young *trees,* Captain Lewrie. Knock more than a few *heads* to flinders. Here, let's load up *all* your carronades, and give it a go!"

"Half a dram more, loose poured atop the bagged charges, and a single cannister atop a stand of grape to each barrel," the lieutenant pointed out. "Spread of two degrees 'twixt guns?"

"Yes, that'd share the grief about. Direct the aim of the guns back there, whilst I see to these two," Wandsworth ordered.

"Aft," Lewrie stuck in, feeling he had to contribute *something.*

"I've my pocket compass," the lieutenant told his senior.

"But of course you do, dear boy." Wandsworth chuckled. "With a bit of luck, and two-and-one-quarter pounds of powder per barrel, we could duplicate these results with the six-pounders, hmm . . ."

"Once you find the proper angle, I'll send a man forrud to the forecastle and he may lay those guns, as well," Lewrie offered.

"Oh no, sir!" Wandsworth countered. "Once we've found our pace way back here . . ."

"Aft," Lewrie supplied again, feeling more than useless now.

"I'll send Scaiff to deal with those," Wandsworth bulled on. "That's his name, d'ye know. Now, let's see . . . hmmm."

This time, all four 24-pounder carronades on the quarterdeck lit off, almost as one, the heavier charges punching the air with an earthquake of sound, and a mountain of roiling smoke, making the ship reel and shiver. For long minutes, with so little wind in the harbour, the gun smoke lingered, only slowly drifting away to let them see the flags waving from the end of the longest pier.

"Think we caused a stir, that time," Wandsworth said. "Thought I heard screamin'... could've been the shot fallin'. Oh, well. Now ... dear me, what *hath* we wrought?"

They had stirred up *something*. Suddenly, there came a crackle of musketry, brisk and urgent; volley fire, followed by a rolling platoon fire up and down the central lines, punctuated by the louder barks of field guns. Piles of smoke began to build in the forests like the thunderheads of a sea-squall, hanging thick and greasy-grey.

"Under assault, dammit," Wandsworth spat. "Stirred 'em to rise up and charge. Stung 'em to move or die, I'm hoping. Half dram less, and the same loads, if ya please!" he shouted to the gunners. "Ready? Stand clear ... by battery ... *fire!*"

This time, they *could* hear faint and thin screaming! A moment before, there had come the chanting, that chilling *"Canga, bafio té!"* shout. *Then* the screaming. The musketry and cannonfire went on for a minute or two, before fading away to a last few sputtered shots.

"Damn this smoke," Wandsworth said, coughing and fanning the air with his hat, as if that would disperse such a gigantic pall. *Proteus* was almost completely wreathed with it. "Ah, here's something ... well, I'm damned! Charge ... *broken*! Shift ... right. Range ... same."

"Easier do we haul in on the springs, Mister Wandsworth," Lewrie reminded him. "How far?"

"Oh, 'bout ten or fifteen degrees, I s'pose," Wandsworth mused, conjuring on his slate, and squinting at it and the shore.

"Mister Langlie? Haul in the stern spring-line."

"Aye aye, sir!"

"Deck, there!" a lookout called down. "Ships off the larboard beam ... workin' into harbour! Five sail ... full-rigged ships! First is a seventy-four!"

Lewrie walked over to the larboard side and raised his telescope, but it was hopeless; *Proteus* was so swathed in spent powder that everything beyond fifty yards from the deck was lost in a bellicose haze.

"What flag?" Lewrie shouted upwards.

"Ours, sir! Leadin' seventy-four is *Halifax*! Know her tops'l patches!" the lookout confirmed.

"Did your brigadier send a small boat for aid?" he asked of the Royal Artillery man.

"Might've, but there hasn't been enough time, surely," Wandsworth replied, acting irritated that his work on his slate was interrupted.

"Perhaps not," Lewrie had to agree, thinking that a small boat would barely have had time to *reach* Port-Au-Prince, and certainly could not have stirred up a rescue force that quickly.

"Just this set of guns, at first," Wandsworth decided, " 'til we are shot in, and then we'll use those up yonder."

"The quarterdeck carronades . . . then the forecastle guns," Lewrie prompted.

"Whatever you say," Wandsworth muttered, bending over a carronade barrel with a triangular piece of metal; graduated in arcane marks and bearing a plumb-bob. "Challenging, this. No dispart sights, and no elevation screws on your long guns . . . just the carronades. Do it by guess and by God . . . oh, well. Ready? By battery . . . *fire!*"

It went on for hours under a blazing hot noonday sun, and well into a sultry, airless afternoon. The guns hammered and bellowed and spewed, 'til even the officers bound kerchiefs over their ears to protect their hearing. *Proteus* reeked of sulfur and rotten-egg fumes, and trickled tendrils of spent powder gases at her planking and seams as if being smoked belowdecks to drive out the rats and insect pests. The swab-buckets and fire-buckets were filled at least twice with water, and the carronade and 6-pounder crews were rotated every half-hour with re-enforcements from the main-battery men, so those relieved could search for a patch of shade and sluice down a tot of water, panting for a single breath of clean air.

Shift left, shift right on the spring-lines; reduce the charges and loft murder shorter; add a dram or dram-and-a-half, and spew grape and cannisters of musket balls, sometimes solid roundshot in conjunction with a slightly greater range, all around the perimeter of the town. Wherever there was an upsurge of enemy activity, the guns were there, shot sleeting into the dense forest and undergrowth to the point that, whenever the smoke cleared a bit, they could see whole new *clearings*, whole new *glades*, that their guns had made.

"By God, Captain Lewrie, d'ye know, there just might *be* something in this indirect fire twaddle!" Wandsworth chortled, clapping his hands together over and over in glee. "There's an article in it, for certain. Some mathematics to be worked out, so others could copy what we've done, but . . . hmmm. Dare I imagine it could someday be termed the Wandsworth System, hey? Usin' naval guns as mortars, and usin' flag signals t'mask one's own batteries? Woolwich Arsenal, t'be sure, but . . . ! Perhaps the Royal Academy, too, for the *science* of it?"

" 'Scuse me, Cap'um," Foster, the Yeoman of the Powder, said as he scampered past the First Officer, after receiving permission to be on the quarterdeck. "We've run clean outta made-up cartridge bags for the carronades an' six-pounders, and fired off almost three whole kegs o' powder. Haveta break out another, Cap'um . . . outta the *second* tier."

"How long?" Lewrie asked, nigh deaf and having to lean close to hear what the fellow was saying.

"Quarter hour, Mister Bess the Gunner's Mate says, sir."

"Very well, thankee, Foster. Captain Wandsworth?"

"Hey?"

"Captain Wandsworth?" Lewrie repeated, louder and nearer.

"Heard ye the first time, no need t'shout, d'ye know, Captain Lewrie," Wandsworth said, cupping a hand to his ear, even so.

"We have to cease fire! Out of made bags, and low on powder!"

"Uhm, sir . . ." Foster added, still on the quarterdeck, most likely for a breath of air himself, Lewrie didn't wonder. "We're low on grape and cannister, too. Mighty low. We can make up stands from the twelve-pounder supply, but it'll take some time, Cap'um."

"Low on grape and cannister, too!" Lewrie shouted to Wandsworth.

"Yes, I could *use* a glass!" Wandsworth shouted back, beaming.

Exasperated at the bobbing, grinning fool, Lewrie took hold of Wandsworth's slate and wrote his message down.

"Oh! Silly me!" Wandsworth barked. "Yes, we'll cease fire!"

And the silence, after so long, was almost painful.

Lewrie took out his watch and opened the face, shocked that it was nearly 5 P.M., an hour into the First Dog. He looked forward and saw a ship's boy, smeared with powder stains from serving as a monkey to a forecastle gun, peering into a sandglass and ready to ring the ship's bell to mark the hour. Someone may have done that for all the time they'd been firing, for all Lewrie knew; to his senses, *everything* rang, by then.

"Mister Coote?" Lewrie called down to the waist to the purser. "How is the scuttle butt?"

"Bone dry, sir. I've sent hands to break out another cask. And the rum issue was cancelled, as well. Should I . . . ?"

"Aye. Fetch it up. Bosun? Be ready to pipe 'Clear Decks And Up Spirits,' soon as the water and rum are on deck," Lewrie bade. "Make it a *full* measure, Mister Coote. No 'sippers' or 'gulpers.' "

"How long, sir?" Wandsworth asked, licking dry lips.

"At least a half hour, sorry t'say," Lewrie told him. "We are not supplied with grape and cannister the way your Army guns are. You have what . . . half your caissons full of that, half of roundshot?"

"About that, yessir," Wandsworth agreed.

"We carry about one-in-five loads. We're almost depleted."

"Hmmm . . . perhaps, once yon two-decked ship of the line comes into harbour, I should go aboard her, then," Wandsworth decided, gesturing with his chin towards *Halifax* and her small convoy, that had yet to get within three miles of an anchorage. The wind, as it always did under a long cannonading, had been shot to a funereal stillness, and 3rd Rates were nowhere near as agile or as weatherly in light airs as a frigate. It might be sundown before *Halifax* hauled up within hailing distance, much less gun-range.

"She may not be able to anchor as close inshore as us," Lewrie speculated. "Might be better, did we borrow grape and cannister from her. She mounts twenty-four pounders, those should fit into our carronades. But once the six-pounder stands and bags are gone . . ."

"Ah, I see," Wandsworth seemed to agree. "And, did Scaiff and I 'shift our flags,' as it were, we'd have to recalculate our figures for the height of her gundecks, distance from shore, and all. I agree. Better we borrow than let that ship supercede us, Captain Lewrie."

"Uhm . . . sorry I have to ask, Captain Wandsworth, but . . . once it's dark, what do we do?" Lewrie wondered aloud.

"Ah, well . . . hmmm!" Wandsworth said, tugging at an ear, as if trying to get it to work properly once more. "Now that's a poser, if I do say so. Can't see signals from my men or yours, after dark. We could fire blind, since we know we're striking beyond our trenchworks. But, do the Samboes pull back to rest, we'd be wasting our shot in harassing fire. Might keep 'em awake, might not."

"And then once they come at our troops in the morning, we would *really* be low on effective shot," Lewrie grimly concluded.

"Well, it may be moot, after all, sir," Wandsworth said with a weary grin. "Surely, those ships coming into port are here to take us off. Another day of this, and we'll have everything loaded aboard the little ships, and won't leave the Samboes a torn shoe or dirty sock."

"One may pray," Lewrie said, nodding with hopeful agreement. He was weary, too, even from mostly standing and pacing about, on his feet for hours. He strode over to the larboard side, hands pressed against his kidneys to ease the kink in his back, arching it, and lifting his feet high and shaking his calves to spur life back into them and ease the slow burn in his soles.

"Signal, sir!" Midshipman Grace yelped. "From *Halifax* . . . our number. 'Up Anchor' and . . . 'Make Way' sir. She's spelling out . . ."

There was a much longer string of code flags to interpret.

" 'Clear . . . Way . . . To Quays,' sir!" Grace puzzled out slowly.

"Damme, do we move, Mister Wandsworth's calculations'll be off, and he'd have to start from scratch," Lewrie muttered. "Mister Grace? Hoist 'Unable,' followed by 'Am Engaged.' And we can only hope all of this gun smoke'll tell 'em what we've been up to."

A new cask of water was fetched to the main deck; the Marines, with muskets and fixed bayonets, and fife and drum, ceremoniously got the gay red-and-gilt rum keg to the forecastle belfry, and the people began to queue up for their tots, chattering and laughing along as the merry tinkle of the string of copper measuring/drinking cups jangled.

"She repeats her first signals, sir," Mr. Grace said, turning a worried eye to his captain, knowing that there was bad blood between Captain Blaylock and Lewrie already.

"We'll explain, once in hailing distance," Lewrie said, though feeling that he was in for a "cobbing," no matter what he did.

Boom-boom-boom-b'boom. The drums began once more, now that the punishing guns, the ones that struck from nowhere, had ceased. A shot sounded, a thin and weak *crack!* from a lone musket. A desultory spatter of two more, a gust of gunfire, then the field guns began to bark anew. There was a massive shout, a challenging roar that caused a blizzard of musketry in reply, and then things fell silent again.

"Flag's waving!" Wandsworth's deputy, Scaiff, pointed out.

"Need us again, I expect. My my," Wandsworth grieved wearily.

"Your midshipman fellow's runnin' off inland," Scaiff said.

"Who? What?" Lewrie snapped, returning to the starboard side. "What the Devil? He's takin' a horse!"

"Into the woods. Curious," Scaiff said, yawning. "That rum ye issue, Captain Lewrie? Could a poor soldier get a taste? I'm dry as dust."

"Aye, go forrud and tell the Purser you want a tot," Lewrie muttered, intent with his spyglass on the doings ashore, wondering why young Nicholas would go dashing off towards the trenchworks so suddenly.

"Water, sir?" Aspinall offered, coming onto the quarterdeck.

"God, yes, thankee," Lewrie said, turning to accept a tall mug and drain half of it in one gulp.

"Fresh batch, sir. Good an' cool from the orlop."

"Quite fine, quite fine," Lewrie answered, sighing with contentment, and relief. His mouth had been as dry as a private soldier's, a man who'd been biting off cartridges all day. "Toulon's hiding down below, I take it?"

"Down in the midships hold, sir. Like he always does. Poor ol' puss, the guns scare him somethin' pitiful," Aspinall chuckled.

The sound of gunfire in the forest erupted again, louder this time, more sustained and urgent, the volleys of two-ranked soldiers on top of each other as fast as they could load, the artillery crashing a steady tolling up and down the lines.

And men were running down the short streets of the town to the docks, men in red coats bearing weapons, but bearing the corners of a series of blankets, too . . . jogging along as fast as they could, with wounded! Thirty or so sentries who had been guarding the diminishing piles of stores were massing, led by a sword-waving officer who looked very much like that Major James who had come aboard earlier, and were trotting double-time the other direction, into the forest.

Lewrie lifted his telescope to see better, and found a figure in white slop-trousers and a short midshipman's coat, hatless, waving at him! It was Nicholas! And his right sleeve and hand were smeared with gore! He clung with his left hand to a side of a blanket which bore a wounded man, and tears could be seen coursing down his face in terror or grief.

"Andrews!" Lewrie roared for his cox'n. "Away my gig to shore! Mister Nicholas is coming back wounded. Hurry, man, hurry!"

"Awn de way, sah! Furfy, Sharp, you two bastids, ovah de side!"

Lewrie felt glued to the ocular of his spyglass, wishing for a stronger one, ruing his cheapness on his last shopping trip to London chandlers. Nicholas trotted—no, staggered!—closer to the end of the longest pier, four soldiers still bearing their burden—to which he clung with a white-faced death grip—'til they reached the very end and laid it down.

Midshipman Nicholas sank to his knees beside the blanket, then lifted the man in it, taking the wounded fellow by the chin to try to shake him back to consciousness, pointing out towards their ship.

It was Midshipman Sevier . . . as pale as death!

"Row like the Devil, Andrews, they're *both* wounded!" Lewrie bellowed, his innards churning to think that his decision might have gotten *both* lads maimed or killed.

"Eh! Eh! Bomba! Heu! Heu! Canga, bafio té!"

The enemy's chant seemed a cruel mockery.

CHAPTER TWENTY-TWO

*B*oat's comin' alongside!"

"Pass word for the Surgeon Mister Shirley!" Lewrie shouted.

"Signallers are waving once more, Captain Lewrie," Captain Wandsworth pointed out. "Hellish urgent-like? Do you have *any* cannister or grape stands remaining, I think it's needed something desperate."

"Very well . . ." Lewrie began.

"Excuse me, sir, but *Halifax* spells out. 'Up Anchor' and 'Move.' "

"He can go bugger himself!" Lewrie snapped. "Second hoist for *Halifax* . . . make 'request all your cannister and grape-shot.' *That'll* keep that pestiferous bastard busy, Mister Grace. Well? Run and send it!" Lewrie growled, noting Grace's wide-eyed goggling of the stir by the entry-port, where Sevier and Nicholas were being hoisted aboard.

"Aye aye, sir," Grace gulped, and dashed for his flag locker and halliards.

"Mister Foster? Break open the shot lockers and make up charges for the guns, quick as you can, and keep it coming 'til it's completely gone," Lewrie said, wanting to dash to the entry-port himself to see to Sevier and Nicholas. Things were coming too thick and fast to suit him, unlike the long minutes of an evolution at sea.

"Charge yer guns . . . shot yer guns . . ." a grizzled quarter-gunner was intoning to his weary crews, who had set their rum rations down on the quarterdeck, that priceless elixir of ease abandoned for a rare once, in the face of need. Other crewmen who had gone forward for their rum ration had gulped it down then returned to their posts, their prime moment of relaxation and jollity stolen by stern Duty.

Wandsworth and Scaiff fiddled and calculated, gazing heavenward and counting on their fingers, muttering and whispering to themselves before reaching a mutual decision. A quick trot down the deck to see to the elevation, and . . .

"By broadside . . . *fire!*"

The 6-pounder long guns and the stubby 24-pounder carronades lit off together, shuddering *Proteus* anew, refogging her in a reeking pall of powder smoke, and making everyone's ears ring. Seconds later, the sound of musketry ashore rose in volume, crackling down the line of trenchworks like the advance of a brushfire, with the crisp sound of burning twigs. There was a roar of several light field pieces, then a howl of human voices raised in rage or fear or glee, the daft bray of a fox-hunting horn to urge them on, just before another musket volley.

"Samboes broke the entrenchments," Wandsworth found time to say, tugging at his ear again, "and I think we just saw 'em out. Where your midshipman was wounded, I shouldn't wonder."

"Mister Langlie, you have the deck," Lewrie said, going to the gangway where Sevier was being hoisted inboard.

"Easy with him, lads," Mr. Shirley was saying, already clad in his "butcher's apron" of light leather for surgery, his sleeves rolled to the elbows. The grey army-issue blanket was lowered to the deck, already half soaked in gore, and Mr. Shirley sadly shook his head for a moment as the loblolly boys transferred Sevier's body to a carrying board, an eight-man mess table with rope straps to bind the patient to it, and other rope straps for lifting.

Shirley looked up at Lewrie and grimaced in sadness with another wee shake of his head. Sevier had been savaged by thrusts from bayonets or swords; the cloth and lace of his shirt, the flap of his white breeches were cut open, baring the hideous wounds beneath, cloth stained bright red over purpling puckers and slashes. His face was a new-paper white, his eyes unfocused, and his breath a faint, labouring wheeze, with small flecks of foamy blood on his lips.

"Mister Durant, Mister Hodson . . . see to Mister Nicholas, while I see Mister Sevier below," Shirley said, getting to his feet and leading the loblolly boys and their burden to the gun-deck ladder.

"What happened, Mister Nicholas?" Lewrie asked the terrified boy, who stood and shuddered, all but blubbering, as blood dripped from his injured arm.

"S-Samboes, sir," Nicholas replied between chattering teeth, "*Hundreds* of 'em! Broke the line. They were in the trenchworks with knives and bayonets, killin' our people left and right, and laughing fit to bust, sir! Jemmy, he . . . him and the Army signallers against a dozen, and him with just a pistol and his dirk! They got that far behind our lines, sir, before . . . I saw one of the signalmen running and shouting they were all being slaughtered, and I . . ."

What little Mister Nicholas needed, first of all, was a hug and a lap, Lewrie thought, but that was impossible; he was a "gentleman volunteer," a future officer.

"I tried, sir, honest I did!" Nicholas wailed, fresh tears coursing down his cheeks, cutting clean runnels in the filth on his face as he shivered, trying to remain "manful" before the ship's people. "But they were jabbin' him and cuttin' at him after he was down, before we got there, and then they came for me, and they were so big and *horrid*, sir, and if the soldiers hadn't come . . . I lost my dirk, sir. I looked for Jemmy's, too, but they took it 'fore they were run back across the trenchworks. I'm *sorry*, sir! I lost my dirk!"

A gentleman's blade, be it inherited sword or humble dagger, was part of his honour; to Nicholas, he had failed miserably at saving his fellow midshipman and friend, had been bested and wounded when faced with face-to-face combat, and, to top it all, had lost his blade. Sure sign of failure, perhaps even a sign of cowardice, to drop it and run.

The 6-pounders and carronades bellowed again; Lewrie had to wait to speak 'til the echoing roar passed.

"No matter, Mister Nicholas," he said, touching Nicholas on his left shoulder. "You went to his aid like a brave fellow, and helped the Army stop their charge after he rushed to yours. Then you brought him back aboard, so he could be among his shipmates. No shame in any of that."

So he can most-like perish among his shipmates, Lewrie thought.

"Now, let the surgeon's mates tend you," Lewrie said, giving him another reassuring pat on the shoulder before returning to the quarterdeck. But he could hear Mr. Nicholas's cries when they tried to peel his coat off, to cut his shirt sleeve away and lift the cloth from the wound; Nicholas sounded like one of his sons after skinning a knee, and nowhere near a stoic young "gentleman volunteer."

"Ready way up there?" Wandsworth was shouting to the gunners on the foc'sle. "Ready, here? *Fire!*"

Midshipman Grace interrupted Lewrie's gloomy thoughts. "*Halifax* has hoisted another signal, sir. It's 'Captain Repair on Board.' "

"We still fly 'Unable' and 'Am Engaged,' Mister Grace?" he asked, hands in the small of his back.

"Aye, sir."

"Haul 'em down, then rehoist 'em in reply," Lewrie said with a snarl. "He don't like that, he can go fuck himself."

"Uhm . . . aye, aye, sir!" Grace said, blushing and tittering.

By dusk, when the wagging signal flags could no longer be read and *Proteus* had shot away her last stand of grapeshot, her last cannister of musket balls, even the lot scavenged from pre-made loads for the 12-pounder great-guns, the ship fell silent.

Halifax had not responded to her call for shot, but had anchored about a cable's distance away in deeper water, along with the merchant ships she had escorted into Mole Saint Nicholas.

Rather surprisingly, those hired ships had become beehives of activity, disembarking boatloads of soldiers who were quickly rowed to the beaches and quays, followed by heaping piles of supplies, ammunition, and field guns.

When the last shot had been fired, Lewrie called for his cox'n and boat to be rowed over to *Halifax.* Pointedly, he did not change to a clean uniform, nor scrub his face and hands; the greyness of his uniform from the gun smoke fog would speak for him.

"Excuse me, sir," Mr. Shirley said, just before he could leave the quarterdeck for his gig, and a salute from the side-party. "That poor lad Sevier passed over, sir. And Mister Nicholas . . . the slash on his arm quite shattered it. We had to take it off, just below the shoulder, Captain."

Lewrie blanched. "Nothing else to be done?"

"No use of it, now, sir," Mr. Shirley replied, "and no feeling in it at

all. Half-severed, already, and why he didn't exanguinate on the dock
before your boat fetched him is a wonder, Captain."

"Very well, then, Mister Shirley," Lewrie said with a mournful sigh.
"You did your best for him . . . for them both. Thankee."

"We were lucky with you, sir," Shirley admitted. "Those boys,
well . . . there's only so much modern medicine may do, sorry to say."

"Well, then . . ." Lewrie lamely said in answer, unconsciously massaging his left arm, and turning away.

"*Damn* you, Captain Lewrie! Damn you for blatant insubordination and
arrogance!" Captain Blaylock howled, as soon as Lewrie had been let
into his great-cabins under *Halifax*'s poop. "You frigate captains are all
alike, damn your blood . . . swaggerin' cock-a-hoops who think they
hung the bloody *moon*! I will lay formal charges before Admiral Parker
and see you court-martialed! I'll see you *broken*, d'ye hear me?"

"That is your right, sir," Lewrie wearily replied, prepared for a "cobbing" since mid-afternoon, and steeled beforehand for any abuse that the
choleric Captain Blaylock had in his shot-lockers. "It will also be my
right to point out to the court that I was unable to clear the mooring,
since I was engaged in supporting the Army ashore. With testimony
from the Royal Artillery officers aboard at the time, or the testimony of
Brigadier Sir—"

"Blazing away at nothing!" Blaylock bellowed back. "Firing off blank
charges, just to excuse your insolence! Firing blind!"

"Indirect fire, sir . . . lofting grape and cannister to harass the slave
troops," Lewrie pointed out.

"There's no such bloody *thing*!"

"There is now, sir," Lewrie responded, almost ready to chuckle in
genuine insolence, too tired and sad to let Blaylock's insults get to him.
The only thing that irked was the presence of *Halifax*'s lieutenants,
summoned aft to watch their captain take the hide off an upstart. Lewrie
snuck a peek from the corners of his eyes at them; some of the six
seemed to enjoy the show, though the much put-upon Duncan and others
seemed ashamed of the spectacle, their eyes on the painted deck covering.
Disputes between Post-Captains, personal or professional in nature—

most especially taking another officer to task or upbraiding a midshipman, petty officer or mate—was not to be done in public. If there was no way to find privacy, it was to be done out of earshot, with no noticeable vitriol or raised voices.

Good *officers*, good *captains don't do it this way*, Lewrie told himself; *but Blaylock, well . . . says it all, don't it?*

"It's impossible, damn your eyes!" Blaylock insisted.

"Then I suggest you ask of Captain Wandsworth, Royal Artillery, sir," Lewrie coolly rejoined. "He's rather proud of what we did, and is simply panting t'write a paper on it for the Royal Society. Oh, I dare say he'll take all the credit for it, call it the Wandsworth System of Supporting Fires, but he needed Royal *Navy* guns to do it, sir."

Lieutenant Duncan and three others stifled smirks of glee, even snorts of taboo laughter. There then came a rap on the door.

"Come!" Captain Blaylock snarled, and a wary-looking midshipman entered the great-cabins. "Well, what the Devil is it?"

"Excuse me, Captain sir, but Brigadier General Sir Harold Lamb has come aboard, and . . ." the boy managed to stutter.

"Well then, fetch him in, damn yer eyes!" Blaylock snapped.

The midshipman gulped, reddened, and dashed out of sight, coming back a long moment later to hold the door open while an Army officer and an aide-de-camp entered the great-cabins, ducking under the beams overhead, and almost managing not to knock their white wigs askew, or bang their noggins on the polished oak.

"Captain Blaylock?" the general officer in all the gilt lace and gimp enquired, fanning his sweaty face in the close warmth of the cabins.

"Sir Harold, sir . . . welcome aboard," Blaylock said, turning as unctuous as anything and practically oozing from behind his desk to go seize the brigadier's hand. "A glass of something cooling, hey? Well met, sir, well met. Our arrival was more than welcome, I'm bound."

"And without notification, Captain," General Lamb said. "Yes, I am a touch dry."

Blaylock snapped his fingers at his steward, who sprang to the wine cabinet for glasses and claret.

"I've despatches from General Maitland for you, Sir Harold. He related to me, verbally, though"—Blaylock all but simpered to be "in the know" from the elevated Maitland's own lips—"that your troops were to be re-enforced with the garrisons of Gonaives and Saint Marc. We picked them up on our way, d'ye see. The other small ports twixt here and there were to concentrate on Port-Au-Prince. From the sound of it ashore as we arrived, I got my convoy in just in the nick of time, haha!"

Sir Harold took a seat without being bade, opened wax seals upon his orders, and shifted under a coin-silver overhead lanthorn to read them quickly, reaching into his ornate coat for a pair of spectacles that he held close to the page like a quizzing glass. He looked up briefly as Blaylock's steward placed a glass of wine on a small round table by his chair, nodded his thanks, then returned to his letters, a deep frown growing on his wrinkled face.

"That should be all, gentlemen, you may go," Blaylock said to his lieutenants. "You too, Lewrie. I will send *you* a letter aboard in the morning," he warned, turning pointedly frosty and stern.

"*You're* Captain Lewrie?" Sir Harold brightened, lowering letter and specs and rising to his feet, dodging a deck beam at the last moment as he came to Lewrie, hand out. "Spoke to Wandsworth. God *bless* you, sir, you and your ship! Never *seen* the like in thirty years as a soldier! Without your good offices, I dare say my lines would be completely rolled up by now, and an entire regiment massacred!"

" 'Twas a risky experiment, General," Lewrie said, shaking hands with Lamb. "But with your Captain Wandsworth's able and eager direction, him and his aide Lieutenant Scaiff, we thought it worth trying. Spur of the moment, all that?"

"Which succeeded admirably," Lamb prosed on, pumping away with belated joy. "Your two brave lads, who went ashore to signal?"

"One passed over, sir. The other lost his arm," Lewrie related, turning sombre again. "Should've sent older men, Commission Officers, or gone ashore myself, instead of . . ."

"Weren't to know, Captain Lewrie," Lamb assured him. "War ain't predictable, or clean. You pick men for such, send 'em off with your fingers crossed, even those in a 'forlorn hope' to breach the walls of a fortified position, never knowin' what the butcher's bill will be. The sorry price to pay for holdin' command over men. But, our duty. Should've seen him, Captain Blaylock, him and his ship this morning," he told the stricken Blaylock, who stood with mouth agape in anguish. "Put out boats and *rowed* his ship into the shallows, and just in your 'nick of time,' too, else I and most of my troops would've been slaughtered long before you rounded the *far* point. Ah, but we surely know we can count on the Navy to save our hides, hey, sir? Do you let me make free with your claret, I'd admire to offer a toast to Captain Lewrie and his ship . . ."

"HMS *Proteus,* sir," Lewrie supplied, beaming with pleasure; and sensing salvation from Blaylock's bile, *and* a court-martial.

"Saw Major James lead a re-enforcement inland, General Lamb. I wonder how he fared?" Lewrie asked, as Blaylock's steward fetched out another glass and poured a brimming bumper. "Is he well?"

"Caught 'em strung out and disorganised, he did, sir. Carved 'em thin as a roast at a two-penny ordinary!" Lamb boasted. "Gave 'em the bayonet and ran 'em back into the woods . . . where your grapeshot and cannister strewed 'em six ways from Sunday! Oh, James got a cut or two, and I doubt his tailor'd approve, but he's main-well. I will tell him you asked of his welfare?"

"I'd appreciate that, sir," Lewrie replied. "Brave fellow."

For a complete nit-wit, Lewrie qualified to himself; *but even they sometimes have their uses.*

"Takes one to know one, as my granny always told me, Captain Lewrie!" General Lamb chortled. "Well, sirs! To Lewrie and *Proteus,* huzzah!"

"Lewrie and *Proteus,*" Captain George Blaylock said in chorus, the smile on his face patently false, his teeth grinding all the while.

"We'll have need of that sort of support in the morning," Lamb said, once they had tossed back their wine and the steward circulated with a cut-glass decanter to top them up. "L'Ouverture's laddies ain't done, not by a long chalk. Even re-enforced, we'll be hard-pressed."

Think I'll rub Blaylock's nose in it, Lewrie maliciously thought; *like a puppy in his scat. Use the upper hand now . . . or lose it.*

"I'd like to oblige you, Sir Harold, but I've fired off the last of my grape and cannister, along with an entire tier of powder kegs, and have only roundshot left. Oh, we could make up new stands of grape and bag musket and pistol balls easily enough," he breezed off, before turning his gaze to Captain Blaylock, ". . . were there some about."

Lamb swivelled about to peer at Blaylock, almost catching that worthy's outraged scowl; which expression was rapidly amended to the genial, slack-lipped smile of a doting uncle.

"Surely, Captain Blaylock, your ship's magazines should be positively stiff with the proper munitions," General Lamb suggested.

"Ah," Blaylock answered with a petulant snap of those lips as he contemplated his ship of the line being plundered a *second* time. "Um, I expect they are, *but* . . . now we've landed two more regiments and two batteries of six-pounders, this . . . indirect fire will be unnecessary, hmm? And, should such *still* be required, would it not better serve to shift *Proteus* to the outer harbour . . . now her quiver's spent, and let *Halifax* take her place?"

Go on, go on, step right in it! Lewrie inwardly gloated.

"My carronades and chase-guns are mounted an entire deck higher than Lewrie's, after all. Hence, less risk of accidentally firing on your soldiers, Sir Harold? And 'tis a business fraught with risk, as it is."

"Captain Wandsworth *could* recalculate his sums, I s'pose, for *Halifax*'s greater height;" Lewrie allowed, as if reluctant to accept. "Damme, though, it cuts a bit rough t'be supplanted, now we've got it down to a science."

"Finish what you started, d'ye mean, Captain Lewrie?" General Lamb quite sympathetically imagined.

"Aye, something like that, Sir Harold," Lewrie said, making his "confession" seem a hard-drawn thing. "Then there's the excitement, I must allow. Blockade work was gettin' boresome in the main, and then here came this marvelous chance for *real* action, and . . . for us to up-anchor and move down-harbour as a guardship . . . well. We'd be *worse* than useless. Not patrollin', not makin' a contribution. . . ." he concluded, all but piping at his eyes in sadness over "not doing his bit."

"Since *Proteus* has exhausted her magazines," Blaylock said, getting a sly-boots look on his phyz that Lewrie, for a moment, dreaded with crossed fingers hidden in his lap. "There's no reason for Lewrie to idle here, at *all*. *Halifax* can handle anything that arises."

Got you, ya greedy, glory-huntin' bastard! Lewrie thought, trying *not* to leap up and whoop in gleeful triumph. *It'll be the onliest way that barge of yours gets* your *name in the papers!*

"Oh, sir, now . . . !" he pretended to protest; not *too* loudly.

"Perhaps a quick return to Kingston would be in order, Captain Lewrie," Blaylock casually suggested. "To replace your lacks, hmm?"

"Surely, there must be someplace closer, someplace not so deep down-wind o' the Trades, though, sir," Lewrie grumbled. "That would take *Proteus* far from her patrol area, and at such a parlous time . . ."

He left off the "tsk-tsk" inherent in his "respectful" gripe.

"Then down to Port-Au-Prince." Blaylock brightened. "There's a storeship in port now, which freed my ship to escort the convoy here, and guard the evacuation of Gonaives and Saint Marc. Got my guns back, too," he added with a prissy "so there" sniff of retribution.

"Well, if needs must, then of course, sir," Lewrie said, almost tail-wagging eager to serve, no matter how humbly. "Wherever we are needed."

"Do you sail in the morning, then, Captain Lewrie," General Lamb told him, "I'll send a letter of appreciation aboard your ship before you depart, expressing my undying thanks for your actions today. And a copy to your Admiral Parker, as well . . . to let him know what a paragon he has in his command."

"You do me too much honour, Sir Harold," Lewrie vowed modestly though eating up such approbation like plum duff. That letter would get posted in the news back home, getting *his* name in the papers!

"Nonsense." Sir Harold waved him off. "Captain Blaylock can write a properly appreciative report of his own, hey Captain Blaylock?"

"Why, I . . ." Blaylock responded, mouth agape in high dudgeon and shock for a raw second, before turning bland and agreeable once more. "But of course, Sir Harold. Anything to oblige," he stated, obviously weighing the cost of a refusal against the present goodwill of a rich and knighted senior officer.

"Do you wish, then, to take my anchorage tonight, sir?" Lewrie prodded, shamming some more eagerness. "There's still enough light . . ."

"You would not *mind*, sir?" Blaylock asked, leery of his offer to cede the place of honour so quickly.

"It will give Captain Wandsworth more time to do his sums before dawn, sir," Lewrie replied, rising as if dismissed, the decision having already been made. "And, being toothless, I can accomplish no more."

"Makes sense, sir," General Lamb commented, nose in his glass.

"Aye, up-anchor and stand down below the port, Captain Lewrie," Blaylock said, draining his glass and rising to his own feet as if to begin the evolutions for moving his ship that instant. "Do let me walk you to the deck, Captain Lewrie."

"An honour, sir," Lewrie replied, lying most pleasantly.

Blaylock, for Lamb's benefit, even went so far as to thread his right arm through Lewrie's left, as if they were now as close as cater-cousins on the way to the door.

"Do *not* make the mistake of trying to best me again, Lewrie," Blaylock muttered from the side of his mouth once they were out of Sir Harold's earshot, still beaming like an admiring papa. "I've *years* more experience at Navy politics than any jumped-up, ill-bred jackanapes of a 'dashing' frigate captain. You finagled me once back in Port-Au-Prince, and robbed me of guns. I s'pose you think you did it again, tonight, hmm? Well, let me tell you something. Oh, I will pen you a *modicum* of praise for your damn-foolery, but stress the horrid risk you ran of killing our own troops, and one never knows, does one . . . the Samboes just might've had artillery in those woods, and any casualties from grape or cannister I can always lay at *your* feet, and there goes your good odour . . . boy!"

"Don't you run the same risk, sir?" Lewrie pointed out. "After all, it'll be your guns, tomorrow."

"Tomorrow's accidental dead can always become yesterday's dead . . . on *paper*, Lewrie," Blaylock whispered, evilly beaming. "And just who d'ye think will do the writing once you're gone . . . Lewrie."

"You will, of course, sir," Lewrie levelly responded.

"That's right, that's exactly right!" Blaylock softly crowed.

"Unless it's Sir Harold writing Admiral Parker, should *you* kill some of his men, sir," Lewrie pointed out. "Then it's on your head."

"Ah, but in my case, Lewrie, t'will be an unfortunate accident, a mistaken signal from Army artillerymen."

"Well, since you seem to have everything covered, sir, I'll go back aboard *Proteus* and shift anchor," Lewrie said, outwardly uncaring and eerily calm in the face of such a threat.

"Goodbye, little boy-captain." Blaylock sniffed. Again, for the benefit of General Lamb, he raised his voice for a proper parting sentiment. "Have a safe and quick voyage to Port-Au-Prince."

"Thankee, sir," Lewrie said, conversationally loud as well, but dropped his voice to a whisper again as he stuck out his hand, forcing Blaylock to take it to make a decent show. "Before I go, though, you should know, sir . . . without grape or cannister, *Proteus* cannot guard the harbour tonight."

"Against what?" Blaylock asked, with a snort of derision.

"Cutting-out expeditions by L'Ouverture's men, sir. An attempt to blow you sky-high, sir."

"Oh, tosh!" Blaylock actually giggled at the very idea.

"You did not read my report about the four boats we intercepted, sir? When they saw that they could not escape us, they turned and lit their cargoes of powder, tryin' to take us with 'em. They've dozens of small boats up and down the coast, I'm bound . . . out of reach of the Army's trenchworks. Who knows what they'll be up to, now they have been stung so bad by naval gunfire . . . hmmm, sir?"

Blaylock looked as if he'd sneer for a moment, dismissing such a threat, but then went blank as he realized that it *was* possible, and that his precious ship was now at the point of danger.

"By God, you . . . !"

"Do you have your report aboard by Six Bells, sir, to accompany Sir Harold's, I b'lieve I can breast the slack of the tide and work my way out on the land-breeze. If you please, sir."

Didn't think o' that, didya? Lewrie gloated some more; *the first ship out of here's mine, carryin' your damned despatches.*

"By God, I'll have your arse for this, Lewrie!"

"If you say so, sir," Lewrie rejoined, his voice dead-level and his eyes going from calm blue to steely grey. "If you say so."

CHAPTER TWENTY-THREE

*P*ort-Au-Prince was a much more crowded harbour than when *Proteus* had last lain there, and this time, when sailing down the north channel past Ile de Gonaves, instead of the exotic and otherwordly cries of a myriad of brightly coloured island birds, the overlying sounds were of distant field-pieces, thumping flat and hollow, the faint crackle from musket volleys, and the brooding, menacing thud of *voudoun* drums.

An ancient stores ship, HMS *Grampus*, lay at anchor. Once a tall and proud 2nd Rate of 90 guns, she was now a tar-smeared and filthy old barge, little better than a mastless receiving ship or prison hulk, so bereft of upper masts that *Proteus*'s people could conjure that the only way the old warrior could have gotten over from Kingston was under tow.

"Cain't see dot *L'Oi*—dot *Songbird* we took, sah," Cox'n Andrews pointed out, shading his eyes to scan the crowded harbour.

"Well, damme, I'd hoped . . ." Lewrie said, having counted on the prize being there, so he could get Lieutenant Catterall and Midshipman Adair back aboard to re-enforce his depleted petty officers and leaders. "Mister Coote?" he called, shrugging it off. "You'll take the cutter under Mister Elwes to *Grampus*, once we're anchored. Grape shot, cannister makings, and powder first, mind. We're naked without them."

Their last night at Mole Saint Nicholas, without grape or cannister, he'd paced and fretted a move by L'Ouverture's men with an armed double watch on deck, armed Marines in the fighting tops, and both eyes skinned for any suspicious shadow or drifting log in the water, worried that his malicious warning to Captain Blaylock had been borrowing trouble for himself.

"Mister Langlie, once Mister Coote returns, begin loading. I'll be ashore, to find out what aid we may render. Or what we're to do."

"Aye, sir. Though I don't suppose they'll ask for indirect fire here," Langlie commented, taking off his hat to mop his forehead with his coat sleeve. "Our Army's too far inland for that."

"And I doubt General Maitland's staff runs to lunatics, such as our friends Wandsworth and Scaiff," Lewrie replied, softly japing him.

"That, too, sir," Langlie chuckled, turning his attention to the draw of the sails and their course. "Half a point a'weather, helmsman."

Two hours of mopping his face, swatting flies and pesky mosquitoes, dipping up water now and then from the communal bucket at General Maitland's headquarters, and Lewrie had even less of a clue as to what *Proteus* should do once she was re-armed.

At last, coming from a tall set of double louvred doors leading to a parlour converted to offices, he spotted a blue-and-white uniform *not* worn by the Royal Artillery but by a Post-Captain of his own service, and Lewrie practically pounced on him, naming himself.

"Captain Lewrie, is it?" the officer asked, once he'd spoken.

"Aye, sir."

"Nicely . . . of *Obdurate*," the officer replied, and his name fit him most appropriately. Nicely was a square older fellow with pepper-and-salt hair, still thick and wiry, a man possessed of the merriest blue eyes and a permanent tan, his countenance fixed in perpetuity in a benign half smile, as if pleased as punch with his place in the world, his lot, and the progress of all that he surveyed.

"You're senior officer present, sir, I take it. Any orders for me?" Lewrie asked. "Askin' of the Army, well . . ."

"You were off to patrol the north shore," Nicely mused, fingers to his lips to recall him, before snapping his fingers as he got it.

"Aye, sir, but we put into Mole Saint Nicholas a few days ago, and shot away all our grape and cannister. Now that *Grampus* is here, and we may re-arm—"

"Shot it *all* away? Tell me," Nicely said, leading him by dint of personality down the hall towards the front doors. After he'd related the whole tale, Nicely let out a loud "Whew!" of amazement.

"Damme, but you've been a busy lad, Captain Lewrie. You have a written account? O' course you do. Give it me. That laving bowl and the bucket's fairly fresh. Avail yourself whilst I look this over."

Lewrie swabbed his face and neck once more, and ladled up a dipper of water, sipping off half and using the rest to swirl the dipper's ladle clean before slinging it on the stone steps of the commandeered mansion, where the water steamed on the hot, sun-heated stones.

"Damn! Are they trying to shift supplies east to invade Santo Domingo, the best use for your ship would be right back on the station you left!" Nicely grumbled, fanning himself with the sheaf of paper in their airless oven of a hallway. "No love for the Dons, understand, but I wouldn't wish L'Ouverture on the demons of Hell. Soon as they're in charge here, they'll be over the border quick as you can say 'knife,' and God help the Spanish, then. This . . . indirect fire may prove useful here in a few days. I'm afraid I must order you to stay, Lewrie."

"I understand, sir," Lewrie answered, nodding and smiling as he contemplated another visit ashore, and a *rencontre* with that Henriette. With a qualm, too, for this time, should he have to fire over the head of British troops, he wouldn't have Wandsworth or Scaiff to "carry the can" should things go wrong. Perhaps Captain Blaylock would get his wish after all, and he'd end up slaughtering British soldiers by error! *His* error! Quickly followed by a court-martial, Blaylock testifying that he'd "told him so," and . . .

"Excuse me, sir, but you said . . ." Lewrie plumbed at last. "If L'Ouverture is in charge? Of Port-Au-Prince?"

"Should have said 'when,' rather," Nicely told him, turning sombre. "Mole Saint Nicholas re-enforced with troops from Saint Marc and Gonaives . . . thereby ceding those little ports to L'Ouverture, do you see. Us here in their South Province and West Province concentrating forces at Port-Au-Prince and Jacmel, on the south coast. We've given up Little and Grand Goave, Arcahele just north of here . . .'twas that or get their garrisons massacred. L'Ouverture's unleashed his armies on us in an all-out effort, and frankly the swarthy little bugger is beating our poor Army

like a cheap drum, Lewrie. Your coming here is much like 'out of the
frying pan, into the fire.' "

. "Well, damme!"

"Couple of days back, it was run or die, up at Croix de Bouquets . . .
routed Maitland's troops and ran 'em clean out of the Plain de Cul-de-
Sac," Nicely explained. "Flank units gave way under hellish swarms of
'em, then the center lost heart and scampered before they could be cut
off and encircled. Abandoned guns, caissons . . . wounded? That's not
over five miles from here. Our six or eight thousand healthy and present,
'gainst fifty or sixty thousand of theirs? Damme, I suspect we'll be asked
to evacuate the Army in a few days. A total muddle, Lewrie. Complete
and utter."

"Dear Lord," Lewrie said with an authentic qualm and a gulp of
amazement. "Who'd've ever thought it possible?"

"*Know* Captain Blaylock, do you?" Nicely asked of a sudden, and
with a less than "nice" expression on his phyz.

"Not really, sir. Not 'til our convoy here, oh . . . weeks ago."

"Had praise for your actions. Faint praise, but some is better than
none," Nicely pointed out, picking up a used towel with which he
sponged and mopped his face. "Aahh! Lord, it's so hot and still!"

They despise each other, Lewrie quickly schemed; *damme, perhaps the
truth'll serve for a rare once! Navy politics, feuds, and jealousy, Gawd! But
I do need a patron out here . . . bad!*

"General Sir Harold Lamb insisted that he do so, sir, whilst I was
present, so he could hardly refuse him," Lewrie said, daring a cynical
grin. "I'd already angered him in Kingston harbour, and I think he
blames me for having guns stripped from his ship once we brought a
convoy here. And, whilst engaged against the Samboes, I rejected his
summons to go aboard *Halifax* 'til we were out of munitions and targets.
Munitions which I requested from his ship . . . which request was ignored, too, sir."

"His loss of guns was my doing," Nicely said, grinning after he had
dried his face. "What *did* you do in Kingston harbour?"

"My libertymen sang too loud and woke him at midnight, sir."

Nicely found that delicious, and uttered a bark of laughter.

"You'll do, Captain Lewrie," Nicely told him, "you'll do quite well.

Tomorrow morning, once laden, take up a closer anchorage to the shore. I shall put a flea in General Maitland's ear regarding this indirect fire business . . . have him second his most experienced artillery officer aboard your ship. There's always the possibility that if the enemy presses Maitland back to the town environs, we may have to try it on, and see if there's anything to it . . . and how well you do."

"Aye aye, sir," Lewrie said, getting the wind up, again.

"I'll forward your report to Admiral Parker at Kingston, with a recommendation of mine own," Nicely promised. "Is there anything else I may do for you, Lewrie?"

"I sent in a prize with my Third Officer and best midshipman in charge of her, sir. I lost two midshipmen at Mole Saint Nicholas, and I need my people back."

"Can't," Nicely brusquely said. "Sent her on to Jamaica, with all those French privateersmen. I'd no place to secure them. She's in the hands of the Prize Court, though, so there'll be some reward coming . . . should that be a comfort."

"Oh well, then," Lewrie said with a sad shrug. "Short-handed a tad longer. Promote a couple of quartermasters or mates as acting midshipmen? Uhm . . . when the Army buckled and broke, sir . . . do you know anything about the Fifteenth West Indies regiment? An old friend of mine commands it."

"You don't mean that fop Colonel Beauman, do you?" Nicely asked, a look of distaste on his face.

"Oh *no*, sir!" Lewrie all but gasped. "I know Colonel Beauman, from long ago, but . . . I refer to Colonel *Cashman*!"

"Oh, *him*!" Nicely laughed, throwing back his head. "One devil of a fellow. That's alright, then. Pity, though, about him and his regiment. There's a bit of a stink, after the battle up at Croix des Bouquets. Not in good odour with Maitland since. Your friend lives, though, have no fears on that score. They're somewhere along the lines, fairly close to town, I believe."

"Well, that's good," Lewrie said, letting out a breath of pent worry. "Whilst we're loading, do you not have anything for me to do, sir, I'd very much like to look Cashman up."

"Shouldn't be a problem," Nicely decided. "God keep you, then,

Captain Lewrie. We'll surely speak again, as long as this poor siege lasts. *Adieu*, sir." Nicely and Lewrie doffed hats, then Nicely strode out into the torrid sunshine, reaching into his left sleeve for a handkerchief, and sneezing as the full brunt of the sun struck him, before stomping briskly towards the quays.

The staff officers at the commandeered headquarters were loath to loan him a horse, but Lewrie cajoled them after a long palaver and rode up the streets out of town. The paving stones gave way to silty dirt and sand, the last tumbledown shanties and hovels of Free Blacks and *petits blancs* were left behind, and the undergrowth grew thicker and closer to the track, reaching overhead to interlace and block off the sun, making multiple swaying dapples of soft green light along the eerie tunnel through the woods.

Maybe this isn't such a good idea, Lewrie thought, drawing his thin-shanked, weary mare to a halt. He took off his hat to fan himself and swabbed his cheeks and chin of dripping sweat on his right sleeve. Though he was in deep shade, there was no relief from the heat and, perplexingly, it felt even warmer than under the crushing sizzle of the sun; airless, too, the heat muggy and close, and so humid that he could feel his breath *flow* in and out like running water.

Eeriest of all, it was ominously quiet—but for the throb of those damned drums, and the hum and buzz of mosquitoes, tiny bees, and large flies that swarmed his sweaty horse and sweaty self.

When first he'd entered the woods, there had been a faint hum of town doings astern, and the ring of axes thwocking into timber some-where ahead. Exotic birds had screeched and hooted, crickets and grass-hoppers had sawed and fiddled and cheeped, frogs had croaked and whatever-the-hell-they-weres had rustled and whined. Now, all was si-lent; but for the deep waggon ruts in the dirt track and the imprint of army boots along the verges where soldiers had slogged to avoid the puddles, he could conjure that he was the only human in the trackless forest, the only person to have come this way in days!

Maybe I don't like Cashman that much! he told himself considering turning around and going back aboard ship, with grim remembrances of the underlying terror of wild wastelands he'd felt as a young midshipman in the woods of the Yorktown peninsula in the Virginia Colony before the siege began. His future brothers-in-law, Governour and Burgess Chiswick, had taunted him about skulking Red Indians, Rebel snipers, and irregulars just waiting to lift his hair, cut his throat, and carve off his privates, whilst screeching with glee and dancing above his half-dead body!

Lewrie could not see half a decent pistol-shot in the forests on either hand, the dirt track a demi-lune forming the bottom of the view down a telescope's tube, and . . .

He heard a jingling-plashing-thumping approach up ahead and round the slight bend in the road! He groped for the double-barreled pistol in his waistband, thumbing the right hammer back to half-cock, his legs tightening about his mount, and ready to saw the reins to run back into town, heels pressed to the mare's belly, about to thump her to her fastest gait.

"Oy, thank God!" a soldier, a Corporal, cried as he came round the bend on a horse. He was a wizened little fellow, not as big as a minute, clad in a tunic that had faded from red to pink, and stained white breeches, his walnut-tan face grizzled with several days' worth of whiskers. A short musketoon was slung across his back, and across the saddle in front of him lay several lengths of chain.

"Ah!" Lewrie snapped, very much relieved, de-cocking his pistol.

"Thort I wuz t'onliest man alive fer a bit there, sir," the old veteran merrily cackled, pacing his horse up next to him. "Spooky ol' place, 'ese woods, sir."

"Indeed," Lewrie "windily" agreed. "I'm looking for the whereabouts of the Fifteenth West Indies."

" 'Bout a mile an' a bit straight on, sir, then veer right along the lines, first track ya come to. Woods open up so's ya can see your way, not a quarter-mile yonder, where a big plantation wuz, an' you're fair-safe, then . . . among soldiers, beyond 'em fields an' all, sir."

"Thankee, Corporal."

"Be glad t'get outta th' woods, meself," the corporal said, taking a swig from a wood canteen. "Get 'ese trace-chains fixed, so's me major's waggon'll draw again. Why, do I not find a handy smith, h'it'd take me all this day an' night, sir! Major'd not expect me t'risk 'is road after dark, sir . . . no, 'e wouldn't!"

The "water" in the man's canteen smelled hellish alcoholic to Lewrie's nose. An experienced old hand, the corporal obviously wanted any excuse to toddle off and dawdle over his errand, getting a shot at a decent meal, a thorough drunk, and a woman before having to go back to the Army's misery.

"You goin' up to h'arrest some o' them officers from 'at regiment, sir, 'em Fifteenth? Good Lord knows somebody should, th' cowards. 'Tis said, sir . . . some of 'em rode off an' left 'eir men t'die or get took by 'em dark devils. Won't see 'at in an *English* regiment, nossir, but . . . wot can ya h'expect from such an idle lot, sir?"

"Visiting a friend," Lewrie answered.

"I'll ride on then, sir, an' keep safe," the soldier bade him, saluting for the first time, with a leery expression for anyone with a friend from among that regiment's officers.

"Same to you, Corporal," Lewrie rejoined, doffing his hat, and clucking his mount into motion once more.

CHAPTER TWENTY-FOUR

*H*e found the Fifteenth at long last, after casting rightwards past the fork in the road, slowly walking his mount along the rear of several other units' encampments and entrenchments.

Lewrie had seen defeat and despair often enough in his eighteen years of service, and this army was showing all the signs of it. Care wasn't being taken of equipment, but for personal arms. Uniforms were still mud and grass-stained, and the clotheslines were not the usually crowded rows of bunting. The soldiers looked hang-dog and lethargic.

When he got to the lines of the Fifteenth West Indies, it was even worse. There were very few tents, replaced with brush arbors or mere awnings stretched beneath the trees, where exhausted, sick, and hollow-eyed men lolled nigh-insensible to everything around them, not even raising their heads at the rare sight of a naval officer on horseback. What tents remained contained the wounded . . . and the still-neat line of larger pavillions for officers. One, the largest of all, he took for Ledyard Beauman's; that was where some fashionably dressed and rather clean officers had gathered, raising a merry din as if they were enjoying themselves, where fine horses stood cock-footed and shivered their skins and lashed their tails and manes against the flies, blowing and nickering now and again in exasperation or boredom.

Lewrie dismounted and led his horse down the lines until coming to a sizable pavillion with a large fly, and two sides halfway rolled up. He recognised the coat hanging on a nail driven into the tentpole in front. From within there came the sounds of snores.

"Hallo, the house," he called, rapping on the pole.

"Ummph!" came a querulous, half-awake plaint.

"Wakey wakey, lash up and stow, you idle bugger," Lewrie japed.

"Alan?" Cashman croaked, coughing and clearing his throat before sitting up on his sagging cot. "What the bloody hell're you doing way out here?" he asked, swinging his booted legs to the ground.

"Came in search of good cheer," Lewrie said, kneeling down and tying his reins through a rusty iron ring set in a tethering-stone.

"Came to the wrong bloody place if you did . . . more fool you," Cashman grunted, scrubbing his face with dry hands and yawning broadly, reaching for a towel to soak up his sweat. "No joy here, believe me."

"Ran into a soldier on my way here . . ."

"Not hard t'do, that," Cashman snorted, taking the lid off his tin water pail and dipping out a ladleful to swish around his mouth and spit out. "We're lousy with 'em. Least, we were."

"Said you'd had a spot of bother, recently. Asked if I was up to arrest anyone," Lewrie said, ducking under the tent fly to sit on a folding camp stool and fan himself with his hat. How Cashman slept under canvas was a wonder to him; the temperature felt as if it had increased by a full twenty degrees inside the tent.

"Wish *someone* would!" Christopher spat, dipping up more water, this time to guzzle down. "My luck, though, they'd come for me."

"What happened?" Lewrie asked, waving off Cashman's offer of a crooked, local-rolled *cigarillo*.

"Feel like a stroll?" Cashman asked, fumbling with his tinder-box and striking flint on steel several times before getting the lint burning, with which to light his *cigarillo*.

"Not really, it's hotter than the hinges of Hell."

It was no matter to Cashman, who, now puffing away, stood and pulled on his waistcoat, coat, hat, and sword-belt and led the way out to the bare and sandy tramped ground of the encampment.

"We'll go up and take a look at the lines," Cashman announced, setting off for the woods to the east. Lewrie could but shrug before following him; at least, from Cashman's initial pace, it would be the slow, ambling sort of stroll he had in mind.

"That purblind, Goddamned *fool* back there!" his old friend said at last, once out of earshot of the officers' lines. "He got us halfway massacred . . . and now swears it wasn't any fault of his! I've lost a third of the regiment, dead or wounded, and the rest're so terrified, I doubt they'll be worth a tuppenny shit the next time they face those devils of L'Ouverture's."

"How?" Lewrie asked.

"Why, by being himself, Alan," Cashman said, the scorn dripping. "By bein' his merry little, useless, witless self! General Maitland put us out on his left flank, braced by a veteran regiment of regulars on the extreme left. Heard about the battle we had t'other day, at Croix des Bouquets? The 'Port-Au-Prince Derby'?"

"Only that there was one," Lewrie told him.

"Had us some trenchworks, not much, 'bout waist-deep, with the bushes and such cut and cleared a couple of hundred yards out beyond," Cashman explained as they threaded through a worn path into the woods towards their new front. "Caltrops in the grass and all, two guns on the line for help. 'Bout a half-hour before sunup, here the darkies came, the sun in our eyes. Advance party, a 'forlorn hope,' that had most-like spent all night creepin' through the grass to us? Sprang up at the first volley, and got into the trenches with their cane-knives and short spears. Some o' them just fire-hardened canes or branches, if you can feature it. I'd kept two companies back for just such an emergency, and brought 'em up myself. First time in real action, our lads, so a fair number broke, no matter what the sergeants did t'keep 'em steady . . . you know how that is."

"I'm with you," Lewrie said, idly swatting a mosquito that landed on his cheek.

"Don't *do* that!" Cashman snapped in a hoarse whisper. "It draws fire. The darkies snipe at any sound, and some of 'em are dab hands at shootin'. Not just muskets out there . . . some have *jaeger* rifles and rifled huntin' pieces . . . took 'em from their dead masters' plantation homes. Sometimes they take a blind shot, at night especially. T'keep us awake and scared, mostly, but every now and then, they'll wing some poor bastard."

Sure enough, a second later there came the sharp crack of a gun from the distant woods, the faint warble of a ball passing over their heads, and a spattering of leaves. Native birds screeched in sudden alarm and took wing, sounding like a musket volley as they beat their wings and crashed through the limbs and leaves.

"You were sayin'," Lewrie prompted as they began to walk on.

"First waves came on, runnin' flat-out," Cashman continued with his tale of woe. "Not a *one* of 'em armed, not with muskets, actually. Socket bayonets jammed on sticks, that sort o' thing, and we're firin' by platoon volleys, wastin' lead on 'em, and the smoke's gettin' thick like it always does, and up comes Beauman, the chuckle-headed bastard! You could *hear* 'em breakin' without seein' 'em. Yellin' and hollerin' fit t'bust, at first, then steppin' on the caltrops and howlin' like a pack o' ramcats . . . wounded and dyin' weepin' and wailin'? I decided t'send the two reserve companies back to the rear, but Beauman wouldn't hear of it. Wanted 'em formed twenty paces behind the trenchworks and him behind 'em. Personal bloody guard, even if their charge was broke and bloodied. It was over, d'ye see, Alan. L'Ouverture and his generals, they'll trade half a regiment just t'count your guns, see if they can find a weak spot, before they send in the troops with muskets. We had 'em beaten, with only eight companies . . . them slidin' off to our left, and catchin' more Hell from the regulars."

"Feeling about for your flank," Lewrie intuited.

"Damme, we'll make a soldier of ya, yet," Cashman chuckled with a sour amusement. "That's exactly what they were doin'. Right professional of 'em, really. Fightin' falls off on our front, the gun smoke clears, we've laid out an even hundred or so, and the lads're feelin' right pert, and cheerin' like 'billy-oh.' Then the firin' picks up on the far left, and you could hear a charge against the regulars, where they'd found the flank, and field pieces firin' cannister and grape into 'em. You could *just* see the men of the Ninth Hampshires wheelin' about, refusing the flank with three or four companies and a gun, bent back at right angles. That's when Beauman lost it for us, the simple sonofabitch."

"What'd he do?"

"Took the two reserve companies, the light and grenadier company from our line, and ordered 'em to re-enforce the Hampshires," Cashman growled, slashing at the undergrowth with a stick. "We *told* him we'd lose touch on both *our* flanks if he did it, that the Cuffies would see it and hit our six remainin' companies, soon as he moved . . . the Hampshires needed help, they'd ask for it, a reserve regiment was in our rear for just such a thing, but he wouldn't listen. Wanted to do somethin' grand, I s'pose. Had hold of his bridle, and he lashed at me with his ridin' crop, sittin' up there on his big grey horse, so arrogant and dumb! Off he goes, with his favourites drawin' out their swords and *yelpin'* for it. All his bloody neighbours and debtors, hot for bloody *fame!* Well, even before they set off, and filed the grenadier company and light company out of line, the Hampshires had smashed the Samboes and didn't *need* the help, but . . . he was already in motion and I was left t'string at what was left, to cover the front."

"And the slaves hit you again," Lewrie said, half-knowing the worst.

"A big attack, that time, Alan old son," Cashman said, sighing with disgust and sorrow. "Damn' near a brigade, in a big block column, maybe two hundred across and might've been fifty deep, the front ranks with muskets this time, and skirmishers out front in pairs. I sent a galloper after Beauman, t'warn him what was comin' and how we needed all our lads back, soon as dammit, but they were on us before he could stir his slack arse up. *Damn* him!" Cashman spat, slashing hard at the weeds, as if it were happening that instant, and not several days ago.

"The line broke?"

"No, we held! Men goin' down like nine-pins, but we held for as long as we could," Cashman said. "Sent another galloper back for the reserve regiment . . . warn 'em, d'ye see? Well, here comes help at last, Beauman with our four companies, but I look back at him, and do ya know what I see? He's formin' 'em a hundred yards *behind* the line! We're on our own! Oh, he's trottin' back and forth, wavin' his sword and makin' his stallion rear, all glorious-like. Might've seen it in a damn' painting, I s'pose . . . but he ain't helpin' *us!* After my lads see 'em, all lined up and ready . . . then see the enemy comin' at a dead run with bayonets levelled, well . . . *that* was when we broke, and no holdin' 'em.

Thought it looked safer to the rear. That tore the line wide open, our wounded are gettin' butchered, and the Cuffies are rollin' up the right flank of the Hampshires and the left of what regiment was on our right, and the race was on! Those units pivoted companies backwards, to refuse, and our lads took it for a retreat. So did Beauman, damn him, and he's shoutin' for us *all* t'fall back on the reserves, and I'm yellin' 'No!' but our people're dyin', no matter if I could've held 'em, then it's Devil take the hind-most.

"I *tried* t'organise volley fire . . . front rank fires and falls back ten paces t'reload whilst the second rank fires? But Beauman and his damn' pets were orderin' 'em t'run, so once the first rank retired they took off for the woods, and not a second later, the second rank, and it's a complete rout, Goddammit!"

"That's where the whole army broke, then?" Lewrie asked.

"The very place," Cashman said with a sneer, "and it's all *our* fault. Oh, I got' 'em stopped, once they ran out of breath, and formed 'em up, what was left of 'em. Even got 'em t'go forward again, t'help the reserve regiment. No help from Beauman or his beau-dandies! They scampered off *God* knows how far to the rear! Didn't even see 'em 'til late in the afternoon, when the whole army had fallen back, but they'd had time t'get their stories straight, and met up with General Maitland first and fed him a tale of woe . . . how no one could've held against such a horde, no matter their *valiant* efforts! Blamed the regular regiment, the Hampshires for gettin' flanked . . . and me, for being unable to control the line!"

"Surely you protested, Kit!" Lewrie barked in outrage. "You've witnesses . . . you could even demand a court t'clear your name."

"Sent Maitland a written protest, with a list of witnesses, but the way things are goin' it'll be months from now 'fore a court can be seated . . . and where's my witnesses then? Half stand a fair chance o' dyin' on a darky's bayonet long before I need 'em," Cashman groused.

"And in the meantime, Beauman's free t'say anything he chooses, and lay the blame on you," Lewrie realised.

"Kingston and Spanish Town papers are owned by some of his *very* best friends, too," Cashman said, continuing his litany of anger. "After we lost so many local men, I'll be lucky I'm not hung before a court could sit . . . or 'De-Witted,' like that Dutchman got pulled to wee pieces by a mob with their bare hands."

"The sales price of your lands wouldn't matter much then, hey?" Lewrie commented, using a stick to whack some tall weeds himself.

"Even if I prevail at the court-martial, I'll still be ruined," Cashman spat. "Better I just challenge him, put a ball in him, and be done."

"Kit, for God's sake!" Lewrie said, frowning. "You can't just shoot him or carve him up! You'd have to resign your commission, and then you'd *never* get a court. Lieutenant colonels can't duel colonels, anymore than I could duel an admiral. Have t'be a civilian before you can 'blaze' with a senior officer. Otherwise, we'd have eighteen-year-old generals and admirals, and all my lieutenants would be ten! Want a promotion . . . want command? Just eliminate the next highest over you! Besides," he added, "your Maitland ain't a complete fool. He *must* know that Ledyard's got the forehead of a hen, and you're the one who saved what was left. Think it over . . . compose a letter of your own for the Jamaican papers, laying it all out. Believe me, no amount of money or power's going t'make people believe *he's* the better soldier. Any man who's had dealings with him'll most-like already think him a dunderhead."

"Might work," Cashman allowed. "But if it doesn't, and I don't get my court, then I'll have no choice but to resign my commission . . . and *then* duel him. If you're still around, I'll ask you to be my second."

There was no way that a friend, and a gentleman, could turn away from such a request; Lewrie could only dumbly nod his head and accept.

"If there's no *other* solution . . . and if that's the only satisfaction you'll have, then . . . aye, of course, Kit. I'll second you."

"He refuses, I'm proved right, *and* shown him up for a coward," Cashman said, looking wolfish with anticipated delight. "Does he take me up on it, then I'll *kill* him! Think I could sail away happy after that. Thankee, Alan. I knew I could count on you."

"What friends are for," Lewrie replied, feigning agreement. He had no doubts that Cashman could blow Beauman's heart clean out with a pistol or carve him to chutney sauce with a sword. What sorrowed him was the fact that once the deed was done his old friend would be penniless, and too suspect to ever go for a soldier again. His lot would be ignominous exile, perhaps to those southern United States that he'd disparaged.

"Think my writing General Maitland could help?" Lewrie offered.

"Oh, please!" Cashman sneered with bitter amusement. "Support from a *sailor* who wasn't even there? Hardly. But thankee for the offer, Alan old son. Hmmm . . . gettin' on for late afternoon. Best we get you back to town. The darkies begin to play up at night."

Sure enough, the drums had begun again, and that infernal chant could be heard far off in the eastern jungles.

> *"Eh! Eh! Bomba! Heu! Heu!*
> *Canga, bafio, té!*
> *Canga, moune de le!*
> *Canga, do ki la!*
> *Canga li!"*

"What language *is* that?" Lewrie asked, chilled to the bone once more by the sounds. "And what does it mean?"

"Some African tongue from the Ivory Coast, where they came from," Cashman told him, starting to lead them back toward the tent lines. "I was told it means 'We swear to destroy all the whites, and everything they own. Let's die if we don't.' Way they fight, *I'd* believe it."

"Anything I can send to ease your misery?" Lewrie asked him.

"Can't thing of anything, no," Cashman sadly told him. "Keep a sharp eye peeled, mind. There's always skulkers along the roads after dark."

"Oh, thankee for tellin' me!" Lewrie barked. "I was nervous enough ridin' up here alone in broad daylight!"

"You could always stop in town at Jean-Pierre's and look up yer little Henriette." Cashman snickered. "There's a spur t'move ya along."

"Way Port-Au-Prince is fallin' apart, I'm better off aboard my ship," Lewrie admitted, a knot of unease growing between his shoulder blades—where the musket ball, spear, cane knife, or poisoned arrow might strike were he unwary, or just plain unlucky on his lone ride back. "'Tis not a sailor's fight, this sort of . . ."

Cashman cocked an eye at the sky, and the place of the sun. He clapped Lewrie on the back, suspiciously near that knot of unease, as if he suspected his qualms, then chuckled.

"Nothin' like a little dread t'keep you cloppin' along faster. Think there's time for the stirrup-cup at my tent, then we'll get you on your way 'fore twilight gets too deep. There'll be a last rush of troops and officers on the road 'bout now, so it shouldn't be too bad."

"But keep my ears open and my head swivellin'?" Lewrie queried, suspicious of such blithe reassurances.

"Reins in yer left, cocked pistol in yer right," Cashman intoned.

And Lewrie made it a quick stirrup-cup, both he and horse antsy to the faint chorus and the vibrating drums.

"Canga, bafio té! Canga, moune de le!"

Lewrie took the salutes from the side-party, doffed his hat, and stepped inboard, just as the late afternoon heat began to dissipate in the face of a freshening breeze off the sea, as the sun sank lower in the west. Lt. Langlie and the Surgeon, Mr. Shirley, were awaiting him on the starboard gangway, looking anxious.

"Excuse me, sir, but this order came aboard for you, about one hour ago," Langlie said, offering a single sheet of paper, folded over and sealed with a tiny daub of wax. Lewrie took it and split it open.

"Aha," he sighed, making a face. "I see. Well, damme."

"Bad news, sir? Pardon my curiosity," Langlie enquired.

"Seems that General Maitland and Admiral Parker have struck a bargain with our foe, L'Ouverture, Mister Langlie," Lewrie informed him, his weariness taking over after days of enforced activity and briskness. "Since we now hold untenable positions in Saint Domingue, and to spare the further 'useless effusion of blood,' " he went on, dripping sarcasm, "Maitland has proposed an armistice. Once he receives L'Ouverture's assurances that the civilian populations of Jacmel, Mole Saint Nicholas, and Port-Au-Prince will be spared any 'reprisals,' we depart."

"Depart, sir? But . . ."

"Strike our tents and sail away," Lewrie spat, wadding up the order. "Abandon 'em to the 'good offices' of L'Ouverture's men, tuck our tails twixt our legs, and slink off . . . without even a last bark at 'em. We're to prepare to embark the Army and all its stores, and sail back to Kingston."

"Well, damme, sir," Langlie groaned, removing his hat to swab his forehead and shake his head in sorry wonder. "They beat us."

"Aye, it appears they have," Lewrie said. "Mister Shirley, the Army hospitals are filled with wounded. You'd best prepare for some of them to be put aboard."

"Of course, sir," Shirley replied, hemming and hawwing a bit, though. "There is another matter that you must know first, Captain."

"And what's that?" Lewrie asked, suddenly filled with a defeatist lassitude.

"Several of our people are sick, Captain," Shirley told him in a gruff mutter, all but wringing his hands in despair. "So far I cannot tell you with any certainty whether it's malaria or Yellow Jack. Three hands show the fever, sweats, and headaches of malaria—along with the requisite icy chills—but two more also exhibit pains in the back and limbs one would expect to see with a case of Yellow Fever, so I cannot—"

"Oh God, no!" Lewrie blanched, his worst long-lingering dread for the ship at last confirmed. "Only five, so far?"

"As of the start of the First Dog Watch, sir, but it could be a dozen more by sunup," Shirley grimly prophecied. "You are aware how quickly it can spread, Captain."

"Aye, I am," Lewrie sadly whispered. "Let's hope that *chichona* bark extract avails, Mister Shirley. Keep me informed, and make them as comfortable as you can. Anything you need . . ."

He turned away and went to the quarterdeck bulwarks to peer out at the now dark and brooding shore of the anchorage. Port-Au-Prince, its docks and streets near the harbour, was lit by torches and faint lanthorns where soldiers and sailors off the stores ship laboured at the mounds of munitions and rations—this time to start reloading them for evacuation. Despite General Maitland's truce, the dull crack of a musket now and then broke the twilight's serenity along the lines deeper in the trackless jungles.

For nothing, Lewrie thought, groaning with weary cynicism; *'twas all for nothing. Nicholas and Sevier, Seaman Inman . . .*

Toussaint L'Ouverture, a plump little Black man, unschooled in weapons and tactics, and his army of tag-rag-and-bobtail former slaves with agricultural tools, had beaten the British Army! He had no way to fathom the "how" of it, except ... to think that L'Ouverture's victory, and the uneasy peace which might follow it, was for the best. Every experience he had with slavery, the more he was put off by it, just as Cashman was. In the face of such an amazing debacle, even a rake-hell as casually "churched" as he could shrug and think it God's Will.

That wasn't to say that it didn't rankle, though; the bitter cup of defeat's gall had never been easy for Lewrie to swallow, ever since his first taste of it in 1780. And pondering the disgrace of sailing away after being bested by illiterate Blacks, by hordes of beasts with the musk of over-worked demons and not a jot of Christian mercy, not a jot of civilisation to their souls ...! Truce or not, what would keep L'Ouverture's hordes from butchering everyone indiscriminately ... when they massacred *petits blancs* and townsfolk in an orgy of gore, would *that* be God's Will, too? What would *their* Inquisition be like?

The *voudoun* drums in the hills and forests throbbed on as they had since weeks before. Tonight, though, they sounded less funereal, though just as ominous. Now the drums almost had a lilt, a celebratory liveliness, and Lewrie could conjure images of men and women capering and leaping in the savage glare of bonfires, flaunting finery stolen from the dead, brandishing cane knives, spears, and muskets, firing rounds off at the moon and whooping like victorious Muskogee Indians in Spanish Florida.

"Just thank God I'll never have t'set foot on *that* shore again," he whispered. "And you bastards are welcome to it."

For now, he had a crew to worry about, another debacle blooming on his own decks. Impossible as it might prove to be, to save his men from almost always fatal plagues, he didn't think it God's Will, or a form of punishment from On High that his poor sailors should suffer so for being unwitting pawns against the Saint Domingue Blacks' eventual freedom. Perhaps God would take their innocence into account and spare them ... or help him find a way to save them!

BOOK THREE

Sed ti qui vivum casus, age fare vicissim, attulerint.
Pelagine venis erroribus actus an monitu divum?

But come, tell in turn what chance has brought you
here, alive. Come you driven in your ocean-
wanderings, or at Heaven's command?

AENEID, BOOK VI 531-533
PUBLIUS VIRGILIUS MARO "VIRGIL"

CHAPTER TWENTY-FIVE

*W*e may consider ourselves fortunate," Sailing Master Winwood said, rapping his knuckles lightly on the wheel drum of the idle helm for luck, even so.

"Fortunate . . . aye, sir," Lt. Catterall replied with a roll of his eyes. "Eight dead so far, and thirty helpless with fever below. Why, with a run of luck such as that, I'd stake the family fortune."

"Consider the lot of those poor devils aboard the other ships," Winwood pointed out, gesturing across Kingston Harbour. "Nigh half of their men down sick or buried. Consider the lot of the soldiers we brought off from Saint Domingue, sir. A full third of them are dead, and now interred ashore. No, sir, for my money, *Proteus* has come off rather easily, for all the time we spent close to that pestilential shore. Even as a good Christian, which I hope I am, I must confess I find a certain comfort in the tales told about *Proteus* and her almost inexplicable birthing . . . and about our captain. Though the tales of his last ship, *Jester*, and the tales about our own, smack of heathen, pagan old sea-gods, the idea of him, and us with him, being guarded by a benevolent Divine hand are a form of solace in the face of Life's unfairness."

"Comforting, aye, Mister Winwood, but . . ." Catterall replied with a faint shrug; it was too warm for wider gestures. Catterall, a happy-go-lucky Deist and cynic, found Mr. Winwood's mysticism amusing. "The captain may be spoken of as a lucky captain, and his ships lucky by association, but . . . t'would *take* a pagan sea-god to deem *us* worthy in his sight."

That left unspoken the bald fact of Captain Lewrie's adultery, his recent dalliance with a half-caste Port-Au-Prince whore, the rumour of which had made the rounds belowdecks, usually accompanied by hoots of appreciation and admiration, rather than disapproval or envy.

"Ahem," Mr. Winwood commented by clearing his throat, blushing at the unsaid reminder of their captain's human frailty.

"But God loved even his King David . . . Bathsheba notwithstanding," Catterall drolly posed. "Something like that, sir?"

"Ahem," their priggish sailing master reiterated, tongue-tied and unable to respond to such wordly japing without violating his vows not to curse.

"The proof of the statement that God loves a sinner, in hope of his eventual salvation, or has use of him in His majestic plan, stands before me, sir," Winwood finally answered, glowering a touch.

"Point taken, sir," Catterall rejoined with a wink and chuckle. He was, in fact, rather proud of his repute as a rake-hell and a pagan, so Mr. Winwood's comment caromed right past him. "And I will stand in humble abeyance 'til His fated use for me is revealed."

"Uhm . . . excuse me, sirs, but the captain is coming off shore," Midshipman Elwes informed them, approaching them from his vantage point on the starboard bulwarks. Sure enough, the quick use of a glass showed one of the ship's larger boats stroking away from the piers, where it had landed another funeral and burying detail.

"Very well, Mister Elwes. Summon the side-party," Catterall instructed.

"Permission to mount ze quarterdeck?" Surgeon's Mate Durant, more laconic and weary than ever, requested from the base of the starboard ladder from the waist.

"Aye, come up, sir," Catterall allowed. "How's old Wyman?"

"I regret to inform you, sir, zat the poor man 'as just now gone away from us," Durant told him, wiping his hands on his apron, using a French phrase for departure from Life.

"Well, damme," Catterall muttered, face creasing in genuine sorrow; though taking an involuntary step away from Mr. Durant, as if to flee

Death's miasma . . . or the noisome reek of the Yellow Jack's last agony, when the victim voided his bowels, after many days of inability, and spewed up dark, bloody *vomito negro*. The stench of Wyman's dying clung to Durant's apron, bare arms, and very hair, like a whiff off the River Styx.

"That will make you Second Officer, Mister Catterall," Winwood needlessly pointed out. "And young Mister Adair an acting lieutenant."

"Indeed," Catterall said in a whisper, realising the enormity of their loss, and the onerous weight placed on his shoulders as a result.

"God help us, then," Winwood sniffed. "God help us all. 'Tis a horrid toast, 'to a bloody war or a sickly season' . . . so we may attain our desired promotions."

"Uhm . . . yes," Catterall said to that, turning away and feeling like a weary Atlas, sobered for once from all sarcasm.

God, not another *damn' funeral,* was Lewrie's first thought, once he had gotten the dismal news of Lt. Wyman's death. The first men who had died had been buried at sea, cleanly and neatly. The last five—no, six, Lewrie had to remind himself—were interred in the military cemetery outside Kingston. They lingered longer in the mind; the plots of mounded earth and simple wood crosses not quite so . . . forgettable, but more permanent, and seemingly, eternally dispiriting.

In the last few days, administering the Last Rites had become a daily chore, supplanting all the other cares a captain should have for his ship, and the mellifluous prose of the Book of Common Prayer cloying and banal, the litany *so* familiar that he could almost recite from memory, as if declaiming passages from Caesar's *Gallic Wars* at school.

Lewrie looked over at Midshipman Grace, feeling pangs of sympathy as the lad stumbled about the gun-deck as if in a trance, red-faced but dry-eyed after their last trip ashore in the cutter . . . to bury his grandfather, the canny Nore fisherman they'd known simply as the Older Grace. Now Mr. Grace's father, too, lay insensible beneath an awning stretched over the boat-tier beams up forrud by the foc'sle belfry, by turns shivering and teeth-chattering under three blankets, or sweating buckets and thrashing for relief from malaria. Arthur "The Middle"

Grace *might* recover, Mr. Shirley believed; it was malaria, not the Yellow Jack, and *chichona* bark extract was lengthening the calm periods 'twixt bouts, though he was still as weak as a wet dish-clout. Young Grace stumbled forward and knelt by his father's pallet, taking his hand and clinging and patting it.

"How's he doing?" Lewrie asked Durant in a soft mutter.

"It comes and goes, sir," Durant said, heaving another of those Gallic shrugs of his. "Improving, I venture to say."

"Mister Shirley?"

"He is resting, *Capitaine*. Ze strain 'as been 'orrible. It is a wonder, so enervated he 'as become, zat he 'as not succumbed himself. So far, it is ze old and weak, ze very young who fall ill and die."

"Any more cases?" Lewrie asked, crossing his fingers.

"Two, *Capitaine* . . . Seaman *Ordinaire* Harper and Landsman Drew," Durant mournfully went on. "Both, 'owever, display no sign of Yellow Jack. Only ze malaria. And zey are strong."

"But only one death today," Lewrie insisted.

"Ze poor Lieutenant Wyman, *oui* . . . but zere are two more 'ands who 'ave the Yellow Jack, and near ze last stages of ze malady, sir. I cannot imagine zey will see tomorrow's dawn."

"Damn, damn, damn!" Lewrie spat, weakly thumping a fist atop the cap-rail of the starboard gangway bulwarks. "I'm *tired* o' this, Mister Durant. There must be something more we can do."

"We do all zat medicine knows, sir," Durant objected. "*Chichona* extract at the first sign of sickness, salt water clysters and all the fresh water zey can drink, to ease ze constipation, and lack of . . . my English . . . pissing in zose wiz Yellow Jack. Better air on deck, shade and coolness? Mister Hodson smokes ze ship below wiz faggots of tobacco, we scour wiz vinegar and salt water, we root out ze rats and cockroaches, no one 'as lice or fleas. But it is all so confusing zat we 'ave both malaria and Yellow Jack at once together, *Capitaine*. Is ze *chichona* bark *good* for zose wiz the Yellow Jack, or harmful? Is fruit juice helpful, or does it produce more bile, zat, I zink is a symptom of Yellow Jack, and contributes to the *vomito negro*? Ze liver and ze kidneys of men who die of Yellow Jack, when examined after death, are ruined. It explains ze lack of piss, ze constipation, but ze why, or ze how . . . ?"

"And we've pumped the bilges so often, you could *eat* down there. There's no ordure, the pump-water comes out bright and clean," Lewrie wondered aloud. "We've burned loose gunpowder, buckets of tar, not a damned preventative that's *supposed* to work, works!"

"Water casks emptied, scoured wiz vinegar and sea water as well," Durant sadly agreed. "It was most odd, though, sir ... ze water casks we filled once we reach Jamaica? When we open zem wiz Mister Coote an' his mate, I find ze top of ze water thick wiz little nits. Set aside in a glass I cover wiz gauze, I find zat mosquitoes hatch out. I read of zis, regarding slave ships calling at Dahomey ... zat zey found nits in fresh water taken from running streams, as *well* as still pools. Wiz ze gauze, I filter ze water, skim ze tops, before we stow clean casks bellow, zis time. And ashore, *Capitaine,* pardon ze expense, but we found a shop zat sells extract of citron, and candles made wiz citron."

"They smell good, aye ... better than the mess-decks do now, at any rate," Lewrie agreed, with a firm nod of his head. "*How* expensive?"

"Cheaper zan ze *assafoetida* herbs, Capitaine," Durant said right quickly, to justify what was surely an unauthorised outlay. "Besides, ze *assafoetida* is very 'ard to find, at present. *Mais non,* ze merchant assures me zat, if citron candles, or if a mix of hot tar and citron oil, is lit and let smoulder and fume, ze house where they burn does not suffer malaria or Yellow Jack."

"Damme, a cure?" Lewrie exclaimed with great relief.

"For, uhm ... women of ze house, it seem, *Capitaine,*" Durant said, with a weasely look. "Men, who are about business outside ze home, are just as vulnerable *but,* sir, zose *inside* are protected! Ze citron, I believe, exudes a *sweet* miasma, countering ze *bad* miasmas zat cause malaria and Yellow Jack! Regard, *Capitaine,*" Durant said, becoming agitated and cheerful, waving off Lewrie's just-as-sudden scowling. "You go into ze forest, you find ze poisonous plant or weed. But every time, growing close by, is ze antidote! Nature will 'ave her balance, *n'est-ce pas?* Every *grand-mère,* your grannies, know of zis! Sickness follows contact wiz ze shore, but after a week or two at sea ze number of ze stricken diminishes ... until ze next contact wiz shore. Citron candle and citron tar smoke-pots burning below, by the hatchways, perhaps hung all about ze upper deck after dark, *blocks* ze insinuation of tropical miasmas, sir!"

"How much?" Lewrie asked again, arms crossed in leeriness.

"Twenty pound, ten shillings, five pence, *Capitaine*. Five pound of my own, some from Mister Hodson—zough he does not believe, he will grasp at ze straw, *n'est-ce pas?* Some from Mister Shirley, because he is desperate, and ze rest, uhm . . . from ship's funds, sir."

"For . . . perfume," Lewrie scoffed; for that was the only use he knew of for citron . . . other than colouring or zesting desserts.

"Please, I beg you, let me try it, *Capitaine*. Ze merchant says it is well recommended on ze Spanish Main, by ze Portugese in Brazil!"

"Oh, for God's sake, Mister Durant, he sold you a bill o' goods!"

"If nozzing else, *M'sieur Capitaine*, ze citron seems to drive ze pesky mosquito away," Durant insisted, playing his final card.

"Aye, then . . ." Lewrie finally relented. "If for nothing else but a good night's sleep, without all that buzzin' and swattin'. I'll let you try it. S'pose we could write it off as an experiment."

"God bless you, *Capitaine* Lewrie! *Merci, merci beaucoup!* You will see . . . I 'ave made up ze hot tar and citron oil already . . ."

"Thankee for asking first . . . sir," Lewrie scowled, turning away to go below to his cabins. "Mind you, this turns out to be a cure for malaria and Yellow Jack, put me down for a *large* share of the profit."

"But of *course, M'sieur Capitaine* . . . guaranteed!" Durant said with a gush, grandly doffing his plain hat and sweeping it down to the deck as he bowed his gratitude before scrambling down the ladder for the main companionway hatch, and his medical stores below.

The transom sash windows were open wide, the glazed panels in the coach-top overhead were propped open, and a canvas wind-scoop ventilator caught what little air stirred in the millpond-still harbour, but his great-cabins were still stifling. Lewrie stripped off his formal funeral finery and changed into a worn pair of white slop trousers, trading his fancy Hessian boots for a dowdy pair of calfskin slippers. He sat at his desk with a "top-silver" palmetto fan, clawing his neck-stock off and opening his shirt.

Aspinall brought him a glass of sugared lemon water, silently padding about as if fearful of catching Lewrie's eye. He'd been that deferential and insubstantial ever since the first deaths. Lewrie had a sip, and pondered which onerous task he'd undertake first. Sighing, he plopped his feet atop his desk and slouched down in his chair, feet aspraddle and crotch aired; it was too warm and humid to cross ankles.

There was the matter of letters to write to the dead mens' kin, but at the moment he felt too enervated, and too steeped in death, to tackle that chore. Besides, he had exhausted all the stock platitudes he knew for grief, and it wouldn't feel quite right to pen an identical letter to all, like an Admiralty form for indentures or broken spars.

With so many dead, dying, or bedridden for weeks as they healed, there was the Watch-And-Quarter Bill to be amended, but Lewrie thought that would best be done in concert with Lt. Langlie and the midshipmen, who worked more closely with the hands than he. Perhaps have them all in for a "working" breakfast? There was a cook to be discovered among the crew, since poor old lamed Curcy had been one of the first to pass over, and the food issued since had been positively vile. Foster, the Yeoman of The Powder, would move up to Gunner's Mate to replace poor Mr. Bess, whom they'd buried the last morning; he'd find another man handy with canvas and needles to replace the Sailmaker's Mate, young Hickey. If things went on as badly as they had so far, fully half of those thirty sick men presently laid out flat would die before the week was out, he realised, and the survivors wouldn't be worth tuppenny shit for two or three weeks more. Only two Ordinary and two Able Seamen were lost so far, but a fair number of the sick were the spryest topmen, the young and experienced hands a ship could not do without. And their replacements were half a world away, due on the next hired supply ship and not expected to arrive before the end of hurricane season, 'round October or November when the bulk of the "liners" returned from Halifax.

And always had first choice, damn them, their captains, and the seniority and favouritism that dictated the new mens' dispersement!

Not wishing to think about Watch-And-Quarter Bills, Lewrie had another sip of sweet lemon water and scowled, one eye asquint, at his desk . . . at his mail from England. After the first rushed reading, he wasn't so sure that he wanted to revisit those, either!

"Damme, pile it on, why don't You?" he muttered to God or Fate. "And thankee that trouble usually comes in threes!"

Plague, uselessness, and his personal life; each one a horror!

The letters from his father Sir Hugo had been the easiest stood, and had contained more pertinent information. What little he'd gotten from Caroline had been pure vitriol!

For it seemed that *another* of those damned, anonymous "My dear friend, you simply *must* know . . ." epistles had turned up on Caroline's doorstep, and this time whoever the Devil wrote them had known all and had *told* all regarding his visit to Theoni Connor's London town house, the day after Caroline had stormed off for Anglesgreen in high dudgeon; how Theoni had coached down to Sheerness and had cohabited as man and wife with him for an entire week before *Proteus* had sailed! The anonymous writer had even named the inn and the placement of their set of rooms, How early their candles were snuffed . . . !

So much for 'time heals all wounds,' Lewrie glumly thought, once he'd read Caroline's lone, accusatory missive; *and you can chuck 'least said and soonest mended' and 'absence makes the heart grow fonder' over the side, too!*

And damn his father, but he wrote about as superciliously as he *looked*, with passages of sympathy interspersed with others bearing the tone of "I told you so!" or even sour amusement, as if writing one of his old cronies from the Hellfire Club or his first regiment about the peccadilloes of a total stranger, over which they could both crow!

"Sophie continues rather wan," Lewrie read, "though she has taken up of late with the company of Richard Oakes, one of Harry Embleton's fellow roisterers—one with some sense, at bottom, at the very least— who is a Captain of Cavalry in the local Yeomanry militia, and shapes well as a soldier. Pity he's a first son, not down for a set of colours like his brother Roger. He will, however, inherit substantial acreage, and may be thought a prize catch in these parts (dull as they may be). You *are* aware, though, that somewhere along the line, to Caroline's great Furor, you evidently gave permission for Sophie and your own First Officer, Lt. Anthony Langlie (a worthy unknown to me) to correspond. The Arrival of a letter from Jamaica is become a momentous Event in your household."

"And when the Devil did I do that?" Lewrie muttered to himself, vowing that he and young Langlie were due a heart-to-heart meeting, soonest! A rather loud one, he expected.

"Caroline, of course, dismissed the very idea at once, damning *all* Sailors as highly suspect, which vocal and insistent disapproval has, given Sophie's contrary Nature, made her the more eager to correspond. Just recall how your earlier disapproval of Harry Embleton almost drove her to elope with him to Gretna Green!"

And damn his father some more, but he'd found it so amusing that he simply *had* to relate how "... once Services were done two Sundays past, inspired perhaps by Rev. Goodacre's sermon on the forgiveness of Sins, your little Charlotte accosted all and sundry in the church yard with the pronouncement that '*My* daddy's a sinner, *and* a filthy beast!' in her usual loud and *piercing* voice, extolling the congregation for their prayers. Embarassing, of course, but quite droll, you must admit. 'Out of the mouths of babes,' as it were, hey?"

Droll, hell! Lewrie thought, squirming anew in long-distance embarassment; *and Caroline* not *so quick to shush her, either!*

That was followed by a long plaint as to how *he* was being "cut" or snubbed by the local gentry, forced to spend more time on his farm— *alone!*—or being positively *driven* to flee up to London, where his new town house was shaping main-well, and plans for a gentlemens' *hôtel* and lodging club were coming together quite nicely, thankee very much, and the London Season was lively and provided him much distracting *Solace* and diverting Amusement, in *their* time of Troubles!

As to those Troubles, "... but your brother-in-law Governour is hellish exercised, nigh to choleric Frenzy, by your Faithlessness, and swears that he saw it coming years before, but could not dissuade you, or his Dear Sister, from your Folly. He now goes about swearing that, had he the Occasion to confront you *visage contre visage* as the French say, he would quite gleefully do you in for the Shame you have brought upon the Chiswick Name, the gentlemanly constricts of a Duel bedamned."

Lewrie had himself a skeptical snort over that threat; Governour was approaching twenty stone in weight, and getting out of *bed* lately was enough to turn his '*visage*' choleric! *Damn* swords or pistols; if it came to that he'd challenge him to a foot race and see who keeled over first!

Back during the Revolution, when Governour was as lean and sinewed as a young panther, it would have been a different proposition, but good living and prosperity had taken its toll.

On that score, his father had further written ". . . when last I took my mid-day meal at the Red Swan Inn, the churl actually dared to banter *me*, your carcass not being immediately available. I quickly informed Mr. Chiswick that, should he desire an early Death, I was more than willing to oblige him. Did he desire Pistols at twenty paces, I would await his Seconds, though it was no affair of mine, and that his use of my Presence as an excuse for his disgraceful and boastful Behaviour would not be tolerated even by a gentleman of only the slightest acquaintance with you. I further informed him that I found all his Ranting to be due to your Absence, and *not* a thing he would do in your Vicinity. Then, following that slur, did he wish Aggrievance, I told him that I would meet him that Instant on the side lawn with a small-sword. Alan, the weather has been most cooperative this spring, and you should see how Verdant the countryside is become. The side yard, your lawn, and my new-sodded ones, have come up something wondrous to behold, do you care to know.

"He made a great Show of Apoplexy, but side-wise demurred, not refusing *exactly*, and stated that his Argument was with you, not your poor old Father. At which shilly-shally I brusquely informed him of the consequences of his rash Intemperance, assuring him that once you were returned to England, you would be *more* than willing to confront him in any manner he wished, and to temper his utterances with the sure certain, and fatal, Risk to his self in Mind. . . ."

And set me up for a killin' duel, Lewrie gloomed; *thankee very damn much, you old braggart! You* never *did me any favours, did ya?*

Sir Hugo further carped that he now took his custom to the Olde Ploughman Inn, and that, sterling beer notwithstanding, he had never been so bored in his life, nor entered such a seedy establishment than that, comparable to a tumbledown Irish *shebeen* or Hindoo *arrack*-dive! Poor him, being forced to rub elbows with the common folk!

It seemed that Caroline, in a raging snit, had determined that all plans for Hugh to take colours as an Army officer, or even *see* the slightest glimpse of sea water all his born days, much less go in his father's (disreputable!) footsteps as a Midshipman in the Royal Navy, were quite well "scotched," too. Sewallis and Hugh, *she* had written him, would board away this fall, at a school which stressed Christian and Classical preparation for the civilian, country gentry life, if not a career in the *clergy*; which decision Sir Hugo had deemed a mortal-pity in *his* letter, decrying the waste, of Hugh at least, who was so suited for a military or naval career.

Caroline had portrayed the school differently, of course, and spitefully implied that it was the least expensive she could discover that still held the acceptable *ton* for Hugh and Sewallis's entry into Society; that they could no longer count upon "their oft-absent, and indifferent Father" in his "meanness" to fund a better schooling.

Their new school was small, she'd written, but not too far away, in Guildford, and was run by a renowned and respected High Church rector and his equally virtuous wife, well recommended by the Reverend Goodacre.

". . . at least your Sons will grow up in proper Fear of the Lord, under a *strict* Christian tutelage that imparts modest and humble Moral Behaviour, even if *you* were deprived of such, sir. Sewallis and Hugh, I vow, will never emulate you!"

And, to his greater sorrow, Caroline no longer thought that any purpose would be served by any correspondence from *him*, nor would they be allowed the distraction of writing back. His sons had greeted that edict with much wailing and weeping, she had confessed, but ". . . the least said, soonest mended,' and 'out of sight, out of mind.' I know that boys shed their Grief after a Season, unlike girls. After a time, the rigours of Education, the distractions of games and healthy sports would engross their interests, making your memory an *eminence gris*, one best left unseen and un-thought of. Hence, sir, sooner or later quite *justly* Forgotten, as all Ogres merit!"

Damn, but that felt so unfair! Right, so he'd strayed; rather like a rutting bull run from his pasture, admittedly, but . . . to turn his children against him, actively encourage their hatred, break their hearts and *send* them weeping and snuffling, just for spite and revenge, well . . . that was simply *too* much! Lewrie shook his head in sorrowful wonder that his sweet and gentle wife, who made such a "do" about the works of Christian charity and forgiveness, would go so far as to seem a Medea, who would *slay* her children to get her own back against that bootless Jason!

Poor little tykes, was his first thought; *Wonder what this will cost me,* was his second.

In comparison, the thick packet of letters from Theoni Connor, one for every week he'd been gone, were a drink of cool water, ambrosia of the Olympian gods, rather than the gall and dirt that Caroline had offered up. Oh, they were so chatty, so informative about her doings, how her firstborn Michael was sprouting, and how much joy *their* son Alan James Connor provided her, now that he was toddling and beginning to babble almost comprehensible words! Scandals in Society (in which theirs didn't signify, thankee Jesus!), political rumours from supper parties among the powerful, notice of naval actions farther afield from his own bailiwick . . .

And firm, devoted, fond, and teasing Love!

Most especially, the *non*-judgmental kind of Love. To her lights he was still a Paragon, a Hero, her own True Blue Heart of Oak, one who could do no wrong, and ". . . though we may never dare show our Affection in Public, yet every night I clutch my pillows, proud to be your *Amour,* dear Alan, and sometimes find it hard to eschew a ringing Declaration of the fact of Us to one and all, and bedamned to their disapproval."

You just keep up that eschewing, old girl! Lewrie thought, with a groan or two for the consequences, squirming some more in his chair, groping at his crutch in remembered fever, and thinking that he should write her back, *instanter,* to warn her about that anonymous scribbler so eager to ruin his life. Sooner or later he could find a target for his bile closer to home, and heap calumny on her, as well.

But it was so hot and still, and he was so very tired and worn down to a nubbin by his cares, that any task involving anything more of him than slouching and brooding felt quite beyond him at the moment.

Faintly, he heard groans from up forrud and below on the mess-deck. There came a retching noise, a weak "Oh God, save me!" from one of the sick or dying, he knew not which, as one of the fevers caused a sailor to void his stomach.

There was nothing he could do to help them, he now realised in grim sorrow. Durant's citron-tar fumes would avail, or not, and only

God would decide—it was beyond him. All he could do was bide his time 'til the next death, the next drear funeral, the next grief.

He closed his eyes, lolled back his head, and tried to nap, to find at least a little mindless, temporary escape in unaware sleep.

CHAPTER TWENTY-SIX

*N*ow it was fourteen hands dead and buried.

Proteus still lay immobile from her best bower and stern kedge anchors, moored seemingly forever in a Slough of Despond, days after the ships of the line had departed to "summer" on the North American Station at Halifax; taking with them hundreds upon hundreds of whole, fit, and *healthy* sailors, their crews made up to full capacity or even beyond—sailors Lewrie would have happily killed for, just for some of them, the merest pittance of re-enforcement.

Was there a single bright spot to their situation, Mr. Durant had provided it; for the liberal use of smouldering, guttering citron candles and hot tar and citron oil pots seemed to have cut the number of new men infected almost to nothing, even still moored near the miasmic Jamaican shore, which should have been a ready source of new infection.

Oh, there were still over forty hands sick or staggering weakly on light duty as they mended, and of those sick, Durant expected at least five or six more to succumb, mostly to Yellow Jack, which was a much more pernicious disease. The bulk of the crew who had gone sick had caught malaria, which was manageable with *chichona* bark extract; a man could live with malaria, despite the unpredictable recurring bouts that would follow him the rest of his days, Hodson and Durant had assured him.

The Surgeon could no longer assure Lewrie of anything; he was the thirteenth corpse to be laid to rest ashore, wearing out his strength in caring for others. Cox'n Andrews had expressed the thought that Mr. Shirley had perished of shame and guilt, for not being able to do more, or save more.

That had presented Lewrie with a vexing problem, of explaining to Durant that his warrant as Surgeon's Mate was predated by Mr. Hodson, making him senior, and earning him promotion to Acting-Surgeon instead of Durant. Durant had taken it with seeming good grace, disappointed though he was. Hodson was risen from a doctor's apprentice before he joined the Navy, whilst Durant had been a trained and certified doctor in France before the Revolution and the Terror, educated even beyond the usual, damned-near as well as a university educated Englishman who could merit the prestigious title of "Physician," and be addressed as a "Doctor" instead of the "Mister" of a mere surgeon. Lewrie had tried to assure him that it was the perverse way of the service, *not* a slur upon his nationality. Mr. Durant had squinted his eyes in the faintest expression of pain—Hell's Bells, perhaps in frustration, or simple bitterness in the face of British prejudice—and had said no more.

"I assure you, Mister Durant, my reports to superiors mention your stalwart efforts, your acumen, and your dauntless fervour, along with your countering sweet miasma theory with the citron oil extract," Lewrie had stressed, almost going to his knees to beg his pardon, "and I *know* who is the better man, but damned seniority rules me, else I'd name you in charge this instant, sir! The staff-captain . . ."

Durant had merely shrugged philosophically once more, then gone forward and below, and Lewrie was sure that he'd lost him. As if one more thing could go wrong.

Aye, the staff-captain, Sir Edward "Bloody" Charles, too! When Lewrie had taken his reports over to Giddy House and Fort Charles, he had found a *new* source of worry and aggravation! This time, there had been no "chummy" glass of claret for him, no clubman's wing chair.

"Captain Blaylock describes you pretty-much as I expected you to turn out, Captain Lewrie," Sir Edward had gravelled from behind his desk, face as frownish as a stout bulldog's, "rash, intemperate, self-centred, obstreperous, and nearly insubordinate! Ah, but you will have your own way, *go* your own way, orders bedamned, will you not?"

"I consider that an unfair characterisation, sir," Lewrie told him, as reasonably and as moderately as he could.

"*I* decide how you are characterised, sir!" Sir Edward had barked in full dyspepsia. "I'm also aware of your foolhardiness over this 'indirect' gunfire support. Good God, man, you could have killed half our own soldiers!"

"But I *didn't*, sir! General Sir Harold Lamb was most appreciative of it. He sent Admiral Parker a letter about it, I have a copy of it," Lewrie had shot back, unable to stifle his combative nature in the face of an injustice to his repute. "Captain Blaylock of *Halifax* seemed eager to emulate our work, next morning. Did he, sir?" Lewrie asked, "Did *he* kill anyone from our side when he took my anchorage, sir?"

"No, he did not," Sir Edward had truculently admitted, "but he only fired a few rounds before our troops, re-enforced by the regiments he landed, retook enough of their old perimeter beyond the range of his carronades. Poor Blaylock . . . lost his First Lieutenant, Duncan, along with three seamen. Shot from ambush, Captain Lewrie, by sneaking, low-down skulkers! Bad as 'Jonathon' riflemen! Officers deliberately targeted, bah!"

Poor Duncan, Lewrie thought, feeling fey and queasy; knew *I was talkin' to a dead man, last time I saw him! Price you pay, when you go huntin' fame and glory.*

"My condolences, sir, but I lost two midshipmen under much the same circumstances," Lewrie had replied.

"And a damn' good reason never to engage in such hare-brained idiocy," Sir Edward had glowered. "Only a perfect lunatic'd dare it, Captain Lewrie . . . someone daft as you, I dare say. Aye, we received Sir Harold's letter, but he's a bloody *soldier*, so what does he know of things? Both Admiral Parker and I concur in deeming your experiment à mad-hatter exercise, and are considering sending a letter of censure to Admiralty. Unless you are thinking of ever doing it again, hmmm?"

Things had gone downhill from there.

No, the ships of the line needed every fit sailor they had, to work them North, so *Proteus* could not have a one of them. Sir Edward feared that, with the Fleet so reduced by fevers already, sending him healthy men would be "good money after bad," since *Proteus* was still a raging pest-house, where valuable hands would quickly sicken and die.

And no, neither the shore hospitals nor the other vessels could at present spare a Warrant Surgeon to replace poor Mr. Shirley; with so many ill to tend no Surgeon's Mates were available, either. So Lewrie would have to "soldier on" short-handed.

No, the cost of citron oil and candles could not be reimbursed from Admiralty funds; did Captain Lewrie wish his ship to "smell" nice and cover the funk of vomit, that was his own lookout and the costs could come from his own pocket.

"Sir, here's my report on how Surgeon's Mate Durant reduced the rate of infection by the use of citron oil, much like the purchase of fresh fruit eliminates scurvy, which *is* covered by Admiralty—"

"Well, if your rate of new infection is dropping so precipitously," Sir Edward had haughtily sniffed, "you really do not have need of a Surgeon or extra Surgeon's Mate, do you?"

"I still have fourty hands sick, and they need care, sir! With so many so weak, on light duties, barely able to rise from their beds, sir . . ."

"Then you may remain in harbour 'til they're well, and take joy of the port, sir." Sir Edward had chuckled over the rim of a glass of claret. "Though, with your crew still infectious, there will be no more shore liberty, you understand. Might not even be able to fetch off the bumboatmen and their doxies 'til your diseases have passed and gone." Oh, but he'd enjoyed ordering that! "You will *not* place your ship 'Out of Discipline,' therefore. Do *you* wish, as I gather you *do,* to amuse yourself ashore—you and your officers—liberty will be allowed to you and them, of course."

Sir Edward had had himself a hearty simper over that'un, as if gossip about Lewrie's personal life had made its way as far the West Indies, at last.

"Speaking of officers, sir," Lewrie had said, leaping for the opportunity and letting the slur slide off his back like water off a duck's, "I am one Commission Officer and two Midshipmen short."

Sir Edward had gotten a crafty look, had simpered and chuckled to himself a tad, as if contemplating which of his many lieutenants on the West Indies Station was possibly the most despised and useless to the Fleet . . . whom he could lumber on Lewrie.

Lewrie had realised that Sir Edward would rather prefer to deny him everything, but that was too blatant an act of prejudice, one that could be documented and complained about to officials in London. And, sure that Sir Edward was a top-lofty prig, who would have no use for a Midshipman come from the lower deck, up "through the hawsehole," he'd further said, "I *s'pose* I could promote a pair of Quartermaster's Mates or a pair of literate seamen as acting Midshipmen, sir, but . . ." he winced, as if the very idea was disgusting to him as well.

"No, no," Sir Edward had countered at once, waving off the idea and sloshing a few drops of wine over the papers on his desk. "Better I send a brace of young gentlemen aboard your ship . . . along with a new officer, your lingering maladies notwithstanding. I'll think of someone . . . promising and aspiring." Then he'd gotten a fresh sly look.

That had almost put a cold chill down Lewrie's spine, sure that Captain Sir Edward Charles would saddle him with his *very* best slack-wits, drunks, or droolers.

"But you cannot spare a Surgeon or Surgeon's Mate, sir?" Lewrie had queried, as if it were inexplicable to him.

"With hundreds—nay, thousands—more sick or dying, sir? I think not!" Sir Edward had harrumphed. "You must do your best with what you have in that regard, for I cannot spare anyone."

"Very well, sir. And once *Proteus* is pronounced clean of disease once more, may I have your permission to hold recruiting 'rondys' ashore, sir?"

"But of course, Captain Lewrie," Sir Edward most grudgingly allowed, knowing that the first sign of a press gang or recruiting party setting foot ashore would stampede every able-bodied male on Jamaica to the hills, the threat of death at the hands of the Maroons, bedamned!

"Once manned close to requirements, sir, what would be my orders after that?" Lewrie had pressed.

"Why, put back to sea to patrol, Captain Lewrie." Sir Edward had come nigh to sneering. "Admiral Parker and I will remain here through hurricane season. I think a close patrol of Hispaniola . . . both the French half which we just abandoned as well as the Spanish half—you *do* recall we're still at war with the Dons, do you not? That'd suit quite admirably. Since you have trouble following orders, perhaps a roving commission, 'til you run out of rations, would do quite well. Time apart, to ponder your . . . faults."

" 'Out of sight, out of mind,' sir?" Lewrie had dared say.

"*Completely* out of mind and sight, Lewrie. Completely!"

"Very good, sir."

Lewrie loafed on the quarterdeck, under a vast sailcloth awning stretched beam-to-beam to provide a welcome bit of shade and cool dimness. For some reason, the awning seemed to create a breezeway that drew zephyrs beneath it, the way a tent never would. The awning trapped the smell of tar and citron-oil pots, now "doctored" with liberal doses of ground sulfur to "improve" their efficacy, but that was a small price to pay for a breeze to chill the sweat on his shirt and "ice" him down in the process.

Despite the many ill, ship-work continued; stays still had to be tensioned, worn running-rigging still had to be spliced, rerove, or replaced; sails still had to be hung and dried to prevent mildew, and the Sailmaker still had to sew and patch. Emptied kegs still had to be undone and the staves bound up for re-use; decks still had to be scrubbed and washed, laundry still had to be aired, along with bedding, from the gun-deck sleeping quarters, and most certainly from the sick bay. His crew, those of them still on their pins, were having a "make and mend" day, almost a "Rope-Yarn Sunday" of purposeful idleness free of drills, with lashings of fresh fruit and scuttle-butts of fresh water on hand. The gig, launch, and cutter were over-side, angling out from the single bow-painters so their seams and caulking, their planks, could soak up water and swell back to water-tightness.

More hot tar sulfur smells arose from the gun-deck, where hands knelt and crept as they plied heated loggerheads over freshly tarred deck seams to melt the tar and oakum into the gaps to restore water-tightness against the rain, as well. Lewrie saw Midshipman Grace by his father's side, helping him take tentative, weak steps to get his strength back, now that the last bouts of fever had left him.

Lewrie also saw his two new Midshipmen, Mister David Burns, and Mister George Larkin, and he could not help but scowl at them. Burns was a pimply, dark-haired scarecrow, a mouth-breather who gulped quite often . . . else he'd have drowned in his own spittle. His family had left it late, and had only sent him to sea at fourteen; now, with one certified year at sea, he *still* gawped about as if just wakened from a trance, wondering where the Devil he was. He was *blankly* pleasant, a perpetual cypher whom Lewrie was sure had been hustled off to sea for the Navy to care for, for his "young but widowed" mother surely could not, or would not, and probably had promising prospects for remarriage if *only* she disposed of her hopeless "git." It was an old story.

Young George Larkin was most-like born an unwelcome bastard, an Anglo-Irish by-blow of a wealthy absentee landowner and some daughter of a poor tenant. He was stout, almost knobbly at elbows, knees, and shoulders, possessed of an unfortunate nose so "Irish pugged" that it was more swinish than anything else—he stood a fair chance from drowning did he look up at a driving rain—topped by an unruly shock of straw-coloured hair. Larkin, at least, had *some* wits about him, a cheerful mien, and an ever-eager anxiousness to please and perservere; quite unlike poor Mr. Burns, who tended to stare, gape, and gulp a lot, with his eyes only half focused on the task at hand. Larkin was poor as a church mouse, his uniform a seedy *mélange* of issue slop-clothing and the cheapest coat, waistcoat, and hat ever found in a trash pile, or looted from a corpse. He was sixteen, with three years of duty at sea, and was at least tarry-handed. Naturally, the crew had taken to the little ape, as they never would with Mr. Burns. They'd pity Burns and *try* to keep him from tripping over his own feet, but . . .

Lewrie had conferred with Mr. Winwood and at his recommendation had promoted one of his Master's Mates to make up the sixth midshipman that *Proteus* rated. Jemmy Merriam, now *Mister* James Merriam, was mid-twenties and as salty as anyone could wish. Though it was hard to be a "gentleman-to-be" over former forecastle messmates, Merriam was, so far, coping. But, at the same time, Merriam was junior to everyone in the orlop cockpit, even to Burns, Larkin, and little Grace! And how he kept a straight face below with them in the off-duty hours, Lewrie had no idea.

Try as he might, Sir Edward just *couldn't* conjure up a replacement Lieutenant for them, so Mr. Adair had been confirmed as an officer. Lewrie strongly suspected that Captain Charles had had a few "runners" in mind, each about as thick as an anchor stock, but *might* have felt that Burns and Larkin were trials enough for his least-favourite captain on station. Even he, at the last, could not be *utterly* vindictive!

Lewrie had just settled down in his folding canvas and wood deck chair (a contraption that most other "sea-dog" captains would look upon as dangerously luxurious) with his feet up on the taff-rail flag lockers, pennywhistle to his mouth and Toulon curled up napping beside his feet on the lockers. He essayed a scale, then launched into a gay hornpipe, when the midshipman of the watch shouted.

"Hoy, the boat, there!" Mr. Larkin shrilled.

"Hoy, the ark!" a booming voice rejoined. "Is Noah aboard?"

"*Who,* sir?" Larkin gawped, never expecting such a challenge.

"Your captain, laddy! Buggerin' camels, is he? Both male and female, did he take aboard?" the voice posed, rather loudly.

"Aye, he's aboard, sir! And who would *you* be, come a'callin'?"

"Colonel Christopher Bloody Cashman, the Lord of Plunder!"

Lewrie whooped in glee and got to his feet, his music forgotten.

"Captain, sir," unfortunate Mr. Burns said, doffing his hat as he came to the quarterdeck, "but there's a drunk soldier alongside, is asking for you, and . . ." He gulped a time or two, fretfully.

"Tell him I'm fucking a zebra," Lewrie said with a chuckle.

"I can't tell him . . . *that,* sir!" Burns said, so embarrassed that his face paled, making his acne stand out like bubonic buboes.

"Make it 'carnal knowledge of'—never mind, I'll tell him," Lewrie said, gladly trotting to the entry-port to lean over and wave.

"Permission t'scamper up that wee ladder thing, sir!" Cashman cried, standing unsteadily in the gently rocking rowboat. "I've come t'get you drunk, Admiral Lewrie, and I'll not be denied, dammit all!"

"The zebra I was stuffin' was a *virgin,* you reprobate, so this had better be good!" Lewrie called down, to the great amusement of his crew.

"Half dozen o' Jean-Pierre's best bubbly, Admiral Noah!" Cashman promised, displaying a bottle from a straw-packed case at his feet in the rowboat's bilges.

"Aye, then . . . scamper on up that ladder thing, General Cashman!"

CHAPTER TWENTY-SEVEN

So this is the infamous Toulon," Cashman said, stripping away his scarlet tunic, neck-stock, and waistcoat as a seaman fetched in the crate of bottles. He tossed his uniform at the starboard-side settee, then plunked into an upholstered chair, reaching out to the desk where the cat sat, hunkered down over his front paws, uncertain of this newcomer's antecedents. "Meow, puss. Killed any rats lately?" he asked as he offered fingers under Toulon's nose. A moment later and Toulon was on his side, tail lashing, and head writhing in bliss to be petted.

"Fickle bastard," Lewrie grumbled. "Ah, Aspinall, kindly take the tompion from the muzzle of one of those bottles, and run it out in battery for us, will you? There's a good lad."

"What *is* that smell?" Cashman asked, wrinkling his nose.

"Tar, citron oil, and sulfur," Lewrie chuckled. "Our Surgeon's Mates are still tinkerin' with the formula, but it's cut the number of men who come down sick, *and* run off the flies and mosquitoes."

"Like Satan breakin' wind under clean sheets." Cashman hooted.

"Takes our minds off the bilges and the pea-soup farts," Lewrie told him as Aspinall produced a loud *Thwock!* and a flying cork, which made Toulon scramble to his paws and fly off the desk to intercept it. Good flutes were filled, the bottle stood on the desk, then Aspinall faded back into his tiny pantry. "Damn' fine, even warm. Aahhh, damn fine," Lewrie said after a first tentative sip.

"We'll not see its like this side of Paris any longer," Cashman mourned. "Jean-Pierre and *Maman* escaped Port-Au-Prince, and took all their wine cellars with 'em . . . their cooks, *their* families, and their best girls. Hired a schooner, emptied their house o' furnishings and plate, chests and *chests* o' money, and all, and headed for Charleston."

"Mighty tempting target, all that pelf," Lewrie speculated with a frown. "Who's t'say the crew won't turn pirate for an hour or two, and have 'em over the side?"

"Took a half dozen o' their bully-bucks armed to the teeth, and their girls and kin, as well," Cashman snickered, topping them up once more. "Doubt they'd have any trouble on that score. By the by, your darlin' Henriette sends her love. When in Charleston, look her up, she says."

"That'll be the day," Lewrie scoffed.

"Must've made a hellish impression on her, old son. But then, you have that effect on all the willin' little biddies, don't ya, hey?"

"Hah!" Lewrie replied, even while wondering if even Cashman had heard rumours from Home, by now. "So, what's the occasion?"

"Alan, my boy, we're havin' a wake, a proper old Irish wake, in honour of someone . . . *somethin'* that just died," Cashman grimly stated.

"You came to the wrong place to celebrate death, Kit. I've lost fourteen so far, with five or six more lookin' peaky," Lewrie objected.

"Miser," Cashman countered. "I lost nigh half the regiment, by now . . . shot or butchered on Saint Domingue, or to the fevers. Already mourned them. No, I refer to the regiment itself, and my military career with it."

"They'll disband 'em?" Lewrie gawped, sitting up straighter.

"In the process," Cashman spat. "Called us 'excess to requirements,' now we've no major campaign to . . . wage. Oh, there's still a deal o' work wantin' down on Grenada and Saint Vincent, takin' on the Black Caribs and the *real* Caribs, but it's no concern of ours."

"They'll chuck Ledyard Beauman, then," Lewrie surmised. "God, I can understand sheddin' him, but you! General Maitland had you on his staff last year, you told me. Surely, *he* doesn't mean to tip you out with the bathwater?"

"Double-dealin' sonofabitch," Cashman growled, tossing back his glass so quick that half of it flooded his shirt-front. "He and that L'Ouverture were correspondin' all the time, did you know it? Secret

negotiations were goin' on, even whilst we were bleedin' and sweatin'
in those woods, fightin' like we really *meant* it! Men died, while he was
dancin' to and fro with our enemy. Hell, the last week before the evacuation, we fought L'Ouverture seven times, he *beat* us seven times . . .
but each time there'd be secret letters flyin' back and forth. 'Well, ya
lost here, my dear Maitland, so will ya give in? No? Then how 'bout
this'un?' Maitland sayin', 'Didn't we bleed ya enough, still have soldiers
and arms for another try, m'dear Toussaint?' 'Oh Dear, now will you
pack it in, *mon cher* Maitland?' Pah! Even did Maitland get down on his
hands and knees and beg me to stay with the colours . . . even throw in
fellatio . . . I'd still spit in his Goddamned face!"

"Well, I never," Lewrie said with a groan, as disgusted as Kit Cashman. He had lost Sevier and Nicholas, Inman and Shirley, and poor old
Lt. Duncan had died, all those lost to malaria and Yellow Jack had died
in a sham? As a way to save a general's reputation, before some amateur
Black rebel slave out-soldiered him? "The bastard!"

"Won't get him titled," Cashman sarcastically snickered. "No 'thanks
of the Crown' for him, when he goes home. If Maitland'd stuck it out,
L'Ouverture would've strewed us dead on the beaches, he'd've had another week, so I can see the temptation to sign *anything* and get out.
L'Ouverture, Dessalines, Petion, and Christophe . . . they're damn' good,
Alan. Samboe versions o' Julius Caesar, with more troops under their
command than Xerxes brought to Greece. Poor-armed, but even so, they
just swamp right over you, pick up the guns from their dead, and keep
right on comin'. Fine, they beat us fair and square, and so what. What
really irks me, though, old son . . ."

Cashman leaned forward on his elbows on the desktop, grating deep
in his throat, with eyes slit in fury.

"He wrote his letters behind the backs of his own *men*, damn him!
He could've *told* us, after the first couple o' defeats and he saw how
things stood, he could o' told *us* he was negotiatin', he could o' asked
for a *truce*, and I'll lay you any odds ya wish, old Toussaint L'Ouverture
would've granted it . . . he didn't want any more o' *his* men killed, either.
Hundreds o' men would still be alive, the battle that broke my damn'
regiment need never've been bloody *fought*!"

"Maybe L'Ouverture would have gone right on and fought us, Kit.

Drivin' out a white, British army's one thing, but slaughterin' them to the last man on the beaches is another. His message to the world."

"Us leavin' with our tails t'wixt our legs ain't *enough* of a message?" Cashman waved this off, leaning back in his chair and tossing down his fresh glass of champagne. "Shit, Alan. That's shit, and ya know it. L'Ouverture ain't through fightin', there's still the Spaniards in the east he wants t'take on, there's still that half-caste General Rigaud down in South Province against him. There's probably some of his very own generals just slaverin' like hounds for a shot at power, too. No, L'Ouverture wants t'stay alive, and in charge, liberate the entire island of Hispaniola—hell, the whole damn' West Indies, he needed t'husband the army he had! He's too smart t'throw it away on gestures and messages to the world. S'truth."

"So, what'll you do?" Lewrie asked, stretching to refill his own glass. "Resign, or wait to be retired?"

"Ask for a court," Cashman told him, brightening a touch. "Get my record cleared . . . make sure everyone knows for certain it was that fool Ledyard who lost it for us. See, Alan . . . Maitland and his staff are lookin' for scapegoats, and damned if I'll play 'goat.' Maitland holds a court-martial and blames Beauman for losin' him the battle that cost him the entire campaign, why, he can go back to England smellin' like a bed o' spring roses! The regular Army'll love it, 'cause what can ya expect from Yeomanry, militia volunteers, and amateur officers? Pile up a big, smelly heap o' shit over here, then you hardly notice the reek from over yonder, d'ye see. Then, no one'll take Maitland to task for 'conspirin' with the enemy.' That's what you can *deem* secret letters with the foe. You could almost call it treason, and that's a hangin' offence, no matter what your rank or titles."

"He'll never allow it," Lewrie said after a long moment to mull it over. "Ya don't think Ledyard Beauman doesn't know about Maitland and L'Ouverture negotiating already? Better for Ledyard, his lawyer will know of it, and how to use it. The Royal Navy's just as eager to cover its arse when someone's mucked it, I know, I've seen it close at hand, Kit. Better for Maitland to explain to Horse Guards that he was grossly outnumbered and swamped by bloody *waves* of fanatics, then only opened negotiations when he saw he had no chance to win. He saved his army, he saved the civilians on Saint Domingue by wangling a promise that L'Ouverture wouldn't take reprisal on 'em. Remember, Kit, I was at Yorktown, and—"

"Oh, that tale again." Cashman waved it off.

"Lord Cornwallis had had his arse kicked from the Cape Fear to Yorktown, *then* got himself stuck like a bung in a barrel, countin' on the Fleet t'save him. Did Graves, Hood, or Denby pay for failing him? Christ no, they didn't. Did Cornwallis pay for losin' the last army we'd be able to raise, losin' the war, for losin' the Colonies at one stroke? Hell no to that, too! They still love him. This latest rebellion in Ireland we've heard about, that French landing under General Humbert, they're sending Cornwallis t'sort it out."

"So Maitland won't pay, either?" Cashman said as he squinted at his old friend; rather "squiffily," by then.

"End of his active career, most-like, Kit, and no honours, but he'll flap away as free as a dove, with not a harsh word said to him, you just watch and see," Lewrie prophecied, "and everyone'll say, 'What a pity, when just one more regiment, one more battery, just a wee bit more luck and we'd have conquered the place, and we're better off out of there, anyway,' d'ye see? He'll write his memoirs and prove it wasn't a bit of *his* doing, and nothing'll get in the way of that. So, before you pile up your stink, he'll shed you and Ledyard, disband yer regiment, and then it's 'least said, soonest mended' for everyone."

"Not for me, damn yer eyes," Cashman thundered, "it's my honour, my good name that's dragged in the mud! Without a court it'll always be me who funked it, t'will be me who's whispered about, *laughed* about! I'll not have it, Alan, if I have to challenge Maitland, too, once I'm a civilian!"

"Oh, don't talk rot, Kit," Lewrie scoffed, half worried now.

"The Beaumans have already begun white-washin' his odour," Kit snapped, repouring from the bottle, which was already deeply drained. "Their newspaper friends, those papers sent to England on the packets. Two, three months more, and I'll be all over the London rags as the one who cut and ran. People in town, already . . . I'm bein' snubbed. Goin' to the other side of the street when I walk by, gazin' skyward with a 'cut sublime' . . . out at our camp. Wives and children, widows, come to find what happened to their menfolk, and I . . ."

In the privacy of Lewrie's great-cabins, the indomitable Christopher Cashman began to snuffle and swipe at his eyes with his shirt sleeves, making Lewrie wince in pain for him, yet avert his eyes so as not to stare too directly and shame him. To see someone unmanned . . .

"Private soldiers know the truth, they try t'tell their folks, but the way they still *glare* at me, Alan, it's so . . . !" Cashman wept.

Suddenly, he smashed a fist on the desktop, so hard he made the glasses, the bottle, inkwell, and correspondence box jump.

"*Damn* Beauman! Damn him and his kin, damn all those rich, stuck-up bastards and bitches t'Hell and gone! They'll ruin me to save *that* useless, Goddamned pinch o' pig shit, take all I have! Take my honour and all I've done before, run me outta Jamaica like an 'untouchable' Hindoo, too low caste t'swamp out a toilet . . . make me sell up for a pence to the pound and lose ev'ry farthing I've invested here . . . well, I'll not have it. I'll find a way t'get my own back, if it means that I murder Ledyard, or murder 'em all!"

"Now you're really talking rot, Kit!" Lewrie spat back. "Think with your head, not your pride, for God's sake. Want t'end up hanged? *Then* where's your honour, or your good name, hey?"

Lewrie tossed back his own glass of champagne, then took assay of the bottle on the desk. Talking fools out of idiocy was dry work; he bent down to extract a second bottle from the wood case and ripped away the lead foil, gave the cork a twist, and opened a replenishment, topping them both up. And tossed Toulon a new "play-pretty."

"Duelin' him's better, remember duelin'?" Lewrie asked once he had taken another deep sip. "What you talked about on Saint Domingue, not two weeks ago? I'll stand as your second, God help me. *Let* 'em retire the both of you, there's no King's Regulations preventing two *former* officers from fightin'. You blow great holes in him or slice him to pork chops, there's your revenge. But he'll cry off, I'd bet, and that'll *prove* he's the liar, *and* a coward to boot. Then you're able t'sell up, justified. Might not get full price even so, but the buyers'll be gettin' a fair bargain, and not robbin' ya blind."

"He *can't* deny me, Alan, his brother'll make him, so . . ."

"So you kill him all legal-like, and take *shilling* to a pound," Lewrie snapped, nigh exasperated with trying to make sense to a drunk. "A twentieth or tenth of yer worth beats poverty all hollow, old son."

"And the bastard'll be dead," Cashman said, half to himself, as if the end result had just occurred to him; beginning to beam as if he had just discovered the joy of it.

"That's the point . . . ain't it," Lewrie maliciously grinned.

"Don't know," Cashman said, sighing and reaching for the fresh bottle for a refill, shaking his head like a disappointed tot, denied a "surprise" from town by a thoughtless daddy. "Doesn't seem enough, somehow. Not by half, it don't."

"Well, you could have him raped by a cart horse, first," Lewrie suggested, throwing his hands aloft and sinking back in his chair. "My God, Kit, what *is* enough? Besides your honour, your good name, reasonable profit from your properties, and public acquittal, that is?"

"I dunno," Christopher said with a semi-drunk shrug. "Pillage his lands, burn his house down . . . poison his wells and livestock? An end to the whole Beauman line . . . his sister Lucy, excepted."

"Aye, spare the whores and the simple," Lewrie sneered. "*They,* at least, have their uses."

"Run his slaves off to the Maroons in the mountains?" Cashman fantasised, blood and thunder and gore a'bubble behind his eyes.

"Spare me a half-dozen strong'uns when you do, Kit. I'm sorely in need of hands," Lewrie suggested. "Hell's Bells, even if they're nought but simple-minded soldiers, I'd gladly take some of your wharf rats when your regiment gets broken up. Need fresh Marines, too . . ."

"They'll parcel 'em out to t'other under-strength units—oh," Cashman said, perking up like a wakened cat, and sitting more upright, almost managing to resemble "sober." His phyz became suffused by a grin, one of the sly sort, filled with impish mischief, slowly, like a high-latitude sunrise. He peered at Lewrie, then winked!

"What?" Lewrie demanded, perked to the edge of his own chair.

"How many Marines did you say you were short, Alan?" Cashman enquired, with a soft, smugly satisfied chuckle.

"We could use five," Lewrie told him, delighted at the offer he thought was coming. Not that he'd relish gaining hands from a friend's misfortune, but neither was he loath to refuse soon-to-be unemployed volunteers. Not when he'd considered stopping American merchant ships once back at sea, and press-ganging anyone who had even a slight English accent or the slightest error in his citizenship certificate; and God knew three-quarters of those were bogus, or given (or sold!) by an American consul like so many cough lozenges.

"I'll have a word with the best men I have," Cashman promised.

"Hallelujah!"

"There's still some have a taste for soldierin'," Cashman said, tittering with impending glee, "or so calf-headed I can talk 'em into it. But, Alan . . . *but!*"

"But, mine arse," Lewrie quipped. "What? Tell me, you sot!"

"You don't mind Black sailors, do you, Alan?"

"Not a bit. Already have some. Think I always have had, every ship I've ever served. They're good hands, too, so . . . no, it don't signify if they were Eskimos," Lewrie assured him. "Your *slaves?*"

"How many d'ye think you'd need, then?" Cashman asked, avoiding the query, though hugging his sides in a tittering fit.

"A round dozen'd suit," Lewrie allowed. "Make landsmen of 'em, for pulley-hauley chores. Some young'uns might make topmen, sooner or later. And damme," Lewrie began to enthuse, "I'd kill for just one older one who knows how to cook decent for an hundred or so. Would it be too much to ask, for one of 'em t'be a cook?"

"Oh, I think we can arrange that," Cashman promised, becoming even more mystifying.

"You're not askin' me to *buy* your slaves, are you, Kit?" Lewrie asked, growing wary of a sudden. "Damme if I'm that keen on slavery, after all you told me, and damned if I can afford 'em, not even at a shilling to the pound, so . . ."

"Not mine, Alan old son. And free . . . scot-free."

"Whose, then?" Lewrie said with a chary scowl.

"Ledyard Beauman's," Cashman hooted, slapping the desktop.

"Mine arse on a band-box!" Lewrie exclaimed in wonder.

"It'd be sweet, wouldn't it?" Cashman managed to say, just about wheezing with mirth by then. "Sweet revenge, for one. You sail out to Portland Bight, soon some dark night, and abscond with some of his slaves. Young'uns, like you said, so they haven't been branded or had their backs whip-scarred yet, so who's t'say whose they are, once on your ship? I know some Black freedmen who can get to 'em and promise 'em they'll be free, if they ship with you. What d'ye say?"

Lewrie fell back into his chair, astounded by the idea, giving the proposition a *hard* think, beginning to chew a thumbnail. Taking slaves, *liberating* slaves, was just about the worst crime in the West Indies, right up there with horse theft, and a hanging offence.

Damme, but I do need 'em hellish-bad, he thought.

But the risk of getting *caught,* and the ramifications, would be equally hellish-bad. He'd be stripped of his command, court-martialed, cashiered, and sent home in disgrace at the very least—sent home to face a termagant wife, disaffected kiddies, and another scandal as bad as this one, with Theoni and his bastard! The Navy was all that he knew, and without a civilian career, he'd be in debtors' prison before a year was out, he just knew it.

Before that, though, there'd be the civil courts here on Jamaica that would most-like "scrag" him by the neck, so why worry about infamy in England?

"Sooner or later, someone'd talk, Kit," Lewrie schemed. "Sass from a slave who didn't get to go . . . damme, don't ya think they'd *miss* 'em? Raise the hue and cry, remember there was a frigate offshore the night they scarpered, and put two and two together?"

"Ledyard, none of the Beaumans, would know one of their slaves by sight 'less they were house servants," Cashman said dismissively of his qualms. "No brands, no worries. First off, they'd hunt 'em northward, if they thought they'd run off to join the Maroons. And you can depend on me t'plant that rumour . . . even offer t'lead the hunt!"

"But later . . ."

"I'll be sellin' up anyway," Cashman went on, "puttin' my own slaves on the block, so who's t'say I didn't sell you some o' mine . . . with a certified bill of sale t'prove it? Or manumitted 'em before ya lured 'em aboard? We can forge some papers, give 'em other names . . ."

Like father, like son, Lewrie thought, recalling Sir Hugo's doings back when he'd "press-ganged" him into the Navy, so he could get his paws on the supposed inheritance from Granny Lewrie way off in Devon— because he'd needed the money "hellish-bad" to clear his debts before he lost his St. James's Square house and got slung into prison himself! His father had ended up running to Oporto in Portugal after *his* scheme had gone "belly-up."

Lisbon's nice and cheap, Lewrie speculated; *if all else fails. A rogue on the run could live well, there. Wine's good . . . hmmm.*

"I'll even throw in a cook, from my own stock," Cashman cooed.

"Well, if we sent ship's boats inshore on a moonless night and kept *Proteus* hull-down . . ." Lewrie muttered. "Hellish row, though. Like a cutting-out expedition? I'd never be able t'let 'em take shore liberty with the other hands, though."

"Do ye think *they'd* want t'run the risk any more than you, hey? Those you get, the ones I said I sold, *could've* been sold to a trader from the Bahamas who took 'em away, so your name never appears in it. What d'ye say, Alan?"

"You know I'd have to sail off to Hell and gone, right after," Lewrie pointed out. "I wouldn't be here to second you when you duel Ledyard. Reprovisioned, I'd be gone for four or five months at the least, do I not run out of hands for prize crews."

"Right, so I kill him first, *then* we steal his slaves," Cashman merrily suggested. "It'd make sense that they'd run, with him dead and no wife or heirs t'take 'em over, and God knows where they'd get sold after."

"I'd be in port 'til you and he get retired, then you duel him, then we steal his slaves?" Lewrie scoffed. "Captain Sir Edward bloody Charles won't let me linger a minute more than necessary."

"So I get someone else t'be my second, I s'pose," Cashman decided, disappointed. "Wanted you there, t'savour the moment, if for no other reason, but perhaps it's best you were gone when it happens. Less way t'link your name, the slaves' disappearance, and all."

"Hmmm . . ." Lewrie gnawed a cuticle more deeply, giving it another hard think. Perhaps it would be best, he thought, to be well to windward when the shit started flying. He and his clerk, Padgett, could do up freedmens' papers for his new "volunteers". . . .

And it would be a grand jape on that ass Ledyard Beauman.

"What are the dues, d'ye think . . . to join the Slavery Abolition Society?" he said, offering his hand across the desk.

CHAPTER TWENTY-EIGHT

*H*oy, the boats!" Lieutenant Langlie hissed into the darkness, as HMS *Proteus* fretfully rocked and rolled on the scend, three miles off Portland Point.

"Blackbirds," Cox'n Andrews hooted back, and everyone gathered on the gangway let out a huge sigh of relief. Moments later the boats were thudding against the hull, and people were scampering up the man-ropes and boarding-battens, eyes and teeth gleaming in wonder and delight, reflecting the single lanthorn they'd dared display.

There were only eleven of them, ten youngsters and one thicker, older man with grizzled grey hair. They came with small packs of possessions bound up in cast-off pillowcases or shirts; barefoot, wearing ragged nankeen or sailcloth trousers worn gauzy-thin by work, loose and ending above the knees; topped with shapeless, stained pullover shirts without collars, just neck-holes, and equally frayed.

For a long moment, they just stood in stupefied wonder, taking in the height of the masts, the guns, the mazes of rigging, and most of all, the sea of white faces confronting them; shying into a tight group, elbow to elbow, as if this suddenly seemed like a bad idea and the price of freedom too high.

"Sure, and I hope one o' ye knows how t'cook!" Landsman Furfy cried, breaking their stricken tableau.

"Ah does," the older man said. "Gideon's me name."

"Welcome aboard then, mate!" Furfy gushed, stepping forward to take him by the hand and pump it energetically. "Shoulda *seen* what we been doin' with good rations, it'd sicken a goat!"

"You boys come on, now," Morley, one of the Black seamen, urged, stepping forward and waving to the other half-dozen fellow Blacks among the crew to join him, making the newcomers nervously grin. "Don't be standin' round. Cap'um wants ya t'see th' Surgeon's Mates, get bathed, an' into new clothes. Make yer marks an' sign ship's books?"

"Cold rations a'waitin'," another promised, "then a bit o' kip in yer new hammocks. Last 'all-night-in' ye'll have."

"*Who* de cap'um?" one of the newcomers asked, peering about.

"Him, dere . . . Cap'um Lewrie," Morley pointed out.

Lewrie had thought it best to turn out in his newest uniform to welcome them aboard, to impress them from the first. He stood apart on the quarterdeck, hands behind his back.

The youngster came toward him, eyes alight as if he'd seen Jesus, and fell to his knees at his feet. "T'ankee, massa, t'ankee!"

"Oh, for God's sake," Lewrie muttered, wondering again if this was a bad idea, himself. "Don't do that. Get up, man. I'm not your 'massa,' I don't own you."

No, the Navy does, and if that ain't a sort o' slavery, I'll eat me hat, Lewrie had to think as he helped the youngster up.

"What's your name, young'un?"

"Calls me Cambridge, sah. Cambridge is all."

"Your mother's choice?" Lewrie asked. "Or your master's?"

"Nossah," the teenager shyly grinned. "Mama call me Noble."

"Noble you'll be, then."

"Noble Lah . . . Lewrie?" he carefully pronounced.

"God, no!" Lewrie had to bark in amusement. "I'm in enough of a stink with my wife already. Uhm . . . Noble . . . Hood. Hood's a great admiral in the Navy, a knacky fighting man. Noble Hood."

"Yassuh, Noble Hood," the boy happily agreed.

"We'll let you choose new names, all of you," Lewrie told them in a louder voice. "Names that'll never fetch your old master's suspicion. Once on ship's books, with papers showing you as free men, you won't have to fear being taken. So think it over whilst you see the Surgeon's

Mates, Mister Hodson and Mister Durant. Then we'll fit up the wash-deck pump . . ."

That idea seemed to make them shy back together.

"All sailors do it when they sign aboard a new ship," Lewrie explained patiently. "Wash off the shore stinks and . . . get *baptised* in salt water, like a church baptism, when babies get named," he extemporised quickly.

"Don't nobody baptise *us*, sah," the older man, Gideon, said in a jocular tone. "Dot fo' white folks."

"Then it's about time, ain't it, sir?" Lewrie quipped.

"Did they not *church* you?" Mr. Winwood asked of a sudden, coming forward and sounding indignant. "Did they not tell you of being washed in the blood of the Lamb, of being good Christians?"

"Preach at us, now an' then, sah," one told him. "Dey *say* dot we arter be good Christians, but . . ."

"Baptism *and* a washing, then," Winwood enthused, clapping his hands at the prospect, "to cleanse your souls as you take your free names . . . to wash slavery from you forever, and baptise you as sailors, the finest calling in the world. Recall . . .'twas *sailors* that Jesus first made his disciples, 'simple fishermen and sailors. Let me, sir?" he almost pled, turning to Lewrie. "I'll attend to it."

"It appears I've gained sailors, and you, converts, sir," Lewrie chuckled.

"Pray God, sir, that I have . . . souls delivered up to the Lord."

"I'll leave you to it, Mister Winwood. Soon as you may. We're almost on a lee shore, and need to get out to sea before dawn, before they clap us all in prison."

"My word on't, Captain Lewrie," Winwood fervently assured him.

"Mister Langlie? Run the ship's boats 'round astern. We'll tow them 'til after Dawn Quarters," Lewrie ordered. "Let's get way on her and make an offing . . . Sou'east-by-East, for now."

"Aye aye, sir," Langlie replied, still looking worried.

Lewrie clapped his hands behind his back once more and paced to the railing overlooking the waist, feeling like breaking out into jig-dancing; it had worked, they had pulled it off, and (hopefully!) no one was the wiser! He saw Andrews and the last of the boat crews climbing up to the deck, and went forward to speak to him.

"How did it go, Andrews?"

"Lawd o' Mercy, sah," Andrews answered, shaking his head sadly, "I'd forgot how evil dey treat people. Warn't one o' dot Mista Ledyard Beauman's big plantin's, just a drunk overseer t'watch 'em, so I think we got away clean, but you never see such mis'ry. Mamas an' papas come down to de boats t'see 'em away, sah . . . weepin' and whimp'rin' like dey never see dey children again. But soft, so'z nobody'd hear. Blessin' us fo' gettin' 'em free, no matter what de cost, 'coz de sea can't be no worse'n bein' field hands dey whole lives. Tellin' 'em, 'Don't worry 'bout us, we'll lie good,' an' swearin' nobody'll talk true. Dey pick names outen a hat fo' de ones t'come away with us, sah. I tell 'em . . . dey be earnin' money good as a white sailor, maybe dey come back some day an' buy dey brother's or sister's freedom, too, buy dey mamas and papas out. You an' me know dey most-like can't, but . . . slaves live on hopes, like waitin' fo' de Second Comin'.'"

" 'Next year in Jerusalem,' " Lewrie muttered. To Andrews's puzzled look, he explained, "What the Jews say, for better times coming."

"Yessah," Andrews replied with a shrug. "Good."

Langlie had gotten *Proteus* moving, at last, the steady Nor'east Trades now coming up her stern as he directed the crew to wear her off the wind, before rounding up on larboard tack to the Sou'east.

"Somethin' odd ashore, though, sah," Andrews continued.

"Someone see you?" Lewrie almost blanched in alarm.

"Nossah, some *thing*," Andrews said, sending a premonitory shiver up Lewrie's back. "Ya know dey's seals in dese waters, sah. Dey's been hunted almos' out, but dey's some still about?"

"Seals?" Lewrie exclaimed, feeling fit to burst with fey dread of the old pagan *cess* that seemed to follow him, from HMS *Jester* to a new frigate, a benign and benevolent sea god's "protection."

"Dey started barkin' and splashin', an' I thought ever'body was gonna die o' fright 'til we saw what dey was, sah." Andrews chuckled. "Swam out with us, dey did, rollin' an' snortin' so close, dey made it hard t'keep de stroke fo' de oarsmen. Leadin' us, sah, out to de *deep* water. Stayed with us almos' right to de side, sah, den disappeared."

Lewrie dashed to the landward, the larboard side, to peer out almost anxiously for a glimpse of them, but the night was black and the sea was ebon, with only tropic starlight to gleam off whitecaps and horses as the deep ocean waves met the shore, and the rebounding echoes of those that had crashed on the beaches hours before.

There! he thought, espying a misplaced whitecap between wavetops in a trough, the faintest, quickest glimpse of a head, a flash of *eyes,* as briefly chatoyant as a cat's from the single burning lanthorn, lambent and large *approving* sea-hound's eyes. . . .

Then the apparition was gone as if it had never been, as if he had wished it to be, leaving him grinning when he should have been deflated with disappointment and dread of his crime.

"Damme, if I don't feel we've done something right, tonight," Lewrie said. "Even was it wrong."

"Aye, sah."

There came a whoop as a new-come was hosed down under the force of the wash-deck pump, turning and shivering naked, along with a laugh from his waiting companions and the off-watch crew who'd gathered for the show, encouraging him to make the best of it.

Mr. Winwood came forward, a bared sword in his right hand, once the fellow was through, urging everyone to hush. He laid the blade on the man's right shoulder, as if conferring knighthood, and said, "With God as my witness, I christen thee in a new life and a new name. Put on sailor's clothing and be known as . . ."

"Abraham," the former slave supplied, in an awed tone.

"As Abraham Howe. Welcome aboard, lad!" Winwood cried, laying the sword on his left shoulder then the top of his head, eliciting a round of applause from the sailors, and two dozen hands to be shaken.

"Uhmm . . . Andrews," Lewrie murmured.

"Aye, sah?"

"You might, uhm . . . pass the word among the crew. About those seals? Might make them easier of mind about our little raid," Lewrie suggested.

"Oh, *aye,* sah!" Andrews laughed, tumbling to it. "By de way, sah?

Don't know if ya ever knew it, but my slave name was Caesar, sah. My ol' massa name me after some damn' ol' Roman," Andrews said in a soft voice, as if daring to suggest a first-name basis.

"Want to pick another whilst Mister Winwood's dolin' 'em out?" Lewrie replied with a tentative chuckle, feeling that there was an accusation in there someplace. It stung, in fact, since he *had* known it, ages before, but had quite forgotten it; like any seaman aboard ship, Andrews was "Andrews" or "Coxswain," known by his place and his duty, with nothing more required between a common seaman and an officer. If Andrews, to hide his identity in the Navy, had chosen a new name, a new *first* name, when he'd run away, he'd never bothered to learn it, either!

"Think ah'd have t'strip an' bathe, sah?" Andrews asked, a tiny mocking edge to his voice.

"Mister Winwood's Church of England, not a Dissenter, so total immersion's probably not necessary," Lewrie said, tongue in cheek, to jape Andrews out of whatever "pet" he was in. "A wee dribble atop yer head'll be all." Damn, he *still* couldn't recall his first name!

"Ah'll stick with the one ah got then, sah," Andrews said, as if weary of trying. "Too many ship's books, an' those fake papers you and Mistah Padgett done for me, already got it down."

"I'd admire, did you have a word with our new volunteers, once they're named and settled in," Lewrie went on as if Andrews had not put him on the spot, for whatever bloody reason. "Cruel as it was, they might be feeling a touch homesick."

"Missin' dey mamas an' daddies, sah," Andrews expounded. "And worryin' 'bout how bad de beatin's and whuppin's gonna be when dey is missed. Gonna be a ruckus raised. White folks is antsy enough 'bout runaways and rebel slaves, already."

"You don't think they'd talk, do you?" Lewrie asked suddenly.

"I think dey'd *die* fo' dey say a word, sah," Andrews told him, turning to face him in the darkness for a moment. "Deir sons is free, and dot's all dot matters. De massas are fooled, with a scare put on 'em, and dot sort o' victory's worth all de lashes dey can deal out."

"But they'll still be homesick," Lewrie pressed.

"Aye, sah, dey will. And I'll talk with 'em, and try to ease dey minds."

Matthew! Lewrie suddenly recalled, after frantically dredging his memory; *his first name's Matthew!*

"I'd admire that . . . Matthew Andrews."

"Aye, sah."

In the faint gleam of the single lanthorn, Lewrie could see his eyes brighten.

"Carry on, then, Cox'n."

BOOK FOUR

Saepe trucem adverso perlabi sidere pontum?
Saepe mare audendo vincere, saepe hiemem?

How oft under unkindly stars thou glidest over the
savage deep? How oft in thy daring thou conquerest
the sea, and oft the storm?

CATALEPTON, IX 47-48
PUBLIUS VIRGILIUS MARO "VIRGIL"

CHAPTER TWENTY-NINE

*P*roteus now had a distinguished list of names on her books for all the world to wonder at; there was a Howe, a Hood, an Anson, even a Byng. There was a skinny little runt going by George Rodney, another by Hawke, yet another was now a Cook, a massive teenager who still was growing (if such a thing were possible for someone already built like Atlas) was named Jones Nelson. And, of course, there was a Groome, to reflect his slave duties as a horsetender; a Carpenter, a Saw-yer, even a Brewster, for a slightly older fellow who'd tended the vats where the molasses had been turned to rum. Along the same line, *Proteus* boasted a Newcastle, a Bass, and a Samuel Whitbread, in honour of their favourite imported English beers; even if they'd never been *allowed* a taste, the stone bottles and names emblazoned on them had been thought of as a white man's, their masters', ambrosia.

What *Proteus* did *not* have, though, were skilled sailors, for the new "volunteers" were farmboys, landsmen, and "new-caught fish," about as ignorant of the sea as any clerk press-ganged from a Wapping tavern in London. And, to beat all, for the first few days the bulk of them were seasick, as *well* as homesick!

Lewrie had decreed a "sea school" be formed, with the experienced tars, both White and Black, as the "bear leaders," to guide the newcomers about, name the myriad items of rigging and sails, and get them ac-quainted with their future duties. During this time, none were to be "started," even the stupidest.

Their frigate stood out from Hispaniola far to the Sou'east, to cruise along the southern shore of Saint Domingue, well out of sight from the port of Jacmel or any shore watcher, most especially of other Royal Navy ships that might get near enough to "speak" her and wonder where *Proteus* had gotten all of her ham-fisted, puking amateur Black sailors.

And her newcomers had had a lot to which to adjust, besides the homesickness and nausea. The first few days, they'd been dazzled by their spanking-new slop-clothing uniforms, the "privilege" of stockings and brass-buckled shoes (hastily put aside except for Sunday Divisions) never bought for field hands, the art of sleeping in a properly spread and hung hammock and its rolling-up each dawn, of scrubbing decks, and pulley-hauling—eating!—alongside White sailors. They had been at first amazed then incongruously daunted by that closeness, as if it were perhaps too *much* egalitarianism to digest at one sitting.

Certainly, their first sight of White sailors being "started" by the bosun and his mates on their way aloft to trim or shorten sail before the almost-daily squalls had been a revelation; even if Lewrie never allowed petty officers to use the stiffened rope starters in real anger, just as instructive incentives to quicker action. And while it had been weeks since a man had merited a dozen lashes from the cat-o'-nine-tails, whilst lashed barebacked to an upright hatch grating, the idea of punishment for *anyone* in violation of the Articles of War that Lewrie had read weekly had sent them first into giggling fits, then a sombre reflection about upright behaviour, and just what they had gotten themselves into.

And the novelty of three square meals a day, with portions at least twice the victuals they had ever gotten as slaves, even on the rare holidays, was a wonder! For the first time in ages, Lewrie was just about dumbfounded to hear people rave over boiled salt meats, the pease pudding, or even the burgoo! And as for the daily rum rations, and the small beer . . . ! The newlys agreed, though, that the rock-hard ship's biscuit was a peril to all mankind, but the currant duffs and the weekly figgy-dowdys were just handsome-fine. Even a "Banyan Day" of cheese, beer, biscuit, and gruels pleased them, for now.

Then there was the matter of arms drill.

No one in the West Indies or the New World ever put weapons in a Black's hands, nor even in his close proximity for fear of revenge murder or full-blown rebellion. Even Black freedmens' rights to own weapons was strictly regulated. Here, though, the newlys were expected to become proficient with cutlass, hatchet, boarding pike, musket, and pistol, and were even allowed to purchase clasp-knives to hang on their belts (with the tips blunted like everyone else's) even if used for nothing more than whittling in off-duty hours, or for cutting their tough meat portions.

"Most enthusiastic students ever I did see, sir," Lt. Devereux told Lewrie one morning off Santo Domingo, the Spanish half of Hispaniola, as the hands shot at towed kegs from the taff-rail. "Even do I halfway suspect ulterior motives."

"Such as, sir?" Lewrie asked.

"Well, sir, there's bound to be one or two using us as a school for later rebellion . . . like Irish volunteer soldiers who get paid by our Army to teach 'em how to fight us?" Devereux said offhandedly, as if he was merely joshing, after all. "Where else might young Black men get the chance to learn weapons-handling as good as any European soldier or sailor? Or, do you come to it, sir, the art of the great-guns, and the use of artillery?"

"Over yonder, with L'Ouverture and his bully bucks," Lewrie responded, jerking his chin northward. "Or with our Jamaican Maroons."

"Exactly, sir," Devereux said with a sage nod, but with a wink, as well. "But we got 'em young, so perhaps serving aboard our ship, where they'll get firm but fair and humane treatment, will be a civilising influence against rebellious thoughts."

"Don't make me rue my decision, Mister Devereux," Lewrie said, with a mock shiver. "I've qualms enough, already."

And how I let Cashman talk me into it, I'll never *know!* Lewrie thought anew; *He's corruptin', and I'm weak and corruptible, just as he said. Always have been, and I doubt the sorry old plea of 'drink and bad companions' will excuse me in court!*

"Damme, but that wee Rodney fellow is a cracking shot, sir . . . e'en with our poor old muskets!" Devereux exclaimed.

Little "George Rodney" had plumbed a round right in the center of the keg lid, in the second that it had swirled about end-on to the ship's stern, and at a creditable seventy yards, too! Sergeant Skipwith pounded him on the back in congratulations, and his mates whooped in shared glee, whilst Rodney's face lit up in ecstatic joy.

"Wonder what he could do with my Ferguson rifle, or with one of those fusils?" Lewrie said. "We might detail him in the main-top as a sniper when we go to Quarters, alongside your Marines, 'ey, Mister Devereux? *Make* him a Marine . . . ?" Lewrie japed with a wide grin.

"Well, uhm . . ." Lt. Devereux demurred, wincing and sucking his teeth. "That might present a problem, sir. There have *never* been any Black Marines, and did we wish to experiment, as it were, my men would resent it mightily . . . most especially our five new volunteers we got from your Colonel Cashman's disbanded regiment."

"I don't really intend to kit him out in pipe-clay and a red coat, Mister Devereux!" Lewrie said with an amused snort.

"Those five are West Indies-born and bred, or have lived here so long they've taken on local prejudices, sir," Devereux explained, "and strictures against armed Blacks most of all. Their regiment was lily-white, and you *know* how little mixing there is in island society."

"Outside the sheets, that is," Lewrie dryly commented.

"Uhm, aye, sir," Devereux agreed shyly. "So, should we station Rodney with a musket at Quarters, it might be best did he shoot from the bulwarks, but not in the tops with the Marines, sir."

"Are they disgruntled, you're saying?" Lewrie demanded.

"Only *mildly,* sir . . . so far," Devereux replied, his usual air of elegant detachment slowly shredding. "They're happy, in the main, for another chance to 'soldier,' with their pay, uniforms, and rations. They're adapting well to most aspects of shipboard life . . . so much so that they're already expressing the usual low opinion of sailors, and the superior air of Marines. None *seem* to be future disciplinary problems, though they're tough men, sir. No raging drunks or troublemakers have reared their heads . . . yet. A ship, though, with so many of her people Black . . ."

"So their only plaint is against our Black sailors?" Lewrie asked. "Damme, sir . . . it's not like they haven't seen ten Blacks to each White settler already, ashore, haven't seen ships stationed out here for three

years or more with half their British crews perished, and God knows
who mannin' 'em?"

"They have, sir, but . . ."

"Damme, are they so disgruntled they'd blab where we got 'em?"

"Oh, no fear of that, sir!" Devereux was quick to reassure him.
"Their disgust with that Colonel Ledyard Beauman is so great that they
found our little raid rather delightful. Frankly, Captain, they despise him
worse than cold, boiled mutton, and think what we did was a *grand*
buggering! No, the only fear I have concerns desertion, sir . . . should
they hear of a chance to see Colonel Cashman duel the hen-headed
bastard, and run off to cheer him on!"

"I see," Lewrie said, calming, but still furrowing his brow in contem-
plation of a new threat. "*That's* a comfort . . . I think."

"About fusils, sir . . ." Devereux said, with a shifty look in his eyes—
eyes usually steeled with rigid Marine rectitude. "Our new men were
trained on, and equipped with, fifty-four calibre fusil muskets. While
they're no match for German *jaeger* rifles, or Yankee Doodle Pennsylvania rifles, fusils *are* more accurate than Brown Bess. Your friend Colonel Cashman sent us extremely good marksmen, born to shooting and
hunting. So I was wondering, uhm . . ."—Devereux coughed gently into
a fist to cover his scheming—"should you have another opportunity to
speak with Colonel Cashman, sir, might it be possible that he could
obtain some fusils for us? With his regiment disbanded, their arms will
rust away in an armory, and you just *know* how the Army will insist
everyone use seventy-five calibre Tower muskets just to ease problems
with ordnance supplies, so . . ."

"You wish to arm our Marines with fusils, then, sir?" Lewrie asked,
rocking on the balls of his feet with a stern glower on his face. "Opposing
the 'wisdom' of our Lords Commissioners of the Admiralty?"

"Oh, not all of them, sir, just a dozen . . . a *half*-dozen fusils." Devereux squirmed. "The Army surely would not miss so few. Was a swap
possible . . . our Short Sea Pattern muskets for fusils, well . . ." righteous
Lieutenant Devereux muttered like a housebreaker chatting plans for his
next robbery in an ale house. He coughed into his fist again.

"But too hard to explain to the Ordnance Board and our own su-

periors when *Proteus* pays off, Mister Devereux," Lewrie told him, with
a knowing leer and a tap on the side of his nose. "Why, damme if they
didn't charge us for 'em! And I doubt the local Army staff would find
it easy to explain, either, how a dozen or more weapons went missing.
Might charge *them* for 'em, too! Besides, as far as the Army is concerned,
Horse Guards, and God Almighty ordained the use of the Tower Musket,
Long Land Pattern, calibre seventy-five. Might've been etched into the
tablets Moses brought off the mountain, for all I know."

"But we could claim—"

"Damme, sir!" Lewrie barked with amusement. "D'ye mean for me
to *steal* 'em for you, Mister Devereux? Since I'm such a dab-hand at
stealin' slaves for sailors?"

"Well, I would not characterise it as *stealing*, sir, exactly," Devereux
said, tucking his hands behind his back (perhaps to keep them a *semblance*
of clean!) whilst his phyz reddened with flusterment, and jutting his chin
horizon-ward.

"You've another synonym handy, I take it, sir?" Lewrie teased, snickering to see their stolid Marine officer so discomfited.

"A mere half-dozen would suit, sir. Well, perhaps ten, or the dozen,"
Devereux all but begged. "For our new men, and those already aboard
who are demonstrably good shots. Why, think of the possibilities, sir!"
he wheedled. "Skilled men in the tops equipped with fusil muskets could
decimate an enemy's officers and mates at one go, sir! We could cripple
any ship we face with one accurate volley!"

"Even does our staff-captain, Sir Edward Charles, oppose such a
practice of targeting officers and gentlemen as savage and barbaric, Mister
Devereux? I am ordered never to engage in such, tsk tsk."

"Well, sir, what actually happens, and what is written up in a report
are two horses of another colour," Devereux slyly posed. "I do also
recall our recent competition with the American frigate . . . and how the
Hancock's men out-shot ours. Do we ever fight them, *they* will not feel
such nice compunctions against shooting *us*, sir. And neither would
French naval infantry, or bloody-handed privateersmen."

"Granted," Lewrie allowed.

"And I must own, sir, that the Yankees' superior arms and skill did
irk me. And fill me with envy," Devereux confessed. "Recall our fight

with those rebel slaves off Monte Cristi, sir. Had we possessed fusils, accurate long-range musketry would have slaughtered them long before they could get close enough to detonate their cargoes of powder. And done it more cheaply than using our great-guns, too, sir. Improve our, uhm . . . efficiency 'gainst small privateers and smugglers?" Devereux fantasised, aswell with ideas and barely disguised impatience.

"Hmmm," Lewrie sobered, pondering that galling event and weakening a trifle.

"And, have we not, sir, with you as our guide, already set an example as being more than ready to, uhm . . . extemporise if needs must, Captain?" Devereux pled.

"Extemporise," Lewrie scoffed as they paced forward to amidships of the windward gangway. "Now, *there's* a word that covers a multitude of sins. Damn my eyes, Mister Devereux. Are you pissing down my back? 'With me as our guide'? Christ on a crutch!" he snorted dismissively.

"We may not be able to swap for them, sir, but your friend the colonel could, ah . . . spirit them away for us?" Devereux schemed. "Or fusils *could* be explained away as personal weapons of our officers and gentlemen midshipmen, sir. Kept aft in the gun-room or your cabins . . .'til we get a chance to go ashore and *hunt*? Sporting arms, sir, aha! After all, fusils arose as officers' weapons back in the Seven Years' War, so they could appear as common soldiers to French or Indian sharpshooters, and not be targeted as leaders . . . but didn't wish to bear the burden of a Brown Bess musket. A fusil is much lighter . . ."

"No, we must *never* overburden officers," Lewrie laughed aloud. "They've enough stress, already!"

Hmmm, though. . . .

Personally, he liked the .54 calibre fusil musket, and had from his first experience with them, with Kit Cashman, at the tail end of the American Revolution, even fetching off one as a memento of their failed expedition up the Appalachicola River in Spanish Florida. And where was it now? Hanging over the mantel in his private office/study at home in Anglesgreen . . . that is, had Caroline not sold it or given it away out of bloody-minded spite.

"If all else fails, sir, we could claim we captured them off a suspect merchantman, or a privateer, or . . ." Devereux hinted.

"You wish 'em hellish-bad, don't you, Mister Devereux?"

"I do, indeed, sir!" Devereux vowed, childishly hopeful.

"Even if that means sailing back to Kingston for 'em and exposing our new hands to recapture? Us into court? Or letting your new Marines ashore for liberty, where they might brag and get us hung?"

"Well, uhm . . ." Devereux shied, with a painful squint. "Do you put it that way, sir . . . I know it's a risk, but I still think that did we have them, it would be in the ship's best interests, Captain."

"Dear me, Mister Devereux," Lewrie said, checking their pacing, and with a sad shake of his head, "but I do believe we've managed to corrupt even such a proper young fellow as you! Society ought to lock us all away as a threat to the Public Good."

"And the Navy hasn't, sir?" Devereux chirped, suddenly elated, yet gesturing at the bare, featureless horizon. "Could you but try to speak to your old friend, Colonel Cashman . . ."

"Well," Lewrie hemmed and hawed.

"And whilst you do that, sir," Devereux rushed on to pose, "I've an idea about that 'indirect' fire. Those slave boats were too far for grenadoes, you recall? But, did we have, say, three or four small coehorn mortars in the tops, mortars we could extemporise to the metal stanchions and forks for the swivel guns, we could fire explosive shell—steep plunging fire!—right onto an enemy's decks, like that Colonel Shrapnel's fused exploding case-shot, and . . . !"

Six Bells chimed from the forecastle belfry, precluding further thought on that subject; the first was trouble enough, to Lewrie's imagination. Six Bells; eleven of the morning, and a half hour 'til the welcome pipe of "Clear Decks And Up Spirits" for the issuance of the rum ration.

"One bit of devilment at a time, if you please, Mister Devereux. I'm not as young as I once was, d'ye know," Lewrie told him, grinning. "Too much audacity at one sitting leaves me breathless these days."

Lt. Langlie came up to join them, doffing his hat.

"Six Bells, sir. Permission to secure from arms drill?"

"Very well, Mister Langlie," Lewrie replied, now properly stern. "Make sure they're well cleaned and oiled before stowing. Does time permit, have the senior hands instruct the volunteers in basic knots."

"Very good, sir," Langlie replied, in his own properly crisp manner, yet sharing a meaningful glance with Devereux, as if they both were in on things.

"Anything else you wish, then, Mister Devereux?" Lewrie queried. "A 'whore transport' to trail us about, perhaps?"

"A what, sir?" Devereux gawped, this time wholly surprised.

"Ask Andrews about it," Lewrie suggested. "It's an old tale. And you, Mister Langlie."

"Sir?" Langlie paused, halfway to turning and saluting.

"*You'd* not turn up your nose at a personal, sporting, hunting fusil, I take it?" Lewrie grinned. "What, the *entire* gun-room?"

"Well, uhm, ah . . ." Langlie flummoxed, sharing another glance with Devereux, as if to ask what trouble he'd gotten into, now.

"Damme, but I begin to fear we're a ship filled with conspirators from keel to truck." Lewrie snickered.

"One might term it, ah . . . *aspiring*, Captain," Langlie replied.

"Aspiring, hey? Hmmm . . . works for me. Carry on, Lieutenant Devereux. Mister Langlie, a word, sir."

Devereux saluted and left, a bounce in his step, as if eager to inform the other officers that they'd be getting fusils, by hook or by crook. Langlie stood and waited, as a perpetually put-upon First Officer should, waiting for *another* heavy shoe to drop on his head.

"I am informed by the latest post that you and my ward, Sophie de Maubeuge, are in correspondence, Mister Langlie," Lewrie said. "And I am also informed that my permission was granted. Exactly when *did* I allow such, Mister Langlie? Hmmm?"

"Why, uhm . . . at Chatham, sir!" Langlie said, reddening, and of a need, perhaps, to cough into *his* fist for cover. "The last night we lay at anchor, when we dined your family aboard, and held the singing and such, sir? Sophie, uhm . . . Mistress de Maubeuge, the Vicomtesse, rather, said that she'd spoken to you about it, and had received your permission, so I *assumed* . . ."

"Sound a tad more French when she told you, did she?" Lewrie asked, still stern-faced.

"Well, as a matter of fact, aye, she did, Captain. A tad."

"Do you have the pleasure of seeing her face-to-face again, do keep in mind that when she's scheming, she sounds more French than English,

Mister Langlie," Lewrie informed him. "I did not give her leave to write you."

"Oh God, I'm sorry, sir, I . . . !" Langlie exclaimed. "I beg your forgiveness, and . . . I never meant to! *That's* what you meant about conspiring, just now."

"Oh, hush, Mister Langlie," Lewrie wearily told him, waving one hand dismissively. "After knowing you for a year, I rather doubt you're the sort to trifle with the girl, or tarnish my family's reputation . . . assumin' such a thing's *possible*, these days."

"Uhm, ah . . ." Langlie began to agree, then thought better of it. His mouth worked, as if trying to bite his tongue, or stifle a titter of amusement—the sort of laugh that would never do his career or his professional relationship any good.

"Uhm, yayss, quite," Lewrie chuckled, archly sarcastic over his own repute. "You wish to continue corresponding?"

"I do, sir."

"And I'm to assume that Sophie is of the same mind? Despite the distance involved?" Lewrie asked. "And the temptations of local beaus?"

"I may only gather . . . ah, assume, at *present,* sir, that she is not averse to receiving my letters," Langlie stammered.

"Many a slip, 'twixt the crouch and the leap," Lewrie allowed, slapping his hands together behind his back and gazing aloft. "Well then, since you ain't poxed, drunk on duty, breakin' out in purplish spots, and can eat with a knife and fork, Mister Langlie . . . I'll let this stand. Just don't do anything momentous at long distance, d'ye hear me? God knows how long it'll be before we're back home again, and God only knows what home there'll be to welcome you, if there is a home at all."

"Thank you, sir! Thank you so . . . !" Langlie cried.

"Carry *on,* Mister Langlie!" Lewrie insisted, shooing him away. "Carry on."

"Very good, sir," he said, doffing his hat eagerly, clumsily, rapturously aquiver, and his face a perfect portrait of bliss.

"You may not thank me, later, d'ye know, sir," Lewrie cautioned. "The wife now despises the Navy worse than God despises the French, if such a thing is possible, and that'll put you right in the middle of it, right in the line of fire, d'ye see? You're *asking* for trouble, Mister Langlie."

"I'll bear the risk, sir . . . gladly," the young officer vowed.

"Then you're an idiot, God help you. Women, sir! Mine arse on a band-box!" Lewrie snorted. "Oh, go shove on a rope or something, sir, do! Shoo! And quit that bloody . . . beaming!"

"Aye aye, sir!" Langlie said, doffing his hat, even making a wee bow in *congé*, absurdly formal aboard ship; and *still* grinning like the worst Lunatick in Bedlam, but almost back to a professional bearing.

Well, it's his poor arse, Lewrie decided to himself, pacing aft to his quarterdeck; *he's been warned.*

CHAPTER THIRTY

Puerto Rico, Lewrie thought, eying the landmass that had risen from the sea a little after Dawn Quarters; *and the Mona Passage. Now what do we do? North-about Santo Domingo, or run back along the south shore, close in?*

Out to the East'rd lay golden isles, the storied cays that had featured in his youth, the Danish Virgins and below them the beads-on-a-necklace of the Leewards, each a little gem, and this morning almost presaged by how the sea glittered gold, lapis, and sun-silvered.

Are they poxed, too? he asked himself; *now it's Fever Season is there a safe lee shore anywhere in the West Indies?*

Lewrie hung in the larboard mizen shrouds, just at the beginning of the cat-harpings, coat, hat, and neck-stock ˉoff, and savouring a cool morning breeze, the scent of salt and iodine, and a faint fishy tang of shorelines up to the Nor'east. He lowered his telescope and gazed down and in-board to *Proteus*'s gangways and gun-deck, where sailors crowded round in untidy knots, some still licking their chops after a breakfast remnant, as they formed up by gun-crews a bit before the call was piped for drill on the artillery.

For a miraculous change, they looked healthy and fit again, the last ravages of the fevers left astern and ashore. There were formerly half-dead men who now strode about and joshed with their fellows; there were those who had never been infected, no matter how often they'd gone ashore or slept on deck for coolness when anchored; there were the local lads who might have suffered malaria or the Yellow Jack when babies and now were immune, as was he.

With a word, Lewrie could order the ship to beat up through the Mona Passage, round the eastern tip of Hispaniola, and re-enter her old patrol grounds to the north . . . with the fresh Nor'east Trades blowing so strong that feverish miasmas would always lie alee, and no one else might fall ill.

With a word, he could put *Proteus* about, turn his back on those golden isles of the Leewards and the Virgins (though he had a yen for a glimpse of them once more) and then the Trades would brush across the island of Hispaniola, wafting God only knew what nastiness right down on them. At sea, with the deck and bulwark railings pitching and tossing, they could not employ Mr. Durant's tar-and-citron pots to counteract the foul miasmas that brought disease with sweet ones. Surely some who had not yet succumbed ran the risk of another exposure; those debilitated the first time might not survive a second.

Lewrie slowly collapsed the tubes of his telescope, each click of the tubes seating a step towards a decision. He turned his body to peer forward, past the spread of the main and fore courses, and the upthrust bow sprit and jib-boom, and the anchor cat-heads. A day more on this course to the Sou'east would take *Proteus* deep into the waters between Saint Thomas and Saint Croix, where privateers and smugglers were two-a-penny during the Revolution in his "green" days.

Though some could call it poaching, Lewrie told himself with a wry grin. The Royal Navy squadrons based out of English Harbour, down at Antigua, prowled those seas when they could spare vessels from the blockade of troublesome Guadeloupe, whilst he and his frigate were beholden to Kingston and the West Indies Station.

Ostensibly, every British warship answered to Admiral Parker, and his headquarters at Kingston, from the Bahama Banks to Trinidad, from the Antilles to the shoal waters of the Spanish possessions far to the west, such as New Spain and the Isthmus of Panama, so . . . would trolling a *touch* more East'rd really be poaching? It could be excused . . . couldn't it?

The Leewards were a tempting lure, and not just for him alone. The rare Dutch merchant ships still at sea would try to succour their colonies;

if they threaded past the blockade in European waters, that's where they would first strike the West Indies. The supposedly neutral Danes, and those pesky Swedes, would be up to their old games of shipping contraband goods and arms, turning a blind eye to ships from belligerent nations in their harbours; merchantmen, privateers, and the odd ship of war that came calling. American vessels, despite the undeclared war against France, still traded with the Danes, the Dutch, and the Spanish . . . and probably with the French isles, as well, for they were a mercenary lot for all their protestations, and losses to French privateers.

Puerto Rico, well in sight now, and the Danish Virgins would be a grand place for smugglers and contrabanders to break their passages, refit and resupply, perhaps take a little joy of shore liberty before their long jogs home, or put in for shelter from storm winds in those marvelous natural harbours and bays that yawned so emptily . . . and so covertly, the perfect hidey-holes for nefarious doings.

With the telescope now shortened and safely slung over his left shoulder, Lewrie faced the shrouds and took several cautious steps upward on the ratlines, up where the futtock shrouds of the mizen top intersected the side-stays, until the futtocks almost brushed his bared scalp; where a man would have to make a choice . . . either take the seamanly ascent out-board by hanging from the futtock shrouds, or confess his lubberliness and snake between to follow the side-stays' easier "ladder" to the mizen top platform, through the lubber's hole.

The arms they'd recovered . . . Yankee-made arms.

American ships trading along the Spanish Main, at Tampico, Vera Cruz, Cartagena, Caracas, and Port-Of-Spain, the Dutch isles of Curacao would most-like take the most direct route back North, using the Mona or the Windward Passage. Or they could go round-about, skirting the lee side of the Antilles.

What had that Captain Wilder of *Bantam*, and Kershaw of the U.S.S. *Hancock* frigate, told him . . . that they would make a rendezvous point to form American convoys in the lee of St. Kitts? As far to the East'rd, as well up to windward of the Trades as possible, leaving half an ocean of sea-room alee, 'til entering the Old Bahama Channel, or passing west of New Providence yet east of Andros through the Bahamas on their way home. Then, should they meet contrary winds, they wouldn't end up wrecked on a lee shore.

Lewrie realised that a *guilty* Yankee trader could sell all the arms and munitions he wished, pick up an innocent cargo for the return voyage, and then lumber along in convoy with other ships, protected by the guns of his spanking-new and uncurious navy!

Laughin' all the way, Lewrie sourly thought; *Bugger it, it ain't like we're chained like a guard dog. We're not even on a long leash!*

The staff-captain's written orders, when they'd come aboard at last, had pretty-much instructed him to toddle off and make a nuisance of himself 'til Hell froze over . . . on their enemies, for, a change. He had an open-ended, roving brief to chase his own tail if of a mind, in any body of water under Admiral Parker's writ—just as long as *Proteus* was not "in sight" to plague his seniors' sensitive humours.

Lewrie squirmed about, carefully shifting feet and hand-holds, to peer Nor'westerly. Hispaniola was under the horizon, Saint Dominque most likely an ocean of gore by now, as old grudges were avenged upon the losers, and Spanish Santo Domingo could most likely now be aflame, as L'Ouverture led his rag-tag armies over the border to "liberate" all the island. Santo Domingo had never amounted to much, really. It was the windward end of Hispaniola, too dryed by the Trades for plantation agriculture, and bereft of mineral wealth. There were, his advisories had informed him, vast ranches raising cattle, pigs, and goats, enough grains grown for domestic use but little for export, and most of that land but sparsely populated, its grandees rather shabby in the main, and most of its people and slaves living hand-to-mouth. *Boucanieros,* those who cooked, salted, and jerkied meat along the coast, were mostly leftover pirates' descendants, still living and dressing in skins off their goats. *Barbecana,* their product was; two words introduced into English as "buccaneers," and outdoor roasting parties becoming popular in the United States, Cashman had told him . . . "barbecues."

Well, that problem, as far as *Proteus* was concerned, was over and done with, for now; a trifle to be isolated and left to fester or expire on its own, and the small tenders, cutters, and schooners of the West Indies Squadron would manage that chore. To turn North and race down either the north or south shore would probably be fruitless.

He turned again, just as carefully, to face forrud, taking one hand to swipe his unruly hair back into a brief semblance of neatness.

"Nuisance they wish, then it's a nuisance they'll get," Lewrie whispered to himself under the flutter-drum of the winds, and suddenly feeling much happier. "Just like Goodyer's Pig, 'never well, but when in mischief'!" he chuckled.

In his mind's eye, he could already see the abyssal royal-blue seas of the Virgins and the Leewards, could almost feel the thuds and thumps up through the stays to his fingers and boot soles of a vessel crossing those "square" waves that could blow up on brisk days, where the chop could be four feet high, with barely six feet between crests . . . and the rocky-gold islets and cays breezed past in constant parade, their beaches the palest new parchment colour and the shoals the palest glass green.

The steep slopes, the palms and palmettoes, the rounded pastures and cane fields, the "balds" with the pretty, pastel windmills slowly rotating and waving in greeting . . . drawing him on. . . .

He closed his eyes, drew a deep, pleasing breath of ocean scent, and nodded as he made his decision. If nothing else, it would·be like a homecoming.

And, did it prove fruitless, or he got *caught* poaching, a quick run back downwind to his own kennel was possible.

CHAPTER THIRTY-ONE

$\mathcal{H}$MS *Proteus* hauled her wind and bore away Sou'Sou'east to cut below the western tip of Saint Croix, then take an easy, hill-gentled cruise along that island's southern shore in its lee. Bowing to full winds past the eastern end she stood on for fifteen nautical miles before coming about to starboard tack, to clear the shoals of the Lang's Bank, then headed Nor'west in deep water, roughly aimed for the Salt Island Passage into Sir Francis Drake's Channel. The winds were a tad perverse, though, backing a point, so by dusk she was nearer the small and rocky isles of Norman and Peter Island, where she fetched-to for the night just before full sunset. Cocked up to the night winds as she was, she would make a slow and quiet sternway back out to deep and safe waters to the Sou'west.

The skies were clear and strewn with stars, the winds soughing softly, and the motion of her hull easy, a slow and stately rocking to and fro, the' slightest measured pitch and toss as the dark, abandoned bulks of slightly larger Peter Island, and lower Norman Island, wafted rightward off the larboard bows.

It was such a rare event that some of the hands begged for line and hooks, using salt-junk as bait, and soon were hauling up catch after catch, whooping with delight to land fish without battering them to bloody rags whilst the ship was underway. Bonito, red snapper, even a small shark came thrashing up over the bulwark's, and their new Black cook, Gideon, called for more firewood and lit off the grills, expertly gutting, heading, and slicing them into steaks, pausing only to spit tobacco juice from his ever-present quid as he sprinkled salt, pepper, and lime juice over the sizzling slabs. Though there was salt-pork in the steep-tubs already, the fish would augment the usual rations quite nicely, he assured everyone, easily enlisting help among the crew.

"Gon' eat good, boys!" Gideon boasted. "De fish, he eat sweet! What de white folk sometime call 'surf an' turf,' dey have beef wif a fish? Woll, we havin' 'surf an' *sty*!' Mo' firewood, heah! Cut me a mess o' dose lemons, too, Noble! Mistah Morley, ya done wif 'at pompano fo' de cap'um's table? Woll, hand dem steaks heah, fo' he perish o' de hungries!"

Lewrie's nostrils twitched and his stomach rumbled with anticipation as the heady fumes flowed aft from the galley funnel. A sweet dark whiff of rum on the wind caught his senses, as well. The senior hands and mates *always* found a way to cache smuggled rum. It appeared that some of it was being used to flavour the fish. His nose wrinkled as he caught the other scent, the musk-sweet and oily reek of Mr. Durant's miasma pots along the windward side, set in hollows delved into the tubs of sand kept for gun crews' traction, firefighting, and deck scrubbing.

"We'll look as lit up as a whaler with her try-pots goin'," he groused to Lt. Langlie, as he watched Durant and Hodson proceed aft in dodderers' crouches, bent over with prepared pots and burning punks in their hands. "So much for anonymity . . . or hiding our presence."

"Not that we've seen anything more than fishing boats and local traders as of yet, sir," Langlie counseled. "Fredericksted Harbour on the west end is little used according to Mister Winwood, and Christiansted on Saint Croix's north shore is shallow and rocky. The only good commercial *entrepôt* is Charlotte Amalie, yonder on Saint Thomas, so—"

"Ah-moll-yah," Lewrie corrected. "The locals say Ah-moll-yah, not Am-ah-lee, Mister Langlie. Aye, it was a right pirate's hole, in the old days. Smugglers, privateers, slavers . . . only saw it from off shore, but perhaps tomorrow. I'm told it's a pretty little town. We aren't at war with Denmark. We might even request a pilot and anchor for a day and night. Our old Sailing Master once told me that above the town, on the island's spine, there's a vista where one may sit and look east, all the way down Drake's Channel . . . Drake's Seat. Said he sat up there himself, like a king on his throne, the old buccaneer. I'd rather like t'do that, myself. See all the isles, all the way out to Virgin Gorda and Anegada . . . prettiest view in the whole Caribbean, I've heard tell. What Heaven must seem, for sailors."

"For those few of us who'll be admitted through the Pearly Gate, sir," Langlie softly joshed, massaging his middle as his stomach emitted a genteel growling. In the dark, Lewrie could *feel* him wince at his unthinking words, having put his foot in it again.

"More than you'd imagine, Mister Langlie," Lewrie said, after a brief pause and a short snort of amusement; mostly at Langlie's wary shadow-dancing around him. "I've always held that sailors ain't *great* sinners, in the main. Their needs and wants are simple and their sins are minor and venal . . . not outright wicked or cruel. Their lives and livelihoods are too precarious, and the sea's too big for them to go off tyrannical or murderous. Oceans keep the fear o' God on 'em, and keep 'em looking over their shoulders. Superstition, perhaps; fear of the Lord, perhaps, as well. Who knows? *There* lies your true evil, sir, your true wickedness," Lewrie concluded, pointing at the faint loom of light, roughly where Charlotte Amalie lay, on the Nor'west horizon.

"So . . . shore's the trouble, sir? And what little time a tarpaulin man spends there is . . . ?" Langlie puzzled out.

"Respite, sir," Lewrie snickered, mocking his own pretensions to philosophy. "Respite." And Langlie chuckled with him, easier and honestly this time.

"The stink-pots may help, sir," Langlie said of a sudden, as an almost companionable silence extended perhaps a bit too long. "With the ship lit up like a whaler as you said, who'd imagine we're a ship of war? Whales *might* be taken in these waters . . . if they swim through the Turk's Passage a bit north and west of here, as you told me, sir."

"Accidental . . . *camouflage*, as the French would say?"

"Pray God it's a fortuitous choice, Captain," Langlie answered, in all seriousness.

" 'Scuse me, Cap'um . . . Mister Langlie, sir," Aspinall said as he appeared at their side on the quarterdeck, "but that Gideon fella's got yer supper ready. Big slab o' pompano, pease puddin', boiled tatties, and some o' that cornmeal sweet bread o' his, and Toulon's goin' nigh frantic t'claw the dish cover off. Best come quick, beggin' yer pardon . . . else he'll have it all."

"There wasn't a portion for him?" Lewrie hooted with mirth.

"Aye, there was, sir, and not a morsel left. Gone quicker'n a wink, and still lustin' after yours," Aspinall warned him.

"It appears I must go below or go hungry, Mister Langlie. Do you have a good supper of your own."

"Aye, sir. Goodnight. And we'll see what fortune the morning brings," Langlie said, doffing his hat.

"Surely, it'll be good, Mister Langlie," Lewrie paused to say, returning the salute, "since we've already managed the miracle of the Loaves and Fishes!"

HMS *Proteus* hauled her wind Sutherly and got underway one hour before Dawn Quarters would normally be stood, with only a cursory try at scrubbing decks to perfect cleanness. She stood Sou'east–Half South for awhile to gather speed and clear any shoals, until she was roughly even with the Salt Island Passage, then tacked about to take the winds on her starboard quarter, and, under reduced sail, loped Westerly, to prowl close to the southern coast of Saint John, for a peek into Coral Bay before angling off toward Saint Thomas to look into the Pillsbury Sound which separated the islands, and held several tempting hurricane holes where privateers and smugglers could lurk.

Saint John, Lewrie recalled as he loafed by the windward rails with a spyglass, had been a productive island, with many plantations of sugar cane, before a slave rebellion had slaughtered most of the White owners and driven the rest away. With British and French help back in a rare example of "tween wars" cooperation, the slaves had been massacred, but not before the fields had been burned to stubble, the houses, presses, barns, and mills destroyed as symbols of cruel subjugation. A renascence had never occurred, and Saint John brooded in a sleepy, funeral silence, with most of the arable land going back to jungles, and left alone as if accursed. Perhaps it was, Lewrie speculated.

Coral Bay, between narrow headlands on her Sou'east corner, was one of the great, but unused natural harbours in the world, and were the Virgins in British hands, would have supplanted Kingston for Navy use ages ago, since it lay so much further up to windward of the main passages to the West Indies. And once out of the main channel, Coral Bay funneled out into narrow leads to North and Nor'west, into hurricane holes, the worst winds and storm surges blocked by headlands and narrow but high peninsulas.

"If not there, sir, there's Pillsbury Sound," Mr. Winwood was saying, pointing at a carefully tacked down chart. "There's eleven to fifteen fathom right up it, where it splits round Grass and Mingo, Congo and Lovango Cays. There's a Windward Passage, narrow but practicable for in-bound vessels, of the same depths. A Middle Passage to the west of Grass Cay, and a long, narrow but useable channel between Thatch Cay and the north shore of Saint Thomas."

"Great escape routes, aye," Lewrie commented, after returning to the binnacle cabinet and the traverse board. "That last'un leads out to deep water, past Hans Lollick and Little Lollick, I see. What about Red Hook Bay, here, at the east end of Saint Thomas? And Saint James Bay . . . these little inlets?"

"Very shoal, sir, and exposed to the Nor'east Trades, but with decent holding ground. Hard sand bottom," Winwood opined. "But a wee privateer or a small trading schooner might be able to put in there. Pity we don't have something similar, as a tender, to explore, sir. There are anywhere from four to nine fathom for anchoring, but so very many shifting sand shoals."

"Well, we'll just have to stand in close as we dare, but keep our heads, won't we, Mister Winwood?" Lewrie tried to tease the man.

"Somewhat close, sir," Winwood mournfully lowed; their Sailing Master was an impossible sobersides, and would not recognise a jape if it kicked him in the crutch. "And there is the matter of Danish sovereignty, Captain. Within the three-mile limit, inside which we at this very moment stand, we have no jurisdiction."

"Does Denmark have a frigate in these waters, sir?" Lewrie shot back. "Any forts outside Charlotte Amalie, with more than a corporal's guard to man a few rusty guns?"

"I have not *heard* of such reinforcements, sir."

"Then bugger 'em," Lewrie decided. "Ah! We're nigh to the west end of Norman Island. We'll be able to see deep into Coral Bay within a minute or two."

"Sail ho! Deck, there!" a foremast lookout cried, dancing with delight on the narrow cross-trees. " 'Cross the point! Two sail standin' outta the bay! Two points off the starboard bows!"

Lewrie sprang forward along the starboard gangway to the break of the forecastle in his eagerness, his expression joyous and wolfish, creating excitement in the hands he passed, in those clustered below on the gun-deck. Perhaps it was "uncaptainly" to show feelings, exciting people for nothing, especially if he could not deliver, but he could not help himself.

He raised his glass. It was that magical, dim time of the dawn before the sun was truly up and everything was soft twilight, the sea and clouds and sky pearly blue-grey, the isles and cays muted and dark. Against that background, two dark hulls stood out starkly, their sails ghostly white, before sunrise revealed them to be a weary and stained tan. There was a large schooner, and a chunkier, dowdier brig or snow, both bound Sou'west, just clear of Leduck Island and headed out as if to pass Ram Head, and not three miles off! And their flags . . . !

One was French, the schooner; the brig was a Yankee.

First out of his mouth was a loud whoop, followed by orders he shouted back to the quarterdeck through cupped hands. "Mister Langlie, hands aloft to set t'gallants and shake out the reefs in the courses! Mister Winwood, steer direct for Ram Head and cut them off!"

He whirled back to face the two suspicious vessels again, experience juggling courses and possible speeds. The schooner and brig had the initial advantage, almost completely exposed to the Nor'east Trade wind, but were deep up the bay. Was *Proteus* partially masked from the full force of the morning winds, she could deploy thousands more square feet of sail more quickly, and her waterline was longer; slower to accelerate, but once she had a bone in her teeth she'd be the fastest off the wind.

The American brig bore the same limitations of all square-rigged ships; she would find it hard to go to windward, to point as "high" as a fore-and-aft rigged vessel like the schooner, so the only way she had to escape would be to run like a scalded cat for Charlotte Amalie and throw herself on the mercy of the Danish authorities. She *could* round

Ram Head and surge up Pillsbury Sound, with the winds abeam or just a bit abaft, and go for the Middle Passage or the Leeward Passage.

Lewrie looked aloft at the commissioning pendant streaming from the main-mast truck. The Trades were weak, as they always were in good weather round dawn, weak but steady from the Nor'east, so he thought a try up the Middle Passage from Pillsbury Sound, abeam the winds, out of the question. It would be too slow. No, he thought, if she tried that she would head for the incredibly narrow and treacherous Leeward Passage. He stowed that thought away as improbable.

The schooner, though, was much more manoeuvrable and it was not out of the question for her to spin about almost in her own length and try to run Sou'east, abeam the Trades, and pass astern of *Proteus* at a rate of knots, hoping that the brig would be considered the most valuable prize. With her greater speed, she might dare the risk of broadsides hurriedly ranged and fired. The schooner might dodge right past before a gun could hurt her, and show them a clean pair of heels.

"Don't think of that, don't think of that," Lewrie muttered on his way back aft, pacing sideways to keep his eyes on the brig and the schooner. "Just panic and *run*, you bastards."

"Courses, tops'ls, and t'gallants all set, sir," Lt. Langlie reported as Lewrie gained the quarterdeck. "Outer flying jib, the inner, and the fore top-mast stays'l set, as well."

Lewrie looked aloft for confirmation, also noting that the main and mizen t'gallant stays'ls filled the spaces between the masts, as they had since they'd come about off Salt Island Passage, to make best use of the weak predawn Trades without showing too much aloft for an enemy to espy and be warned off.

"Were they smart, they'd turn and run back up the bay and get ashore," Catterall commented, still coatless and fiddling with his neck-stock. "We'd get the ships if they don't fire them, but the crews would escape us."

Lewrie spun on his heel to glare at him, freezing Catterall in mid-*toilette*. "Then let us pray our Chases are bereft of your great experience, sir. Let's pray they're bumbling idiots . . . sir!"

Catterall gulped and shrugged into himself as his hammock-man held out his coat to don, and he slipped into it as if it were armour.

"Everyone down from aloft, Mister Langlie? Good," Lewrie said. "Now, beat to Quarters. Mister Catterall?"

"Sir?" the hapless Second Officer replied, now dressed but still trying to shrink away.

"Tell off an armed boat crew, with six or eight Marines, and be ready to board one of the prizes, should we be fortunate."

"Aye aye, sir! Mister Towpenny! A boat brought up from towing astern to short stays!"

Lewrie turned back to their Chases, relieved to see that they were still mindlessly intent on fleeing, holding their course, aiming to get round Ram Head into deeper water and run almost due West, with the schooner ahead, of course, and steering a bit further out from the land, almost as if she would challenge *Proteus* and protect her consort. The French *tricouleur* stood out boldly from her gaff, swung by the wind to lay against her mainsail. But *Proteus* was hitting her stride, now, and beginning to surge forward with a purposeful bustle, the apparent wind keener and brisker, and her stout hull "talking" to him in groans and swashings as she parted the rather calm seas like a broad farmer's plough through rich loam.

Gun-ports were hinging up and out of the way on the schooner's larboard side, at least five that Lewrie could see, and she was coming a point "lower" to intersect their course, her gaff-hung sails arcing away from them into mere slivers to cup more stern wind.

"I make the range as under a mile, sir," Langlie said.

The schooner was most likely a French privateer, Lewrie thought, judging her lines more critically. As fine and lean as she appeared, she couldn't bear the weight of more than eight or ten guns, and those could not be much more than 6-pounders. "Man's a bloody Lunatick!" he grunted. "Mister Langlie, I'll thank you to shoot his grandiose dreams to flinders."

"Very good, sir! Mister Catterall, Mister Adair . . . on the uproll, and open upon her!" Langlie shouted down to the gun-deck.

The schooner opened first, wreathing herself in a sudden bank of sulfurous fumes, the sound of her artillery a muffled stutter; five guns as Lewrie had surmised, and terrier-sharp by the sound of them—6-pounders, or more likely 4-pounders.

Shot shrieked overhead, a splash was raised far out to starboard and the ball skipped high enough to chew a small segment of a bulwark railing and strew stowed hammocks in the racks like wakened worms.

"On the up-roll . . ." Catterall could be heard yelling, *"fire!"*

The air was moist and cool with sea mist. *Proteus*'s guns roared and reeled back in-board almost as one, making not only a deep bank of gun smoke, but an instant fog of tortured air, each gun's eruption standing for a moment as a horizontal sea-spout from the muzzles, and making thirteen distinct smoke-and-fog rings that quickly merged into a cloud that only slowly drifted away to larboard and alee as *Proteus* sailed beyond it, leaving a semi-opaque, surface-level cumulus astern.

"Hit . . . hit!" Langlie was noting, striving for professional detachment, though almost dancing on tip-toes. "Three . . . four . . . six!"

"There is a nasty shoal, sir," Mr. Winwood muttered, coming to Lewrie's left rear. "Eagle Shoal, 'tis called, almost dead ahead, by our charts. They're coming to us, so . . ."

"A turn away will not increase the gun-range, aye," Lewrie said quickly, with only a slight turn of his head to acknowledge him. "Two points alee, and keep us clear."

He only had eyes for their targets, now. The schooner had taken the worst of their exchange, with holes punched in both her sails, and sections of her bulwark torn open, a low deckhouse afore her wheel shot up, and her inner jib flying loose of both controlling sheet and halliard. His hands took time to cheer as they swabbed out, thumb-stalled vents, and began to wave the powder monkeys forward with fresh charges borne in flash-resistant leather cylinders.

The brig, still flying an American flag, was hugging closer to the shore of Saint John, as if to shave Ram Head by a boat-hook's reach. Urgent signals were now flying from her lee main-mast.

"She'll pass inside the shoal, Mister Winwood?" Lewrie queried.

"The brig, aye, sir. The schooner, though . . ." Winwood replied with a wince, as if watching an imminent coach accident.

"Schooner's bearing away," Langlie noted. "Ready, down there?"

Gun-captains waved their hands clear of the guns; Catterall had his sword poised on high, nodding eagerly. "On the up-roll . . . *fire!*"

"She's standing directly onto the shoal, sir!" Winwood said.

"The brig displays this month's coded signals, sir!" Midshipman Elwes suddenly cautioned, with some alarm.

"He's a lying dog, then," Lewrie snapped, between explosions from
their guns.

"But, sir! Really, they're this month's signals!" Elwes protested, eyes
wide in fear of error.

"We ain't firin' on *her*, Mister Elwes," Lewrie took the patience to
say to him, direct. "Do you recall our first encounter with Yankee merchantmen? If she's innocent, what's she doin' in company with that Frog
privateer? Once our smoke clears, hoist a signal for her to heave to and
prepare to be boarded. If she obeys, fine. If she doesn't . . . then we *will*
fire into her."

"Aye, aye, sir," Elwes said, doffing his hat before dashing off aft to
his flag lockers and halliards.

Once again, both the schooner and HMS *Proteus* had mounded the
sea with ragged thunderheads of smoke and fog-roil from their guns. A
moment later, the schooner sailed clear of hers, presenting her lines side-
on, her hull pocked with 12-pounder impacts, and the upper gaff of her
foresail hanging limp and the sail bagged out alee.

Then she struck the shoal, jerking to a complete stop, her mastheads
swaying forward, gaffs and booms swinging forward abruptly. Running
rigging snapped, heavy lower booms ploughed through shrouds and
ripped them loose from the dead-eyes, ripped dead-eyes from the chain
platforms! Her bow rose up as if cresting a boisterous wave . . . but remained at that angle, her bow sprit and jib-boom almost vertical.

Proteus's crew groaned aloud, making "Ooohh!" sounds as if in fellow
sailors' sympathy, before recalling that the ship over there *was* French,
after all, and began to jeer and cat-call.

"Someone send for Mister Durant!" Lewrie chortled loudly. "And
ask him how one says 'Oops, oh shit' in *French*!"

"Do you still wish her boarded, sir?" Langlie asked, after the hilarity
had faded and the quarterdeck people had returned to duties.

"Aye, I do, Mister Langlie," Lewrie decided after a long moment to
think it over, weighing risk to his sailors against the need for a confirming document as a privateer. "Send *two* boats with Mister Catterall, and
a larger boarding party. He's to capture her captain or a mate, if possible,

with her Letter of Marque and Reprisal. Does the rest of the crew get ashore, so be it, and let 'em be the Danes' problem. Do they not fire her as they abandon, have our people do it. Instruct him to menace them, but not get into a melee. Do you think he may manage that, Mister Langlie?"

"He's an energetic, simple-minded brute, sir, so I expect that he may," Langlie chirped back with a wry grin on his features.

"Very well," Lewrie announced. "Let's fetch-to and despatch our boarding party, quick as we can. Mister Elwes, what answer did we get from the brig?"

"Can't really make it out, sir, it's all higgledy-piggledy," the boy replied, dashing from aft to a skidding stop at his summons.

"He's a liar and a conspirator, as I suspected, then. Thankee, Mister Elwes. Keep 'Fetch-To' aloft, and think of a way to make that 'Insistent.' Carry on, sir."

Proteus didn't wish to drown any of her boarders by proceeding at full tilt when they scrambled down into the boats, surfing along at the end of short painters, barely held in check by straining coxswains and bow-men with boat-hooks. She would have to slow down and take in sail, steering more for Ram Head with the wind abeam to "make a lee" so the sailors and Marines could disembark down her larboard side.

"Let's make it fast, Mister Langlie," Lewrie said. "Scandalise her and clew up sail in 'Spanish reefs.' Brace in yards, abeam."

"Aye aye, sir!"

Lewrie swung his telescope up and extended the tubes. The brig was almost to the tip of Ram Head, standing off not a cable's distance from the shoals.

"How much water would she have, that close inshore?" Lewrie asked his Sailing Master.

"I make it about fifteen fathom, sir, near the point," Winwood answered as *Proteus* swung her bows Nor'Nor'west, and the yard parrels cried as they were swung about to point the weather arms directly into the wind, the sails now flogging helplessly as they were clewed up at the centres, leaving untidy, thrashing bags suspended like ancient teats at the outer ends, with only jibs, stays'ls and the spanker still keeping way on her.

"Damn!" Lewrie griped. "She'll get a lead on us."

"Ah . . . sunrise, sir," Winwood pointed out, pulling his watch from a waistcoat pocket, as if to confirm dawn's predicted timeliness and heaving a smug, satisfied sigh of approval.

"Very good, sir," Lewrie said with a grateful smile, thinking, though; *Such an easy man to please. Just give him exactitude!*

Scant minutes later, *Proteus* was once more under full sail and under way, thrashing back toward her previous speed in pursuit of the American brig, which was now flying stuns'ls in addition to her royals and t'gallants. Lewrie and Winwood stood close together by the double wheel and binnacle cabinet, ticking off landmarks on a chart as the seamarks almost raced past to starboard as the Chase spun out westward for the shelter of Charlotte Amalie.

Cabrithorn Point, Lameshur Bay, and White Point, then the wide, shallow expanse of Reef Bay. Dittlif Point rose up along the southern shore of St. John, then Rendezvous Bay beyond that long, arrowing peninsula, and Bovocoap Point looming up, with the brig dashing along as close as she could inshore, with *Proteus* standing further out to seaward, just a tantalising bit out of gun-range from her 6-pounder bow-chasers; almost, but not quite yet. . . .

"She is steering dead-on for passage below the Dog Rocks, and Little Saint James Island, it seems, sir," Winwood cautiously opined, toying with his waistcoat buttons. "There is a long shoal, parallel to the shore, below Dog Rocks, with a narrow pass of thirteen fathom between, however. Her captain knows these waters well, we must infer."

"Wants t'brush us off," Lewrie sourly grunted.

"Aye, sir. Once beyond Dog Rocks, though, does she intend the direct route inside of Buck Island before taking a slant into harbour, there are even more shoals."

"Which would force us out alee of yonder Buck Island, and out of any hope of overtaking, if we continue on this course?"

"Aye, sir," Winwood gloomily reiterated, "though I cannot find any indications that the shoals are *particularly* shallow. The charts show some soundings of six or seven fathom. Deep-laden ships would go well clear of the shoals, but that may be sign of too much caution on their captains' parts. With our maximum laden draught of three fathom aft by the keel and rudder skeg . . . it makes no sense for him to think that we'd be *completely* daunted. Perhaps he knows more than our chart may tell us, the location of an old wreck . . ."

"Perhaps he learned his lore of the local waters in very large, deep-draught ships, Mister Winwood," Lewrie said, trying to put a good face on it despite his qualms of running aground, "under one of those cautious captains of yours. She's down to *her* draught waterline, same as us, and she can't draw more than twelve or fourteen feet. Show me your rocks and shoals, let's—"

"Deck, there!" a lookout screeched. "Chase is changin' course! Turnin' away Nor'west!"

"She's only a bit beyond Bovócoap Point," Mr. Winwood protested in a splutter. "That'd take her . . ."

"Into Pillsbury Sound, Mister Winwood," Lewrie snapped. "Maybe this 'Jonathon' captain doesn't think he'd keep enough lead on us to enter Charlotte Amalie before we caught him. If he *really* knows these waters, he must think he holds a high card over us."

"But there's no way out of the Sound, sir. The wind's wrong to weather the Middle Passage, leaving that Leeward Passage past Thatch Cay!" Winwood gawped. "Narrow as a town creek, it is, the soundings uncertain . . ."

"We'll follow her, Mister Winwood," Lewrie told him. "We will not let her get away that easily. Once past the point yonder, shape course Nor'Nor'west, and follow her . . . wherever she goes."

CHAPTER THIRTY-TWO

S ir, I'm bound to point out that this is risky," Winwood said in a mortified whisper as they bent over the chart pinned to the traverse board, once *Proteus* had come about and was now dead-astern from the American brig, perhaps a mile-and-a-half behind. "My duty as——"

"I know, Mister Winwood," Lewrie said, cutting him off quickly, eyes intent on the chart, and the pair of brass dividers in his hand. "Pillsbury Sound's deep, sir! Twelve to eighteen fathoms all the way to the islets and cays. And nice and wide for the most part 'til you are forced to choose a passage out of it. The Windward Passage is out, and does she try the Middle Passage, she'll be full-and-by, sailing at the ragged edge of this morning's wind . . . *without* her stuns'ls spread, than-kee Jesus, which means we'll drive right up her transom long before she can get to it. Your Leeward Passage *is* narrow, but not more than a quarter of a sea-mile . . .'bout two cables wide, 'twixt Thatch Cay and the north shore of Saint Thomas. Bags of room!"

Mr. Winwood uttered a soft complaint that sounded mightily like a cross between a moan and a well-muffled belch.

"Does she wish t'keep her stuns'ls rigged out for speed, she'll *have* t'use the Leeward Passage, Mister Winwood." Lewrie chuckled.

"The *narrows*, though, sir, here . . ."

About three-quarters of a mile due North of Cabes Point, halfway between Coki Point and the southeastern tip of Thatch Cay, there lay an indistinct indication of a shoal, stippled to show sand, which meant *extremely* shallow. On the scale chart they were perusing, a man could have mistaken it for a thumb smudge of ink, a tea stain from previous use. The vague extent of the shoal didn't leave much north of it, and there was another fan-like shoal round Thatch Cay's extremest tip, and that *did* have a sounding—one-half fathom—a scant three feet!

"He'll go south of the shoal, Mister Winwood, where there are soundings of seven to ten fathoms between the shoal and Coki Point," Lewrie insisted, "keeping well off the wind, under stuns'ls, hugging Thatch Cay a tad, once round your shoal, and giving little to loo'rd."

"Does he *get* past the shoal, sir, but—"

"Then it's his bottom that's ripped open, not ours. And we'll do all we can to save her people . . . obeying the law of the sea."

"Does he know of a wreck in there, though, sir . . ."

"The sun's barely up behind us, sir," Lewrie countered quickly. "The very *best* time of the day to see underwater obstacles ahead, *long* before we run afoul of 'em. And with the extreme clarity of the seas hereabouts . . . really, Mister Winwood! One could read a newspaper at six fathoms down. Does our Yankee captain yonder know of a wreck in the channel, then let him use *his* forefoot to dredge for it. Save us a deal o' gunpowder, it would! Wrecks shift, over time."

"Very well, sir," Mr. Winwood finally agreed, though not without a premonitory shiver. "Though I have expressed my reservations . . ."

"The fault will be mine, sir," Lewrie told him with a grim nod of his head before laying down the dividers and standing back up. "I will so note it in the log. Speaking of . . . Mister Elwes? Cast the log, if you please. Mister Pendarves? Hands to the fore-chains with the short leads, and two hands on the bowsprit to keep watch for any shoals or obstructions!"

Lewrie walked back to the stern and raised his glass. The privateer, and their boats, were now out of sight, and there was no smoke visible, had either the French or their own people set her afire. He pursed his mouth and chewed at its lining in worry of all that could have gone wrong. Even alee of the stranded schooner, they were too far away to hear the pops of muskets and pistols; only cannon on the schooner's decks might rumble over the sound of the wind, which would be a bad sign.

No news is good news, Lewrie told himself, turning forward.

Spotting the three other midshipmen standing idle without duty, he put Grace, Larkin, and Burns to work, taking bearings on sea-marks to either hand, and employing their scant knowledge of trigonometry for a range to them.

"Eight and three-quarter knots, sir," Midshipman Elwes reported.

"Thankee, Mister Elwes. I see you've hoisted 'Immediate' above 'Fetch-To'—very good. I doubt she'll respond any time soon, so keep at it with the knot-log, about every ten minutes or so," Lewrie bade him. "I do believe we've gained a touch on that brig, already."

"Aye aye, sir!" Elwes yelped with joy, dashing aft again, full of importance over his assigned task.

From the windward rails, it looked as if they *had* drawn closer to the Chase; more details could be made out that were indistinct before . . . or maybe it was simply full daylight that made him wish it so. *Proteus* was surging along, her wake bone-white atop the light green sea of Pillsbury Sound, heeling a bit to larboard and leeward, masts raked forward a touch, and groaning over it. Sailing almost downwind, the pace wasn't as apparent as it would be working closer to weather. The ship was sailing just as fast as the wind could blow, so there was no exhilarating rush and bustle that plucked at hats, clothing, and flesh, no bursting showers of salt-spray booming over the fore rails, but *Proteus* was moving quite well, gracefully and almost effortlessly. A *touch* on her lee "shoulder," Lewrie deemed her, but . . .

"Mister Langlie, run out the starboard battery, and run in the larboard to the recoil ring-bolts. Let's get her flatter on her keel," he decided of a sudden. "There's just enough wind for that to make a difference. A quarter-knot more, perhaps?"

"At once, sir," Langlie agreed, pacing forward to the quarter-deck railings with his brass speaking-trumpet in his hands.

On very light winds sometimes doing the opposite helped, Lewrie had learned from better men than he; *force* the lee hull downward, off of upright, and a ship would angle her masts and sails more horizontal and "ghost" on a scant breeze that would leave her luffing and boxing the compass, else. Especially along a near shore.

"Eight-and-a-*half* knots, sir!" Elwes shouted from the taff-rail.

"Very good, Mister Elwes!" Lewrie shouted back, allowing himself a small grin. *Damme*, he thought; *but they beat it into you, you hang about ships long enough, you're bound t'learn a little something! Even are you a lazy toad, and half a fraud!*

"I do believe we're within Range To Random Shot, sir," Langlie said as they drew level with Cabrita Point on St. Thomas. "Shall we pester her with the bow-chasers?" he asked, eager for action.

"No, not yet, Mister Langlie," Lewrie finally decided. "Do we open on her at extreme range, we'll appear desperate. Make them *think* they're ahead of the game, d'ye see, and we're firing before we haul our wind and let 'em escape? Now, do we hold fire 'til we're right up her stern . . . when she's nervous about getting round the shoal in the middle of the channel, that's something else. Keeps 'em lookin' aft and chewin' their nails. We look . . . implacable. That'll give 'em a pause or two. Then they're half-beaten."

"Oh, I see, sir!" Langlie puzzled, frowning over it. "We are *Nemesis*, the inescapable old Greek god. And them, mere prey!"

"More like a dangerous duellist, whose fearsome reputation precedes him, Mister Langlie," Lewrie snickered back, always one to prefer a cruder simile. "One smirky grin at his opponent cross the grass, and the other poor bastard collapses with the farting faints!"

Onward they stood, pressing closer and closer to the brig; now at three-quarters of a mile range, well past Cabrita Point and nearing Coki Point, the brig now committed to the Leeward Passage, too far down to the West to tack and stand for the Middle Passage. For a time, the frigate had the best of the winds from the Nor'east, beginning to post nine knots at the last casts. Two-thirds of a sea-mile . . .

"Deck, there! Chase bears off to loo'rd! Spreadin' stuns'ls, again!" a foremast lookout cried.

"She's nearing the narrows," Mr. Winwood said. "Bearing off to the south channel before the shoals."

"Open upon her now, sir?" Langlie pressed.

"Aye, Mister Langlie. Keep 'em busy," Lewrie assented.

The 6-pounders up forward barked and recoiled, the spent powder smoke winging off westward as a solid blot, again. Far off, one ball raised a great splash near the brig's larboard quarters, the other one whipping cross her decks and deflating her spanker for a moment as it tore a neat hole right through it.

"Mark you well, where she turned, Mister Winwood," Lewrie bade. "Where our first shot struck short? Surely there's deep water there."

"Aye, sir," Winwood mournfully fretted.

Lewrie raised his glass again as the 6-pounders heaved back in from their second tries. The brig's spanker now seemed to be in twain, as if a major seam had split wide open, leaving the upper half hanging properly from the gaff-boom, but with the loose-footed bottom forced open and flagging, as if ripped from one bolt-rope edge to the other, and *that* wouldn't help her steering!

Another 6-pounder roundshot struck quite near her larboard quarter again, caroming far enough this time to raise a tiny smudge of engrained dirt and splinters from her, just a'fore her quarter galleries. The second was too high, but it clipped her right in the starboard main-stays and futtock shrouds below the main-top platform, sending a visible shiver up her upper masts like a tuning fork. Those shrouds would be weak, that mast in danger of falling sooner or later.

"Half-mile, I make her, now, sir!" Langlie crowed, enthused.

"Ready to put the ship two points alee, Mister Langlie, once we are above Coki Point," Lewrie cautioned.

A third salvo from the bow-chasers was spot-on, the lee cannon scoring her third direct hit that chewed away some of the brig's larboard bulwark near the break between her quarterdeck and her gangway. The starboard cannon was still firing high, which error one of their quarter-gunners was correcting, loudly and foully, but that roundshot ploughed through the brig's main tops'l and shot a stuns'l boom and sail clean away. And that would slow the brig down right smartly!

"Eight fathom . . . eight fathom t'this line!" the starboard hand in the fore-chains called out.

"Coki Point's abeam, now, sir," Winwood warned them.

"Helm a'weather, Mister Langlie, and bear off!" Lewrie barked. "Two points, no more. Trim for a Fair Wind, course West-Nor'west!"

There was *some* disturbance at the channel narrows, a perturbation of silted water over the shoal, the "knuckle" that the brig left as she wore off, perhaps from the splashes of their gunfire. *Proteus* was turning well before it, though, easing the set of her sails and yards to run with the wind a bit more astern, still fairly flat on her keel, with her batteries still run out or run in.

"Bless me, we're right astern, within a half-mile of her!" Mr. Winwood rejoiced. "And well shy of the shoal, it appears."

Lewrie tried hard not to mock him, making his face stern, busy with his telescope. "Now, pepper her steady, Mister Langlie. Keep us pinched a tad closer to Thatch Cay, too. Nothing to loo'rd."

"Aye, sir. Quartermaster, half a point to weather, and nothing to loo'rd," Langlie parroted as the 6-pounders erupted again.

The brig was trying to pinch up, too, but not succeeding, since she sat heavy-laden and heeled a bit more to leeward than the frigate.

"Twelve fathom! *Twelve* fathom t'this line!" a leadsman cried.

Lewrie heaved a large but well-concealed *whoosh!* of relief at that news; though Thatch Cay and St. Thomas felt close enough to hit with a well-flung rock, before the channel began to widen. They were past the highest ground of Thatch Cay, the tall hill at its easternmost tip where the large fringe of sand shoals lay, so the winds could gust across more directly, without flukey diversions, and *Proteus* began to *sing*, striding up the brig's stern relentlessly.

"Quarter-mile range, sir. We could try the carronades, next!" Langlie hooted.

"Do so, sir. Grape-shot her masts and sails!" Lewrie agreed.

With his glass he could espy her after-guard, officers and mates gathered on her small quarterdeck, looking aft, gawping and pointing at him. Two gun-ports were open in her taff-rail bulwark, and men sweated and heaved to ready a pair of stern-chasers, whilst others gesticulated and most-like swore—a great many mouths were open and a fair number of fists were being shaken at them, at any rate.

The brig's guns fired at last, before his own bow-chasers and starboard carronade—the one not blocked by jibs—could. Roundshot came keening down the deck to starboard, sending everyone on the gangways flat on their faces; the second ball thrummed past the hull to larboard, almost close enough to peel paint, but struck far astern in a series of skip-splashes.

"As you bear . . . *fire!*"

The 6-pounders, with quoins jammed well in, yelped, and the carronade, aimed higher, let out a stentorian belch of smoke and flames. Two roundshot ravaged the brig's stern, shattering transom boards and windows, while the grape-shot in the carronade struck higher, shredding the spanker gaff-boom and the bare cro'jack yard above it, tearing chunks from the main-top, making those already-weakened starboard ratlines and shrouds ripple as sinuously as a crawling snake, her upper topmast canting to leeward of a sudden.

"Under a cable, now, sir!" Midshipman Grace crowed, hopping on his toes in glee.

"Mister Devereux," Lewrie said. "One file of Marines and sharpshooters to the forecastle, and clear her quarterdeck by fire when you think you have the range." By God if they weren't sailing right up her stern, almost ready to jab their jib-boom over her helmsmens' heads!

The westernmost spit of Thatch Cay passed abeam to starboard; from a quick peek at the chart still pinned to the traverse board, Lewrie could see that the safe channel bent due West for a time, then sharply North. Mandal Point on Saint Thomas loomed upwards, 277 feet in the air, with shoals at its feet churning soapy-white foam where tide, current, and scend collided, long before the prettier breakers along the narrow beach. The brig *must* bear up for Hans Lollick Island, and deep water . . . though now without her spanker to balance her helm she could not. Did she try to close-reach, she'd wallow and dither, near the wind then off, like a wounded lizard's death-crawls.

Instead, *Proteus* steered up windward, while the brig sagged to leeward, the range closing even more, to within musket-shot, *Proteus*'s larboard broadside up-wind of her on her starboard quarter.

"Mister Langlie!" Lewrie shouted. "Open the larboard ports and stand by to load!"

The gun crews, the bulk of them frustrated 'til now, leapt for the tackles and tompions as the port lids hinged upward, baring inner paint in a row of stark red squares above her gunwale. Marine sharp-shooters and sailors with good eyes continued a spatter of musketry at the enemy's decks, making her helmsmen steer by squatting down below the bulwarks and craning up to steer by pendant and sail-set, instead of by compass, making the rest of her crew drop from sight.

A white cook's apron appeared over her starboard side, waved frantically. Men stood and waved arms and hats, shouting as loud as they could for mercy as those brutal 12-pounders' iron muzzles were trundled up to the ports to dip, rise, and slew left or right in aiming before a full broadside.

"We strike, damn you! We strike, don't fire, please!" someone in a cocked hat was howling. "Hold fire and we'll lower our colours, for God's sake, hold!"

Two or three cowering members of the after-guard rose up above the quarterdeck bulwarks and cut the halliard for the flag, that came fluttering down to trail in the water, even as others dared, after a moment or two without musket fire, to free braces and sheets, spilling the last wind from the brig's sails.

"Fetch-to, Mister Langlie, and get the last boat led round from astern. You will take the boarding party," Lewrie said. "Take Mister Pendarves the Bosun with you, and the rest of Mister Devereux's men."

"Aye, sir."

"Cargo manifests, ship's papers, and correspondence before all else, sir!" Lewrie urged. "Inspect the holds later. Quickly, man . . . before they ditch 'em or set 'em afire."

"A fair morning's work, Captain," Mr. Winwood was saying, now that the folderol and danger was past. "Two prizes before breakfast. And a passage through shoal waters that'll make them sit up and cheer back in London."

"We'll see, sir. We'll see," Lewrie cautioned. Though he did feel rather joysome, himself.

CHAPTER THIRTY-THREE

A present for you, Captain Lewrie," Lt. Devereux said after he had returned aboard and had taken the salute from the side-party. He held out a knitted wool sack that covered something long and narrow and over four feet long. He was beaming with secret delight.

"What the Devil?" Lewrie muttered aloud as he took hold of it, and felt the hidden object's hardness and leanness. Imagining that he knew what it might be, he stripped off the woolen cover as quick as a child might rip open a birthday present. "Oh, dear Lord, how lovely!"

It was a Pennsylvania rifle, octagonal-barreled, fitted at butt, barrel-bands, and firelock plates with shining brass, the hinged cover to the patch-box in the buttstock also bright brass, and the stock all of a highly polished, ripply-striped bird's eye maple! It was indeed lovely, one of the finest examples of the gun-maker's art that he had ever seen outside of a set of custom duelling pistols; even the plates were engraved so finely that he suspected only a magnifying glass could reveal the detailing.

"Fresh from Philadelphia, sir," Devereux said proudly, "and the work of a master craftsman."

"You've one for yourself, Mister Devereux?" Lewrie asked, lifting the piece to aim at the sky and sight down the long barrel, noting the silver bead on the muzzle's top, and the cut-steel notch sights at the rear, near the fire-lock. "Was this the only one, I'd understand . . . envious as all Hell, but . . ."

"One for myself, too, sir, near its twin," Devereux confessed with a little laugh, "and one of lesser quality for every officer and midshipman . . . as private hunting weapons, ha ha! Two dozen, in all."

"Personal possessions of yon brig's mates?" Lewrie frowned.

"No looting of a prize, sir . . . part of her cargo. Withheld as uhm . . . evidence for the Prize Court?" Devereux snickered.

"By God, we *have* corrupted you!" Lewrie laughed. "But this is magnificent, I must own. Find yourself some coehorn mortars, too?"

"No, sir, but those'll come. Ah, here's Mister Langlie, coming aboard with even better news. I'll let him tell the rest."

Lewrie almost pounced on Langlie, primed to eagerness.

"She's the *Sycamore*, sir, out of Philadelphia," Lt. Langlie reported, after he'd taken the salute, doffed his hat, and had been given his own covered rifle up from the boat below the entry-port. "A native tree, I s'pose, or the name of an Indian tribe. Her master was wounded, and is still aboard. Rather panicked by the thought of expiring, sir, so he was open to questions . . . between prayers and pleas for his last will and testament to be taken down, that is."

"Will he live?" Lewrie asked.

"His wounds are more fearful than mortal, sir. Mister Durant is of the opinion that he's more likely to pass over from fret than shot," Langlie chuckled. "He openly confessed that he's been smuggling to the French for some time. With most of their overseas trade curtailed, 'tis a lucrative endeavour, I gather. He also admitted he's run arms to L'Ouverture on Saint Domingue. Now his country is all but at war, any large cargoes or arms and powder would have been suspicious, and expensive, with the United States Navy the best customer, so he made arrangements through French agents in Philadelphia to meet the privateer and transfer her arms aboard his 'innocent' ship."

"What's his cargo, then?" Lewrie asked, absently stroking his new rifle.

"Two thousand stand of arms, Charleville muskets with leather accoutrements, two thousand pairs of boots and shoes," Langlie intoned as he read from a list he pulled from a coat pocket. "One hundred and twenty thousand pre-made cartridges and twist paper, shot and powder for half a million more . . . four six-pounder Gribeauval Pattern pieces of artillery with caissons, limbers, harness, and the essentials for a battery forge-waggon. Blankets, slop-trousers, cross-belts, shakoes, and other uniform items, bayonets, infantry hangers, and officers' quality swords . . . most of it recently snuck into Guadeloupe aboard a Frog frigate, sailing *en flute*, sir. A real treasure trove."

Turning up in Kingston, with that brig astern and the British flag flying over the American, *would* represent a treasure, a "golden shower" of prize money, Lewrie was mortal-certain.

"There's also an innocent cargo of molasses and sugar, Captain," Langlie went on. "Saint Domingue coffee, tea, and cocoa would have put *Sycamore* far ahead of the game, once they'd unloaded the arms."

"Just their bad luck, but to our good. This is documented? We have them by the 'nutmegs' about this, for certain?" Lewrie demanded.

"Every bit of it on paper, sir, even the captain's private log. It was well hidden, but not destroyed. Mister Neale, our Master-At-Arms, was part of my boarding party and he and his Ship's Corporals, Burton and Ragster, are old hands at knowing where sailors hide things."

"And what they made off with, God only knows . . . or cares, with all this on our plate," Lewrie chortled. "And the rifles *were* part of the cargo?"

"Ordered specifically, sir. L'Ouverture's people are mad for 'em. Yours, sir . . . do you look close, you'll find it engraved with Toussaint L'Ouverture's name, sir. It was to be a present to one of his generals, a man named Dessalines."

"God almighty!"

"We also found three men aboard whose certificates are 'colourable,' sir," Langlie told him. "As English as Bow Bells, and with so obvious a set of frauds, they were pathetic. Should we press 'em, sir?"

"But of course," Lewrie said with a sly grin. "I'll not turn up my nose at volunteers . . . willing, or no. Muster 'em on the gun-deck, and I'll have a word with 'em. We're making sternway onto the shores of Saint Thomas, and need to haul off. The wind's veered half a point North'rd, and we're on a lee shore. Might have to sail all the way to the western end of the island, then beat back to pick up Catterall and our boarding party. . . ."

"Excuse me, sir," Mr. Winwood suggested, coming to his side and looking to Lieutenant Devereux expectantly. "With the wind veered so, it would be possible to stand back down this Leeward Passage, here, with the wind almost abeam, and be off Ram Head in less than two hours. I, uhm . . . I must say, Mister Devereux, those are dashed handsome rifles."

"You are welcome to take your pick from the lot, Mister Winwood. As a private, personal hunting weapon," Devereux assured him.

"And a handsome gesture, too!" Winwood actually enthused, come over all a'mort with greedy pleasure.

"Our prize is secure and in good order, Mister Langlie?" Lewrie asked him. "No troubles from her crew or mates?"

"Secure, sir, and ready to proceed. The crew disarmed and our Bosun, Mister Pendarves, and trusted hands to back him up in guarding them," Langlie confidently stated. "Very little real damage done."

"Very well, gentlemen. Let's get under way back down the Leeward Passage. We know it, now, and I know when I've stretched my luck in unfamiliar waters for the day. Better the Devil you know, hey? And not an inch to loo'rd this time. Hmmm . . . stern kedge anchors readied for dropping, just in case this pass holds a last surprise . . . right?"

Lewrie reluctantly surrendered possession of his new rifle into Andrews's care, then went down the starboard ladder to the waist where three seamen stood hang-dog, awaiting their fate. Lewrie put his hands in the small of his back and faced them. One, the youngest, hopefully a teenaged topman, stared back fearfully, eyes blared and swallowing in shuddery gulps. One stouter, older fellow dared glare back at him in a sneer. The third, a lanky-lean man in his middle thirties, couldn't meet his eyes, but darted his glance about or found the grain of wood deck planks intriguing, his flat, tarred hat pulled low over his brow.

"Well, lads, you're caught, fair and square," Lewrie told them. "False certificates so badly done, if you paid more'n a shilling each for 'em, you got swindled. What names you use? Your own, or aliases?"

The young one, at least, perked up to that statement, glancing at the sneering man in alarm for a second.

"Don't signify," Lewrie went on, naming himself and his frigate. "You're runnin' from debtor's prison, termagant wives, or whatever, I don't care. We've had fevers, and we're short-handed. You're British, no matter how you protest it. You all wish to be 'John Bull' or 'Billy Pitt,' so be it, 'cause I've more need of you than the authorities back home. 'Tis becoming a tradition aboard, for people to take new names when they sign on. The pay's less than merchant service, but the rations are fair measure and decent quality. We don't flog unless you're a *total* bastard, and as you've seen this morning, we're lucky with prize money. A man . . . a boy, could do worse. How much is that Yankee captain owing you?"

"N-nigh on twelve pounds, sir," the youngest said in a shy voice. Merchant captains were infamous for "crimping" off their crews near the end of a voyage; when met by a Royal Navy vessel In Soundings of home waters, they'd gladly give up all but the merest few required to work into port, and pocket their pay—sometimes with connivance with officers of Impress Service tenders.

"I'll screw it out of him, and it's yours, lad," Lewrie vowed, "and pay a *willing* volunteer the Joining Bounty . . . no matter which name he puts down in ship's books. Oh, it'll go to pay for what kit you don't have, but we'll fetch your sea-chests aboard so you'll have most of what you need already, and save a bit with our Purser, Mister Coote. He's a fair man, can you believe that of a 'Nip Cheese.' So, what's it to be? Volunteer and make the best of it, or be pressed, and begrudge me to the end of your days?"

"Willy Toffett, sir, and I'll volunteer, then," the teen said with a relieved smile. "Main topman, I was."

"And you, sir?" Lewrie asked the second, who still glared, but with a resigned and bitter air of helplessness.

"Press me and bedamned," he gravelled, halfway surrendering to Fate, but determined to go game. "And put me down as Toby Jugg. With two 'Gees,' " he almost snarled, but with a sardonic smile to excuse it.

"Your choice, then," Lewrie allowed. "Rating?"

" 'Twas an Able Seaman, aboard *Sycamore*."

"Then Able you'll be rated, here, with the extra pay that goes with it," Lewrie promised, though that did nothing to mollify the man.

"Had a woman and girlchild on Barbados," Toby Jugg groaned. "Never see 'em again, now. Poor as church-mice and . . ."

"Your Joining Bounty could be sent on to them," Lewrie hinted.

With tears beginning to well in his eyes at the thought of not seeing his woman and daughter for years, his face clouded and taut, he nodded his assent, still unable or unwilling to accept his lot. A man who might have been pressed before, Lewrie suspected, unwilling to give his right name for fear of punishment for desertion.

"And you, sir?" Lewrie asked the third, who still could not meet his eyes except in brief, darting glances.

"Ships is ships, I reckon," the man said with a defeated sound. "Aye, I'll sign on, volunteer. Me name's George Gamble, and I was an Ordinary Seaman . . ." he muttered in a Midlands "Mumbletonian" accent.

"Landsman, ya were," Toby Jugg snorted in derision, "and cack-handed, at that, ya lubber!"

Gamble raised his head and hat brim high enough to glare daggers at his "shipmate" for a second. "Damn' captain cheated me, he did! I'm rated Ordinary, and well ya know it. Just 'coz he already had all the seamen he needed, and too cheap t'pay me due ratin', was the reason."

"Coulda signed aboard another ship," Jugg quibbled as if Lewrie wasn't there.

"Oh aye, an' me broke as a convict, and all me pitiful advance gone t'pay off me crimpin' landlord for his rat-hole lodgin's—"

"Some other time," Lewrie interrupted "We'll try you as an Ordinary Seaman, Gamble. I'm Landsman-Poor, at the moment. Do you have any certificates from past captains to show your rating?"

"Uh, nossir. Lost 'em 'tween ships, or somone stole 'em whilst I was sleepin' ashore."

"Sold 'em for drink, more like," Jugg scoffed.

"Enough!" Lewrie snapped. "You'll volunteer, Gamble?"

"Aye, sir . . . s'pose I'll haveta," the man replied, ducking his head again.

"Very well, then. Once we've a way on her, see the First Lieutenant, Mister Langlie, and he'll enter your names in our ship's books, then draw your issues from the purser," Lewrie told them, pleased that all but one of them seemed docile. He suspected that Gamble might be a King's Bad Bargain, and nothing better than a Landsman, after all; from the sound of his former shipmate, and the simpery grin on the young Willy Toffet's face as they had their little tiff, he suspected that Gamble might end up making more enemies than friends among the crew, by shirking duty. But Bosun Pendarves and his mates, with their starters, could light a fire under his shifty, idle arse.

He returned to the quarterdeck as *Proteus* began to pay off from fetched-to to larboard tack, and began to gather way for a reach down the Leeward Passage to Pillsbury Sound. Lt. Langlie had reduced sail, since there was no more need for "dash" to catch a prize. The winds were cooperating, too; veered to Nor'east-by-North, and weakening as the morning warmed. There might be two or three hours more of gentle sailing before the tropic heat created stronger gusts, and fresh veers or backings. By then, they could be back off Ram Head and beyond, in deep water and miles from any shores or shoals.

"Deck, there!" a lookout called down as *Proteus* neared the mouth of Pillsbury Sound. "Smoke round the headland, four point off the weather bows! Small boats under sail, too, d'ye hear there?"

The smoke was as thin as a pipesmoker's for a minute or so, then quickly became a belching gush of darker, thicker smoke on the far side of Ram Head, flame-driven upwards by a catching conflagration. Lewrie began to worry and fret about the safety of his boarding party. It had been too *long* for the French to have fired the ship to prevent seizure, but hours too late for Catterall to have done it, he thought.

"Two boats, sir, under lug-sails," Langlie prompted, turning his attention closer in. "Ours, I do believe."

"A point of lee helm and close them, then, Mister Langlie."

"Aye, sir. Quartermaster, helm alee one point."

Within half an hour, Lewrie could feel a true sense of relief, and one of accomplishment, too, for the boats *were* theirs, and in the ocular of his glass, he could make out faces and put names to them in quick inventory, realising that every man jack he'd disembarked would return safe and sound, and with no sign of blood or bandages to mark any wounded, either.

Lieutenant Catterall was standing up in the stern-sheets of his boat, whooping and hollering, waving exuberantly as *Proteus* and her prize brig fetched-to once more. Catterall pointed astern, threw out his chest proudly, and polished his fingernails on the white facings of his uniform coat, beaming fit to bust.

His boat swung round to the starboard, lee entry-port, where he was first up the man-ropes and boarding-battens to give his report, taking the salute due him from the side-party offhandedly, and almost swaggering as he doffed his hat.

"A Frog privateer, right enough, sir," Catterall boasted, "the *Incendiare*, she was called. Quite apt, now she's lit up like a pile of winter deadfall, haha! Crew of ninety, all told, before she struck the shoal, and mounted eight six-pounders." He related the important facts of her demise; for captured privateers, the best most crews would receive from a Prize Court would be "head and gun money," mere shillings paid out for each crewman and each piece of artillery. "No prisoners, sorry t'say, Captain. She was well and truly stuck on the rocks 'til the Final Trump, and nigh awash aft, when we gained her. The Frogs had departed in their own boats for the island. But they were in such a rush they abandoned all her paperwork. Not her Letter of Marque, sorry, but her box of correspondence in her master's cabin. There's more than enough proof of her being a privateer. Why it took me so long before we lit her off, and headed back to sea, d'ye see, sir? Since I can make out French rather well . . ."

"Oh, aye!" Langlie muttered under his breath, rolling his eyes.

"Well, I do, Anthony," Catterall objected, "though I don't say it well as I read it. I decided that goin' over her with a fine-tooth comb for documents'd be best. Glean some insight into what the Frogs are intending, where they operate, and such."

"Exactly as I would have, Mister Catterall," Lewrie praised him. "Good, quick thinking, that. Let's get your party back aboard, first, get the boats a'tow aft, then we'll discuss what gems you may have discovered. Enough of import to please Admiral Sir Hyde Parker and his staff-captain, one would hope?"

"Er, aye, sir!" Catterall replied, taken all aback for a moment to be the object of praise, instead of the odd grudging grunt of acceptance, and a muttered "carry on."

"No hope of salvage, though?" Lewrie had to ask.

"Smashed all to pieces up forrud, sir, her keel snapped in two abaft her forecastle, and half her knee timbers and planking spraddled or gone, to amidships. Just hangin' on the shoal, she was, sir. Sorry."

"No need. She's out of business, and her crew's marooned ashore on a rarely visited island," Lewrie said with a shrug. "They can sail over to Charlotte Amalie and be interned, but it'll be months before an exchange can be arranged through the local French consul. The prize we took more than makes up for it. And . . . do you talk sweetly to Lieutenant Devereux, perhaps he'll gift you with one of the items he captured off her. 'Tis something you'll drool over, trust me."

"Oh, ah . . . well, sir!" Catterall said, beaming at a good day's work, and glancing about greedily for a sight of the Marine officer.

The boarding party was coming aboard then, sailors and Marines tramping the starboard gangway and the after ladder to the waist, with their arms removed from bandoliers and baldrics, ready to be put back in the arms chests. They were crowing over their own deeds, getting chaffered by those who'd stayed aboard as to who had had the best adventure, or had accomplished the greater deed.

"You new men," Lieutenant Langlie ordered, "assist Mister Towpenny at leading the boats aft to their towing painters."

Lewrie was standing by the rails and nettings overlooking the waist, just about to clap his hands together with satisfaction, when he glanced down. One of his recently "volunteered" hands, the one who went by George Gamble, looked up, aghast, his mouth dropping open and his tanned face paling in shock, darting a look at Mr. Towpenny, who stood on the inner edge of the starboard gangway over his head, still burdened with cutlass, pistol, and musket as part of the boarding party.

"Hennidge?" Mr. Towpenny exclaimed of a sudden, just as aghast. "*Martin* Hennidge?" he added, this time scowling, the name spat out in loathing. His musket came up quickly.

Lewrie jerked his head back to look at Gamble, who started like a deer at a dog's barking, quickly lashing out to seize a musket from a seaman who'd been idling with a messmate, the butt on the deck, and one forearm draped casually over the muzzle as a hiking stick. Gamble scampered forward, musket at port-arms, and using it as a bludgeon to either hand to clear his way!

"*Mutineer*, sir!" Mr. Towpenny cried, putting his musket to his shoulder as if to aim. "One of the Hermiones! Knew him years ago, I did . . . know him anywhere!"

"Proteuses, seize that man!" Lewrie barked.

"Keep back!" the fugitive sailor shrieked, spinning to face the crew and levelling his musket to point at them from his hip. "Leave me be, or by Christ I'll shoot at least one o' ye! Keep back, I say!"

He swung the muzzle back and forth, frantically, daunting the few hands who had obeyed Lewrie's order. He climbed the larboard companionway ladder near the focs'le belfry to the gangway, near the larboard anchor cat-heads.

"Sir!" the seaman who had lost his musket called up. "Sir! 'At musket ain't *loaded*! Mister Catterall wouldn't let us back aboard wif one!"

Lewrie tipped the sailor a wink, drew his sword, and took off at a quick trot down the larboard gangway. "Give it up, Gamble, or whatever your name is!" He forced himself to look stern and menacing, sure that the joke would soon be on their "armed" mutineer.

Hennidge looked down to his piece, used one hand to make sure it was at full cock again, and raised it, aiming at Lewrie's heart.

"Won't be taken, I *won't*! Back, ya tyrant, or I'll kill you, if it's the last thing ever I do!" Hennidge cried.

"Murder another officer, would you?" Lewrie snarled, sword extended and almost within reach of the muzzle. "There were *ten* slaughtered aboard *Hermione* . . . in their beds! Those not enough for you, Hennidge? Thrown overside, still alive but bleeding, even the wee midshipmen who pleaded for their lives. Have a hand in that, did you? *Did* you, you traitor?"

"An' all of 'em torturin' devils!" the man shot back, jabbing at Lewrie as if his musket had a bayonet to keep him back out of reach of his sword's tip. "They *all* deserved what they got, and more! *Officers*, God above! You're *all* monsters! Navy, merchant . . . !"

"The Spaniards didn't treat ya right?" Lewrie taunted, parrying with his hanger, forcing the sailor backwards. "No shower o' gold for handin' 'em a British frigate? No commission in their navy, no reward for you? Drop that musket . . . now! It's over. Nowhere to go . . ."

He grazed his sword blade down the musket barrel and forestock, threatening to slash the man's left wrist and fingers if he kept proper hold of it, forcing him back against the bulwarks, with no place to escape, sure that this made a great raree-show. "Give up!" he roared in the man's face.

Leap and lunge! Left hand round the muzzle to lever it up and away, right fist smashing his hanger's hilt and curved hand-guard into Hennidge's nose, making it explode in crimson, eyes crossed in pain!

Left knee into the crutch as he bulled forward, for good measure!

Give, before ya get! Lewrie snickered to himself.

As Hennidge dropped to his knees, Lewrie stepped back a pace and yanked hard to tear the useless musket away. Hennidge found breath to howl, right hand still clawing to keep his weapon by the fire-lock and one finger inside the brass trigger-guard, and . . . *BLAM!*

"*Holy shit!*" Lewrie screeched, flinging away the hot muzzle from his left hand. "You *bastard*!" he added, raising his sword and bringing the hard pommel down atop the man's head for sheer spite, as the spent powder smoke wreathed round his head and shoulders.

From sheer terror, Lewrie coshed him on the head again!

Sailors and Marines were beside him in an eyeblink to take hold of the mutineer and drag him toward the companionway to the gun-deck.

Fat lot of help you *shits were!* Lewrie fumed, gasping fit to a swoon, and his bowels dangerously loose; *Unloaded, hey? Mine arse on a band-box! Why, he could've . . . killed me! Aye, make a great show, now he's out cold! Pitch in, and look organised . . . if not brave!*

"I'll have that sonofabitch in irons . . . double irons, at once, Mister Catterall!" Lewrie roared, once he'd got his breath back, picking on the first officer he spotted within easy reach. "Someone check my cabins for the list of descriptions of *Hermione* mutineers we were told to look out for. See Mister Padgett, my clerk, quickly now!"

"No need, sir," Mr. Towpenny assured him from the gun-deck. "I knew him. You peel off his shirt, here, you'll find two tattoos. He had one on his left upper arm, a Killick Anchor atop a heart. Seen it often enough when we were in *Queen Charlotte* t'gether, sir. Over his right shoulder blade, there should be a Saint Paul's Cross, in green ink . . . protection 'gainst drownin', the tattoo man in Plymouth told him, sir. He's Martin Hennidge, sure enough, I'll swear a Bible Oath to it at a court, Cap'um. And admire t'see him hang for his sins."

Padgett came forward with the list, quickly raked out of the desk drawers aft in his cabins, and the written description, including tattoos, fit Gamble/Hennidge to a Tee.

Lewrie sheathed his hanger and stepped down to the gun-deck as Hennidge was sluiced with a bucket of sea-water and awakened, spluttering and moaning, already fettered and shackled to a 12-pounder shot.

"Sling his sorry arse below on the orlop," Lewrie ordered in a mellower mood. "Bread and water, only. Mister Langlie?"

"Here, sir."

"Our prisoner, and his return to justice, is more important than continuing our cruise," Lewrie instructed. "Once well Sou'east of the island yonder, shape course for Kingston."

"Aye, sir," Langlie replied, a foolish expression of awe, mixed with both relief and joy on his face. "Beg pardon, sir, but that deed was . . . just about the boldest, damnedest thing, ever I did see! You went for him without a blink, a thought for your safety . . . !"

Lewrie made the appropriate, and expected, deprecating gestures and clucking sounds, as if it was really nothing much, though all the while thinking: *S'posed t'be safe as houses. Un-thinking is the word for it! Damme, there must be easier ways t'keep a good name! Got to get aft . . . 'fore I squit my breeches!*

"Don't quite know, myself, Mister Langlie," Lewrie said with a shake of his head, as if puzzled, heading sternward along the gangway. "Thank God for Mister Towpenny, or we'd have had this man aboard for years, all unknowing. *Thought* his story was queer, but . . ." Lewrie shrugged again.

"I'd admire to shake your hand, sir!" Langlie earnestly cried.

"Well, if you must, Mister Langlie," Lewrie answered, trying on a humble chuckle as he took hands with him, keeping a pleasant grin on his face, though he was, by gastric necessity, rather impatient.

"Three cheers for the Captain, lads!" Lt. Catterall yelled, not to be outdone. "Hip hip . . . !"

HMS *Proteus* trembled with the strength of their enthusiasm, the cheers almost feral in their intensity. And Lewrie caused a further outburst, when he drew out his pocket watch, noted the time, and said that after such a strenuous and rewarding morning's work, once they'd shaped course for Jamaica, the rum cask would be got up and everyone would "Splice The Mainbrace," with full and honest measure for all.

He did not stay on deck to share rum with them, though. He got the retrieved musket from a Marine private and stepped down to the gundeck to return it to Ordinary Seaman Fawcett, who had lost it.

"Not *loaded*, was it?" he hissed, almost in the lad's ear, as he leaned close. "*Not* charged or primed, hey?"

"Oh Gawd, sir, I'm sorry!" Fawcett gulped, eyes abrim with tears and shaking like a leaf. "I *thought* 'twas, oh Jesus . . . !"

"You're an idiot, Fawcett! The blitherin' sort!"

"Yessir?" the sailor cringed in dread and sorrow.

"Oh, for God's sake," Lewrie relented, stepping back, his urgent needs denying him a good and proper rant. "Go get your rum, and we'll say no more about it. But, by God you'll never, *ever* fetched a loaded weapon back aboard, again . . . will you."

He went up the ladder to the quarterdeck, stiff-legged and his buttocks pinched; struck a "captainly" pose for a second, hands behind his back, then ducked aft quickly. Bounding down the stern ladder to his cabins, he stripped off hat, coat, waistcoat, sword and belt, and dashed into his private quarter-gallery, slamming the door on Aspinall and a welcoming brandy. Even so, he barely made it. Fear, belated or not, worked its way on him better than an enema from Mr. Durant's clysters; so loose, rank, and gaseous that he had to fan the air.

After a moment or two, though, he had to laugh out loud. "God, people get *knighted* for less, and . . . !" Captain Alan Lewrie, RN, wheezed, biting on a fist to keep from *braying*, for all the world to hear.

"Don't know how fame and glory strike other people," he giggled, "but by God, they have an effect on me! Hee hee!"

"Out in a bit, puss!" *Mew*! Toulon cried, pawing the door.

CHAPTER THIRTY-FOUR

*L*ewrie had Lieutenant Langlie and Lieutenant Catterall in for a working supper, with Mr. Durant to aid in the translations. They had captured a brace of hogs from the brig *Sycamore*'s manger, quickly run over to *Proteus* in the cutter, and done to a crackly turn by their new ship's cook. Being a Yankee brig, she'd also carried several sacks of cornmeal which had gone into skillets to bake sweet, chewy muffins or pone bread for all hands, to replace hard ship's biscuit for a day or two. Mushy peas with melted cheese sauce, and breaded and fried onion accompanied the tender pork roast, making a fine victory feast, with promise of a piping-hot apple dowdy to come. It was only after a round of port, with some biscuit and cheese, that the papers from the French privateer *Incendiare* were fetched out for study.

The bulk of it was dry, boresome, and innocuous; lists of needs and expenses for cordage, spars, canvas and tar, shot, powder and cartridge flannel (all pleasingly hard to come by on Guadeloupe at present, they noted), and the problems among her crew; the everyday life of a working ship.

Much more interesting were the former captain's letters from at least three ladies of Guadeloupe, all dated within days of each other, of a blue-hot ardent and salacious nature, which had them all guffawing, along with the former captain's attempts at draft letters that tried to keep them sorted out without repeating himself. Even racier was an unfinished and forlorn missive to his wife in Bordeau, practically weeping blue ink over missing her so grievously!

A good supper, fresh bread (of a sort), and the promise of prize money to come had them all in an expansive mood, Lewrie noted. Even Mr. Durant seemed to have laid aside his disenchantment over Hodson's place as the senior Surgeon's Mate, for the nonce, and joined in the mirth, holding up his end of the table conversation and putting down a fair and manly share of wine, even cracking droll jests before they got down to the business at hand. And in that business, letters that *Incendiare*'s captain had received provided bright gems of interest.

"This'n from his wife, sir," Lt. Catterall said, holding up a page for better light from the four-lanthorn chandelier that swivelled and swayed over Lewrie's glossy dining table, "she writes that things are hotting up in the Mediterranean. An Admiral de Brueys—sounds as if her family knows his—has taken command of a three-decker by the name of *L'Ocean*, and a large number of line-of-battle ships . . . uhm, accompanied by over an hundred transports, for an expedition bound for somewhere."

Durant hid a snicker behind his port glass; it was true, then, that Catterall *could* read French, but couldn't pronounce it worth a tinker's damn, as he tried to expand eruditely. After two bottles' worth, he should have known better, Lewrie thought.

"In his journal, zere is similar mention," Mr. Durant stated, setting down his glass and opening a salt-stained book of ruled pages. "Ah . . . he speculates about zis armada, sirs. He is certain zat some tremendous victory will be won, and . . . rumour gained from Guadeloupe officials about one possible aim being ze island of Malta."

"Damme, that'd cut the Mediterranean in half," Langlie said. He refilled his port glass from the decanter that circled larboardly round the table as he spoke. "And with no help from the neutral and beaten Italian states, and Austria out of things, that'd leave Admiral Jervis where he was two years ago . . . chased back to Gibraltar or Lisbon."

"He regrets zey do not come to ze West Indies, sirs," Mister Durant read on, "and retake Martinique, or other former colonies . . . ah! Apparently, a General Bonaparte is in charge, and has a grander scheme in mind. He writes that perhaps the Balkans are the aim—"

"Bonaparte?" Lewrie grumbled, slapping the table. "Why, I've met the little bastard, in '93! Ran me out of the Adriatic, too, when he invaded Italy in '96, and beat the Austrians and Piedmontese like a dusty rug. Almost bagged me on the Genoese coast once, too. He's a dangerous man, I tell you. Never trust the dwarfish, gentlemen. He's no bigger than a minute, but slipp'ry as an eel. . . ."

It need not be said that Lewrie was, by then, most cheerily in his cups, since he'd—By God—earned it, and was damned grateful to have breath in his body for use between sips. Unloaded? *Jesus!*

"Well, if he's busy conquering someplace Dago-ish, we'll not be plagued by him this summer at least," Catterall snickered, only a wee bit sozzled. His robust constitution came with a "hollow-leg."

"No ships to spare to oppose us. Good," Langlie contributed.

"And with their Atlantic ports blockaded so close, where else'd the Monsieurs get frigates or corvettes, with their Toulon fleet busy?" Catterall snorted.

"So the West Indies'll be safe 'til our 'liners' come back from Halifax, at the end of hurricane season," Lewrie reasoned out.

"Uhm . . . he expresses worry about American frigates, sirs," Mr. Durant continued, flipping through the private journal. "He was pursued by one off Dominica . . . he was run one hundred miles in a day."

"Recent?" Catterall demanded, eyes beginning to unfocus, after all, and starting to sound "bull-horned" drunk.

"Recently, yes, Mister Catterall," Durant replied.

"Must've been that *Hancock*, then," Catterall said with a grunt.

"I'd've run, too," Lewrie jokingly confessed, "whether she was over-sparred and un-handy, over-gunned or crank. She's a fearsome and fast beast."

"Privateers stand no chance on ze coast of America, now," Mr. Durant paraphrased. "Zey return to Caribbean waters, uhm . . . he suspects more American frigates . . . ah! Here is something, sirs. After ze break in relations, Paris determines to re-enforce zeir navy here . . . what ships zey may spare from Brest and L'Orient, bringing fresh troops and arms. . . ."

Durant made a shrug and a *moue*.

"He rejoices, for L'Ouverture's victory over General Maitland," Durant cautiously said, "he congratulates ze *noirs* of Saint Domingue, and writes of hopes zat zey may be directed west to an invasion of Jamaica, rather zan east against Spanish Santo Domingo. But he does not trust zem, sirs, nor does he like zem. If zey go east, Spanish harbours might be closed to privateers."

"Be a good thing," Catterall huffed. "Tally-ho, Toussaint!"

"A *mission diplomatique* is to be sent to L'Ouverture, soon, as I read zis!" Durant cried, making them all sit up and take notice of such news. "Important officials who will ask L'Ouverture to reconcile with General Rigaud in South Province, so zeir armies may combine to attack Jamaica! And ask for a time of rest, so zey may build up his supplies first, and assemble suitable transports!"

"We must get this news to Kingston, at once," Lewrie declared. "Then rush right back, and hunt the delegation ship!"

"Pipe dreams, sir," Langlie sadly said. "Their hopes for a try at Jamaica, that is. That'd take lots of ships, not a gaggle of potty little fishing boats, nor all their privateers as escort. Can't be done without proper ships of war, even with our ships of the line away 'til October or November."

"Unless Bonaparte really means to hit the Indies, not something in the Mediterranean," Lewrie objected. "I told you he was devious as the Devil! Look at the way he gammoned half a dozen brilliant Austrian generals by sayin' one thing, demonstratin' one thing, but doin' quite another fifty miles away. Anything more on that line, Mister Durant?"

"Zere is another entry, quite recent, *Capitaine*," Durant said, after wetting a finger to turn the pages. "Before he sails north, to rendezvous with ze brig we capture, uhm . . . many privateer *capitaines* meet with an officer sent from Paris on the frigate zat delivers ze arms we take, a *Capitaine de Vaisseau* . . . a Post-Captain. He is under the Governor-General Hugues, to coordinate. He writes, 'If United States have turned belligerent, prey upon their merchantmen, those of useful burthen, and *capture* sufficient transport for future expeditionary use. Then, as re-enforcements arrive, under escort by ships from the Atlantic squadrons, both French and *noir* forces will combine for a descent upon islands now occupied by Albion,' . . . that is to say, us, gentlemen. The *capitaine* of *Incendiare* describes the new arrival as a most energetic and inspiring man . . . zough he expresses a troubling fear of him, due to his monstrous appearance, and his reputation as an ardent and ruthless *chasseur* of Royalists and seditionists during Ze Terror. He names him *Le Hideux*," Durant said, turning the book about so they could see the entry for themselves.

"Huh? Beg pardon?" Lewrie stammered, wishing that his senses were not quite so foxed, or his eyes so mutinous at focusing. "*Le Hideux*, did he call him?" He felt a cold, fey dread invade his body.

No, can't *be!* he quailed inside; *I killed the dog! Didn't I?*

"*Oui, Le Hideux, Capitaine.*" Durant blithely continued reading from the journal. "Apparently, zis officer is deformed by many cruel wounds. He wears a black mask over ze right half of his face and his eye, to cover a blinding and a livid scar, it is rumoured. He has a bad limp, and must wear an iron brace over his boot to stand and uses a cane . . . which must be awkward for him, since his right arm is gone at ze shoulder. His name, he notes . . ." Durant paused. "*Mon Dieu!*"

"Guillaume Choundas!" Lewrie spat. "Mine arse on a band-box!"

"You know of him, *aussi, Capitaine?*" Durant asked, shivering.

"I killed him," Lewrie whispered. "Swear t'Christ, I *thought* I did, back in '96." He stared blank and pale at the far partitions.

"Sir?" Langlie gawped, eldritch-struck by such a reaction from his captain, by such an ominous, rabbit-across-one's-grave dread. "Did you say you . . . *killed* him, sir? Then . . . ?"

"Who is the bastard, then, sir?" Catterall asked, impervious to superstition; nigh impervious to anything, by then.

"A fiend from Hell's deepest pits, Mister Catterall," Lewrie at last managed to say, after mastering himself. "A fiend who just won't die, no matter I've had my whacks at him two or three times. An evil, clever, murderin', bastardly gullion of a Malouin corsair, who thinks he has some Breton, ancient Celtic destiny, since Julius Caesar conquered the Veneti. Mad as a March Hare, but clever . . . oh, so clever!" Lewrie told them, shaking his head in queasy wonder, and pouring himself more port, a brimming bumper, with hands that barely shook despite his shock.

"Paris couldn't have *picked* a better foe to send us. Dangerous as a crate o' cobras, and not a jot o' mercy in his thrice-damned soul. He puts a squadron together in these waters, and he'll raise mayhem as sure as I'm born. Sew your arses shut, and keep yer backs to a wall."

He felt another sinking feeling in his innards, and knew that it was not the result of indigestion or a tropical fever. "You gentlemen will, I pray, excuse me for a moment," he bade, tossing off his glass of port at one go, then shoving his chair back so hard that it nearly tipped over, its feet catching at the painted canvas deck cover. They rose in kind as he headed aft for his quarter-gallery again.

"Whew!" Lt. Catterall softly marvelled, clawing for the bottle to charge his glass. "Never heard the like! If this . . . what was he, this Choundas, is that bad, and his presence in the West Indies upsets the captain so, well . . . he must be Satan incarnate."

"You asked if Captain Lewrie had heard of him, *too*, did you not, Mister Durant?" Langlie enquired more sombrely, but also in a mutter that would not carry far aft. "What do *you* know of him?"

"Rumours of him before my family and I escape Toulon in '93, Mister Langlie," Durant fretfully informed them, frowning hard. "And what he did to zose who could not flee ze Republicains when Toulon fell. Six thousand guillotined, shot, or bayoneted in ze surf, wading out and pleading for just one more boat. Guillaume Choundas was one of those who purged ze Toulon fleet and ze city. He *loves* ze guillotine, ze torture . . . poor helpless women, and especially little girls in terror of him. He slaughter his way south from Paris, to every naval port, an enthusiastic agent of Ze Terror. I had not thought of him in years, *Grace á Dieu!* But now . . . pardons, gentlemen, but I fear it will be a very bad zing for him to appear."

"But, surely . . . !" Langlie protested in a splutter that sounded half bemused, now. "He's but one man, in charge of a pack of tag-rag-and-bobtail privateers . . . that's like herding cats!"

"No insult meant, Toulon," Catterall grumped, winking at Lewrie's pet, who was hunkered on all fours with his tail tucked about his front paws on the sideboard, his eyes half slit in the dim lanthorn light as eerily as a witch's familiar. He'd meant to jape, but the atmosphere had gotten to him, too.

"Charge of *nothing*," Langlie persisted, sterner now. "He might get the use of a frigate or two, that's all, and we've what . . . seventy or more ships out here? And we've Captain Lewrie, as brave and smart a scrapper as ever trod a quarterdeck! And we've *Proteus*, surely the finest frigate in the whole Royal Navy! *We'll* settle this Choundas."

"Got old Lir," Catterall whispered. "Don't forget the tales of seals and selkies, the old sea-god's favour and all, and the uncanny good fortune that follows the Captain from ship to ship. What did for our first commanding officer at Chatham? What did for that mutineer, Rolston, the night we transferred him after we escaped the Nore? No, lads, don't forget we've luck on our side. Why, the Captain's taken the man half apart, already! Shot off his arm, by the sound of it . . . probably did the carvin' on his phyz, too, I shouldn't wonder, maybe was the one who lamed the bastard, as well!

"One more encounter with Captain Lewrie, and this Choundas'll have t'sign his name with his prick like that Buckinger feller, does all the stunts at the raree shows 'thout arms or legs, hey? And keeps Mistress Buckinger a happy woman, 'tis said!" Catterall chortled, more loudly than necessary. "He don't scare me, this Guillaume Choundas or howsomever ya say it! Bring him on, I say!"

"Hear, hear!" Langlie cheered, drumming the tabletop.

"And, *m'sieurs*," Durant slyly commented, tapping the side of his head, "after so many disasters to his person . . . who is to say that he, Choundas, just may be in dread of *rencontre* with ze *capitaine, n'est-ce pas?*"

"Hear, hear!" Langlie chirped, merry once again, hastening to top their glasses. "The Captain gets one more shot at him, and it will be *finis* for Choundas. After this morning, I doubt that there's anything on Earth that'd daunt our captain for more'n a second!"

"Toast, toast!" Catterall cried, staggering to his feet.

In the sudden silence, though, as foxed wits tried to dredge up the proper sentiments, there came a sound from the quarter-gallery in the stern, not quite unlike a prolonged, stentorian belch; nor, being in a hero-worshiping and charitable humour, could the assembly term it as resembling a day-long, *fluttery* fart.

Either way, though, it didn't *sound* particularly heroic.

EPILOGUE

*M*ind th' paint, yer honour, sor," Landman Furfy cautioned, as Lewrie's gig bumped against their frigate's hull below the entry-port.

"You do the same, Furfy," Lewrie cheerfully called back, taking in how much ended up on Furfy rather than the gunwale, "else the only thing t'clean you would be neat rum, or turpentine."

"Prefer th' rum, sor ... *bathin'* in it, ah th' wonder!" Furfy replied, pausing on the half-awash work catamaran platform on which he stood, standing back to salute with his paintbrush as Lewrie ascended the battens to the starboard gangway. Pipes trilled, boots clomped in unison, hands slapped shiny, linseeded musket stocks, and sailors took pause in their labours to doff their hats.

"The high-jump, was it, sir?" Bosun Pendarves asked once Lewrie had turned aft to the quarterdeck.

"Guilty on all counts, and to be hung at dawn tomorrow," Lewrie told the hawk-nosed older man with a satisfied nod. "A foregone conclusion, really. Chained, tarred, and caged 'til his bones fall away, then buried off the Palisades at low tide, God knows when."

"We can see it from here, sir?" Bosun Pendarves chuckled, glad for a bit of amusement. Public hangings did that to people, even the primmest. "I'd admire t'see Hennidge get scragged, I would."

"All ships in harbour to send witness parties, Mister Pendarves. And all crews to muster facing Execution Dock," Lewrie said. "You get first thwart in the boat, then choose the rest for me. Best turn-out, mind."

"Oh, aye, sir!" Pendarves beamed, rubbing his calloused hands with gleeful anticipation. "I'll see to it."

Lewrie didn't tell him that he'd send a midshipman with him in nominal charge of the shore party; he thought that Mr. Elwes was tough enough, and "blooded" by longer service, not to shame *Proteus* by casting up his accounts to Neptune at the sight.

He took another look about the ship before going below, and it was amazing what Martin Hennidge's appearance at Kingston had done for his frigate's repute. Canvas, cordage, tar, and oils—paint!—so spitefully and stingily denied before, had appeared in liberal, squanderous amounts, since. Admiral Sir Hyde Parker had been effusive with praise, and had done him the honour of supplying him a copy of a flatteringly fulsome report he would send to Admiralty anent the capture of a *Hermione* mutineer; which report lavishly, nigh luridly, recounted his personal seizure and disarming of Martin Hennidge, with but a hanger against a loaded and cocked musket. Even the staff-captain, Sir Edward Charles, had simpered with outwardly sincere congratulations.

Sycamore's capture, with proof of Yankee Doodle collusion with the French, admittedly had caused a problem with the American consul, and could still result in a chilly rift with their frigates in future, but the burning of a French privateer, the scotching of an arms delivery, and most especially the intelligences he had gained had offset that—as far as Lewrie and *Proteus* were concerned, at any rate. The matter of his pressing three men from *Sycamore*, and one of them a mutineer—as if the United States had deliberately sheltered him—was *not* a matter for discussion from the local American representative! Too bloody embarassing, all round!

So, perhaps for the moment, he could afford to feel smug. But for the Admiral's parting comment as he'd left the court-martial, that he'd count on *Proteus* to put paid to that ogre Choundas! As if it was to be *his* quest, and no one else's!

Lewrie allowed himself a disbelieving shiver as he gained his great-cabins and divested himself of his best uniform, and donned one of his older shirts, without neck-stock, and slop trousers. He went to the desk to give Toulon an affectionate stroking of his belly. In the heat of a Caribbean summer, the ram-cat had taken to sleeping on his back, with all four paws limply stuck in the air. His best response to a petting was a sleepy "*Urrmph*" and a thump and swish of his stout tail on the desktop. Toulon was down for the day, most-like to contemplate shedding.

Lewrie went aft to the transom settee and splayed himself slack-spined on the cushions, his head resting on the sash-window sill for a cool breeze.

Choundas, by God! he thought; *can't the bastard find anything better to do than follow me round the world? I've taken my best shots at him, surely someone'd call me 'out' and send in another batsman to finish him off! 'Thankee, I'd rather not, this time, but do keep me posted.' Bet that'd go down well! Damme, if fame an' glory ain't a cursed buggery . . . do one thing flashy, and they never give you a rest!*

He shut his eyes and crossed his arms over his chest, trying to recall the bastard. From the description Mr. Durant had read, he'd hit Choundas's arm, not the chest he'd aimed for. Two hundred yards, even with a Ferguson rifle, was an iffy shot. Their sword-fight on a beach at Balabac in the '80s . . . hacking that hateful face into ruin with a last-second, blind slash to save his very life! Ham-stringing him and forcing that leg-brace and mask on him, making Choundas stump and limp with a cane evermore . . . ! By now Choundas should be a shambling ogre, the stuff of children's nightmares, an implacable Nemesis tracking him down, a beast to *fear*, but . . . Lewrie found himself grinning a bit, seeing him not as his Doom, but as a crippled . . . clown!

Not as quick as he used t'be, I'll warrant, Lewrie thought as he fanned the front of his shirt for coolness; *it* can't *be his sword and mine crossed, this time . . . he'll order others. No matter how well he chooses, his minions could* never *measure up to* him!

It also struck Lewrie that Choundas wasn't part of that massive French fleet, not part of General Bonaparte's, or of Admiral de Brueys's grand aspirations, either!

Who'd want a man that gruesome in one's entourage! Lewrie felt like giggling; *He'd put people off their feed! Damme, has Choundas had a comedown . . . tsk-tsk?*

The French Revolution had a habit of eating its own; condemning and executing its early firebrands who were too crude, radical, and brutal to present on the world stage, too identified with The Terror, and its excesses and slaughters. They had a habit of turning on each *other*, too, denouncing and guillotining both leaders and followers of losing factions in their ever-shifting grasps for absolute power!

And Guillaume Choundas was surely one of the last of the "judicial" murderers who'd purged the aristocrats from his own navy, then purged the "suspect" who didn't give the Revolution their entire soul.

More than enough reasons to shuffle him off, out of sight; his foul repute, his butt-ugly appearance, his continual embarassment to the glittering, polished "new men!"

Choundas's appearance in the Caribbean, Lewrie thought, was an *exile*; a last chance to redeem himself at best, a callous dismissal to the deadly Fever Isles where he could die, unwanted and un-loved, at the worst. *He'll be desperate!* Lewrie surmised with sudden joy; *he'll take more risks than he'd usually dare, to vindicate his ugly self!*

"Vulnerable," Lewrie whispered aloud, drawing out the word, syllable by syllable, to savour its import. "Third time's the charm, by God?"

He jerked to his feet, ready to scrabble to the quarterdeck to shout this revelation to the world, chest swelling with eagerness for the meeting with his arch foe; eager to shout his suddenly discovered sense of courage, when before he might have trembled in his boots with dread. Choundas, and his machinations, would be the Devil one knows, knew *too* well for terror. If he felt the slightest check on his emotions, it was wariness. He could face Choundas clear-headed, not swooning with anxiety, in future! A shambling, limping, crippled clown!

"Marvellous!" he muttered joyously, aflame to speak to someone, write someone, about this sudden change of heart. But *whom?*

Caroline? No, he'd told her about his early adventures, and of encounters with Choundas. She knew him too well, or thought that she did. He'd been breezy about the man, swaggering as a proper hero must. To express, to confess, that he'd always feared him would be weakness. And to blather on about no *longer* being fearful would be even worse, a *Frenchman*'s insouciant gasconading boasts. There was no way to rejustify himself in her eyes, even did she break the seals and read his letter, instead of using it for fireplace tinder.

Theoni Connor? Again, no. She had always seen him as heroic, and any admission of past dreads would demean him with her. He could explain just who this *bête-noir* was, at least lay out the odds of the possible future confrontation, now they were due to cross each others' hawse, but . . . maybe weaning himself of Theoni Connor was the better course. It was three years before *Proteus* sailed home to pay off, and at least two months each way for letters.

He could write his father, baldly stating, "By the by, that dog we chased in Asia is now here, and we hunt each other. The weather is fine . . ." That might be best, he thought; surely his father would be able to put a flea in Sophie's ear, and that would get back to his own household in short order, reawakening concern for him in Caroline's heart. Again, that was two months' mail packet passage before the news could affect anyone, for good or ill.

Cashman? He felt like telling *somebody*! Cashman, though, was hip-deep in selling up his plantation, was too distracted with his ongoing feud with Ledyard Beauman . . . and his gleeful, cackling preparations for that duel. He was an old friend, a man, a seasoned soldier, so surely *he'd* understand, did a respected, courageous officer relate a *few* twinges of worry over an old foe's reappearance, and how he had found a way to deal with him . . . over a few bottles of champagne?

Perhaps the next time he was ashore, visiting Kit; though that was an *unbearably* long time to sit on the matter. And, when ashore, their time would mostly be spent on the duel, since Cashman meant to hold him to his promise to second him, and the over-formal *punctilio* of the code *duello* would prove exacting.

The curse of command, Lewrie sourly realised, deflating from a brief moment of exuberance; *good tidings or shiverin' shits, there's not a single soul you can tell! The public masque ya wear in Society . . . yer good odour as a hero won't allow it ashore, either!* he thought with a self-deprecating scoff over "hero."

No, he would have to "play" the imperturbable Royal Navy stock character, as seen on stage, saving his innermost feelings only for a "good woman." After all, that was what a life's helpmeet was for, the role in life as stock characters for "good women."

Or bad'uns, who don't parlez any English, Lewrie told himself with a smirk; *to unburden oneself just might be an* active *verb, there! In more ways than one.*

"Aspinall, how are we set for something cold to drink?" Lewrie asked the empty great-cabins, and his manservant popped his head from his small pantry, where he'd been doing some sennet-work napkin rings.

"Pitcher o' cool tea with lemon an' sugar comin' up, sir!"

Lewrie went to the desk and ruffled Toulon's belly fur, tickling him under the chin. The cat awoke in a trice, and after a brief yawn and stiff-legged stretch, he began to wriggle and writhe about, eager for some play, tail whisking again, and his eyes wide.

"You poor old puss," Lewrie said with a sigh, fingers escaping quickly snapped jaws and batting paws for another "attack" upon belly fur, that put Toulon into a fit of flipping from side to side. "May not know it, but you're my onliest audience, Toulon. You've the only ears I can whisper into. 'Cause you're the only one who can't blab."

"Mmmrrph!" Toulon replied, trapping a hand and rasping tongue on a finger.

"I love you, too, you rascal."

AFTERWORD

$\mathcal{P}$erhaps it's not a good omen for Alan Lewrie, but the captains and admirals who participated in the Battle of Camperdown had no luck at all. Too tainted, perhaps, with the worst part of the Nore Mutiny in the spring of 1797, their ships' crews the worst and most threatening to naval and social order (see *King's Captain* for Lewrie's part in it), none of them, even after winning a victory and eliminating a threat of joint Franco-Dutch invasion of England itself, none of them prospered. And one, the captain of *Agincourt*, was cashiered for cowardice.

The way the Dutch fought, close-up and courageous, shattered as many British ships as they lost. None of the Royal Navy ships served for very long after being extensively repaired; nor were any of their hard-won prizes taken at Camperdown worth anything, either. They were bought in, also given extensive repairs, but five or six years later, most of them ended up as non-sailing hulks or harbour receiving ships.

By the way, those purists who might object to the *Orangespruit* frigate being there . . . sure, I knew she was a *very* old warship in '97 and was probably a hulk by the time of the battle, but she was a 36-gunner, and the name was *very* Dutch, and since I know little of Holland beyond tulips, windmills, cheeses, and beers, well . . . I'll not steal a victory from a *real* captain and his capture, and I'll not name a ship *Edam* or *Gouda*, either. Lewrie will get his share of prize money from her taking, and that's all *he* cares about, thankee very much.

⚓

Many thanks to the U.S. Naval Institute Press, and Michael A. Palmer, for *Stoddert's War* regarding the rebirth of the U.S. Navy and its operations during the Quasi War with France in the Caribbean, and thanks to Ty Martin, USN (Ret) and former skipper of *Constitution* for a list of proposed ship names of American frigates that weren't used . . . so I could "borrow" one for the USS *Hancock*. I suspect we will run into *Hancock* and Captain Kershaw again. Mr. Martin's book, *A Most Fortunate Ship*, details *Constitution* and her operations in the Caribbean during the Quasi War, as well as her later illustrious career.

By the way, the founding of Washington "City" and the District of Columbia where President George Washington laid the cornerstone of the Capitol in 1793, was a neat little boondoggle with government money, and some so-called "upright" characters made themselves a "shower o' tin" buying up swampland for a song and selling it for scandalous profits. My my, how things never change!

Thanks also go to "Bosun" Bob Scappini and his rowdy crew up in Rhode Island, who wore themselves out re-enacting a Revolutionary War artillery unit 'til, after shifting battery eleven times one day under a broiling sun, they found one of my books and decided that becoming the "Landing Party" off the American Sloop of War *Providence* might just be a lot cooler, and not involve so much heavy lifting!

They also sent me a tape and lyric book they'd made of sailing chanteys and pulley-hauleys, from which the words to "Nottingham Ale" came. May the Ship's Company & Landing Party "splice the mainbrace"! And beat the Middies from Annapolis, next long-boat race.

Thanks also, again, to Bob Enrione for the year-long loan of a set of books about the Royal Navy and the era from his vast collection, and for attempts to dig up some information about Haiti and the slave revolt.

Haiti, or Saint Domingue . . . well. Ask three Haitians about it and you'll get five differing opinions, and a lot of shifty-eyed looks. Even now, it's an uneasy subject, how their ancestors founded the first independent Black nation anywhere in the world, and a poorly represented topic, too.

I had to order research material, mostly reprinted in generic-bland trade paperback form, done by order from digitized storage, one of which was one of the worst "historical novels" I had ever read, and which shall remain nameless and authorless. *A Brief History of The Caribbean* by Jan Rogozinksi (Meridian Books) was very helpful, and explains the background, from Columbus's arrival, the massacre of the Arawak and Carib Indians, the introduction of sugar cane and necessity of slavery, along with the resultant uprisings and revolts.

The Black Jacobins by C.L.R. James is one of the few informative texts I found about Haiti's history, and the amazing Toussaint L'Ouverture, who would eventually be called the Black Napoleon for his military skill. It was written in 1938, and revised in 1963, and good luck finding one in a bookstore. (James was an admitted Communist who wished all Africa to emulate Haiti!) For those interested, it is from Vintage Books, a division of Random House.

The mutiny aboard HMS *Hermione,* wherein her captain Hugh Pigot (one of Admiral Sir Hyde Parker's favourites, which tells you a thing or two about Parker!) and all his officers, senior mates and most of his midshipmen were murdered, the deed done in part by his own "pets" he'd brought from a previous command, outraged the Royal Navy and all of British society, coming as it did so soon after the Spithead and Nore Mutinies. Pigot was a vengeful, petty, inconsistent, pain-loving beast who turned an adequate crew into maddened desperadoes. It took over twenty years, but about a third of the true culprits and leaders *were* hunted down with implacable, untiring zeal by the Royal Navy. I found *The Black Ship* by Dudley Pope most informative on this mattere.

Let's belabour the obvious—slavery sucks. As Christopher Cashman tells us, it brutalises both the victims, and the victimizer, in the end. Why it is still tolerated in Sudan and other African countries today is beyond me. Just 'cause it's Blacks enslaving Blacks, does that make it too Politically Correct to deal with? Would we be "dissing" some group, whom we must not only tolerate but embrace according to the rules of Diversity and Multiculturalism, if we spoke out against it? Heaven forfend!

Brutality down sooner or later engenders brutality up, as in a "comeuppance," and the record of horrors and atrocities commited during Haiti's War of The Skin are a sickening litany of evil, no matter how "modernists" wish to justify it by claiming that "extremism in the pursuit of (fill in the blank) is no vice," or that the White masters got what they deserved. Thinking like that merits only scorn and derision from rational and realistic people.

Let's also remember that L'Ouverture and Henri Christophe, his follower, *reinstituted* slavery to prop up a shattered economy and get the unskilled "Field Blacks" back on the land where they would not be a perpetually rebellious, unemployed and illiterate under-class, too "dark" to rub shoulders with the lighter-skinned upper-class leaders. Plantations in a broken economy were the only rewards they could give out . . . and what good's a plantation if you don't have people to work it and reap you a profit, hmmm?

Though L'Ouverture has kicked the British out after years of occupation, we're not done with Saint Domingue, yet, not by a long chalk. There's still General Rigaud and other dissidents vying for power, so the arms smuggling and piracy will continue. There's still the Frogs, who wish to conquer the place themselves and restore the old order of things. Once Napoleon Bonaparte became First Consul, then Emperor of The French, he sent one army after another to Haiti/Saint Domingue to subjugate the place, and L'Ouverture ended up betrayed and imprisoned in the icy Maritime Alps in Europe, there to perish from hunger and cold.

That, though, lies in the future, and for now, Saint Domingue is *still* a bug-a-bear for British interests in the Caribbean, a place to be blockaded before their revolution spreads, and that will keep our boy Alan Lewrie busy.

And damme, but don't he *just* have enough on his plate!

His happy marriage (relatively speakin', o' course!) has gone as tits-up as a dynamited bass, his sweet wife is out for blood and/or money—whichever comes first—and he *still* doesn't know whom to shoot who's sending all those "dear friend" letters! His "volunteer" crew is still a problem should anyone ever recognise them as runaway (stolen!) slaves. He did need 'em perishin'-bad, though!

And forgery, as any careful reader of the earlier books knows, does run in the family!

There's Cashman's duel to arrange, Ledyard Beauman's deserved bloody end to manage, if for no other reason than to remove him from the British gene pool so the Ministry of Silly Walks won't get funded 'til the 1960s, and what'll be the up-shot o' that anent Lewrie and his relationships with the other Beaumans?

And, God above, there's Guillaume Choundas to face once more, a "right shower o' bastards" all by himself! Does he discover that he and Lewrie are in the same ocean (trust me, he will) then all sorts of mayhem could break loose. And trust me, such will!

Hey, I didn't nickname the series "Sex, Swords, and Sailing Ships" for nothing, don't ye know! Why, there's even Toulon's love life that hasn't been touched upon, yet, and . . .

Oops. That'd be telling.

For now, in good ol' down-home Southern parlance, "We'll leave the latch-string out for ya", and, as Granny Clampett always said . . . "Ya'll come back now, ya hear?"